Atop the flying griffin, her battle axe lifted high, Diane shouted to Duncan: "The castle! Run for your life. Run to the castle! It's your only chance!"

The horde of hairless monsters had fallen back, driven off by Diane and the charge of the wild Huntsman and his pack—but they would return. As he and his companions ran toward the canted standing stones that lay before the mounded ruins of the castle, Duncan wondered what kind of safety it might offer. If he and his band had to fight again, the castle mound would not afford much protection . . .

As he passed between two of the standing stones, the grass beneath his feet became a different kind of grass— no longer an unkempt meadow, but a well-tended, pampered lawn.

Startled, he looked up and gasped at what he saw. The castle mound was gone. In its place stood a splendid castle, a building out of Fairyland.

Diane, her hair a golden glory in the fading light, still carrying the gory battle axe, was walking across the lawn toward him.

"Welcome," she said, "to the Castle of the Wizards."

Also by Clifford D. Simak
Published by Ballantine Books:

Mastodonia

The

FELLOWSHIP

of the

TALISMAN

Clifford D. Simak

A Del Rey Book

BALLANTINE BOOKS • NEW YORK

A Del Rey Book
Published by Ballantine Books

Copyright © 1978 by Clifford D. Simak

Library of Congress Catalog Card Number: 78-16657

ISBN 0-345-27592-6

Printed in Canada

First Edition: September 1978

Paperback format
First Edition: August 1979

Cover art by Michael Whelan

1

The manor house was the first undamaged structure they had seen in two days of travel through an area that had been desolated with a thoroughness at once terrifying and unbelievable.

During those two days, furtive wolves had watched them from hilltops. Foxes, their brushes dragging, had skulked through underbrush. Buzzards, perched on dead trees or on the blackened timbers of burned homesteads, had looked upon them with speculative interest. They had met not a soul, but occasionally, in thickets, they had glimpsed human skeletons.

The weather had been fine until noon of the second day, when the soft sky of early autumn became overcast, and a chill wind sprang from the north. At times the sharp wind whipped icy rain against their backs, the rain sometimes mixed with snow.

Late in the afternoon, topping a low ridge, Duncan Standish sighted the manor, a rude set of buildings fortified by palisades and a narrow moat. Inside the palisades, fronting the drawbridge, lay a courtyard, within which were penned horses, cattle, sheep, and hogs. A few men moved about in the courtyard, and smoke streamed from several chimneys. A number of small buildings, some of which bore the signs of burning, lay outside the palisades. The entire place had a down-at-heels appearance.

Daniel, the great war-horse, who had been following Duncan like a dog, came up behind the man. Clopping behind Daniel came the little gray burro, Beauty, with packs lashed upon her back. Daniel lowered his head, nudged his master's back.

"It's all right, Daniel," Duncan told him. "We've found shelter for the night."

The horse blew softly through his nostrils.

Conrad came trudging up the slope and ranged himself alongside Duncan. Conrad was a massive man. Towering close to seven feet, he was heavy even for his height. A garment made of sheep pelts hung from his shoulders almost to his knees. In his right fist he carried a heavy club fashioned from an oak branch. He stood silently, staring at the manor house.

"What do you make of it?" asked Duncan.

"They have seen us," Conrad said. "Heads peeking out above the palisades."

"Your eyes are sharper than mine," said Duncan. "Are you sure?"

"I'm sure, m'lord."

"Quit calling me 'my lord.' I'm not a lord. My father is the lord."

"I think of you as such," said Conrad. "When your father dies, you will be a lord."

"No Harriers?"

"Only people," Conrad told him.

"It seems unlikely," said Duncan, "that the Harriers would have passed by such a place."

"Maybe fought them off. Maybe the Harriers were in a hurry."

"So far," said Duncan, "from our observations, they passed little by. The lowliest cottages, even huts, were burned."

"Here comes Tiny," said Conrad. "He's been down to look them over."

The mastiff came loping up the slope and they waited for him. He went over to stand close to Con-

2

rad. Conrad patted his head, and the great dog wagged his tail. Looking at them, Duncan noted once again how similar were the man and dog. Tiny reached almost to Conrad's waist. He was a splendid brute. He wore a wide leather collar in which were fastened metal studs. His ears tipped forward as he looked down at the manor. A faint growl rumbled in his throat.

"Tiny doesn't like it, either," Conrad said.

"It's the only place we've seen," said Duncan. "It's shelter. The night will be wet and cold."

"Bedbugs there will be. Lice as well."

The little burro sidled close to Daniel to get out of the cutting wind.

Duncan shucked up his sword belt. "I don't like it, Conrad, any better than you and Tiny do. But there is a bad night coming on."

"We'll stay close together," Conrad said. "We'll not let them separate us."

"That is right," said Duncan. "We might as well start down."

As they walked down the slope, Duncan unconsciously put his hand beneath his cloak to find the pouch dangling from his belt. His fingers located the bulk of the manuscript. He seemed to hear the crinkle of the parchment as his fingers touched it. He found himself suddenly enraged at his action. Time after time, during the last two days, he'd gone through the same silly procedure, making sure the manuscript was there. Like a country boy going to a fair, he told himself, with a penny tucked in his pocket, thrusting his hand again and again into the pocket to make sure he had not lost the penny.

Having touched the parchment, again he seemed to hear His Grace saying, "Upon those few pages may rest the future hope of mankind." Although, come to think of it, His Grace was given to overstatement and not to be taken as seriously as he sometimes tried to make a person think he should be. In this instance, however, Duncan told himself, the aged and portly

3

churchman might very well be right. But that would not be known until they got to Oxenford.

And because of this, because of the tightly written script on a few sheets of parchment, he was here rather than back in the comfort and security of Standish House, trudging down a hill to seek shelter in a place where, as Conrad had pointed out, there probably would be bedbugs.

"One thing bothers me," said Conrad as he strode along with Duncan.

"I didn't know that anything ever bothered you."

"It's the Little Folk," said Conrad. "We have seen none of them. If anyone, they should be the ones to escape the Harriers. You can't tell me that goblins and gnomes and others of their kind could not escape the Harriers."

"Maybe they are frightened and hiding out," said Duncan. "If I am any judge of them, they'd know where to hide."

Conrad brightened visibly. "Yes, that must be it," he said.

As they drew closer to the manor, they saw their estimation of the place had not been wrong. It was far from prepossessing. Ramshackle was the word for it. Here and there heads appeared over the palisades, watching their approach.

The drawbridge was still up when they reached the moat, which was a noisome thing. The stench was overpowering, and in the greenish water floated hunks of corruption that could have been decaying human bodies.

Conrad bellowed at the heads protruding over the palisades. "Open up," he shouted. "Travelers claim shelter."

Nothing happened for a time, and Conrad bellowed once again. Finally, with much creaking of wood and squealing of chains, the bridge began a slow, jerky descent. As they crossed the bridge they saw that there stood inside a motley crowd with the look of vagabonds about them, but the vagabonds were armed with spears, and some carried makeshift swords in hand.

Conrad waved his club at them. "Stand back," he growled. "Make way for m'lord."

They backed off, but the spears were not grounded; the blades stayed naked. A crippled little man, one foot dragging, limped through the crowd and came up to them. "My master welcomes you," he whined. "He would have you at table."

"First," said Conrad, "shelter for the beasts."

"There is a shed," said the whining lame man. "It is open to the weather, but it has a roof and is placed against the wall. There'll be hay for the horse and burro. I'll bring the dog a bone."

"No bone," said Conrad. "Meat. Big meat. Meat to fit his size."

"I'll find some meat," said the lame man.

"Give him a penny," Duncan said to Conrad.

Conrad inserted his fingers into the purse at his belt, brought out a coin, and flipped it to the man, who caught it deftly and touched a finger to his forelock, but in a mocking manner.

The shed was shelter, barely, but at the worst it offered some protection from the wind and a cover against rain. Duncan unsaddled Daniel and placed the saddle against the wall of the palisade. Conrad unshipped the pack from the burro, piled it atop the saddle.

"Do you not wish to take the saddle and the pack inside with you?" the lame man asked. "They might be safer there."

"Safe here," insisted Conrad. "Should anyone touch them, he will get smashed ribs, perhaps his throat torn out."

The raffish crowd that had confronted them when they crossed the bridge had scattered now. The drawbridge, with shrill sounds of protest, was being drawn up.

"Now," said the lame man, "if you two will follow me. The master sits at meat."

The great hall of the manor was ill lighted and evil

5

smelling. Smoky torches were ranged along the walls to provide illumination. The rushes on the floor had not been changed for months, possibly for years; they were littered with bones thrown to dogs or simply tossed upon the floor once the meat had been gnawed from them. Dog droppings lay underfoot, and the room stank of urine—dog, and, more than likely, human. At the far end of the room stood a fireplace with burning logs. The chimney did not draw well and poured smoke into the hall. A long trestle table ran down the center of the hall. Around it was seated an uncouth company. Half-grown boys ran about, serving platters of food and jugs of ale.

When Duncan and Conrad came into the hall, the talk quieted and the bleary white of the feasters' faces turned to stare at the new arrivals. Dogs rose from their bones and showed their teeth at them.

At the far end of the table a man rose from his seat. He roared at them in a joyous tone, "Welcome, travelers. Come and share the board of Harold, the Reaver."

He turned his head to a group of youths serving the table.

"Kick those mangy dogs out of the way to make way for our guests," he roared. "It would not be seemly for them to be set upon and bitten."

The youths set upon their task with a will. Boots thudded into dogs; the dogs snapped back, whimpering and snarling.

Duncan strode forward, followed by Conrad.

"I thank you, sir," said Duncan, "for your courtesy."

Harold, the Reaver, was raw-boned, hairy and unkempt. His hair and beard had the appearance of having housed rats. He wore a cloak that at one time may have been purple, but was now so besmirched by grease that it seemed more mud than purple. The fur that offset the collar and the sleeves was moth-eaten.

The Reaver waved at a place next to him. "Please be seated, sir," he said.

"My name," said Duncan, "is Duncan Standish, and the man with me is Conrad."

"Conrad is your man?"

"Not my man. My companion."

The Reaver mulled the answer for a moment, then said, "In that case, he must sit with you." He said to the man in the next place, "Einer, get the hell out of here. Find another place and take your trencher with you."

With ill grace, Einer picked up his trencher and his mug and went stalking down the table to find another place.

"Now since it all is settled," the Reaver said to Duncan, "will you not sit down. We have meat and ale. The ale is excellent; for the meat I'll not say as much. There also is bread of an indifferent sort, but we have a supply of the finest honey a bee has ever made. When the Harriers came down upon us, Old Cedric, our bee master, risked his very life to bring in the hives, thus saving it for us."

"How long ago was that?" asked Duncan. "When the Harriers came?"

"It was late in the spring. There were just a few of them at first, the forerunners of the Horde. It gave us a chance to bring in the livestock and the bees. When the real Horde finally came, we were ready for them. Have you, sir, ever seen any of the Harriers?"

"No. I've only heard of them."

"They are a vicious lot," the Reaver said. "All shapes and sizes of them. Imps, demons, devils, and many others that twist your gut with fear and turn your bowels to water, all with their own special kinds of nastiness. The worst of them are the hairless ones. Human, but they are not human. Like shambling idiots, strong, massive idiots that have no fear and an undying urge to kill. No hair upon them, not a single hair from top to toe. White—white like the slugs you find when you overturn a rotting log. Fat and heavy like the slugs. But no fat. Or I think no fat, but muscle. Muscle such as you have never seen. Strength such as no one has ever seen. Taken all together, the

7

hairless ones and the others that run with them sweep
everything before them. They kill, they burn, there is
no mercy in them. Ferocity and magic. That is their
stock in trade. We were hard put, I don't mind telling
you, to hold them at arm's length. But we resisted the
magic and matched the ferocity, although the very
sight of them could scare a man to death."

"I take it you did not scare."

"We did not scare," the Reaver said. "My men,
they are a hard lot. We gave them blow for blow. We
were as mean as they were. We were not about to
give up this place we had found."

"Found?"

"Yes, found. You can tell, of course, that we are
not the sort of people you'd ordinarily find in a place
like this. The Reaver in my name is just a sort of
joke, you see. A joke among ourselves. We are a band
of honest workmen, unable to find jobs. There are
many such as we. So all of us, facing the same problems and knowing there was no work for us, banded
together to seek out some quiet corner of the land
where we might set up rude homesteads and wrest
from the soil a living for our families and ourselves.
But we found no such place until we came upon this
place, abandoned."

"You mean it was empty. No one living here."

"Not a soul," the Reaver said sanctimoniously. "No
one around. So we had a council and decided to move
in—unless, of course, the rightful owners should show
up."

"In which case you'd give it back to them?"

"Oh, most certainly," said the Reaver. "Give it
back to them and set out again to find for ourselves
that quiet corner we had sought."

"Most admirable of you," said Duncan.

"Why, thank you, sir. But enough of this. Tell me
of yourselves. Travelers, you say. In these parts not
many travelers are seen. It's far too dangerous for
travelers."

"We are heading south," said Duncan. "To Oxenford. Perhaps then to London Town."

8

"And you do not fear?"

"Naturally we fear. But we are well armed and we shall be watchful."

"Watchful you'll need to be," the Reaver said. "You'll be traveling through the heart of the Desolated Land. You face many perils. Food will be hard to find. I tell you there's nothing left. Were a raven to fly across that country he'd need to carry his provisions with him."

"You get along all right."

"We were able to save our livestock. We planted late crops after the Harriers passed on. Because of the lateness of the planting, the harvest has been poor. Half a crop of wheat, less than half a crop of rye and barley. Only a small oat crop. The buckwheat was a total failure. We are much pushed for an adequate supply of hay. And that's not all. Our cattle suffer from the murrain. The wolves prey upon the sheep."

Trenchers were set down in front of Duncan and Conrad, then a huge platter with a haunch of beef on one end of it, a saddle of mutton on the other. Another youth brought a loaf of bread and a plate of honey in the comb.

As he ate, Duncan looked around the table. No matter what the Reaver may have said, he told himself, the men who sat there could not be honest workmen. They had the look of wolves. Perhaps a raiding party that, in the midst of raiding, had been surprised by the Harriers. Having fought off the Harriers and with nothing better to do, they had settled down, at least for the time. It would be a good hiding place. No one, not even a lawman, would come riding here.

"The Harriers?" he asked. "Where are they now?"

"No one knows," the Reaver told him. "They could be anywhere."

"But this is little more than the border of the Desolated Land. Word is that they struck deep into northern Britain."

"Ah, yes, perhaps. We have had no word. There are none to carry word. You are the only ones we've seen. You must have matters of great import to bring you to this place."

"We carry messages. Nothing more."

"You said Oxenford. And London Town."

"That is right."

"There is nothing at Oxenford."

"That may be," said Duncan. "I have never been there."

There were no women here, he noted. No ladies sitting at the table, as would have been the case in any well-regulated manor. If there were women here, they were shut away.

One of the youths brought a pitcher of ale, filled cups for the travelers. The ale, when Duncan tasted it, was of high quality. He said as much to the Reaver.

"The next batch will not be," the Reaver said. "The grain is poor this year and the hay! We've had a hell's own time getting any hay, even of the poorest quality. Our poor beasts will have slim pickings through the winter months."

Many of those at the table had finished with their eating. A number of them had fallen forward on the table, their heads pillowed on their arms. Perhaps they slept in this manner, Duncan thought. Little more than animals, with no proper beds. The Reaver had lolled back in his chair, his eyes closed. The talk throughout the hall had quieted.

Duncan sliced two chunks of bread and handed one of them to Conrad. His own slice he spread with honey from the comb. As the Reaver had said, it was excellent, clean and sweet, made from summer flowers. Not the dark, harsh-tasting product so often found in northern climes.

A log in the fireplace, burning through, collapsed in a shower of sparks. Some of the torches along the wall had gone out, but still trailed greasy smoke. A couple of dogs, disputing a bone, snarled at one another. The stench of the hall, it seemed, was worse than when they had first entered.

A muted scream brought Duncan to his feet. For a second he stood listening, and the scream came again, a fighting scream, of anger rather than of pain. Conrad surged up. "That's Daniel," he shouted.

Duncan, followed by Conrad, charged down the hall. A man, stumbling erect from a sodden sleep, loomed in Duncan's path. Duncan shoved him to one side. Conrad sprang past him, using his club to clear the way for them. Men who came in contact with the club howled in anger behind them. A dog ran yipping. Duncan freed his sword and whipped it from the scabbard, metal whispering as he drew the blade.

Ahead of him, Conrad tugged at the door, forced it open, and the two of them plunged out into the courtyard. A large bonfire was burning and in its light they saw a group of men gathered about the shed in which the animals had been housed. But even as they came out into the yard the group was breaking up and fleeing.

Daniel, squealing with rage, stood on his hind legs, striking out with his forefeet at the men in front of him. One man was stretched on the ground and another was crawling away. As Duncan and Conrad ran across the yard, the horse lashed out and caught another man in the face with an iron-shod hoof, bowling him over. A few feet from Daniel, a raging Tiny had another man by the throat and was shaking him savagely. The little burro was a flurry of flailing hoofs.

At the sight of the two men racing across the courtyard, the few remaining in the group before the shed broke up and ran.

Duncan strode forward to stand beside the horse. "It's all right now," he said. "We're here."

Daniel snorted at him.

"Let loose," Conrad said to Tiny. "He's dead."

The dog gave way, contemptuously, and licked his bloody muzzle. The man he had loosed had no throat. Two men stretched in front of Daniel did not move; both seemed dead. Another dragged himself across the courtyard with a broken back. Still others were limping, bent over, as they fled.

Men were spewing out of the great hall door. Once they came out, they clustered into groups, stood, and stared. Pushing his way through them came the Reaver. He walked toward Duncan and Conrad.

He blustered at them. "What is this?" he stormed. "I give you hospitality and here my men lie dead!"

"They tried to steal our goods," said Duncan. "Perhaps they had in mind, as well, to steal the animals. Our animals, as you can see, did not take kindly to it."

The Reaver pretended to be horrified. "This I can't believe. My men would not stoop to such a shabby trick."

"Your men," said Duncan, "are a shabby lot."

"This is most embarrassing," the Reaver said. "I do not quarrel with guests."

"No need to quarrel," said Duncan sharply. "Lower the bridge and we'll leave. I insist on that."

Hoisting his club, Conrad stepped close to the Reaver. "You understand," he said. "M'lord insists on it."

The Reaver made as if to leave, but Conrad grabbed him by the arm and spun him around. "The club is hungry," he said. "It has not cracked a skull in months."

"The drawbridge," Duncan said, far too gently.

"All right," the Reaver said. "All right." He shouted to his men. "Let down the bridge so our guests can leave."

"The rest stand back," said Conrad. "Way back. Give us room. Otherwise your skull is cracked."

"The rest of you stand back," the Reaver yelled. "Do not interfere. Give them room. We want no trouble."

"If there is trouble," Conrad told him, "you will be the first to get it." He said to Duncan, "Get the saddle on Daniel, the packs on Beauty. I will handle this one."

The drawbridge already was beginning to come down. By the time its far end thumped beyond the moat, they were ready to move out.

"I'll hang on to the Reaver," Conrad said, "till the bridge is crossed."

He jerked the Reaver along. The men in the court-yard stood well back. Tiny took the point.

Once on the bridge, Duncan saw that the overcast sky had cleared. A near-full moon rode in the sky, and the stars were shining. There still were a few scudding clouds.

At the end of the bridge they stopped. Conrad loosed his grip upon the Reaver.

Duncan said to their erstwhile host, "As soon as you get back, pull up the bridge. Don't even think of sending your men out after us. If you do, we'll loose the horse and dog on them. They're war animals, trained to fight, as you have seen. They'd cut your men to ribbons."

The Reaver said nothing. He clumped back across the bridge. Once back in the courtyard, he bellowed at his men. Wheel shrieked and chains clanked, wood moaned. The bridge began slowly moving up.

"Let's go," said Duncan when it was halfway up.

Tiny leading, they went down a hill, following a faint path.

"Where do we go?" asked Conrad.

"I don't know," said Duncan. "Just away from here."

Ahead of them Tiny growled a warning. A man was standing in the path.

Duncan walked forward to where Tiny stood. Together the two walked toward the man. The man spoke in a quavery voice, "No need to fear, sir. It's only Old Cedric, the bee master."

"What are you doing here?" asked Duncan.

"I came to guide you, sir. Besides, I bring you food."

He reached down and lifted a sack that had been standing, unnoticed, at his feet.

"A flitch of bacon," he said, "a ham, a cheese, a loaf of bread, and some honey. Besides, I can show you the fastest and the farthest way. I've lived here all my life. I know the country."

"Why should you want to help us? You are the

13

Reaver's man. He spoke of you. He said you saved the bees when the Harriers came."

"Not the Reaver's man," said the bee master. "I was here for years before he came. It was a good life, a good life for all of us—the master and his people. We were a peaceful folk. We had no chance when the Reaver came. We knew not how to fight. The Reaver and his hellions came two years ago, come Michaelmas, and . . . "

"But you stayed with the Reaver."

"Not stayed. Was spared. He spared me because I was the one who knew the bees. Few people know of bees, and the Reaver likes good honey."

"So I was right in my thinking," Duncan said. "The Reaver and his men took the manor house, slaughtering the people who lived here."

"Aye," said Cedric. "This poor country has fallen on hard times. First the Reaver and his like, then the Harriers."

"And you'll show us the quickest way to get out of the Reaver's reach?"

"That I will. I know all the swiftest paths. Even in the dark. When I saw what was happening, I nipped into the kitchen to collect provisions, then went over the palisades and lay in wait for you."

"But the Reaver will know you did this. He'll have vengeance on you."

Cedric shook his head. "I will not be missed. I'm always with the bees. I even spend the nights with them. I came in tonight because of the cold and rain. If I am missed, which I will not be, they'll think I'm with the bees. And if you don't mind, sir, it'll be an honor to be of service to the man who faced the Reaver down."

"You do not like this Reaver."

"I loathe him. But what's a man to do? A small stroke here and there. Like this. One does what he can."

Conrad took the sack from the old man's hand. "I'll carry this," he said. "Later we can put it with Beauty's pack."

"You think the Reaver and his men will follow?" Duncan asked.

"I don't know. Probably not, but one can't be sure."

"You say you hate him. Why don't you travel with us? Surely you do not want to stay with him."

"Not with him. Willingly I'd join you. But I cannot leave the bees."

"The bees?"

"Sir, do you know anything of bees?"

"Very little."

"They are," said Cedric, "the most amazing creatures. In one hive of them alone their numbers cannot be counted. But they need a human to help them. Each year there must be a strong queen to lay many eggs. One queen. One queen only, mind you, if the hive is to be kept up to strength. If there are more than one, the bees will swarm, part of them going elsewhere, cutting down the number in the hive. To keep them strong there must be a bee master who knows how to manage them. You go through the comb, you see, seeking out the extra queen cells and these you destroy. You might even destroy a queen who is growing old and see that a strong new queen is raised . . ."

"Because of this, you'll stay with the Reaver?"

The old man drew himself erect. "I love my bees," he said. "They need me."

Conrad growled. "A pox on bees. We'll die here, talking of your bees."

"I talk too much of bees," the old man said. "Follow me. Keep close upon my heels."

He flitted like a ghost ahead of them. At times he jogged, at other times he ran, then again he'd go cautiously and slowly, feeling out his way.

They went down into a little valley, climbed a ridge, plunged down into another larger valley, left it to climb yet another ridge. Above them the stars wheeled slowly in the sky and the moon inclined to the west. The chill wind still blew out of the north, but there was no rain.

Duncan was tired. With no sleep, his body cried out against the pace old Cedric set. Occasionally he stumbled. Conrad said to him, "Get up on the horse," but Duncan shook his head. "Daniel's tired as well," he said.

His mind detached itself from his feet. His feet kept on, moving him ahead, through the darkness, the pale moonlight, the great surge of forest, the loom of hills, the gash of valleys. His mind went otherwhere. It went back to the day this had all begun.

2

Duncan's first warning that he had been selected for the mission came when he tramped down the winding, baronial staircase and went across the foyer, heading for the library, where Wells had said his father would be waiting for him with His Grace.

It was not unusual for his father to want to see him, Duncan told himself. He was accustomed to being summoned, but what business could have brought the archbishop to the castle? His Grace was an elderly man, portly from good eating and not enough to do. He seldom ventured from the abbey. It would take something of more than usual importance to bring him here on his elderly gray mule, which was slow, but soft of foot, making travel easier for a man who disliked activity.

Duncan came into the library with its floor-to-ceiling book-rolls, its stained-glass window, the stag's head mounted above the flaming fireplace.

His father and the archbishop were sitting in chairs half facing the fire, and when he came into the room both of them rose to greet him, the archbishop puffing with the effort of raising himself from the chair.

"Duncan," said his father, "we have a visitor you should remember."

"Your Grace," said Duncan, hurrying forward to receive the blessing. "It is good to see you once again. It has been months."

He went down on a knee and once the blessing had been done, the archbishop reached down a symbolic hand to lift him to his feet.

"He should remember me," the archbishop told Duncan's father. "I had him in quite often to reason gently with him. It seems it was quite a job for the good fathers to pound some simple Latin and indifferent Greek and a number of other things into his reluctant skull."

"But, Your Grace," said Duncan, "it was all so dull. What does the parsing of a Latin verb . . . "

"Spoken like a gentleman," said His Grace. "When they come to the abbey and face the Latin that is always their complaint. But you, despite some backsliding now and then, did better than most."

"The lad's all right," growled Duncan's father. "I, myself, have but little Latin. Your people at the abbey put too much weight on it."

"That may be so," the archbishop conceded, "but it's the one thing we can do. We cannot teach the riding of a horse or the handling of a sword or the cozening of maidens."

"Let's forsake the banter and sit down," said Duncan's father. "We have matters to discuss." He said to Duncan, "Pay close attention, son. This has to do with you."

"Yes, sir," said Duncan, sitting down.

The archbishop glanced at Duncan's father. "Shall I tell him, Douglas?"

"Yes," Duncan's father said. "You know more of it than I do. And you can tell it better. You have the words for it."

The archbishop leaned back in his chair, laced pudgy fingers across a pudgy paunch. "Two years or more ago," he said to Duncan, "your father brought me a manuscript that he had found while sorting out the family papers."

"It was a job," said Duncan's father, "that should

18

have been done centuries ago. Papers and records all shuffled together, without rhyme or reason. Old letters, old records, old grants, old deeds, ancient instruments, all shoved into a variety of boxes. The job's not entirely done as yet. I work on it occasionally. It's difficult, at times, to make sense of what I find."

"He brought me the manuscript," said the archbishop, "because it was written in an unfamiliar language. A language he had never seen and that few others ever have."

"It turned out to be Aramaic," said Duncan's father. "The tongue, I am told, in which Jesus spoke."

Duncan looked from one to the other of them. What was going on? he asked himself. What was this all about? What did it have to do with him?

"You're wondering," said the archbishop, "what this may have to do with you."

"Yes, I am," said Duncan.

"We'll get to it in time."

"I'm afraid you will," said Duncan.

"Our good fathers had a terrible time with the manuscript," the archbishop said. "There are only two of them who have any acquaintance with the language. One of them can manage to spell it out, the other may have some real knowledge of it. But I suspect not as much as he might wish that I should think. The trouble is, of course, that we cannot decide if the manuscript is a true account. It could be a hoax.

"It purports to be a journal that gives an account of the ministry of Jesus. Not necessarily day to day. There are portions of it in which daily entries are made. Then a few days may elapse, but when the journal takes up again the entry of that date will cover all that has happened since the last entry had been made. It reads as if the diarist was someone who lived at the time and witnessed what he wrote—as if he might have been a man not necessarily in the company of Jesus, but who somehow tagged along. A sort of hanger-on, perhaps. There is not the barest hint of who he might have been. He does not tell us who he is and there are no clues to his identity."

19

The archbishop ended speaking and stared owlishly at Duncan. "You realize, of course," he said, "if the document is true, what this would mean?"

"Why, yes, of course," Duncan answered. "It would give us a detailed, day-by-day account of the ministry of Our Lord."

"It would do more than that, my son," his father said. "It would give us the first eyewitness account of Him. It would provide the proof that there really was a man named Jesus."

"But, I don't—I can't . . ."

"What your father says is true," the archbishop said. "Aside from these few pages of manuscript we have, there is nothing that could be used to prove the historicity of Jesus. There do exist a few bits of writing that could be grasped at to prove there was such a man, but they are all suspect. Either outright hoaxes and forgeries or interpolations, perhaps performed by scriptorium monks who should have had better sense, who allowed devotion to run ahead of honesty. We of the faith do not need the proof; Holy Church does not doubt His existence for a moment, but our belief is based on faith, not on anything like proof. It is a thing we do not talk about. We are faced with so many infidels and pagans that it would be unwise to talk about it. We ourselves do not need such proof, if proof it is, that lies in the manuscript, but Mother Church could use it to convince those who do not share our faith."

"It would end, as well," Duncan's father said, "some of the doubt and skepticism in the Church itself."

"But it might be a hoax, you say."

"It could be," the archbishop said. "We're inclined to think it's not. But Father Jonathan, our man at the abbey, does not have the expertise to rule it out. What we need is a scholar who knows his Aramaic, who has spent years in the study of the language, the changes that have come about in it, and when they came about. It is a language that over the fifteen hundred years it was in use had many dialectical forms.

20

A modern dialect of it is spoken still in some small corners of the eastern world, but the modern form differs greatly from that used in the time of Jesus, and even the form that Jesus used could have been considerably different than the dialect that was used a hundred miles away."

"I'm excited, of course," said Duncan, "and impressed. Excited that from this house could have come something of such significance. But I don't understand you. You said that I . . . "

"There is only one man in the world," the archbishop said, "who would have any chance of knowing if the manuscript were authentic. That man lives at Oxenford."

"Oxenford? You mean in the south?"

"That's right. He lives in that small community of scholars that in the last century or so . . . "

"Between here and Oxenford," Duncan's father said, "lies the Desolated Land."

"It is our thought," said the archbishop, "that a small band of brave and devoted men might be able to slip through. We had talked, your father and I, of sending the manuscript by sea, but these coasts are so beset by pirates that an honest vessel scarcely dares to leave its anchorage."

"How small a band?"

"As small as possible," Duncan's father said. "We can't send out a regiment of men-at-arms to go crashing through almost half of Britain. Such a force would call too much attention to itself. A small band that could move silently and unobtrusively would have a better chance. The bad part is, of course, that such a band would have to go straight across the Desolated Land. There is no way to go around it. From all accounts, it cuts a broad swath across the entire country. The expedition would be much easier if we had some idea of where the Harriers might be, but from the reports we get, they seem to be everywhere throughout the north. In recent weeks, however, from the more recent news that we have had, it seems that they may be moving in a northeasterly direction."

His Grace nodded solemnly. "Straight at us," he said.

"You mean that Standish House . . . "

Duncan's father laughed, a clipped, short laugh that was not quite a laugh. "No need for us to fear them here, son. Not in this ancient castle. For almost a thousand years it has stood against everything that could be hurled against it. But if a party were to attempt to get through to Oxenford, it might be best that they get started soon, before this horde of Harriers is camping on our doorstep."

"And you think that I . . . "

His father said, "We thought we'd mention it."

"I know of no better man to do it," said His Grace. "But it is your decision. It is a venture that must be weighed most carefully."

"I think that if you should decide to go," Duncan's father said, "you might have a fair chance of success. If I had not thought so, we would not have brought it up."

"He's well trained in the arts of combat," said His Grace, speaking to Duncan's father. "I am told, although I do not know it personally, that this son of yours is the most accomplished swordsman in the north, that he has read widely in the histories of campaigns . . . "

"But I've never drawn a blade in anger," protested Duncan. "My knowledge of the sword is little more than fencing. We have been at peace for years. For years there have been no wars. . . . "

"You would not be sent out to engage in battle," his father told him smoothly. "The less you do of that the better. Your job would be to get through the Desolated Land without being seen."

"But there'd always be a chance that we'd run into the Harriers. I suppose that somehow I would manage, although it's not the kind of role in which I've ever thought to place myself. My interest, as it has been yours and your father's before you, lies in this estate, in the people and the land. . . . "

"In that you're not unique," his father told him.

"Many of the Standish men have lived in peace on these very acres, but when the call came, they rode off to battle and there was none who ever shamed us. So you can rest easy on that score. There's a long warrior line behind you."

"Blood will tell," said His Grace pontifically. "Blood will always tell. The fine old families, like the Standishes, are the bulwark of Britain and Our Lord."

"Well," said Duncan, "since you've settled it, since you have picked me to take part in this sally to the south, perhaps you'll tell me what you know of the Desolated Land."

"Only that it's a cyclic phenomenon," said the archbishop. "A cycle that strikes at a different place every five centuries or thereabouts. We know that approximately five hundred years ago it came to pass in Iberia. Five hundred years before that in Macedonia. There are indications that before that the same thing happened in Syria. The area is invaded by a swarm of demons and various associated evil spirits. They carry all before them. The inhabitants are slaughtered, all habitations burned. The area is left in utter desolation. This situation exists for an indeterminate number of years—as few as ten, perhaps, usually more than that. After that time it seems the evil forces depart and people begin to filter back, although it may require a century or more to reclaim the land. Various names have been assigned the demons and their cohorts. In this last great invasion they have been termed the Harriers; at times they are spoken of as the Horde. There is a great deal more, of course, that might be told of this phenomenon, but that is the gist of it. Efforts have been made by a number of scholars to puzzle out the reasons and the motives that may be involved. So far there are only rather feeble theories, no real evidence. Of course, no one has actually ever tried to investigate the afflicted area. No on-the-spot investigations. For which I can not blame . . . "

"And yet," said Duncan's father, "you are suggesting that my son . . . "

"I have no suggestion that he investigate. Only that

23

he try to make his way through the afflicted area. Were it not that Bishop Wise at Oxenford is so elderly, I would say that we should wait. But the man is old and, at the last reports, grown very feeble. His sands are running out. If we wait, we may find him gone to his heavenly reward. And he is the only hope we have. I know of no one else who can judge the manuscript."

"If the manuscript is lost while being carried to Oxenford, what then?" asked Duncan.

"That is a chance that must be taken. Although I know you would guard it with your life."

"So would anyone," said Duncan.

"It's a precious thing," said His Grace. "Perhaps the most precious thing in all of Christendom. Upon those few pages may rest the future hope of mankind."

"You could send a copy."

"No," said the archbishop, "it must be the original. No matter how carefully it would be copied, and at the abbey we have copyists of great skill, the copyist might miss, without realizing it, certain small characteristics that would be essential in determining if it's genuine or not. We have made copies, two of them, that will be kept at the abbey under lock and key. So if the original should be lost we still will have the text. But that the original should be lost is a catastrophe that bears no thinking on."

"What if Bishop Wise can authenticate the text, but raises a question on the parchment or the ink? Surely he is not also an expert on parchments and on inks."

"I doubt," the archbishop said, "that he'll raise such questions. With his scholarship, he should know beyond all question if it is genuine from an examination of the writing only. Should he, however, raise those questions, then we must seek another scholar. There must be those who know of parchments and of inks."

"Your Grace," said Duncan's father, "you say there have been theories advanced about the Desolated Land, about the motive and the reason. Do you, perhaps, have a favorite theory?"

24

"It's hard to choose among them," the archbishop told him. "They all are ingenious and some of them are tricky, slippery of logic. The one, of all of them, that makes most sense to me is the suggestion that the Desolated Lands are used for the purpose of renewal —that the evil forces of the world at times may need a resting period in which to rededicate their purpose and enrich themselves, recharging their strength. Like a church retreat, perhaps. So they waste an area, turning it to a place of horror and desolation, which serves as a barrier to protect them against interference while they carry out whatever unholy procedures may be necessary to strengthen them for another five centuries of evil doing. The man who propounded this theory sought to show a weakening of the evil done for some years preceding the harrying of a desolated land, and in a few years after that a great increase in evil. But I doubt he made his point. There are not sufficient data for that kind of study."

"If this should be true," said Duncan, "then our little band, if it trod most carefully and avoided any fuss, should have a good chance to pass through the Desolated Land unnoticed. The forces of Evil, convinced they are protected by the desolation, would not be as alert as they might be under other circumstances, and they also would be busy doing all the things they need to do in this retreat of theirs."

"You might be right," his father said.

The archbishop had been listening silently to what Duncan and his father had been saying. He sat with his hands folded across his paunch, his eyes half closed, as if he were wrestling with some private thought. The three of them sat quietly for a little time until finally His Grace stirred himself and said, "It seems to me that more study, really serious study, should be made of this great force of Evil that has been loose upon the world for uncounted centuries. We have responded to it, all these centuries, with horror, explaining it by thoughtless superstition. Which is not to say there is no basis for some of the tales we hear and the stories that are told. Some of the tales one hears, of course, are true, in some cases even documented. But many of them are false, the tales of stupid peasants who think them up, I am convinced, to pass off idle hours. Ofttimes, other than their rude horseplay and their fornications, they have little else to amuse themselves. So we are engulfed in all sorts of silly stories. And silly stories do no more than obscure the point. What we should be most concerned with is an understanding of this Evil. We have our spells and enchantments with which to cast out devils; we have our stories of men being changed into howling dogs or worse; we believe volcanoes may be the mouths of Hell; not too long ago we had the story of some silly monks who dug a pit and, descending into it, discovered Purgatory. These are not the kinds of things we need. What we need is an understanding of Evil, for only with an understanding of it will we have some grounds upon which to fight against it. .

"Not only should we get ourselves into a position to fight it effectively for our own peace of mind, for some measure of freedom against the indignity, injury and pain Evil inflicts upon us, but for the growth of our civilization. Consider for the moment that for many centuries we have been a stagnant society, making no progress. What is done each day upon this estate, what is done each day throughout the world, does not differ one iota from what was done a thousand years ago. The grains are cut as they always have been harvested, threshed as they always have been threshed, the fields are plowed with the same inefficient plows, the peasants starve as they have always starved. . . . "

"On this estate they don't," said Duncan's father. "Here no one starves. We look after our own people. And they look after us. We store food against the bad years and when the bad years come, as they seldom do, the food is there for all of us and . . . "

"My lord," said the archbishop, "you will pardon me. I was speaking quite in general. What I have said is not true on this estate, as I well know, but it is true in general."

"Our family," said Duncan's father, "has held these lands for close on ten centuries. As holders of the land, we have accepted the implicit responsibility . . . "

"Please," said the archbishop, "I did not mean your house. Now may I go on?"

"I regret interrupting you," said Duncan's father, "but I felt obliged to make it clear that no one goes hungry at Standish House."

"Quite so," the archbishop said. "And now to go on with what I was saying. It is my opinion that this great weight of Evil which has borne down upon our shoulders has worked against any sort of progress. It has not always been so. In the olden days men invented the wheel, made pottery, tamed the animals, domesticated plants, smelted ore, but since that first beginning there has been little done. There have been times when there seemed a spark of hope, if history tells us true. There was a spark of hope in Greece, but Greece went down to nothing. For a moment Rome seemed to hold a certain greatness and some promise, but in the end Rome was in the dust. It would seem that by now, in the twentieth century, there should be some sign of progress. Better carts, perhaps, and better roads for the carts to run on, better plows and a better understanding of how to use the land, better ways of building houses so that peasants need no longer live in noisome huts, better ships to ply the seas. Sometimes, I have speculated on an alternate history, an alternate to our world, where this Evil did not exist. A world where many centuries of progress have opened possibilities we cannot even guess. That could have been our world, our twentieth century. But it is only a dream, of course.

"We know, however, that west of us, across the Atlantic, there are new lands, vast new lands, so we are told. Sailors from the south of Britain and the western coasts of Gaul go there to catch the cod, but few others, for there are few trustworthy ships to go in. And, perhaps, no great desire to go, for we are deficient in our enterprise. We are held in thrall by Evil and until we do something about that Evil, we will continue so.

"Our society is ill, ill in its lack of progress and in many other ways. I have also often speculated that the Evil may feed upon our misery, grow strong upon our misery, and that to insure good feeding it may actively insure that the misery continues. It seems to me, too, that this great Evil may not always have been with us. In earlier days men did make some progress, doing those few things that have made even such a poor society as we have now possible. There was a time when men did work to make their lives more safe and comfortable, which argues that they were undeterred by this Evil that we suffer or, at least, not as much deterred. And so the question, where did the Evil come from? This is a question, of course, that cannot now be answered. But there is one thing that to me seems certain. The Evil has stopped us in our tracks. What little we have we inherited from our ancient forebears, with a smidgen from the Greeks and a dab from Rome.

"As I read our histories, it seems to me that I detect a deliberate intent upon the part of this great Evil to block us from development and progress. At the end of the eleventh century our Holy Father Urban launched a crusade against the heathen Turks who were persecuting Christians and desecrating the shrines of Jerusalem. Multitudes gathered to the Standard of the Cross, and given time, undoubtedly would have carved a path to the Holy Land and set Jerusalem free. But this did not come to pass, for it was then that the Evil struck in Macedonia and later spread to much of Central Europe, desolating all the land as this land south of us now is desolated, creating panic among those assembled for the crusade and blocking the way they were to take. So the crusade came to naught and no other crusades were launched, for it took centuries to emerge from the widespread chaos occasioned by this striking of the Evil. Because of this, even to this day, the Holy Land, which is ours by right, still lies in the heathen grip."

He put a hand to his face to wipe away the tears that were running down his chubby cheeks. He gulped, and when he spoke again there was a suppressed sobbing in his voice.

"In failing in the crusade, although in the last analysis it was no failure of ours, we may have lost the last hope of finding any evidence of the factual Jesus, which might have still existed at that time, but now undoubtedly is gone beyond the reach of mortal man. In such a context, surely you must appreciate why we place so great an emphasis upon the manuscript found within these walls."

"From time to time," said Duncan's father, "there has been talk of other crusades."

"That is true," said His Grace, "but never carried out. That incidence of Evil, the most widespread and most vicious of which our histories tell us, cut out the heart of us. Recovering from its effects, men huddled on their acres, nursing the unspoken fear, perhaps, that another such effort might again call up the Evil in all its fury. The Evil has made us a cowering and ineffectual people with no thought of progress or of betterment.

"In the fifteenth century, when the Lusitanians evolved a policy calculated to break this torpor by sailing the oceans of the world to discover unknown lands, the Evil erupted once again in the Iberian peninsula and all the plans and policies were abandoned and forgotten as the peninsula was devastated and terror stalked the land. With two such pieces of evidence you cannot help but speculate that the Evil, in its devastations, is acting to keep us as we are, in our misery, so that it can feed and grow strong upon that very misery. We are the Evil's cattle, penned in our scrubby pastures, offering up to it the misery that it needs and relishes."

His Grace raised a hand to wipe his face. "I think of it at nights, before I go to sleep. I agonize upon it. It seems to me that if this keeps on there'll be an end to everything. It seems to me that the lights are going out. They're going out all over Europe. I have the feeling that we are plunging back again into the ancient darkness."

"Have you talked with others about these opinions of yours?" asked Duncan's father.

"A few," the archbishop said. "They profess to take no stock in any of it. They pooh-pooh what I say."

A discreet knock came at the door.

"Yes," said Duncan's father. "Who is it?"

"It is I," said Wells's voice. "I thought, perhaps, some brandy."

"Yes, indeed," exclaimed the archbishop, springing to life, "some brandy would be fine. You have such good brandy here. Much better than the abbey."

"Tomorrow morning," Duncan's father said, between his teeth, "I shall send you a keg of it."

"That," said the archbishop suavely, "would be most kind of you."

"Come on in," Duncan's father yelled to Wells.

The old man carried in a tray on which were balanced glasses and a bottle. Moving quietly in his carpet slippers, he poured out the brandy and handed the glasses around.

When he was gone the archbishop leaned back in his chair, holding out the glass against the firelight and squinting through it. "Exquisite," he said. "Such a lovely color."

"How large a party did you have in mind?" Duncan asked his father.

"You mean that you will go?"

"I'm considering it."

"It would be," said the archbishop, "an adventure in the highest tradition of your family and this house."

"Tradition," said Duncan's father sharply, "has not a thing to do with it."

He said to his son, "I had thought a dozen men or so."

"Too many," Duncan said.

"Perhaps. How many would you say?"

"Two. Myself and Conrad."

The archbishop choked on the brandy, jerked himself upright in his chair. "Two?" he asked, and then, "Who might this Conrad be?"

"Conrad," said Duncan's father, "is a barnyard worker. He is handy with the hogs."

The archbishop sputtered. "But I don't understand."

"Conrad and my son have been close friends since they were boys. When Duncan goes hunting or fishing he takes Conrad with him."

"He knows the woodlands," Duncan said. "He's run in them all his life. When time hangs heavy on his hands, as it does at times, for his duties are not strenuous, he takes out for the woods."

"It does not seem to me," the archbishop said, "that running in the woods is a great qualification . . . "

"But it would be," said Duncan. "We'd be traveling in a wilderness."

"This Conrad," said Duncan's father, "is a brawny man, about seven feet and almost twenty stone of muscle. Quick as a cat. Half animal. He bears unquestioning allegiance to Duncan; he would die for him, I'm sure. He carries a club, a huge oaken club . . ."

"A club!" the archbishop groaned.

"He's handy with it," said Duncan. "I'd put him with that club of his up against a dozen swordsmen and I'd give you odds on Conrad and his club."

"It would not be too bad a choice," Duncan's father said. "The two of them would move quietly and swiftly. If they need defend themselves, they'd be capable."

"Daniel and Tiny to go along with us," said Duncan.

Duncan's father saw the archbishop's lifted eyebrows. "Daniel is a war-horse," he explained, "trained to battle. He is the equal of three men. Tiny is a great mastiff. He is trained for war as well."

31

3

Cedric left them well before dawn, after guiding them to a patch of thick woodland where they spent the remainder of the night. Shortly after dawn, Conrad awakened Duncan and they breakfasted on cheese and bread, unwilling to light a fire. Then they set out again.

The weather had improved. The wind had shifted and died down. The clouds were gone and the sun was warm.

They traveled through a lonely land, largely covered by woods, with deep glens and faery dells running through the woodlands. Occasionally they came across small farms where the buildings had been burned, with the ripe grain standing unharvested. Except for a few ravens that flew silently, as if awed to silence by the country they were passing over, and an occasional startled rabbit that came popping out of one thicket and ran toward another, they saw no life. About the whole country there was a sense of peacefulness and well-being, and this was strange, for this was the Desolated Land.

Some hours later they were traveling up a steep slope through a woods. The trees began thinning out and the woods came to an end. Ahead of them lay a barren, rocky ridge.

"You stay here," Conrad said to Duncan. "I'll go ahead and scout."

Duncan stood beside Daniel and watched the big man go swiftly up the hill, keeping well down, heading for a rocky outcrop that thrust above the ridge. Daniel rubbed a soft muzzle against Duncan's shoulder, whickering softly.

"Quiet, Daniel," Duncan said.

Tiny sat a few feet ahead of them, ears sharp-pricked and bent forward. Beauty moved over to stand on the other side of Duncan, who reached out a hand and stroked her neck.

The silence wore on to a breaking point, but it did not break. There was no sound, no movement. Not even a leaf was rustling. Conrad had disappeared among the rocks. The afternoon wore on. Daniel flicked his ears, again rubbed his muzzle against Duncan's shoulder. This time he did not whicker.

Conrad reappeared, stretched out full length, slithering, snakelike, over the rocks. Once he was clear of the ridge, he came swiftly down the slope.

"Two things I saw," he said.

Duncan waited, saying nothing. Sometimes one had to wait for Conrad.

"There is a village down below us," Conrad finally said. "Black and burned. Except for the church. It is stone and could not burn. No one stirring. Nothing there."

He stopped and then said, "I do not like it. I think we should go around."

"You said you saw two things."

"Down the valley. There were men on horses going down the valley, far beyond the village."

"Men?"

"I think I saw the Reaver at the head of them. Far off, but I think I recognized him. There were thirty men or more."

"You think they're after us?" asked Duncan.

"Why else should they be here?"

"At least we know where they are," said Duncan, "and they don't know where we are. They're ahead of

33

us. I'm surprised. I hadn't thought they'd follow. Revenge can get expensive in a place like this."

"Not revenge," said Conrad. "They want Daniel and Tiny."

"You think that's why they're here?"

"A war-horse and a war-dog would be very good to have."

"I suppose so. They might have trouble getting them. Those two would not change masters willingly."

"Now what do we do?"

"Damned if I know," said Duncan. "They were heading south?"

"South, and west, too. A little west. The way the valley runs."

"We'd better swing east, then. Go around the village and widen the distance from them."

"They are some distance off. Still more distance would be better."

Tiny rose to his feet, swinging around to the left, a growl deep in his throat.

"The dog has something," Duncan said.

"A man," said Conrad. "That's his man growl."

"How can you know?"

"I know all his talk," said Conrad.

Duncan swiveled around to stare in the direction Tiny was looking. He could see nothing. No sign anything was there.

"My friend," Duncan said, conversationally, "I'd come out if I were you. I'd hate to have to send the dog in after you."

Nothing happened for a moment. Then some bushes stirred and a man came out of them. Tiny started forward.

"Leave him be," said Conrad to the dog.

The man was tall and cadaverous. He wore a shabby brown robe that reached to his ankles. A cowl was bunched about his shoulders. In his right hand he carried a long and knobby staff, in his left he clutched a fistful of plants. The skin clung so tightly to his skull that the bones showed through. His beard was skimpy.

He said to them, "I'm Andrew, the hermit. I had

34

meant not to interfere with you. So, catching sight of you, I hid from sight of you. I was out to hunt for greens, a mess of pottage for my supper. You wouldn't have some cheese, perchance, would you?"

"We have cheese," growled Conrad.

"I dream of cheese," said Andrew, the hermit. "I wake up at night and find I am thinking of a bit of cheese. It has been a long time since I have had the taste of cheese."

"In that case," said Duncan, "we'll be glad to give you some. Why don't you, Conrad, take that sack off Beauty."

"Nay, wait a moment," objected Andrew. "No need to do it now. You be travelers, are you not?"

"You can see we are," said Conrad, not too pleasantly.

"In that case," said Andrew, "why not spend the night with me. I'm fair famished for the sight of human faces and the sound of human tongue. There's Ghost, of course, but talking with him is little like talking with someone in the flesh."

"Ghost?" asked Duncan.

"Aye, a ghost. A very honest ghost. And quite a decent one. Not given to the rattling of chains or moaning in the night. He's shared my cell with me since the day that he was hanged. The Harriers done it to him."

"The Harriers, of course," said Duncan. "Would you tell us how you escaped the Harriers."

"I hid in my cell," said Andrew. "It really is a cave and it's not as small and cramped and miserable as a proper cell should be. I fear I am not a proper hermit. I do not go in for the mortifications of the flesh as the more successful hermits do. I dug the cave first to cell-like proportions, as I understood I was supposed to, but over the years I have enlarged it until it's spacious and fairly comfortable. There's plenty of room for you. It's hidden quite away. You'll be secure from all observation, as I would imagine most travelers in a place like this naturally would want to be. The

35

evening's coming on and you must soon seek camp and you can't find a better place than this cell of mine."

Duncan looked at Conrad. "What are your thoughts," he asked, "upon the matter?"

"Little sleep you got last night," said Conrad, "I got even less. This one seems an honest yokel."

"There's the ghost," warned Duncan.

Conrad shrugged elaborately. "Ghosts I do not mind."

"All right, then," said Duncan. "Friar Andrew, if you will lead the way."

The cave was located a mile or so outside the village, and to reach it they passed through a cemetery which, from the variety and condition of the stones, must have been in continuous use for centuries. Near the center of it stood a small tomb built of native stone. Sometime in the past, perhaps in a storm, the heavy trunk of a large oak tree nearby had fallen across the tomb, shattering the small statuary fixed atop it and pushing the covering slab askew.

A short distance beyond the cemetery they came to the hermit's cave, which was excavated from a steep hillside, its entrance well masked by a growth of trees and heavy underbrush and a chattering brook hurrying down a steep ravine directly in front.

"You go on in," Conrad said to Duncan. "I'll unsaddle Daniel, bring in Beauty's pack."

The cave was dark, but even in the darkness it had a spacious sense. A small fire burned on the hearth. Fumbling in the darkness, the hermit found a large candle, lit it at the fire, and placed it on a table. The candle, flaring up, showed the thick carpet of rushes on the floor, the crude table with benches that could be pulled up to it, a badly constructed chair, bins against the earthen walls, the pallet in one corner. A cabinet in another corner held a few parchment rolls.

Noting Duncan looking at them, the hermit said, "Yes, I can read, but barely. In idle moments I sit here by candlelight, spelling out the words and striving at the meanings of the ancient Fathers of the

Church. I doubt that I arrive at meaning, for I am a simple soul and at times a stupid one to boot. And those ancient Fathers, it seems to me, ofttimes were much more involved in words than they were in meaning. As I told you, I'm not really a good hermit, but I keep on trying, although at times I find myself a-wonder at the true profession of a hermit. I have thought off and on that a hermit must be the silliest and most useless member of society."

"It is, however," said Duncan, "a calling that is thought of very highly."

"It has occurred to me, when I've thought deeply on it," said the hermit, "that men may be hermits for no other reason than to escape the labors of another kind of life. Surely hermiting is easier on the back and muscles than grubbing in the soil or performing other menial tasks by which one may win his bread. I have asked myself if I am this kind of hermit and, truthfully, I must answer that I do not know."

"You say you hid here when the Harriers came and that they did not find you. That seems not exactly right. In all our journey we have seen no one who survived. Except one group of ruffians and bandits who had taken over a manor house and had been skillful enough or lucky enough to have been able to defend it."

"You speak of Harold, the Reaver?"

"Yes. How come you know of him?"

"Word travels throughout the Desolated Land. There are carriers of tales."

"I do not understand."

"The little folk. The elves, the trolls, the gnomes, the fairies and the Brownies . . . "

"But they . . . "

"They are local folk. They've lived here since time unknown. They may be pestiferous at times and unpleasant neighbors and, certainly, individuals in whom you can place no trust. Mischievous they may be, but very seldom vicious. They did not align themselves with the Harriers, but themselves hid from them. And they warned many others."

"They warned you so you could hide away?"

"A gnome came to warn me. I had not thought him a friend, for through the years cruel tricks he had played upon me. But, to my surprise, I found that he was an unsuspected friend. His warning gave me time to put out my fire so the smoke would not betray me, although I doubt the little smoke of my poor fire would have betrayed anyone at all. It would have gone unnoticed in the general burning that came about when the Harriers arrived. The huts went up in flames, the haystacks and the straw stacks, the granaries and the privies. They even burned the privies. Can you imagine that?"

"No, I can't," said Duncan.

Conrad came clumping into the cave, dumping the saddle and the packs to one side of the door.

"I heard you say a ghost," he rumbled. "There isn't any ghost."

"Ghost is a timid one," said Andrew. "He hides from visitors. He thinks no one wants to see him. He has a dislike for scaring people, although there's really nothing about him that should scare anyone. As I told you, he is a decent and considerate ghost."

He raised his voice. "Ghost, come out of there. Come out and show yourself. We have guests."

A tendril of white vaporous substance streamed reluctantly from behind the cabinet holding the parchment rolls.

"Come on, come on," the hermit said impatiently. "You can show yourself. These gentlemen are not frightened of you, and it is only courteous that you come out to greet them."

The hermit said to Duncan, out of the corner of his mouth, "I have a lot of trouble with him. He thinks it's disgraceful to be a ghost."

Slowly Ghost took shape above the cabinet, then floated to floor level. He was a classical ghost, white sheeted. The only distinguishing mark was a short loop of rope knotted about his neck, with a couple of feet or so hanging down in front.

"I'm a ghost," he said in a hollow, booming voice,

38

"with no place to haunt. Usually a ghost haunts his place of death, but how is one to haunt an oak tree? The Harriers dug my poor body out of the thicket in which I hid and forthwith strung me up. They might have paid me the courtesy, it seems to me, to have hung me from a mighty oak, one of those forest patriarchs that are so common in these woods of ours, tall trees standing well above the others and of mighty girth. But this they did not do. They hung me from a scrawny, stunted oak. Even in my death I was made sport of. In my life I begged alms at the church door and a poor living I made of it, for there were those who spread the rumor that I had no reason for the begging, that I could have done a day's work as well as any man. They said I only pretended to be crippled."

"He was a fraud," the hermit said. "He could have labored as well as any other."

"You hear?" the ghost asked. "You hear? Even in death I am branded as a cheat and fraud. I am made a fool of."

"I'll say this for him," the hermit said. "He's a pleasure to have around. He's not up on all the ghostly tricks that other ghosts employ to make nuisances of themselves."

"I try," said Ghost, "to be but little trouble. I'm an outcast, otherwise I would not be here. I have no proper place to haunt."

"Well, now you have met with these gentlemen and have conversed with them in a seemly matter," said the hermit, "we can turn to other matters." He turned to Conrad. "You said you had some cheese."

"Also bacon and ham, bread and honey," said Duncan.

"And you'll share all this with me?"

"We could not eat it ourselves and not share it with you."

"Then I'll build up the fire," said Andrew, "and we shall make a feast. I shall throw out the greens I gathered. Unless you should like a taste of greens. Perhaps with a bit of bacon."

"I do not like greens," said Conrad.

4

D uncan woke in the night and for a moment of
panic wondered where he was. There were no points
of reference, just a musty darkness with some flicker
in it—as if he might be in some limbo, a waiting room
for death.

Then he saw the door, or if not a door, an opening,
with the soft wash of moonlight just beyond it, and in
the fire-lit flicker, the bulk of Tiny, lying stretched out
before the opening. Tiny had his legs pushed out in
front of him, with his head resting on his paws.

Duncan twisted his head around and saw that the
flicker came from a low-burned fire upon the hearth.
A few feet away lay Conrad, flat upon his back, his
toes pointing upward and his arms flung out on each
side. His great barrel chest went up and down. He was
breathing through his mouth, and the sucked-in then
expelled air made a fluttering sound.

There was no sign of the hermit. Probably he was
on his pallet, over in the corner. The air smelled
faintly of wood smoke, and over his head, Duncan
could make out the indistinct shapes of bunches of
herbs the hermit had hung up to dry. From outside
came a soft stamping sound. That would be Daniel
not far away.

Duncan pulled the blanket up beneath his chin and shut his eyes. More than likely it was several hours till dawn, and he could get more sleep.

But sleep was reluctant to come. Much as he tried to shut them out, the events of the last few days kept parading up and down his mind. And the parading of events brought home again the rigors of the adventure he had embarked upon. In this hermit cave it was snug enough, but beyond the cave lay the Desolated Land with its freight of evil, with the burned-out village only a mile or so away, the church the only building standing. Not only the Evil, he reminded himself, but a band of evil men headed by the Reaver, who were out to track down his little party. For the moment, however, he could forget the Reaver, who had gone blundering off somewhere ahead of them.

Then his mind went back to that last day at Standish House when he'd sat with his father in the library, that same room where His Grace had told the story of the script writ in Aramaic.

Now he asked of his father the question that had been roiling in his mind ever since he'd heard the story. "But why us?" he asked. "Why should the manuscript have been in Standish House?"

"There is no way to know," his father said. "The family's history is a long one and not too well documented. There are large parts of it that have been entirely lost. There are some records, of course, some writings, but mostly it is legend, stories from so long ago and so often told that there is no way to judge the truth that may be in them. We now are solid country folks, but there was a time when we were not. In the family records and in the legendary tales there are many wanderers and some shameless adventurers. It could have been one of these, traveling far, who brought home the manuscript. Probably from somewhere in the east. As part, perhaps, of his portion of the loot from a captured city or stolen from some monastery or, less likely, honestly purchased for a copper or two as a curiosity. There could not have been much value placed upon it, and rightly so, of

41

course, for until it was placed in the hands of the fathers at the abbey, there was no one who could have known the significance of it. I found it in an old wooden crate, the wood half gone with rot and with mildew on the documents that it contained. The manuscript was tossed in among other odds and ends of parchment, most of which were worthless."

"But you saw or sensed some significance in it. Enough to take it to the abbey."

"No significance," his father said. "No thought of any possible significance. Just an idle curiosity. I read some Greek, you know, and I can make my way in several other languages, although but poorly, but I'd never seen the like of the manuscript before. I simply wondered what it might be and was somewhat intrigued by it, and I thought that perhaps I should put some of those fat and lazy fathers at it. After all, they should be called upon occasionally to do a little work for us, if for no other reason than to remind them where they get their keep. When there's a roof to be repaired at the abbey, we are the ones they come to for the slate and the expertise to put it on. When they need a load of hay, being too trifling to go out and scythe it on their own, they know where to come to get it."

"You must say this for them," said Duncan. "They did quite a job on the manuscript."

"Better that they should be doing that," his father said, "which, after all, is useful work, rather than producing precious little conceits that they employ to spell out the happy hours of someone or other. All scriptoria, and I suspect the scriptorium at our abbey most of all, are filled with artistic fools who have too high an opinion of themselves. The Standishes have held this land for nigh on a thousand years, and from first to last we have given service to the abbey, and as those years went on, the abbey has become more grasping and demanding. Take the matter of that keg of brandy. His Grace did not ask for it, but he came as close to asking as even his good offices allowed."

"That brandy is a sore point with you, my lord," said Duncan.

His father whiffled out his mustache. "For centuries this house has produced good brandy. It is a matter of some pride for us, for this is not a country of the grape. But through the years we have pruned and grafted and budded until we have a vine that would be the pride of Gaul. And I tell you, son, a keg of brandy is not come by easily. His Grace had best use this one sparingly, for he's not about to get another soon."

They sat for a time not speaking, with the fire snapping in the great fireplace.

Duncan's father finally stirred in his chair. "As we have done with the grape," he said, "so have we done with other things. We have cattle here that run to several hundredweight heavier than most cattle in other parts of Britain. We raise good horses. Our wool is of the best. The wheat we grow is hardy for this climate—wheat, while many of our neighbors must be content with oats. And as it is with the crops and live-stock, so it is with people. Many of the peasants and serfs who work our acres and are happy at it have been here almost as many years as the family. Standish House, although it was not known then as Standish House, had its beginnings in a time of strife and un-certainty, when no man's life was safe. It began as a wooden fort, built upon a mound, protected by a pali-sade and moat as many manor houses are protected even to this day.

"We still have our moat, of course, but now it has become a pretty thing, with water lilies and other dec-orative plants growing in it, and its earthen sides well landscaped with shrubs and slanted flower beds. And stocked with fish that serve as sport or food for who-ever has the mind to dangle a baited hook into its waters. The drawbridge remains in place as a bridge across the moat. Ritually, we raise and lower it once a year to be sure it still will work. The country has grown a little more secure with the years, of course, but not so one could notice. There still are roving bands of human predators who show up every now and then. But with the years our house has grown stronger and news of our strength has spread. Not for three hundred years or more has any bandit or reaver or whatever he may call himself dared to throw himself against our walls. A few hit-and-run raids to snatch up a cow or two or a clutch of sheep are all that ever happen now. Although I do not think it is the strength of our walls alone that has brought about this security we enjoy. It is the knowledge that our people still are a warrior people, even if they be no more than serfs or peasants. We no longer maintain an army of idle and arrogant men-at-arms. There is no longer need to do so. Should there be danger, every man of this estate will take up arms, for each man here considers this land his land as much as it is ours. So in a still turbulent society we have created here a place of security and peace."

"I have loved this house," said Duncan. "I shall not be easy, leaving it."

"Nor I easy, my son, at having you leave it. For you will be going into 'danger, and yet I do not feel any great uneasiness, for I know that you can handle yourself. And Conrad is a stout companion."

"So," said Duncan, "are Daniel and Tiny."

"His Grace, the other night," his father said, "carried on at some length about our lack of progress. We are, he said, a stagnant society. And while this may be true, I still can see some good in it. For if there were progress in other things, there'd be progress in armaments as well. And any progress in arms would spell continual war, for if some chieftain or piddling king acquired a new implement of war he need must try it out against a neighbor, thinking that for at least a moment it would give him some advantage."

"All our arms," said Duncan, "historically are personal arms. To use them one man must face another man at no more than arm's length. There are few that reach out farther. Spears and javelins, of course, but they are awkward weapons at the best and once one has cast them he cannot retrieve them to cast them

44

once again. They and slings are all that have any distance factor. And slings are tricky things to use, mostly inaccurate and, by and large, not too dangerous."

"You are right," his father said. "There are those, like His Grace, who bewail our situation, but to my mind we are quite fortunate. We have achieved a social structure that serves our purposes and any attempt to change it might throw us out of balance and bring on many troubles, most of which, I would imagine, we cannot now suspect."

A sudden coldness, a breath of frost sweeping over Duncan, jerked him from his review of that last day. His eyes popped open, and bending over him, he saw the hooded face of Ghost, if face it could be called. It was more like a murky oval of swirling smoke, encircled by the whiteness of the cowl. There were no features, just that smoky swirl, and yet he felt he was staring straight into a face.

"Sir Ghost," he said sharply, "what is your intent to waken me so rudely and abruptly?"

Ghost, he saw, was hunkering beside him, and that was a strange thing, that a ghost should hunker.

"I have questions to ask your lordship," said Ghost. "I have asked them beforetimes of the hermit and he is impatient of me for asking questions that do not fall within his knowledge, although as a holy man one might think he had the knowledge. I asked them of your huge companion and he only grunts at me. He was outraged, methinks, that a ghost should presume to talk to him. Should he think he might find any substance to me, I believe he might have put those hamlike hands about my throat and choked me. Although no longer can I be choked. I have been choked sufficiently. Also, I think, a broken neck. So, happily, I now am beyond all such indignity."

Duncan threw the blanket off him and sat up.

"After such a lengthy prelude," he said, "your questions must be ones of more than ordinary importance."

"To me," said Ghost, "they are."

"I may not be able to answer them."

"In which case, you'll be no worse than any of the others."

"So," said Duncan, "go ahead and ask."

"How come, my lord, do you think that I should be wearing such a getup? I know, of course, that it is a proper ghostly costume. It is worn by all proper ghosts, although I understand that in the case of some castle ghosts the habiliment may be black. Certainly I was not dressed in such a spotless robe when I was strung up from the oak. I was strung up in very filthy rags and in the terror of being hanged I fear I befouled them even further."

"That," said Duncan, "is a question I cannot answer."

"At least you accord me the courtesy of an honest reply," said Ghost. "You did not growl or snarl at me."

"There might be someone who has made a study of such matters who could give you an answer. Someone of the Church, perhaps."

"Well, since I'm not likely soon to meet someone of the Church, methinks I can then do little about it. It is not too important, but it is something that has bothered me. I have mulled upon it."

"I am sorry," Duncan said.

"I have yet another question."

"Ask it if you feel you must. An answer I'll not promise."

"My question," said Ghost, "is why me? Not all people who die, not even all whose lives are ended violently or in shame, assume a ghostly guise. If all did, the world would be filled with ghosts. They'd be treading upon one another's sheets. There'd be no room for the living."

"Neither can I answer that one."

"Actually," said Ghost, "I was not a really sinful person. Rather, I was despicable and no one has ever told me that despicability is a sin. I had my sins, of course, as has everyone, but unless my understanding of sins is faulty, they were very small ones."

"You really have your troubles, don't you. You

46

were complaining when we first met that you had no proper place to haunt."

"I think if I had," said Ghost, "I might be happier, although perhaps it is not intended that a ghost should be happy. Contented, perhaps. It might be proper for a ghost to feel contentment. Contentment, certainly, cannot be proscribed. If I had a place to haunt, then I'd have a task to do and could be about it. Although if it included the jangling of chains and making whooing noises, I would not like it much. If it was just slinking around and letting people catch small glimpses of me that might not be bad. Do you suppose that not having a place to haunt, not having a job to do, may be in the way of retribution for the way I lived? I don't mind telling you, although I would not tell everyone and would not want you to bruit it about, that if I had wanted to I could have done some work, making an honest living instead of begging at the church. Light work, of course. I was never very strong; I was sickly as a child. I recall that it was the wonder of my parents' life that they managed to raise me."

"You raise too many questions of philosophy," said Duncan. "I cannot cope with them."

"You say that you are going to Oxenford," said Ghost. "Perhaps to confer with some great scholar there. Otherwise, why would one go to Oxenford? I have heard that there are many great doctors of the Church gathered there and that among themselves they hold much learned discourse."

"When we arrive," said Duncan, "we undoubtedly will see some of the learned doctors."

"Do you suppose some of them might have answers to my questions?"

"I cannot say for sure."

"Would it be too forward to ask if I might travel with you?"

"Look," said Duncan, becoming exasperated, "if you want to go to Oxenford you can easily and safely travel there yourself. You're a free spirit. You are bound to no place that you must haunt. And in the shape you're in, no one could lay a hand on you."

Ghost shuddered. "By myself," he said, "I'd be scared to death."

"You're already dead. No man can die a second time."

"That is true," said Ghost. "I had not thought of that. Lonesome, then. How about my loneliness. I know I'd be very lonesome if I tried to travel alone."

"If you want to go with us," said Duncan, "I can't think of a thing we can do to stop you. But you'll get no invitation."

"If that's the case," said Ghost, "I shall go along with you."

5

They had great slabs of ham for breakfast, with oaten cakes and honey. Conrad came in from outside to report that Daniel and Beauty had found good grazing in the corner of a nearby hay field and that Tiny had provided his own food by capturing a rabbit.

"In such a case," said Duncan, "we can be on our way with good conscience. The bellies of all are full."

"If you're not in too much of a hurry," said Andrew, the hermit, "there is one service you could do for me, which I would greatly appreciate."

"If it did not take too much time," said Duncan. "We owe you something. You furnished us shelter from the night and good company."

"It should not take too long," said Andrew. "It is but a small task for many hands and the strong back of a burro. It has to do with the harvesting of cabbages."

"What is this talk of cabbages?" asked Conrad.

"Someone made an early garden," said Andrew, "before the Harriers came. Neglected through the summer, it had grown until I discovered it. It is located not too far from the church, just a skip and jump from here. There is a mystery, however . . . "

"A mystery with cabbages?" Duncan asked, amused.

"Not with the cabbages. Not entirely with the cabbages, that is. But with other vegetables. The carrots and the rutabagas, the peas and beans. Someone has been stealing them."

49

"And I suppose," said Duncan, "that you have not been stealing them."

"I found the garden," Andrew said stiffly. "I have looked for this other person, but not too bravely, you understand, for I am not a warrior type and would scarce know what to do if I came upon him. Although I oftimes have told myself that if he were not pugnacious, it would be comforting to have another person with whom to pass the time of day. But there are many fine cabbages, and it would be a pity should they go to waste, or should all be taken by this garden thief. I could harvest them myself, but it would take many trips."

"We can spare the time," Duncan told him, "in the name of Christian charity."

"M'lord," warned Conrad, "leagues we have to go."

"Quit calling me my lord," said Duncan. "If we do this chore of neighborliness we'll undoubtedly travel with lighter hearts."

"If you insist," said Conrad. "I'll catch up Beauty."

The garden, which lay a stone's throw back of the church, displayed a splendid array of vegetables growing among rampant weeds that in places reached waist high.

"You certainly did not break your back to keep the garden clean," Duncan observed to Andrew.

"Too late when I discovered it," protested Andrew. "The weeds had too good a start."

There were three long rows of cabbages and they were splendid heads, large and firm. Conrad spread out a packsack cloth, and all of them got busy pulling up the cabbages, shaking off the dirt that clung to their roots before tossing them onto the cloth.

A voice spoke behind them. "Gentlemen," it said. There was a sharp note of disapproval in the word.

The three of them turned swiftly. Tiny, spinning around to face the threat, growled deeply in his throat.

First Duncan saw the griffin and then he saw the woman who rode it, and for a long moment he stood rooted to the ground.

The woman was dressed in leather breeches and a

leather jacket, wore a white stock at her throat. In her right hand she carried a battle axe, its blade glistening in the sun.

"For weeks," she said, in a calm and even voice, "I have been watching this scabby hermit stealing from the garden and did not begrudge him what he took, for skin and bones as he is, it seemed that he might need it. But I had never expected to find a gentleman of the realm joining him in theft."

Duncan bowed. "My lady, we were simply assisting our friend in harvesting the cabbages. We had no knowledge that you, or anyone, might have better claim to this garden plot."

"I have taken great care," said the woman, "to be sure that no one knew I was about. This is a place where one does not make one's presence known."

"My lady, you are making it known now."

"Only to protect the little food I have. I could afford to allow your friend an occasional carrot or a cabbage now and then. But I do object to the stripping of the garden."

The griffin cocked its large eagle head at Duncan, appraising him with a glittering golden eye. Its forelegs ended in eagle claws; the rest was lion, except that instead of a lion's tail it had a somewhat longer appendage with a wicked sting at its end. Its huge wings were folded far back and high, leaving room for its rider. It clicked its beak at Duncan and its long tail switched nervously.

"You need have no fear of him," the woman said. "He is something of a pussycat, the gentleness of him brought on by extreme age. He puts up a splendid and ferocious front, of course, but he'll do no one harm unless I bid him to."

"Madam," said Duncan, "I find this somewhat embarrassing. My name is Duncan Standish. I and my companion, the big one over there, are on a trip to the south of Britain. Only last night we fell in with the hermit, Andrew."

"Duncan Standish, of Standish House?"

"That is right, but I had not thought . . . "

"The fame of your house and family is known in every part of Britain. I must say, however, that you have chosen a strange time to embark upon a journey through these lands."

"No stranger," said Duncan, "than to find a lady of quality in those same lands."

"My name," she said, "is Diane, and I am no lady of quality. I am quite something else again."

Andrew stumped forward. "If you would excuse me, m'lord, I have grave doubts that the Lady Diane can lay legal, or even ethical, claim upon this garden patch. It was an early planted plot, put in by one of the villagers before the Harriers came with fire and sword, and she owns it no more than I do. If you think back, I never did lay claim to it."

"It would be unseemly," said Duncan, "for us to stand here squabbling over it."

"The truth is," said the Lady Diane, "that he is quite right. It is not my garden, nor is it his. We both used out of it and that I did not mind. But it roused my ire to see interlopers laying claim to it as well."

"I would be willing," said Andrew, "to share it with her. Half the cabbages to me, half to her."

"That seems fair to me," said Duncan, "but somewhat unchivalrous."

"I am no man of chivalry," said Andrew snappishly.

"If yon hermit can provide me with certain information," said Diane, "it may be he can have all the cabbages since then I'd have no need of them."

She dismounted from the griffin and walked forward to join them.

"The information that you seek," said Andrew. "What makes you believe that I might have it?"

"You are a native of the village?"

"Aye, myself and all my folk before me."

"Then maybe you would know. There was a man named Wulfert. He is supposed to have lived here at one time. When I arrived here, after the Harriers had left, I took up residence in the church. It was the only roof left standing. I searched the church for records.

I found few. Not anything of value. The parish priests you people had, Sir Hermit, were careless in their record keeping."

"Wulfert, you say?" asked the hermit. "You say a man named Wulfert. How long ago?"

"A hundred years or more. Have you ever heard of him, anyone speak of him?"

"A sage? A saintly man?"

"He might have posed as such. He was a wizard."

The hermit gasped and put his hands up to his head, his fingers gripping his skull.

"A wizard!" he whimpered. "Are you sure of that?"

"Quite sure. A most accomplished wizard."

"And not of Holy Church?"

"Assuredly not of Holy Church."

"What is wrong with you?" Duncan asked Andrew. "What is going on?"

"In holy ground," Andrew whispered, gasping. "Oh, the shame of it. In holy ground they put him. And him a heathen wizard, for to be a wizard one must be a heathen, must he not? They even built a tomb for him."

"These are strange goings-on," said Conrad. "I find no head nor tail of it."

"No wonder," Andrew cried wildly. "No wonder that the oak should fall upon it."

"Wait a minute, now," said Duncan. "You mean an oak fell upon the tomb? There was a cemetery just the other day."

"Please tell me," said Diane, "about this oak and tomb."

"We passed through a cemetery," Duncan said. "Just a mile or so from here. There was a tomb and a tree had fallen on it. Quite some time ago, it seemed. It still is there, lying across the tomb. The slab covering the tomb had been shoved aside and broken. I wondered at the time why no one had repaired it."

"It's an old burial ground," Andrew explained. "Not used for years. No one bothered. And there may not have been many people who would know who was buried there."

"You think this might be the tomb of Wulfert?" Diane asked.

"The shame of it!" wailed the hermit. "That such be placed in holy ground. But the people did not know, the people of the village had no way to know. Of this Wulfert I have heard. A holy man, it was said of him, who sought refuge from the world in this lonely place."

Duncan asked Diane, "Is this the information that you . . . "

And then he stopped, for there was something wrong. A sudden silence—and that was strange, for there had been no sound before, nothing but the background sound of insects and birds, an ever-present sound one grew so accustomed to hearing that it went unnoticed. And that was it, thought Duncan—the sudden silence was the absence of that background sound. The sudden silence and the strange feeling of expectancy, as if one were tensed for something that was about to happen, not knowing what it was, but rocking forward on the toes to be ready for it.

The others had noticed the silence and perhaps the expectancy as well, for they were frozen in their places, tensed and listening and watchful.

Duncan's hand lifted slowly and his fingers wrapped about the hilt of his sword, but he did not draw it, for there was as yet no solid evidence of danger. But the sense of danger still hung heavy in the air. Diane, he saw, had half lifted the battle axe she held. The griffin had shifted its position and its eagle head was pivoting slowly from one side to the other.

Bushes stirred on the far perimeter of the garden plot and a figure half emerged: a round head, superficially human, thrust forward on a short, almost nonexistent neck set between massive shoulders. Bald—the head bald, the shoulders bald, no trace of hair, not like something that had shaved its hair, but rather something that had never grown hair.

The hairless one, Duncan told himself, the hairless ones the Reaver had told him of that night they stopped at the manor house. Great, white, hairless human slugs that fell short of being human.

54

The sword rasped as he cleared it. He slashed it in the air and the sun glistened off it as he made the symbolic slash.

"Now we'll see," he said, speaking half to himself, half to the Reaver, who had told him of these creatures.

The hairless one rose to full height, emerging from the bushes. It stood a little taller than an ordinary man, but not as tall as the Reaver had led him to believe. It stood on bowed legs, bent forward at the knees, and shambled as it walked. It wore not a stitch of clothing, and the fish white of its bulging torso shone in the sunlight. In one hand it carried a huge knotted club. The club was held nonchalantly, its head pointing toward the ground, as if the club were an extension of its arm.

Behind it were others, stepping out from the trees and bushes to array themselves beside the first. They stood in a ragged line, their round heads thrust forward, tiny eyes beneath bald and jutting brows looking with an interested but contemptuous gaze at those who stood in the garden patch.

They shambled forward, slowly, awkwardly, then suddenly, with no indication they intended to do anything but shamble, they charged, coming in great leaps through the weeds. Their clubs were no longer pointed at the ground, but lifted high, and the chilling thing about the charge was that they came silently. They did not whoop or scream or cry out in any way at all. There was, it seemed to Duncan, a deadliness in the very silence of their attack.

Instinctively, without a thought of what he should do, he stepped forward to meet them. In the lead was the one who had first come into view—Duncan was sure it was the one, although there were no distinguishing marks by which one could be told from another. And this one was coming straight toward him, as if it had marked him out as its special prey.

The club in the hands of the hairless one started to come down and with a quick lunge, Duncan leaped beneath the stroke. His sword arm was back and he drove the blade forward with all his strength. As the sword caught it in the throat, the hairless one tumbled toward him, falling like a severed tree. Duncan threw himself to one side, the sword freeing itself as it ripped a jagged wound through the white, bald throat.

The body grazed him as it fell, throwing him slightly off his balance, forcing him to skip awkwardly for a step or two to maintain his balance. To one side of him was another of the creatures, and even as he skipped to keep his balance, Duncan flung up his blade and cut down at the oncoming hairless one. The whistling edge caught it in the juncture between neck and shoulder and went on through, severing the head and opposite shoulder from the trunk. A gush of blood spurted like a fountain as the head came off.

From the corner of his eye, Duncan saw Diane on the ground, struggling to free herself from the bulk of the body of a hairless one. The outflung blade of her battle axe was smeared with blood, and there was no question that the hairless one on top of her was dead. Towering above her, standing on its hind legs, was the griffin. From one eagle claw dangled a squirming hairless one. The claw was fastened around its head, lifting it so its feet were off the ground, the feet moving rapidly back and forth, as if the hairless one were attempting to run on empty air.

From somewhere, Conrad was yelling at him, "Take heed, m'lord!"

Warned, Duncan ducked to one side, spinning as he ducked. A club caught him on the shoulder, bowling him over. Hitting the ground, he rolled and came swiftly to his feet. A few feet from him one of the hairless ones, perhaps the one that had bowled him over, was lunging at him to strike again. Duncan jerked up the sword, but before he could use it, Tiny struck the hairless one like a foaming fury; powerful jaws fastened on its club arm. The hairless one went down and Tiny, releasing the hold upon its arm, had it by the throat.

Duncan switched around, satisfied that Tiny had the situation well under control—you no longer had to worry about something if Tiny had its throat. Diane had pulled herself from beneath the body of the hairless one and was running toward the griffin, which was facing three of the attackers, striking with its claws, jabbing with its beak. Beneath him lay the body of the one he first had seized, and the three in front of him were beginning to back off.

Just beyond the griffin, Conrad was engaged in a fencing match with two of the hairless ones, all three of them armed with clubs that crashed and splintered as terrific blows were struck, caught, and deflected. A little farther off one of the hairless ones had dropped its club and was running desperately, in full flight from Daniel, who was closing on it, running with outstretched neck and bared teeth. Even as Duncan watched, Daniel clamped his teeth down upon his victim's shoulder and with a toss of his head, flung it high into the air.

There was no sign of the hermit.

With a bellow of encouragement, Duncan ran to aid Conrad in his unequal fencing match. Running, he tripped and fell forward and there was a great throb in his head, a pulsating, red-hot pain that flared until his head threatened to explode. At that point exactly, just before the moment of explosion, the pain went away, only to come again. He did not know when he hit the ground; he felt no impact as he fell. Later, with no way of knowing how much later, he found himself crawling on his belly, reaching out with clawed hands to clutch the ground and pull himself along. The funny thing was that he seemed to have no head. In its place was a tumbled fuzziness that could neither see nor hear. Later—he could not tell how much later or how soon—someone was splashing water on his face and saying, "It's all right, m'lord." Then he was lifted and slung across a shoulder and he tried to protest against it, but he couldn't make a sound and he couldn't move a muscle. All that he could do was sway and dangle on the shoulder.

6

There finally was existence. But that was all—existence. It was a purposeless existence that floated in a place without reference points. It floated in an emptiness that was tied to nothing. The emptiness was comfortable and there was no urge to escape from it or to reach beyond it.

A tiny sound intruded: a faint, far-off chirping sound, and the emptiness of existence tried to push it off or shut itself against it. For it was not meet, it might be destructive, for even so slight a thing as a chirping sound to intrude upon it.

But the chirping sound persisted and it was nearer now or louder, and there was more of it, as if there might be many sources from which the chirps were coming.

The consciousness floated in the emptiness and listened with an enforced tolerance to the chirping sound. And the chirping brought a word. *Birds.* It was birds that were chirping. They were the ones that made the noise. The consciousness reluctantly struggled with the word, for it had no idea what the word might mean or if it had a meaning.

Then suddenly it did know what the word meant and that brought something else.

I am Duncan Standish, said the emptiness, and I am lying somewhere, listening to birds.

58

That was quite enough. That was all it needed, that was far more than it needed. It would have been content if nothing had come at all. For if this much came, there would be more yet to come and that was undesirable. The emptiness tried to shrink away, but that was impossible. Having come to something, it must then go on.

Duncan Standish, no longer an existence poised in a vault of emptiness, but Duncan Standish, something. A man, he (or it) thought, and what was a man?

Slowly he knew. Knew what he was and that he had a head and that a dull throbbing ache pulsed inside the head, with the comfort now all gone.

Duncan Standish, man, lying in some confined space, for now he became aware that he was confined.

He lay quietly to pull all his thoughts together, all those simple things that he had known at one time and only now was rediscovering. But even as he pulled his thoughts together, he kept his eyes tight shut, for he did not want to see. If he did not see, perhaps he could go back to that emptiness and comfort he had known before.

It was no use, however. The knowledge first crept upon him slowly, then came on with a rush.

He opened his eyes and stared up at a high-noon sky seen through a leafy canopy. He raised a hand and a rough stone stopped it, bruising his knuckles. He lowered his eyes and saw the stone, a slab that covered him almost to his shoulders. Resting on the slab was the bole of a large oak tree, the bark scaling off it as if it suffered some ravaging disease.

The tomb, he thought, startled. The tomb of Wulfert, the wizard, unroofed many years ago by a falling tree. And now he was tucked into it.

It was Conrad, he told himself, who had tucked him in the tomb. It was the kind of stupid thing that Conrad would do, convinced all the time he was doing it that it was for the best, that it was perfectly logical and what any man might do.

It must have been Conrad, he told himself. Someone had talked with him, calling him "m'lord" while splashing water in his face, and no one but Conrad would have called him that. And after splashing water in his face, someone had lifted him and carried him on a shoulder, with no effort whatsoever, as if he had been no more than a sack of grain. And there was no one big enough and strong enough to do that as easily as it had been done other than Conrad. And then Conrad had crammed him in the tomb and there must surely have been a reason for doing what he did.

His first reaction was to scramble out, to free himself from the embrace of the tomb, but a sudden caution held him there. There had been danger and there might still be danger. He'd been hit on the head, probably by a thrown club, but while his head still throbbed and he was a little shaky, he seemed to be all right.

Except for the chirping of the birds there was no sound. He listened closely for the rustle of a fallen leaf, a snap of a twig that might tell him someone was nearby and moving. There were no such sounds; the birds, undisturbed, went on with their chirping.

He stirred a little, testing how he lay, and there was a dry rustling under him. Leaves, he thought, autumn-dead leaves that over the years had fallen into the tomb. Dry leaves and something else. Bones, perhaps, the bones of Wulfert, the wizard. With one hand he dug into the debris of the tomb. He could not see what his fingers brought up, for the stone slab cut off his vision, but his fingers told him—dry leaves and certain crumbling fragments that could be powdered bone. There was something, now that he had time to note it, that was digging into his left side, just below his shoulder blade. The skull, perhaps. Would the skull, he wondered, stand up, retain its shape and strength, longer than the other bones?

He shuddered, the fingers of superstitious dread reaching out to touch him, but he fought off the dread. He could not panic and surge howling from the tomb. For safety's sake, he reminded himself sternly, he could share this space with the dead.

He wriggled a little, trying to shift the skull or whatever it might be that was pressing into his ribs. It would not shift and it seemed harder than a skull should be. Maybe, he told himself, a stone that someone, in a flush of mistaken bravado, had chucked into the tomb, before running away as if the Devil were at his heels.

Lying quietly, he listened intently. The birds, flitting from branch to branch, kept up their chirping, but there was no other sound. There was no wind and not a leaf was moving.

He shifted his hand to feel the scabbard at his side and found that the sword was in it. Conrad, meticulous even in the absurdity of what he had done, nevertheless had taken the time to make certain that the blade was secure and ready for use.

Cautiously, Duncan lifted his head to see outside the tomb. The gravestones drowsed in the sun. There was nothing else. Carefully he levered himself up and out, slid to the ground, and crouched beside the tomb. He noted that the stone of which it was constructed was covered by large patches of lichens.

From far down the hill, on the opposite side of the tomb, a twig broke with a snap. Feet scuffed through the fallen leaves.

Duncan quietly unsheathed his blade and, holding it before him, keeping well down so he'd be hidden by the tomb, crept along its base to reach the end of it in order to see who might be coming.

The scuff of leaves moved steadily up the hill. Duncan shifted his weight, getting set for swift action if it should be needed.

In a moment, he could see who it was and let the point of the blade drop to the ground. His breath came out of him with a gush of relief. He was surprised; he had not realized he had been holding his breath.

He stood erect and waved the sword in greeting to Conrad. Conrad came forward with a rush, stopping in front of him.

"Thank the good Lord," he said. "You are all right."

"And you? How are you?"

"Fine," said Conrad. "Knocked around some, but all right. The hairless ones are gone. There is no one around. Had to be sure before I came back to you."

He put a hamlike hand on Duncan's shoulder, shook him affectionately. "You sure you are all right? Seemed all but dead to me. Had to find a place to hide you safe."

"But for the love of God," asked Duncan, "why a tomb? Why hide me in a tomb?"

"Unusual place," said Conrad. "No one would think to look."

"That's right. Conrad, you did fine. Thank you so much."

"The old lord, he told me take care of you."

"I'm sure he did," said Duncan. "And how are the others?"

"Daniel and Tiny are well. They are standing guard behind me. Beauty ran away, but Daniel found her. Daniel has a bruise, high on the shoulder. We licked them, m'lord. We licked them good and proper."

"Diane? The woman?"

"She flew away on the dragon."

"Not a dragon, Conrad. A griffin."

"Griffin, then. She flew away on him."

"Was she hurt?"

"Blood all over her, but I think it came from the hairless one she killed. The hermit ran away. There's no hide nor hair of him."

"Rest easy about him," said Duncan. "He'll be back to get his cabbages."

"What will we do now?"

"We regroup. We talk it over and decide."

"Harriers now know we are here. They'll keep watch on us."

"Maybe it was silly for us to think we could slip through them," said Duncan.

Although at the time they had talked about it, back at Standish House, it had seemed quite possible. The area that had been desolated was large, and it had seemed unlikely that the Harriers could keep watch over all of it, or would even try to keep watch over all of it. Apparently, however, they had worked out some system to guard the approaches to the area. More than likely they used the hairless ones as pickets to keep watch for anyone who might show up. Which could have been why, back in the garden plot, they had faced only the hairless ones and not any of the others that made up the Horde.

"We'll go back to hermit's cave to talk?" asked Conrad. "Maybe spend the night there?"

"Yes, I think so. I expect the hermit will show up. There's something I want to talk with him about."

Conrad half turned to go.

"Wait," said Duncan. "There is something I want to see about."

He led the way around the tomb and leaned down to stare into it.

"I think someone threw a rock into it," he said. "But maybe not. It may be something else."

It was something else. It glistened as no rock would glisten.

He reached in and lifted it out.

"A bauble," Conrad said.

"Yes," said Duncan, "a bauble. And what is it doing here?"

It was as big as a man's fist and pear-shaped. It was covered by a lacy fretwork of gold, inset at the intersection of the fretwork lines with tiny, flashing jewels. Seen through the fretwork was a silvery object, egg-shaped and with a look of heft to it. From the small neck of the pear-shaped outer framework hung a heavy chain that also may have been gold, but was not quite so lustrous as the fretwork.

Duncan handed the bauble to Conrad and once more leaned over the tomb to peer. From one corner a skull grinned out at him.

"God rest you," said Duncan to the skull. Together the two men went down the hill, heading for the cave.

7

"I guess," said Andrew, the hermit, "that I never got around to telling you that besides being a devout man, I'm an arrant coward. My heart cried out to help you, but my legs said for me to go. In the end they overruled my heart and took me out of there as fast as I could go."

"We made out without you," said Conrad.

"But I failed you. I only had my staff but with it I could have struck a stout blow or two."

"You're not a fighting man," said Duncan, "and we hold no blame of you for running. But there is another way that you can help us."

The hermit finished up his slice of ham and reached for a wedge of cheese.

"In any way I can," he said. "It would be my pleasure to be of aid to you."

"This bauble we found in Wulfert's tomb," said Duncan. "Can you tell us what it is? Could it be what the griffin woman was seeking?"

"Ah, that woman," cried Andrew. "You must believe me, please. I had no idea she was here. She hid from me. I am sure of that. She hid and watched me get my poor meals from the garden patch. There must have been some reason for her hiding."

64

"I am sure of that," said Duncan. "We must try to find the reason."

"She hid in the church," the hermit said. "What kind of place is that to hide? It's sacrilege, that's what it is. A church is not a place to live in. It was not built to live in. No proper person would even think of living in a church."

"It was the only place in the village," said Duncan, "that had a roof to cover her. If she were going to stay here she'd have to have someplace to keep out of the weather."

"But why did she want to stay here?"

"You heard her. She was seeking some news of Wulfert. She was searching the church records for some word of him. She knew that at one time he lived here. She might have thought that he left here to go elsewhere, and it may have been that kind of word that she was seeking. There is no way she could have known that he was buried here."

"I know all that," the hermit said, "but why should she be seeking him?"

Duncan dangled the bauble in front of him, and as he did so Andrew reared back in horror, putting as much distance between it and himself as he was able.

"I think she was seeking this," said Duncan. "Do you happen to know what it is? Were there any stories in the village about it?"

"It was a relic," said Andrew. "That's what the villagers thought it was. That's how the olden stories ran. A relic, but a relic of what or whom I don't think I ever heard. Perhaps no one ever knew. The village thought Wulfert was a holy man. He never told them otherwise. He let them go on thinking he was a holy man. It might not have been safe for him if they'd known he was a wizard. Ah, the black shame of it. . . ."

"Yes, I know," Duncan said unsympathetically. "He was buried in holy ground."

"Not only that," cried Andrew, "but the people of the village built a tomb for him. For themselves they were content with crudely carven stones, but for him

65

they spent many days in quarrying great slabs of the choicest stone and more days in dressing it and constructing a place for him to lie. And what is more, there was a great expenditure of wine."

"Wine? What did wine have to do with it?"

"Why, to pickle him, of course. The old tales said he died at the height of summer and that it was necessary to keep him . . ."

"That I understand. But they needn't have used wine. Plain brine would have done as well or better."

"You may be right—better. There is one story that he got rather high before they could lay him in the tomb. But there were those who thought plain brine would be too vulgar."

"So they entombed this wizard with a great deal of work and appropriate ceremony in the belief that he was a holy man. And they buried his relic with him. Perhaps hung around his neck."

Andrew nodded in misery. "I guess, my lord, you have summed it up."

"Don't call me lord. I'm not a lord. My father is the lord."

"I am sorry, my lord. I shall not call you so again."

"How do you suspect that the stories of this Wulfert have lasted so long? A century at least, perhaps several centuries. You have no idea of how long ago this happened?"

"None at all," said Andrew. "There was a date marked on the little statuary that surmounted the tomb, but that was shattered when the tree fell. Although it is not to be wondered at that the stories survived. In a village like this months would go by with nothing, absolutely nothing, happening. So when something did happen, it made a great impression and was long remembered and much talked about. Besides, to have a holy man was a long leg up. It gave the village some mark of distinction no other nearby village had."

"Yes," said Duncan, "that I can understand. And this relic?"

Andrew shrank farther back against the cave wall. "No relic," he said. "It is an infernal machine."

"It does nothing," said Conrad. "It just hangs there."

"Probably it's not activated," said Duncan. "Not working. There may be a certain word to speak, a certain mechanism to be set."

"My advice," said Andrew, "would be to bury it deep or fling it into running water. No good can come of it. We face enough danger and misery without asking for more. Why have you so much interest in it? You say you travel to Oxenford. I do not understand you. You say it is important you get to Oxenford and yet you become overly entranced by this disgraceful thing out of a wizard's grave."

"We travel to Oxenford on the Lord's business," said Conrad.

"Your lord's business?"

"No, the Great Lord's business. Holy business."

"Conrad!" Duncan said, sharply.

Andrew appealed to Duncan. "Is what he says correct? Is this the Lord's business you are on? Holy business?"

"I suppose one could say so. We do not talk about it."

"It must be important," Andrew said. "The way is long and hard and cruel. Yet you have about you something that says the journey must be made."

"It will be harder now," said Duncan. "We had hoped, with only a small party of us, we could slip through unnoticed. But now the Harriers know. We fell afoul of what must have been their picket line and now they'll be watching us. There'll be no step of the way we won't be in their sight. The hairless ones probably will not be the only ones. The whole thing makes me nervous. If they have pickets out, there is something the Horde is trying to protect. Something that they want no one to stumble on."

"How will we go about it?" asked Conrad.

"Straight ahead," said Duncan. "It's the only way to do it. We might try to travel farther east, but I fear we'd find the Harriers there as well. We'd be going a long way out of our way and perhaps not be any safer. We'll go straight ahead, travel as swiftly as we can, and keep close watch."

Ghost had been suspended in one corner of the cave while they had been talking, and now he floated forward.

"I could scout for you," he said. "I could go ahead and scout. The fear of it will shrivel up my soul, if indeed I still have a soul, but for the love of you who have agreed to let me go with you, for a holy purpose, I can do it."

"I didn't ask you to accompany us," said Duncan. "I said I saw no way we could stop you going."

"You do not accept me," Ghost wailed. "You see me not as a thing that once had been a man. You do not . . . "

"We see you as a ghost, whatever a ghost may be. Can you tell me, sir, what a ghost may be?"

"I do not know," said Ghost. "Even being one I cannot tell you. You ask me for one definition and now I'll ask you for another. Can you tell me what a man may be?"

"No, I can't."

"I can tell you," said Ghost, "that it is a bitter thing to be a ghost. A ghost does not know what he is nor how he should act. This especially is true of a ghost that has no place to haunt."

"You could haunt the church," suggested Andrew. "In life you were closely connected with the church."

"But never in it," said Ghost. "Outside of it. Sitting on the steps, begging alms. And I tell you, Hermit, that it was not, all in all, as good a life as I had thought it might be. The people in the village were a stingy lot."

"They were poor," said Andrew.

"Miserly as well. Few of them so poor they could not spare a copper. There were days on end when there were no coppers, not a single one."

"So your lot is hard," Andrew said unfeelingly. "All of our lots are hard."

"There is one recompense," said Ghost. "Being a ghost is not as bad as being dead, especially if, being

68

dead, one should go to Hell. There are many poor souls alive this very moment who know that once they die they will go straight to Hell."

"And you?"

"Again I do not know. I was not a vicious man, only a lazy one."

"But things are looking up for you. You are going with these people to Oxenford. You may like Oxenford."

"They say there is no way in which they can stop me going, an attitude I take to be ungracious of them. But, anyhow, I'm going."

"So am I," said Andrew. "If they will have me, that is. I have longed all my life to be a soldier of the Lord. That was what I thought I was doing when I took up hermiting. A holy zeal burned, perhaps not too brightly, in my breast, but at least it burned. I tried many things to prove my devotion. For years I sat staring at a candle flame, taking time only to find and consume food and take care of my bodily needs. I slept only when I could no longer stay awake. At times I nodded and singed my eyebrows on the candle's flame. And it was expensive. I was at times hard put to keep in candles. And I got nowhere. The candle-watching never accomplished a thing for me. I didn't even feel good about it. I stared at the candle flame, I told myself, so that I might become one of those who were one with the fall of the leaf, the song of bird, the subtle color of the sunset, the intricate web spun by a spider, in this wise becoming one with the universe— and none of this happened. A fall of a leaf meant nothing to me; I could not care less for birds or the songs they sang. I lacked something or the idea went all wrong or those who had claimed success before were only bald-faced liars. After a time I came to know that I was a fraud.

"Now, however, I have a chance to be a real soldier of the Lord. Craven I may be, and with no more strength than a reed, but with my staff I trust that I can strike a lusty blow or two if need be. I'll do my best not to run away, as I did today when danger threatened."

"You were not the only one today to run away," Duncan said sourly. "The Lady Diane, battle axe and all, also ran away."

"But not until it all was over," Conrad said.

"I thought you told me . . ."

"You misunderstood my words," said Conrad. "When the battle started, she was dismounted, but she mounted again and she and the griffin fought. She with her axe, the griffin with his claws and beak. Only when the hairless ones broke and ran did she fly away."

"That makes me feel better," Duncan said. "She had not seemed to be one who would run away. I was the only shirker, then."

"You caught an unlucky throw of a club," said Conrad. "I stood over you to fight off those who came at you. Most of the damage done to the hairless ones was by my lady and the dragon."

"Griffin," Duncan said.

"That is right, m'lord. A griffin. I confuse the two."

Duncan stood up.

"We should go to the church," he said, "and see if we can find the lady. There still is daylight left."

"How is your head?" asked Conrad.

"It has an outsize goose egg on it, and it hurts. But I am all right."

8

The church was not large, but it was a more impressive structure than would have been expected in such a village. Over the centuries pious villagers had labored to erect it, quarrying and dressing the stone, hoisting it into place, laying the heavy slabs that made up the floor, carving the pews and altar and all the other furniture out of native oak, weaving the tapestries to decorate its walls. There was about it, Duncan told himself, a rude simplicity that made for a charm too seldom found in other much larger and more elaborate buildings.

The tapestries had been pulled down from the walls and lay on the flagstones, crumpled and trampled. Some of them had been set afire, but had failed to burn. The pews and other furniture had been smashed, the altar demolished.

Diane and the griffin were not there, although there were signs that once they had been. Griffin dung spotted the stones of the floor; they found the chapel that the woman had used as a sleeping room—sheepskins upon the floor to make a bed, a small, rudely built cooking pit fashioned of stone, and half a dozen cooking utensils.

In the second chapel stood a long table, miraculously still intact. Upon it were spread piles of parchment sheets. An inkpot and a quill pen, fixed to its stand, stood among the litter.

Duncan picked up one of the parchments. It crinkled at his touch. The writing was crabbed, the words misspelled, bordering on the illiterate. Someone had been born, someone had died, a couple had been married, a mysterious murrain had killed a dozen sheep, the wolves had been bad that year, an early frost had shriveled the gardens, but snow had held off almost until Christmas.

He picked up other sheets. They were all the same. The records of years of village nothingness. Births, deaths, marriages, minor local catastrophes. The gossip of old wives, the small fears, the small triumphs— an eclipse of the moon and the terror in its wake, the time of falling stars and the wonder of it, the early bloom of forest flowers, the violent summer thunderstorm, the feasts and their celebrations, the good crops and the bad—all the local historical trivia, the records of a village pastor so immersed in village happenings that he had no other interests.

"She searched all these records," Duncan said to Andrew. "She was looking for some mention of Wulfert, some clue as to where a trace of him might be found. Apparently she found nothing."

"But she must have known that by this time he would be dead."

"Not him," said Duncan. "Not the man himself. That was not what she was looking for. The relic, don't you understand. To her the relic—or, if you insist, the infernal machine—was what was important."

"But I do not understand."

"You are blinded," Duncan said, "by your candle flame, by all your piety. Or was it piety?"

"I do not know," said Andrew. "I had always thought so. My lord, I am a sincere hermit, or I try to be."

"You cannot see beyond your own nose," Duncan told him. "You cannot accept that what you call an infernal machine may have validity and value. You will not give a wizard his due. There are many lands, as Christian as this one, where wizards, however uncomfortable the thought of them may be, are held in high regard."

"There is about them the stink of paganism."

"Old truths," said Duncan. "Old ideas, old solutions, old methods and procedures. You cannot afford to reject them because they antecede Christianity. My lady wanted what the wizard had."

"There is one thing you do not realize," said Andrew, speaking softly. "One thing you have not thought about. She herself may be a wizard."

"An enchantress, you mean. A sophisticated witch."

"I suppose so," Andrew said. "But whatever the correct designation, you had never thought of that."

"I had not thought of it," said Duncan. "It may well be true."

Shafts of late afternoon sunlight came through the tall, narrow windows, looking very much like those shafts of glory that biblical artists delighted in depicting as shining upon saints. The windows were of tinted glass—those that still had glass in them, for many had been broken by thrown rocks. Looking at the few remaining tinted windows, Duncan wondered how the village, in all its piety and devotion, could have afforded that much tinted glass. Perhaps the few affluent residents, of which there certainly would have been very few, had banded together to pay for its fabrication and installation, thereby buying themselves certain dispensations or absolutions, buttressing their certainty of Heaven.

Tiny motes of dust danced in the shining shafts of light, lending them a sense of life, of motion and of being, that simple light in itself could never have. And in back of the living light shafts something moved.

Duncan reached out to grasp Andrew's arm.

"There's something here," he said. "Back there in the corner."

He pointed with a finger, and the hermit peered in the direction that he pointed, squinting his eyes to get a better focus. Then he chuckled to himself, visibly relaxing.

"It's only Snoopy," he said.

"Snoopy? Who the hell is Snoopy?"

"That's what I call him. Because he's always snooping around. Always watching out for something that he can turn to his own advantage. He's a little busybody. He has another name, of course. A name you cannot get your tongue around. He doesn't seem to mind that I call him Snoopy."

"Someday that long-windedness of yours will be the death of you," said Duncan. "This is all well and good, but will you tell me, who is . . . "

"Why, I thought you knew," said Andrew. "I thought I had mentioned him. Snoopy is a goblin. One of the local boys. He pesters me a lot and I have no great love of him, but he's really not a bad sort."

By this time the goblin had walked through the distorting shafts of window-light and was coming toward them. He was a little fellow; he might have reached to a grown man's waist. He was dressed in nut-colored brown: a peaked cap that had lost its stiffening and flopped over at the top, a jerkin, a pair of trousers fitted tight around his spindly legs, shoes that curled up ridiculously at the toe. His ears were oversize and pointed, and his face had a foxy look.

Without preamble, Snoopy spoke to Andrew. "This place is livable now," he said. "It has lost some of its phony smell of sanctity, which was something that neither I nor any of my brethren could abide. The stabling of the griffin perhaps had much to do with it. There is nothing like the smell of griffin dung to fumigate and offset the odor of sanctity."

Andrew stiffened. "You're being impertinent again," he said.

"In that case," said Snoopy, "I shall turn about and leave. You will pardon me. I was only trying to be neighborly."

"No," said Duncan. "Wait a minute, please. Overlook the sharp tongue of this good hermit. His outlook has been warped by trying to be a holy man and, perhaps, not going about it in quite the proper way."

Snoopy looked at Duncan. "You think so?" he asked.

"It's a possibility," said Duncan. "He tells me he wasted a lot of time staring at a candle flame, and I'm not sure, in my own mind, whether that is the way to go about it if one should feel the compulsion to be holy. Although, you understand, I'm not an expert at this sort of thing."

"You seem to be a more reasonable person than this dried-up apple of a hermit," said the goblin. "If you give me your word that you'll hold him off me and will prevail upon him to keep his foul mouth shut, I shall proceed upon what I came to do."

"I shall do all that I am able to restrain him," Duncan said. "So how about you telling me what you came to do."

"I came in the thought that I might be of some small assistance to you."

"Pay no attention to him," counseled Andrew. "Any assistance you may get from him would turn out to be equivalent to a swift punch in the nose."

"Please," said Duncan, "let me handle this. What harm can it do to listen to what he has to say?"

"There you see," said Snoopy. "That's the way it goes. The man has no sense of decency."

"Let's not belabor the past differences between the two of you," said Duncan. "If you have information we would be glad to hear it. It seems to me we stand in some need of it. But there is one thing that troubles me and you'll have to satisfy us on that point."

"What is this thing that troubles you?"

"I presume you know that we intend to travel farther into the Desolated Land, which at the moment is held by the Harriers."

"That I do know," said Snoopy, "and that is why I'm here. I can acquaint you with what would be the best route and what you should be watching for."

"That, precisely, is what troubles me," said Duncan. "Why should you be willing to assist us against the Harriers? It would seem to me that you might feel more kinship toward them than you feel toward us.'

"In some ways you may be correct in your assumption," said Snoopy, "but your reasoning is not too astute, perhaps because you are not fully acquainted with the situation. We have no grounds to love the humans. My people—those folk you so insultingly speak of as the Little People—were residents of this land, of the entire world, for that matter, long before you humans came, thrusting your way so unfeelingly among us, not even deigning to recognize us, looking upon us as no more than vermin to be swept aside. You did not look upon us as a legitimate intelligent life form, you ignored our rights, you accorded us no courtesy or understanding. You cut down our sacred woods, you violated our sacred places. We had a willingness to accommodate our way of life with your way, to live in harmony among you. We held this willingness even when you came among us as arrogant invaders. We had powers we would have been willing to share with you, perhaps in an exchange that would have given us something of value to us. But you had a reluctance to stoop, as you felt, to the point of communicating with us. You thrust yourself upon us, you kicked us out of the way, you forced us to live in hidden places. So, at long last, we turned against you, but because of your ferocity and unfeeling violence, there was little that we could do against you; we have never been a match for you. I could go on for a much longer length of time cataloguing our grievances against you, but that, in summary, my dear sir, is why we cannot love you."

"You present a good case," said Duncan, "and, without admitting it to be the truth in all regards, which I am in no position to do and would not do in any case, I must admit that there is some merit in the words you've spoken. Which proves my point, exactly. Hating us as you must, why are you willing to offer us assistance? Knowing your feelings about us, how can we reconcile ourselves to trusting you?"

"Because we hate the Harriers more than we hate you," said Snoopy. "While you may think so, in your human folly, the Harriers are not our people. We and they stand very much apart. There are several reasons for this. They are pure evil and we are not. They live for evil alone and we do not. But since you humans lump us in with them, through the centuries they have given us a bad name. Much that they do is blamed on us. There are certain areas in which we might have arrived at an accommodation with humans, but the Harriers have foreclosed these avenues to us because their actions and your fuddle-headedness has made us seem as bad as they. When you condemn them, you condemn us equally with them. There are some more intelligent and compassionate humans who, having taken the trouble to know us better, do not join in this condemnation but, sadly, the most of you do, and the voices of the few compassionates are lost in the flurry of hatred that is directed against us. In this invasion of the Harriers, we have suffered with the humans, perhaps not as much as you humans, for we have our small magics that have been some protection for us, magics that you humans could have shared with us had you been willing to accept us. So, in balance, we hate the Harriers more than we do the humans, and that is why we are willing to help you."

"Given such an attitude," Andrew said to Duncan, "you would be insane to trust him completely. He might lead you straight into an ambush. I take no great stock in his professed hatred of the Harriers, even though he warned me once against them. I tell you, there is no assurance of truth in his kind."

Duncan disregarded Andrew. He said to Snoopy, "You say the Harriers are not your people, that you are in no way related to them. Where, then, did they come from? What is their origin?"

"They first appeared," said Snoopy, "some twenty thousand years ago, perhaps longer ago than that. Our legends say this and our people take great care that the legends should run true, unchanged, from generation to generation. At first there were only a few of them, but as the centuries went on, their numbers increased. During that time when there were only a few of them, we had the opportunity to learn what kind of folk they were. Once we learned in all truth the evil that was in them, we were able, in a measure, to protect ourselves. I suppose the same thing happened to the primitive humans who existed in those early days, but the humans, without magic, could do little to protect themselves. Sadly, only a few of those humans, perhaps because they were so primitive, could learn to accept us. Many made no distinction between us and these others whom you now call the Harriers, but who have been known by many other names throughout the ages."

"They first appeared, you tell me, two hundred centuries ago. How did they appear?"

"They just were here, was all."

"But where did they come from?"

"There are those who say they came from the sky. There are others who say they came from deep underground, where they had been penned, but that they either broke loose or overcame the force that penned them there, or, perhaps, that their penance extended over only a certain period of time and that the time-term had expired."

"But they can't be of any one race. I am told they come in all shapes and sizes."

"That is true," said Snoopy. "They are not a race. They are a swarm."

"I don't understand."

"A swarm," Snoopy said impatiently. "A swarm. Don't you know a swarm?"

"He's talking in a lingo of his own," said Andrew. "He has many such words and concepts that cannot be understood by humans."

"Well, we'll let it go at that," said Duncan. "What is important now is what he has to tell us."

"You don't mean you are about to trust him?"

"I'm inclined to. At least we need what he can tell us."

"I can show you the route that may be the safest for you to take," said Snoopy. "I can draw a map for

78

you. There is ink and parchment in one of the chapels."

"Yes, we know," said Duncan.

"A room," said Snoopy, "where a long line of dithering priests sat writing down the inconsequential inanities of irrelevant lives and events."

"I just now," said Duncan, "was reading through some of them."

Snoopy led the way toward the chapel, followed by Duncan, with Andrew clumping crustily in the rear. Conrad hurried to take his place alongside Duncan.

Reaching the chapel, Snoopy climbed upon the table and pawed with his splayed fingers among the documents until he found one that had some white space remaining on it. Carefully he spread it out on the tabletop. Picking up the quill, he dipped it in the ink and made an X on the parchment.

"We are here," he said, pointing to the X. "This way is north." He made a slash to indicate the direction. "You go straight south from here, down the valley, south and a little west. You'll be moving in good cover. There may be watchers on the hilltops. Keep an eye out for them. They probably won't cause you any trouble. More than likely, they'll not attack; they'll just report back on you. Forty miles or so from here the stream flows into a fen—marshy ground, pools of water, heavy growth . . . "

"I do not like the looks of it," said Conrad.

"You turn off," said Snoopy, "keeping to the left bank of the fen. There are high cliffs to your left, leaving a narrow strip between the fen and the cliffs."

"They could drive us into the marsh," said Conrad. "There would be no place to stand."

"They won't come at you through the fen," said Snoopy. "The cliffs are high and unscalable. You can't climb them, certainly, but neither can someone on the top climb down."

"There might be dragons, harpies, other flying things."

Snoopy shrugged. "Not many. And you could fight them off. If they make a ground sally at you, it has to

79

be either front or back and on a narrow front. They can't get around to flank you."

"I'm not fond of it either," said Duncan. "Master Goblin, is there no other way?"

"Many more miles to travel," Snoopy told him, "and even then no farther on your way. Hard traveling. Uphill, downhill. Easy to get lost."

"But this has danger in it."

"Dangerous, perhaps, but bold. A route they'd not expect you to take. If you moved at night, keeping well under cover . . . "

Duncan shook his head.

"There is no place safe," said the goblin. "Not in the Desolated Land."

"If you traveled," asked Conrad, "would you travel as you tell us?"

"I accept the danger," said Snoopy. "I shall travel with you. It's my neck as well as yours."

"Christ save us now," said Duncan. "A hermit, a ghost, a goblin. We grow into an army."

"In going," said Snoopy, "I only show my faith."

"All right," said Duncan. "I take your word for it."

"Down this strand between the fen and cliff you come to a chasm, a gap, a break in the cliffs that cuts through the hills. A short distance only, five miles or so."

"It's a trap," said Conrad. "I can smell a trap."

"But once you leave the gap, you are in what seems fair and open country. But in it sits a castle."

"I shall tread beside you closely," said Conrad. "If a trap this turns out to be, I shall simply cut your throat."

The goblin shrugged.

"You shrug," said Conrad. "Perhaps you want to have it cut."

Snoopy flung down the quill in exasperation. Spatters of ink splotched the parchment.

"What is hard for me to understand," said Duncan, "is that at first you say you will draw a map for us and then you say you will go with us. Why bother with a map? Why not simply say, to start with, that you will go with us and show the way?"

"At first," said the goblin, "I had not meant to go with you. I had simply thought the map. Then, when you questioned my sincerity, I decided that I must go with you, that otherwise you'd have no belief in me."

"What we ask is truth," said Conrad. "We do not ask belief."

"The one," said Snoopy, "cannot go without the other."

"Okay," said Duncan. "Carry on. You said there was a castle."

"An old castle. Moldering away. Falling down. The battlements tumbled. It stinks of great age. I warn you of the castle. You give it wide berth. You do not approach it. On no account go inside of it. It also is evil. Not the Evil of the Harriers. A different kind of evil."

"Wipe all this from your mind," the hermit said. "He is about to get us killed, or worse. Never for a moment can you trust him."

"You make up your mind," said Snoopy. "I've told you all I have to tell. I have tried to be of help and for that you've given me the back of your hand. If in the morning you want to set out, you will find me here."

He jumped down off the table and stalked out of the chapel.

Tiny came pertly into the chapel, walking carefully and alertly on tiptoe. He came up to Conrad and leaned companionably against his leg. Out in the church Daniel was snorting gently and pawing at the flagstone floor.

"Well?" asked Andrew.

"I don't know," said Duncan. "We have to think about it. We must do something. We can't just stay here."

He said to Conrad, "I'm surprised at you. I thought that of all of us, you would have been the one to trust him. Back home you have much traffic with the Little Folk. As you walk through the woods they come popping out to talk with you. It seemed to me that you

81

had an understanding with them. Just the other day you were upset that we had not seen them here. You were worried that the Harriers might have wiped them out."

"What you say is true," said Conrad. "I have a liking for them. I have many friends with them. But of this one we must be sure."

"So you warn him that you'll cut his throat should he lead us astray."

"It's the only way. He must understand."

"Well, then, what do you really think?"

"I think, m'lord, that we can trust him. I only wanted to make sure. I wanted him to understand this was serious and no place for playing games. Little Folk, no matter how nice they may be, are always playing tricks. Even on their friends. I wanted to make sure this one plays no tricks."

"In a situation such as this he'd not be playing foolish tricks."

"That's where you're wrong," said Andrew. "They're always up to tricks, some of them just this side of vicious. I shall keep an eye on him as well. If Conrad does not cut his throat, should need be, I'll brain him with my staff."

9

He had been right, Duncan told himself, back there at the church. They couldn't stay here any longer. They had wasted time and he had the feeling, somehow, that time might be important.

He sat, propped against the cave wall, the heavy blanket pulled up to cover half his body. Tiny lay across the cave's mouth. Outside, just beyond the cave, Daniel stamped and Beauty could be heard moving about. In one corner Conrad snored heroically, gulping explosively between the snores. Andrew, the hermit, wrapped in a blanket on his pallet, mumbled in his sleep. Ghost had disappeared.

He and Conrad could go back, of course, Duncan thought. Back to Standish House. And no one would blame them. The plan from the very beginning had been that a small party, traveling quietly and swiftly, would be able to slip unobserved through the Desolated Land. Now that appeared to be impossible. The shape of circumstances had operated in such a manner as to make it impossible. More than likely it had been impossible from the start. Their collision with the hairless ones had given notice that they were here. The expedition by the Reaver, who had set out to track them down, probably had alerted the Harriers. Duncan wondered what might have happened to the Reaver and his men. If they had come to a bad end, it would be no wonder, for they were an ill-favored and fumbling lot.

He didn't like it, he told himself. He liked none of the situation. The whole adventure had gone awry. Thinking of it, he realized that one of the things he liked least about it were the volunteers they had picked up. Ghost was bad enough, but there wasn't much that could be done about a ghost. The hermit was the worst. He was an old fuddy-duddy with busybody tendencies and a coward to boot. He said he wanted to be a soldier of the Lord and there was no way one could argue against that, just so he kept out of other people's way. The thing about it was, of course, that so far he'd kept out of no one's way. If he kept on with them he'd be underfoot at every turn. But what could be done about it? Tell him he couldn't go? Tell him there was no place for him? Tell him this after they had accepted his hospitality?

Maybe, Duncan told himself, he was fretting when there was no need to fret. Ten to one, the hermit would beg off, would decide at the last moment that there were imperative reasons why he should not venture from his cell.

And Snoopy, the goblin, what about him? Not to be trusted, more than likely, although in some ways he had made an impressive case for himself. They'd have to watch him closely. That could be left to Conrad. Snoopy probably was more than a little scared of Conrad, and he had a right to be. Conrad had not been joking when he'd said he'd cut his throat. Conrad never joked.

So what to do? Go on or turn back? A case could be made for abandoning the journey. There had been no charge placed upon them to face up to great danger, to ram their heads into a noose, to keep on no matter what the hazard.

But the stakes were high. It was important that the aged savant at Oxenford should see the manuscript, and if they turned back now there was a chance he

84

would never see it. The man was old; His Grace had said that his sands were running out.

And now, thinking of it, he remembered something else that His Grace had said that evening in the library of Standish House. "The lights are going out," he'd said. "They are going out all over Europe. I have a feeling that we are plunging back again into the ancient darkness." His Grace, when all was said and done, was something of a sanctimonious blabbermouth, but even granting that, he was not a fool. If, in all solemnity, he had voiced a feeling that the lights were going out, then there was a good chance that they were going out and the olden darkness would come creeping in again.

The churchman had not said that proving the manuscript to be genuine would play a part in holding back the darkness, and yet, as Duncan remembered it, the implication had been there. For if it could be proved, beyond all doubt, that a man named Jesus had actually walked the Earth two millennia ago, if it could be shown that He had said the words He was reported to have said, died in the manner and in the spirit the Gospels reported, then the Church would gain in strength. And a strengthened Church would be a powerful force to hold back that darkness of which His Grace had spoken. For almost two thousand years it had been the one great force speaking out for decency and compassion, standing firm in the midst of chaos, providing men a slender reed of hope to which they might cling in the face of apparent hopelessness.

And what, he asked himself, if once the man at Oxenford had seen the manuscript he should pronounce it valueless, a fraud, a cruel hoax against mankind? Duncan shut his eyes, squeezing them shut, shaking his head. That was something he must never think of. Somehow the faith must be preserved. The whole matter of the manuscript was a gamble, he told himself in all honesty, that must be taken.

He lay, with his head thrown back against the wall of earth, and the agony welled in him. No devout member of the Church, he still was of the Church. It was a heritage that he could not ignore. Almost forty generations of his forebears had been Christians of one sort or another, some of them devout, others considerably less than devout, but Christians all the same. A folk who stood against the roaring and the jeering of the pagan world. And here, finally, was a chance to strike a blow for Christ, a chance such as no other Standish had ever had. Even as he thought this, he knew there was no way he could step aside from the charge that had been placed upon him. There could be no question but that he must go on. The faith, poor as it might be, was a part of him; it was blood and bone of him, and there was no denying it.

10

Snoopy had not been waiting at the church. They had hunted for him, yelled for him, waited for him, but he had not appeared. Finally they had gone on without him, Tiny taking up the point, ranging well ahead and to all sides. The hermit, pacing beside Beauty, followed Conrad, while Duncan and Daniel took up the rear.

Andrew still grumbled about the goblin. "You should be glad that he failed to show up," he told Duncan. "I tell you there is no truth in him. You can't trust any of them. They are fickle folk."

"If we had him with us," Duncan said, "we could keep an eye on him."

"On him, of course. But he's a slippery imp. He could be off and away without your noticing. And what are you going to do about the others?"

"The others?"

"Yes. Other goblins. Assorted gnomes, imps, banshees, trolls, ogres and others of their kind."

"You talk as if there were many of them here."

"They are as thick as hair on a dog and up to no good, not a one of them. They hate all of us."

"But Snoopy said they hated the Harriers even worse."

"If I were you," said the hermit, "I wouldn't bet my life on it, and that is what we are doing, betting our lives on what a goblin told us."

"Yet when Snoopy told us the quickest and the easiest way, you did not contradict or correct him."

"The goblin was right," said Andrew. "This is the easiest way. If it is also the safest, we shall see."

They followed a small valley, heavily wooded. The brook, which had its origin in the spring near Andrew's cave, brawled and chattered along a rocky streambed.

As the valley broadened out, they came upon a few small homesteads, some burned to the ground, others with a few blackened timbers or a chimney standing. Crops that had ripened lay in swaths upon the ground, the heavy heads of grain beaten down by rain and wind. Fruit trees had been chopped down.

Ghost had not put in an appearance, although on several occasions Duncan thought he glimpsed him flitting through the trees on the hillside above the valley.

"Have you seen anything of Ghost?" he asked Andrew. "Is he with us?"

"How should I know," grumbled the hermit. "Who is there to know what a ghost would do?"

He clumped along, fuming, striking his staff angrily against the ground.

"If you don't want to be here, why don't you go back?" Duncan asked.

"I may not like it," said Andrew, "but this is the first chance I've had to be a soldier of the Lord. If I don't grasp it now, I may never have the chance again."

"As you wish," said Duncan.

At noon they halted for a brief rest and something to eat.

"Why don't you ride the horse?" Andrew asked Duncan. "If I had a horse I would save my feet."

"I'll ride him when the time comes to do so."

"And when will that be?"

"When the two of us can work together as a fight-

88

ing unit. He's not a saddle horse; he's a war-horse, trained to fight. He'll fight with me or without me."

Andrew grumbled. He'd been grumbling ever since they had started out.

Conrad said, "I like it not. Too quiet."

"You should be glad of that," said Andrew.

"Tiny would have let us know if anyone were about," said Duncan.

Conrad placed the head of his club against the ground, gouging the soil with it.

"They know we're here," he said. "They are waiting someplace for us."

When they took up the march again, Duncan found that he was inclined to be less watchful than he had been when they started in the morning. Despite the occasional burned homestead and the general absence of life, the valley, which grew wider and less wild as they progressed, had a sense of peace and beauty. He upbraided himself at those times when he realized he had become less alert, but a few minutes later he would fall into inattentiveness. After all, he told himself, Tiny was scouting out ahead. If there was anything around, he would let them know.

When he did snap back to attention, he found himself glancing at the sky rather than at the surrounding hills, and it took him a little time to realize that he was watching for Diane and her griffin. Where could she have gone, he wondered, and perhaps more important, why had she gone? And who could she be? Given the time, he would have tried to find out about her, but there had been no time. The puzzling thing about it all was her interest in Wulfert, a wizard centuries dead, with gray-blue lichens growing on his tomb. More than likely it had been Wulfert's bauble and not Wulfert himself that she had been seeking, although he had no proof of that. He felt the outline of the bauble, which he had thrust into his belt pouch. It made sense, he told himself, that it was the bauble she had been seeking. Wulfert's bones could be of no use to anyone. Perhaps if he really got down to business and examined the bauble, he might be able to pick up some clue to its purpose. Although, he thought, he would be a poor one to do that. An infernal machine, Andrew had called it. Although that could be discounted, for it was the kind of reaction to be expected of the hermit. Should it be a machine, as the hermit had said, infernal or otherwise, he, Duncan Standish, knew nothing of machines. For that matter, he thought, comforting himself, neither did many other people.

Head down, thinking, he ran into Beauty's rear end. Startled, he backed away and the little burro, cocking her head to glance backward at him, unloosed a playful kick that caught him in the knee. It was a light kick, with little power behind it.

Everyone had stopped, he saw, and was staring down the valley. Coming toward them, hobbling, limping and complaining loudly, was an old woman. Behind her, shagging her along, came Tiny.

Conrad said proudly, "Tiny's got him something."

No one else said anything. Duncan walked forward to join Conrad.

The old woman came up to them and flopped down on the ground in a sitting position, pulling her rags about her. She was a hag. Her nose was sharp and pointed, with hairs like spiderlegs growing out of it. More hairs sprouted on her chin. She had no more than half a dozen teeth, and her gray hair hung about her eyes.

"Call off your hound," she shrilled at them. "He drove me like a cow. Gentlemanly about it, I must say. He took no chunks of flesh out of this poor body, as I suppose he could have. But he routed me out of that foul nest I call my home and herded me up the valley. And I don't like it. I don't like being herded. If I had a tithe of the power I once had, I would have frazzled him. But now I have no power. They took all the things I had got together—the owl's blood, the bat's brains, the eyes of newts, the skin of toad, ash from a fire in which a witch had burned, the tooth of a dog that had bitten a priest . . . "

90

"Hold up, grandmother," said Duncan. "Who took this great hoard from you?"

"Why, the Harriers," she said. "Not only did they take them, but they laughed at me gruesomely. Yes, that is how they laughed at me—gruesomely. Then they kicked my big butt out of there and set the torch to my humble hut."

"You are lucky," Andrew told her, "that they didn't hang you or toss you in the blaze."

She spat with disgust upon the ground. "The brutes!" she said. "The bullies! And I almost one of them. Almost of their own. They shamed me, that's what they did. They said, short of saying it, that I was not worth a length of rope or the disturbance of the fire."

"You should be glad they shamed you," Andrew said. "Shame is a preferable alternative to death."

"I had worked so hard," she lamented, "and for so many years. I tried hard to build a professional reputation as a witch upon whom my clients could depend. I studied the cabala and I practiced—I practiced endlessly to perfect my art. I worked hard and sought endlessly for the materials needed in my craft. I hate to think of the midnight hours I spent in graveyards, seeking out the various kinds of grave mold. . . ."

"You tried hard to be a witch," said Conrad.

"Laddy, that I did. I was an honest witch. An honest witch and there are not too many honest witches. Evil, perhaps. A witch must have some evil in her. Otherwise she would not be a witch. Evil, but honest."

She looked at Duncan.

"And now, sir, should you wish to run that great sword through me . . . "

"I would not think of it," said Duncan. "Through another witch, perhaps, but not an honest witch."

"What do you intend to do with me? Since your dog brought me here, what will you do with me?"

"Feed you, for one thing," said Duncan. "That is, if you are in need of food. You look as if you might be. Why should not one be courteous to an honest witch who has fallen on hard times?"

91

"You'll regret the courtesy," Andrew said to Duncan. "Fool around with witches and some of the witchery is bound to rub off on you."

"But this one is scarcely a witch any longer," protested Duncan. "You heard her say so. She has lost all her paraphernalia. She has not a thing to work with."

Tiny had sat down and was regarding her quizzically. He acted as if he thought she belonged to him.

"Get that horrid beast away from me," said the witch. "Although he hides it in a seeming humor, he has a wicked eye."

"Tiny is no wicked dog," said Conrad. "He has no badness in him. Otherwise you would be without an arm or leg."

The woman put her hands on the ground and tried to lift herself.

"Here," said Conrad, putting out a hand. She grasped it and he hauled her to her feet. She shook herself to make the rags fall back in place.

"In truth," she said, "you two are gentlemen. The one does not run a blade through me and the other helps me to my feet. Old Meg thanks you."

She switched her gaze to Andrew.

"This one I do not know about," she said. "He is a sour character at the best."

"Pay no attention to him," Duncan said. "He is a sour old hermit and the day's not gone well for him."

"Witches I have no love for," said Andrew. "I will tell you plain. Nor goblins nor gnomes nor wizards nor any of their ilk. There are too many such in this world we live in. We'd be better off without them."

"You said something about food," said Meg, the witch.

"We have another hour or two of travel before the day is done," said Duncan. "If you could wait that long."

"I have in my pocket," said Andrew, "a small bit of cheese, carrying it in case I should feel faint. If she wants it, she is welcome to it."

"But Andrew, I thought . . . "

"For a woman," said Andrew, "not a witch. Anyone who hungers . . . "

He held out the piece of cheese and she accepted it demurely, if a creature such as she could be demure.

"Bless you," she said.

"I do not accept your blessing," Andrew told her stiffly.

11

Well before the sun had set, they camped, gathering wood, building a fire, bringing water.

"There's no reason to go without a fire," said Duncan. "If there's anyone around, they'll know that we are here."

Meg had ridden Daniel, who had been inclined to prance when she'd first been boosted to the saddle, but later quieted down, going at a deliberate pace to accommodate the rack of bones that rode upon his back.

Conrad, squatting before the fire, raked hot coals off to one side and cooked oaten cakes and rashers of bacon.

Their camp was situated at the edge of a small grove, with the stream in front of them and a sandy stretch of ground running from the water to the grove.

They ate as darkness was creeping over the land. A short time later Ghost came floating in.

"So there you are," said Andrew. "We had been wondering what had happened to you."

"Much afraid," said Ghost, "still I travel very widely. In the open daylight, which is unpleasant for me, I spied out the land."

"How far have you gone?" asked Duncan.

"To where the fen begins. I do not go beyond. Very spooky place."

"And you a spook," said Conrad.

"A ghost," Ghost told him primly. "Not a spook. There is a difference."

"You saw nothing, of course," said Conrad. "Tiny has been out all day as well."

"There are those you call the hairless ones," said Ghost. "A very few of them. To the east, some miles to the east. Several small bands of them. Keeping pace with you. Traveling in the same direction."

"How came Tiny not to see them?"

"I flit must faster than the hound," said Ghost. "Over hill and dale. But frightened. Very frightened. It is not given a ghost should be out in open country. His proper sphere is within a structure, shielded from the sky."

"Maybe they don't even know we are here," said Andrew.

Duncan shook his head. "I'm afraid they do. If not they'd be traveling this same easy route, instead of out there, clambering up and down the hills. It sounds to me as if we're being herded, somewhat less obviously than Tiny herded in the witch. They know, because of the fen, that we cannot go west. They're making sure we don't make a break toward the east."

Meg, the witch, tugged at Duncan's sleeve. "Sire," she said, "those others."

"What is it, grandmother? What others?"

"The ones other than the hairless ones. They are nearby. They squat in outer darkness. They are the ones who laugh gruesomely even as they proceed with your undoing."

"If anyone was here," Conrad objected, "if anyone was near, Tiny would know of them and warn us."

Tiny lay beside the fire, his nose resting on his outstretched paws. He gave no sign that he knew of anything.

"The dog might not know," said Meg. "You are dealing here with something that is more subtle and with a greater capacity for evil and deception than the

95

evil things you encounter in the ordinary run of events. They are . . . "

"But the Reaver spoke of demons and of imps," said Conrad. "He would know. He fought them."

"He used the only names he knew," said Meg. "He had no names for these other ones, which are not seen as often as the demon or the imp. And there may, perchance, have been imp and demon, for the Horde would attract a large gathering of camp followers, all the evil of ordinary kind joining in with them as great gatherings of common people will follow a human army."

"But you did not join with them," said Duncan. "And you said that you were evil. A little evil, you said. That you'd have to be a little evil to be a witch at all."

"Thus you find me out," said Meg. "I only try to be evil. I would be evil if I could, for then my powers would be the greater. But I only try. At times I thought myself of greater evil than I was and I felt no fear when the Horde came sweeping in, for I said to myself most surely they will recognize me and leave me alone or teach me, perhaps, a greater evil. But this they did not do. They stole all my amulets and they burned my hut and they kicked me in the butt, a most uncourteous way in which to treat someone who is doing her poor best to be even as they are."

"And you feel no shame in this quest of evil? You feel it is appropriate that you make yourself an evil one?"

"Only the better to practice my work," said Meg without a trace of shame. "Once a person lays hands upon her life work, then it must make sense that she do the best she can, no matter where her proficiency may lead her."

"I'm not sure I follow you entirely," Duncan said.

"I knew you for no evil one," said Conrad, "when first I laid eyes upon you. There was no evil in your eye. No more evil than one finds in a goblin or a gnome."

"There are those who believe," said Andrew primly,

"that a goblin and a gnome have some taint of evil in them."

"But they're not," insisted Conrad. "They are Little People, different from us, having little magics while we have almost no magic at all."

"I could get along quite comfortably," said Andrew, "without their little magics. Using those small magics they've pestered me almost to the death."

Duncan said to Meg, "You say that there are members of this greater Evil about, even now, outside the camp? That the dog may not be able to detect them?"

"I do not know about the dog," said Meg. "He may detect them and be only slightly puzzled. Not enough to pay much attention to them, not knowing what they are. But Old Meg detects them, ever so faintly, and she knows what they are."

"You are sure about that?"

"I am sure," she said.

"In that case," said Duncan, "we cannot depend on Tiny alone to stand guard against them, as we might have otherwise. We'll have to stand watch throughout the night. I'll take the first watch, Conrad the second."

"You're leaving me out," said Andrew, somewhat wrathfully. "I claim my right to stand my share of the watch. I am, after all, a soldier of the Lord. I share the dangers with you."

"You get your rest," said Duncan. "The day ahead will be a hard one."

"No harder than it will be for you and Conrad."

"You still will get your rest," said Duncan. "We can't hold up the march for you. And your mind must be clear and sharp to point out the way if there should be question."

"It is true," said Andrew, "that I know the trail, for I've followed it many times when I was younger than I am now. But it presents no problems. Any fool could follow it."

"Nevertheless I insist you get your rest."

Andrew said no more, but sitting close beside the campfire, he did some mumbling.

Andrew was the last of them to go to sleep. Conrad stretched out and pulled the blanket over him and almost immediately began to snore. Meg, curled up in a ball beside the saddle and the packs, slept like a baby, at times making little crying noises. Off to one side, Daniel lay down to sleep; Beauty slept standing on her feet, her head drooped, her nose almost touching the ground. Tiny dozed beside the fire, occasionally getting up to march stiff-legged about the camp's perimeter, growling softly in his throat, but giving no indication that there was anything requiring his immediate attention.

Duncan, sitting beside the fire, close beside Tiny, found no trouble in staying awake. He was tensed and on edge, and when he tried to smooth out the tenseness, it refused to go away. No wonder, he told himself, with all of Meg's talk about the Evil being close. But if there was Evil about he could not detect it. If it were there, it rustled in no bushes, it made no noise of any kind. He listened intently for the footstep—or the paw-step or the hoof-step—and there was nothing there at all.

The land drowsed in the liquid moonlight. There was no breeze, and the leaves were silent, unstirring. The only sound was the soft gurgle of the water flowing over a short stretch of shingle between two pools. Once or twice he heard the hooting of owls far in the distance.

He pressed his fingers against the pouch hanging at his belt and heard the faint crinkling of the parchment. For this, he thought, for so frail a thing as these few sheets of parchment, he and the others (the others, with the exception of Conrad, not knowing) were marching deep into the Desolated Land, where only God might know what would be waiting for them. A frail thing and a magic thing as well? Magic in that if it should prove to be genuine, then the Church would be strengthened, and more would find belief, and the world, in time to come, would be a better place. The Evil Horde had its evil magic, the Little People their small magics, but these leaves of parchment, in the last accounting, might be the greatest magic of them all. Without actually forming words, he bowed his head and prayed it might be so.

And, finally, as he prayed, he heard a sound and for a long moment could not be sure what it was. It was so distant, so muffled, that at first he was not sure he heard it, but as he listened intently, it became more distinct, and he could make it out. The sound of distant hoofbeats, the undeniable hoofbeats of a horse, and now another sound, the far-off baying of dogs.

Although never loud, the sounds were distinct and clear. There could be no doubt of it: the wild hoofbeats of a running horse and the baying of hounds, and occasionally (although he could not be sure of this) the shouting of a man or men.

The strange thing about it was that the sound seemed to be coming from the sky. He looked up at the star-washed, moon-drenched sky, and there was nothing there. And yet the sound seemed to come from there.

It lasted only for a few minutes, and then it went away, and the silence of the night closed in.

Duncan, who had risen to make his survey of the sky, sat down again. Beside him, Tiny was growling softly, his muzzle pointed upward. Duncan patted him on the head. "You heard it, too," he said. Tiny ceased his growling and settled down.

Later on, Duncan rose to his feet and walked down to the stream, carrying a cup to get a drink of water. As he knelt beside the stream, a fish jumped in the pool above him, shattering the stillness. A trout, he wondered. The stream might carry trout. If they had time in the morning, they might try to catch a few of them for breakfast. If they had time; that was, if it didn't take too long. For there was no time to waste. The more quickly they were on their way, the faster they got through the Desolated Land, the better it would be.

When the moon had dropped appreciably toward the west, he awakened Conrad, who came to his feet, alert, with no sign of sleep left in him.

"Is everything all right, m'lord?"

"Everything is fine," said Duncan. "There has been nothing stirring."

He said nothing about the hoofbeats and the baying in the sky. As he formed the words in his mind to tell Conrad, they sounded too silly for the telling, and he did not say them.

"Call me a little early," he said. "I'll try to catch some trout for breakfast."

Duncan rolled up his cloak and used it as a pillow. Stretching out on the hard ground, he pulled the blanket over him. Lying on his back, he stared up at the sky. He pressed his fingers against the soft deerskin pouch and heard the soft crinkling of the manuscript. He pressed his eyes tight shut, trying in this manner to put himself to sleep, but behind the closed eyes he conjured up in his mind, without intending to, quite unwillingly in fact, a scene that he could not understand. But then the realization of what his mind's eye, in all the activity of his imagination, was showing him came clear. Impatiently he tried to shake it off, but it would not go away. No matter how hard he tried to shake it off, that figment of imagination hung on stubbornly. He turned over on his side and opened his eyes, seeing the campfire, Tiny lying beside it, Conrad looming over him.

Duncan closed his eyes, determined that this time he would go to sleep. But his mind's vision fastened on a furtive little man who scurried busily about to see and hear all that might be heard or seen among a small band of men who were associated with a tall and saintly figure. These men, all of them, the saintly man as well as his followers, were young, although too somber for their years, too dedicated, with a strange light in their eyes. They were of the people, certainly, for they were clothed in tattered garments, and while some of them wore sandals, others had nothing on their feet. At times the band was alone, at other times there were crowds of people who had gathered to gaze upon the saintly man, straining their ears to hear what he might say.

100

And always, hovering on the edge of these crowds of people, or dogging the footsteps of the little band when it was alone, was this furtive figure who darted all about, never of the band, but with it, listening so hard that his ears seemed to swivel forward to catch the slightest words, his bright, sharp, almost weasel eyes squinted against the desert sunlight, but watching closely, missing no move that might be made.

And later, crouching against a sheltering boulder or hunkering by a small campfire in the dead of night, writing all he'd seen or heard. Writing small so that his parchment would not run out, using every scrap of whiteness to inscribe his labored words, twisting his face and pursing his tiny mouth in the effort to get down the words exactly as they should be, telling in those words all that he had witnessed.

Duncan tried without success to gain a full view of this furtive man, to look him in the face, so that he might judge what sort of man he was. But he was never able to. The face was always in a shadow or was turned away at that very moment when, finally, he thought he'd see the face. He was a short man, almost a dumpy figure. His feet were bare and there were bruises on them from the desert rocks and pebbles; he was dressed in dusty rags, so tattered that he was continually pulling at them in an effort to cover his scrawny nakedness. His hair was long and unkempt, his straggly beard untrimmed. He was not the sort of man upon whom a casual observer would have wasted a second glance. He was a nonentity. He faded into the crowd. He was an unrecognizable and unimportant human among many other humans, a man so undistinguished that he drew no attention. There was nothing about him that made him stand out among all the others; he was engulfed and absorbed by them.

Duncan followed him, trudging steadily and doggedly to keep pace with his furtiveness, attempting to circle him so that he might come head-on at him and so get to see his face. Always he failed to do so. It was almost as if this furtive man was aware of him and was studiously careful either to keep well away from him or, on his approach, to turn away from him. Yet watching for some sign that this other furtive one was aware of him, he could catch no sign he was.

Then someone was shaking him and hissing him to silence. He fought his eyes open and sat up. Conrad was crouched in front of him. His half-clenched hand was raised to the level of Duncan's face, and an emphatic outstretched thumb was pointing across the dying campfire toward the ring of darkness that lay beyond the circle of the campfire's light. There, at the edge of the circle, between the light and dark stood Tiny in a rigid stance, straining forward as if someone held him on a leash, lips curled back to bare his fangs, a low growl rumbling in his throat.

Out of the darkness gleamed two wide-spaced balls of green fire and below them a frog-mouth rimmed by gleaming teeth, and over all of it—the teeth and balls of fire—the impression of a head or face so outrageous in its formation, so chilling in its outline that the mind rejected it, refusing to give credence to there being such a thing. The mouth was froglike, but the face was not. It was all angles and sharp planes and above it rose the suggestion of a crest. And in the instant that Duncan saw it, there was slaver at the corner of the mouth, a drooling hunger that yearned toward the campfire circle but was held from coming out—perhaps by the snarling Tiny, perhaps by something else.

He saw it only for a moment, and then it was blotted out. The balls of fire were gone and so were the sharp and gleaming teeth. For an instant the outline of the face, or the hinted outline of the face, persisted; then it, too, blinked out.

Tiny took a quick step forward, the growl rising in his throat.

"No, Tiny," Conrad said softly. "No."

Duncan surged to his feet.

"They've been around the last hour or so," said Conrad. "Prowling in the dark. But this is the first we've seen."

"Why didn't you call me sooner?"

"No need, m'lord. Tiny and me were watching. They were looking us over only."

"Many of them? More than this one?"

"More than one, I think. Not many."

Duncan put more wood on the fire. Tiny was pacing around the campfire circle.

Conrad spoke to the dog. "Come in. Tame down. No more of them tonight."

"How do you know there'll be no more tonight?" asked Duncan.

"They just looked us over. But now they've decided not to tackle us tonight. Maybe later on."

"How do you know all this?"

"Don't know. Just guess is all. A feeling in the bones."

"They have something planned for us," said Duncan.

"Maybe," Conrad said.

"Conrad, do you want to turn back?"

Conrad grinned viciously. "Just when it's getting good?" he asked.

"I mean it," Duncan told him. "There is danger here. I do not want to lead all of us to death."

"And you, m'lord?"

"I'd go on, of course. Perhaps alone, I could make it. But I don't insist that the rest of you . . . "

"The old lord, he said take care of you. He'd skin me alive should I come back without you."

"Yes, I know," said Duncan. "It has been that way since the time that we were boys."

"The hermit," Conrad said. "Maybe the hermit would go back. He's been bitching ever since we started."

"The hermit," Duncan told him, "is a self-proclaimed soldier of the Lord. He needs this to restore his self-respect. He feels he was a failure as a hermit. Scared witless, he'd still not turn back unless the others of us did."

"Then we go on," said Conrad. "Three comrades-in-the-arms. But what about the witch?"

"She can make her choice. She hasn't much to lose,

one way or another. She had nothing when we found her."

So, no matter what Ghost may have told them, Duncan thought, it was not only the hairless ones who were watching and keeping track of them. Meg had been right. The others were about, had been there all night, perhaps, watching from the darkness. Even when he'd sat beside the campfire during that first watch, they had been out there without his knowing it. And what was more, without Tiny's knowing it. Only the witch had known it. And strange as it might seem, she had not been greatly perturbed by it. Despite knowing they were there, she had curled up beside the saddle and the packs and had slept like a baby, making those little crying noises that had made her seem more babylike.

Perhaps she had sensed somehow that they were safe, that there'd be no attack. And how could she have known, he wondered, and why had those others not attacked? Huddled as they were around the campfire, one swift rush from the outer darkness would have taken care of them—there would have been no way a small party such as they could have stood them off.

And in the days ahead, how would they stand them off? Surely there would come a time when the Harriers would set out to kill them. They would stay vigilant, of course, but vigilance was not the entire answer. If enough of the Harriers were willing to meet death themselves, they could do the job.

Yet, he told himself, he could not turn back. He carried with him a certain talisman that might keep the lights still burning, beating back the ancient darkness. And if he did not turn back, neither would Conrad, neither would the hermit.

Dawn was near at hand. The darkness was filtering from the trees and one now was able to see a ways into the woods. A flight of ducks went over the camp, crying as they flew, perhaps heading for a favorite feeding ground.

"Conrad," he asked, "do you see anything strange?"

104

"Strange?"

"Yes, the way this place looks. It seems to be all wrong. Not the way it was when we camped last night."

"Just the light," said Conrad. "Things look different in the dawn."

But it was more than the dawn light, Duncan told himself. He tried to place the wrongness and was unable to. There was nothing definite that he could put a finger on. And yet it was different. The woods were wrong. The stream was wrong. The sense of things was wrong. As if someone had taken the geography in hand and had given it a slightly different twist, not changing it too much, but enough to be noticed, enough to give a viewer the feeling that it was skewed out of shape.

Andrew sat up, levering himself upright with his elbows.

"What is wrong?" he asked.

"There is nothing wrong," growled Conrad.

"But there is. I know it. It is in the air."

"We had a visitor last night," said Duncan. "Peeking from the bushes."

"More than one," said Conrad. "Only one peeked out."

Andrew came swiftly to his feet, snatching up his staff.

"Then the witch was right," he said.

"Of course she was," said Meg, from where she was huddled by the saddle and the packs. "Old Meg is always right. I told you they were skulking about. I said they were watching us."

Daniel lunged to his feet, took a few quick steps toward the campfire, then paused. He blew fiercely through his nostrils and pawed with one hoof at the ground.

"Daniel knows as well," said Conrad.

"All of us know," said Andrew. "What do we do about it?"

"We go on," said Conrad. "That is, if you want to."

"What makes you think I wouldn't want to?"

"I thought you would," said Conrad.

Meg threw back her blanket, got to her feet, shook her rags into some semblance of shape about her.

"They are gone now," she said. "I can't feel them any more. But they have enchanted us. We are in a trap. There is a certain stench to it."

"I see no trap," said Conrad.

"Not us," said Andrew. "We are not the ones enchanted. It is the place that is enchanted."

"How do you know?" asked Duncan.

"Why, the strangeness of it. Look over there, just above the stream. There is a rainbow shiver in the air."

Duncan looked. He could see no rainbow shiver in the air.

"The Little People sometimes try to do it," Andrew said, "but they do it very badly. As they do most things very badly. They are fumblers."

"And the Harriers are not?"

"Not the Harriers," said Meg. "They have the power. They do a job of it."

It was all insane, thought Duncan, to stand here so calmly, saying there was an enchantment on this place. And yet, perhaps there was. He had noticed the strange way in which the geography seemed to have been skewed about, slightly out of focus. He had not seen Andrew's rainbow, but he had noticed how the place was slightly out of joint. Looking at it, he saw that it still was out of joint.

"Perhaps we should get started," Duncan said. "We can have breakfast later. If we move immediately, we may get out of this strangeness that you call enchantment. Surely it cannot cover a great expanse of ground."

"It will get worse farther on," said Andrew. "I am sure that a deeper enchantment lies ahead of us. If we should go back we might soon be out of it."

"Back is where they want us to go," said Conrad. "Otherwise why enchantment? And we are not going back. M'lord has decided we go on."

He reached for the saddle and threw it on the back of the waiting Daniel.

"Come on," he said to Beauty. " 'Tis time to get you packed."

Beauty flapped her ears and trotted forward so he could put on the packs.

"No one needs to go," said Duncan. "Conrad and I have decided that we will. But the others of you need not."

"You heard me say that I would go," said Andrew.

Duncan nodded. "Yes, I did. I was sure you would."

"And I as well," said Meg. "Faith and there's little in this howling wilderness for an old girl such as I. And I have seen worse enchantments."

"We do not know what may lie ahead," warned Duncan.

"At least with you, there's food," she said, "which looms large in the eyes of a poor old soul who betimes has been forced to eke out her existence by eating nuts and roots, much as a hog would eat, rooting in the woods to find his dinner. And there's companionship, of which I had none before."

"We have no time to waste," said Conrad grimly. He grasped Meg around the waist and heaved her into the saddle.

"Hang on," he said.

Daniel pranced a little, in a way of welcome to his rider.

Conrad spoke again. "Tiny, point," he said.

The dog trotted down the trail, Conrad close behind him. Beauty took up her place, with Andrew trudging along beside her, thumping the ground with an energetic staff. Daniel and Duncan brought up the rear.

The enchantment deepened. The land became wilder than it had been before. Monstrous oaks grew in massive groves, the underbrush was denser, and about it all there was an unreality that made one wonder if the oaks and underbrush were really there, if the boulders had as thick a coat of lichens and the sense of antiquity that they seemed to have. But that was only a part of it. A brooding grimness held over everything. A deep hush pervaded the land, a hush of ominous and forboding waiting, sinister and doomful.

If the oaks had only been monstrous oaks, if the underbrush had been no more than thick, if the boulders had been only ancient mounds of lichens, a man, Duncan thought, could have accepted it. But there was the warping of these ordinary things, the crookedness and bias of them, as if they were not permanently planted in the earth, but were only there for the moment, as if someone had projected a picture of them and was as yet undecided what kind of picture he might want. It was a picture that wavered, as the reflection in a water surface might fluctuate with the almost imperceptible movement of the water, an oscillation, a shifting, a puzzling impermanence. And here and there one glimpsed at times the broken segments of shivering rainbow colors that Andrew had mentioned earlier, but that Duncan had not seen when he had looked for them. But now he did see them—the sort of shimmering color one saw when light shone through thick glass and its rays were scattered into a million hues. They appeared and disappeared, they did not last for long and never were they a complete rainbow arc, but fragments of arcs, shattered arcs, as if someone had taken a perfect rainbow and crushed it in his hands, shattering it, then broadcasting the fragments to the wind.

The valley still remained, and the hills that rose on each side of it. But the faint trail they had been following had disappeared, and now they made their way through the tangled forest as best they could. Conrad was holding Tiny close ahead of him, not allowing the dog the wide range that he had permitted before. Daniel was nervous, tossing his head and snorting every now and then.

"It's all right, boy," said Duncan, and Daniel answered with a quiet whicker.

Ahead of Duncan, Andrew stumped along beside Beauty, thumping his staff with unaccustomed force.

108

Beauty minced beside him, staying close. Unaccountably, she seemed to have taken a fancy to this strange companion. Perhaps she believed, thought Duncan, chuckling at the thought, that now she had acquired a human of her own, as Tiny had Conrad and Daniel had Duncan.

At the head of the column, Conrad and Tiny had stopped. The others came up to cluster with them.

"A swamp ahead," said Conrad. "It blocks our way. Could this be the fen?"

"Not the fen," said Andrew. "The fen does not block the way. It lies to one side and is open water."

Through the trees the swamp could be seen, a spreading marshiness that was not open land, but choked by trees and other heavy growth.

"Perhaps it's not deep," said Duncan. "We may be able to make our way through it, keeping close to the hill."

He moved ahead, Conrad striding beside him, the others trailing in their wake.

Duncan and Conrad stopped at the edge of the water.

"Looks deep to me," said Conrad. "Some deep pools out there. More than likely mud. And the hill you speak of. There isn't any hill."

What he said was correct. The line of hills they had been following now fell away and to their left, as well as toward their right, lay the tangled swamp.

"Stay here," said Duncan.

He stepped into the water. At each step the water deepened, and beneath his feet he felt the squishiness of mud and slime. Before him lay the beginning of one of the pools that Conrad had called his attention to—black as the blackest ink, with a look of oil, of something heavier and more treacherous than water.

He shifted his course to skirt it, and as he did the inky blackness of the water boiled, lashed to fury by something that struggled to emerge from it. A sinuous back humped up and broke through the blackness of the pool. Duncan's hand went to the sword hilt, half drew the blade. The sinuous back subsided and the

109

water once more assumed its undisturbed oiliness. But in another pool a little farther on, the surface exploded in a froth of violence, and out of it shot a vicious head supported by a snakelike body that hurled itself erect, towering above the level of the pool. The head was triangular, not so large as might be expected from the size of the ropelike body. Two horns crowned the scaly head; the cheeks had the appearance of armor plate, pinching down to a beaklike snout. It opened its mouth, and the mouth was larger than the head. Cruel curved fangs projected from the jaws.

Duncan had the blade out by now and stood, holding it, ready for attack, but the attack did not come. Slowly, almost reluctantly, the body slid back into the pool and the head disappeared beneath the surface. The swamp lay quiet and black and menacing.

"I think you'd best come back," said Conrad.

Slowly, step by careful step, Duncan backed out of the swamp.

"No chance to get across," said Conrad.

Andrew came clumping down to where they stood, Beauty mincing along behind him.

"There is no swamp," he said. "There never was a swamp. It is all enchantment."

"Swamp or not," said Meg, huddled on top of Daniel, "a bewitchment such as this can kill you."

"Then what do we do?" asked Duncan.

"We try another route," said Andrew. "We pass the enchantment by. No matter how powerful may be the ones who laid this witchery on us, they cannot lay it over everything. They knew where we were going and it was along that route that the enchantment was laid."

"You mean into the hills," said Duncan. "If we go there, how well do you know this land?"

"Not as well as this valley, but I know it. A few miles from here, due east, there is another trail. A bad trail. Very crooked, up and down the hills. Hard going. But it will take us south. It will take us beyond these hills that block us from the south."

"I think," said Meg, "we best had seek that trail."

12

They found Andrew's trail, but it proved to be the wrong trail. Halfway up a steep hillside it petered out to nothing.

They had left the enchantment far behind them, had escaped from it. Now there were no rainbow tints, no feeling that the landscape had been skewed. The land was the kind of land one would have expected to find. The oaks were honest oaks, the honest boulders had honest lichens on them, the stretches of underbrush were normal underbrush. The feeling of gloom was gone, the foreboding had dropped away.

It had been hard work. There had been no level ground. Constantly they had been traveling steep slopes, or making their careful way down steep slopes, which in some cases was almost as exhausting as the climbing.

Now that the trail had finally disappeared, Duncan glanced up at the sky. The sun was almost at its zenith.

"Let us stop to eat and rest," he said. "Then we'll strike east and try to find the right trail." He said to Andrew, "You are sure that there is one."

Andrew nodded. "I've traveled it, but only a few times and that many years ago. I am not well acquainted with it."

111

The trail had been lost on a small shelf of fairly level ground, extending for not more than a few yards before the steep slope took up again. Conrad gathered wood and started a fire. Daniel and Beauty stood with hanging heads, resting from hard travel. Tiny flopped down on the ground.

"We could use Ghost," said Conrad, "but he is far away, spying out the land ahead of us."

"I'll say this for Ghost," said Andrew. "I have a lot more respect for him than I had before. It takes real courage for a ghost to go out in broad daylight and do the kind of job that he's been doing."

A gray shadow moved among the trees below them.

"There's a wolf," said Duncan.

"There are a lot of wolves around," said Andrew. "More than there ever were since the Harriers came."

Another gray shadow followed the first, and farther down the slope was yet another one.

"At least three of them," said Duncan. "And there may be more. Do you think they might be following us?"

"Nothing to worry about," said Conrad. "A wolf is a coward. Face up to one and he runs away."

Meg put her arms around herself, hugging herself, shivering a little. "They smell blood," she said. "They can smell blood before there is any blood."

"Old wives' tale," said Conrad.

"Not a tale," Meg said. "I know. They know when death is coming."

"Not our blood," said Conrad. "Not our death."

A wind had come up and far down the hill it could be heard moaning in the trees. The ground was thick with fallen leaves. And over all of it was a somberness, the sense of autumn, a psychic warning against the coming of the snow. Duncan felt a faint unease, although there was nothing, he told himself, to be uneasy about. In just a short time now they would find the right trail and be on their way again, following a harder road than they had first intended, but on their way at last.

How many more days, he wondered, and was

amazed that he had no idea. Once they were through these hills, more than likely, they would make faster time. So far they had not hurried, but gone along at an easy pace. Now was the time, once they were squared around, he told himself, to really cover ground.

"If Snoopy were only here," said Andrew, "he would know the way, how to find the trail. But that is wishful thinking. There is no honor in him. Even when he told us, when he gave his word, he had no intention of being any help to us."

"We'll make out without him," Duncan said, a sharpness to his words.

"At least," said Conrad, "we walked out of the witchery that was laid for us."

"The witchery, yes," said Andrew. "But there will be other things."

They ate and then moved on, striking toward the east, or as close to east as was possible, for in this tangled, tortuous land there was no such thing as heading in any one direction. There were diversions— a bad lay of ground, a particularly steep climb that they tried to skirt, a tangle of fallen trees they must go around. But, in general, they trended toward the east.

The sun went down the sky and there was still no sign of any trail. They moved through a region that had no trace of men, or of there ever having been any men. There were no burned farmsteads, no cuttings where timber had been harvested. Ancient trees stood undisturbed, hoary with age.

From time to time they caught glimpses of wolves, but always at a distance. There was no way of knowing if they were the same wolves they had seen earlier.

We are lost, Duncan told himself, although he said nothing to the others. Despite all that Andrew said, all that he professed to know, there might not be a trail. For days they might keep plunging into the great wilderness and find nothing that would help them, floundering in confusion. Perhaps, he thought, it might be the enchantment still at work, although in a

113

less obvious manner than had been the case before.

The sun was almost gone when they came down a long slope into a deep glen, rimmed by the hills, as if it might be sunk into the very earth, a place of quiet and shadows, filled with a sense of melancholy. It was a place where one walked softly and did not raise his voice. The light of the sun still caught the hilltops above them and gilded some of the autumn trees with flaming color, but here night was falling fast.

Duncan hurried ahead to catch up with Conrad.

"This place," said Conrad, "has an evil smell to it."

"Evil or not," said Duncan, "it is a place to camp. Sheltered from the wind. Probably we'll find water. There must be a stream somewhere. Better than being caught on some windy hillside."

"I thought to catch sight of something ahead," said Conrad. "A whiteness. Like a church, perhaps."

"An odd place for a church," said Duncan.

"I could not be sure. In this dark, it is hard to see."

As they talked they kept moving ahead. Tiny had fallen back to walk with the two of them.

Ahead of them Duncan caught a glimpse of whiteness.

"I think I see it, too," he said. "Straight ahead of us."

As they progressed a little farther they could see that it was a building—for all the world like a tiny church. A thin tall spire pointed toward the sky and the door stood open. In front of it a space had been cleared of underbrush and trees, and they went across this space filled with wonder. For there should not be a church here, even a small one. Round about lived no one who would attend it, and yet there it stood, a small building, like a toy church. A chapel, Duncan thought. One of those hidden chapels tucked away, for one obscure reason or another, in places that were off the beaten track.

Duncan and Conrad came to a halt in front of it, and Andrew came hurrying up to them.

"Jesus of the Hills," he said. "The Chapel of the Jesus of the Hills. I had heard of it, but had never

114

seen it. I had no idea how to get to it. It was a thing spoken of half in wonder, half in disbelief."

"And here it is," said Conrad.

Andrew was visibly shaken. The hand that held the staff was trembling.

"A holy place," said Duncan. "A place of pilgrimage, perhaps."

"A holy place only recently. Only the last few hundred years," said Andrew. "It stands on most unholy ground. In earlier times it was a pagan shrine."

"There are many holy places that were raised on areas that once were special to the pagans," Duncan told him. "In the thought, perhaps, that the pagans would more readily accept Christianity if the places of worship were built on familiar ground."

"Yes, I know," said Andrew. "Reading in the Fathers, I ran across some mention of such thoughts. But this one—this was something else."

"A pagan shrine, you said. A place of the Druids, most likely."

"Not the Druids," said Andrew. "Not a shrine for humans. A gathering place for evil, where high carnival was held upon certain days."

"But if such were the case, why was a chapel built here? It would seem to me this was a place the Church had best avoid, for a time at least."

"I do not know," said Andrew. "Not with any certainty. There were in the olden days certain militant churchmen who perforce must seize evil by the horns, must confront it face to face . . ."

"And what happened?"

"I do not know," said Andrew. "The legends are unclear. There are many stories, but perhaps no truth to any of them."

"But the chapel's here," said Conrad. "It was allowed to stand."

Duncan strode forward, went up the three shallow steps that led up to the chapel door, and through the door.

The place was tiny, a dollhouse sort of place. There was one window on each side made of low-grade colored glass that glinted in the fading light, and six pews, three on each side of the narrow aisle. And above the altar . . .

Duncan stared in horror. He gagged and knew the bitterness of gall gushing in his mouth. His stomach knotted at the sight of the crucifix that hung behind the altar. It was carved out of a large oak log, all of it in one piece, the cross and the carven Jesus hanging on the cross.

The crucifix was upside down. The figure of Christ was standing on His head, as if He had been caught in the midpoint of a somersault. Filth had been smeared upon Him and obscene sentences, written in Latin, were painted on the wood.

It was, Duncan thought fleetingly, as if someone had struck him hard across the mouth. It was only with an effort that he kept his knees from buckling. And even as he reacted to the profanation and the sacrilege, wondered why he should—he, the mildest of Christians, with no great piety or devotion. And yet a man, he thought, who risked his neck and the necks of others to perform a service to the Church.

The crucifix was a mockery, a gusty whoop of pagan laughter, a burlesque of the Faith, a hooting, a ridicule, a scoffing, and, perhaps as well, a hatred. If the enemy cannot be conquered, at least he can be ridiculed and laughed at.

Conrad had pointed out that despite the pagan ground on which it had been built, the chapel had been allowed to stand. And in this observation there was implicit the question of why it had been allowed to stand. And this, the reversed crucifix and the violence that had been done it, was the reason. Years ago a man of Christ had come, a militant man intent on ramming Christianity down a pagan throat, and had built the chapel. And now the joke had been turned upon him and the chapel stood a mockery.

He heard the gasps behind him as Conrad and Andrew saw the crucifix and caught, for an instant, the impact of the horror.

Duncan whispered at them, "A mockery. A living

116

mockery. But Our Lord can stand that. He can take a little mockery."

The chapel, he saw, was clean and well cared for. There was no sign of the ravages of time. It had been swept but recently. It had been kept in good repair.

Slowly he began to back out of the door, Conrad and Andrew backing with him. On the steps outside sat a huddled Meg.

"You saw," she said to Duncan. "You saw?"

Dumbly, stricken, he nodded his head.

"I did not know," she said. "I did not know we were coming to this place. If I had, I'd have told you, stopped you."

"You knew what was here?"

"I had heard of it. That was all. Heard of it."

"And you do not approve of it?"

"Approve of it? Why should I disapprove of it? I have no quarrel with it. And yet, I would not have had you see it. I've eaten your food, ridden on your horse, your great dog did not tear hunks of flesh from me, you ran no sword through me, the big one reached out his hand to help me rise, he boosts me onto the horse. Even that sour apple of a hermit gave me cheese. Why should such as I wish any ill for you?"

Duncan reached down and patted her on the head. "It's all right, grandmother. We take it in our stride."

"Now what do we do?" asked Andrew.

"We spend the night here," Duncan said. "We are worn out with our travels of the day. We're in no shape to go on. We need some food and rest."

"Not a bite of food will I be able to swallow," said Andrew. "Not in such a place."

"What do we do then?" asked Duncan. "Go running out into the hills, fighting through the woods in the dark? We'd not make a mile."

Thinking, even as he said the words, that were it not for Andrew and Meg, he and Conrad could go, leave this pagan place behind them, find a safer camping place. Or keep going all the night, if that were necessary, to put some distance between them and the Chapel of the Jesus of the Hills. But Andrew's legs were tottery from the punishment they'd taken, and Meg, although she probably would deny it, was near the end of her endurance. Back at the hermit's cave he'd worried about the volunteers they were taking on, and here was evidence that he'd been right in worrying.

"I'll get some wood and start a fire," said Conrad. "There's a stream over to the right. I heard running water there."

"I'll go and get some water," Andrew said. Duncan, watching him, knew the kind of courage it had taken for him to offer to go alone out into the dark.

Duncan called Daniel and Beauty in, took the saddle off Daniel and the packs off Beauty. Beauty huddled against Daniel, and he seemed quite content to have her there. The two of them, Duncan thought, know as well as we that there is something wrong. Tiny prowled restlessly about, head held high to catch any scent of danger.

Meg and Conrad did the cooking at the fire that Conrad lighted only a short distance in front of the steps leading up to the chapel. The lights from the flames of the fire washed across the whiteness of the tiny structure.

Up on the hill to the west a wolf howled and was answered by another from the north.

"Some of those we saw early in the day," said Conrad. "They are still around."

"The wolves have been bad this year," said Andrew.

The glen, as full night came down, held the dank wet feel of fear, of danger walking on soft pads, moving in on them. Duncan, feeling this, wondered if this sense of apprehension arose from having seen the defamation of the crucifix, or if it would have been present if there had been no chapel and no crucifix.

"Conrad and I will do double watch tonight," said Duncan.

"You're forgetting me again," said Andrew, but with something in his voice that sounded to Duncan as if it might be relief.

"We want you rested," said Duncan. "The both of ou, so that we can put in a long day tomorrow. We'll start as soon as we can see. Well before full morning ight."

He stood beside the fire, staring out into the dark. t was hard, he found, not to take alarm at an magined shape or an imagined noise. Twice he hought he saw movement out beyond the campfire ircle, but each time decided it was no more than his magination, sharpened by the fear that he sought to onceal but could not, himself, deny.

The wolves occasionally howled, not only from the west and north, but from the east and south as well. This country, he told himself, was crawling with the peasts. However, the howls still were from a distance; he wolves did not seem to be moving in. They might come later, Duncan told himself, after they had worked up more courage, and the activity about the campfire had quieted down. Although of wolves, they need have no fear. If they came in, Daniel and Tiny would wreak havoc on them.

If there were anything to be feared, it would be omething other than the wolves. Remembering, once again he saw the frog's mouth full of teeth, the glowing eyes, the suggestion of a face that was made up of smooth planes and sharp angles—the face that had stared out at them from beyond the campfire of the night before. And the snaky evilness that had surged out of the black pool in the swamp.

Meg called them in for food and they squatted round the fire, wolfing it down. Andrew, despite his assertion that he would not be able to swallow a single morsel, did full justice to the meal.

There was little talk, only a sentence now and then and of inconsequential things. No one talked about what they'd found inside the chapel. It was as if all of them were busy in an effort to wipe it from their minds.

But it was not a thing, Duncan found, that could be wiped away. Never for a moment since he first had seen it had it been more than a short distance from his consciousness. Mockery, he had told himself, and it was that, of course, but it also would be, he thought, more than mockery. Hatred, he had said, almost as an afterthought. But now, having thought on it, he knew that there was in it as much hatred as there was mockery.

And that was understandable. The pagan gods of ancient days had a right to hate this new faith that had risen something less than two millennia ago. But he chided himself that he should think of the pagan gods as somehow legitimate in their hatred, that he should admit, even parenthetically, that they had existed and did now exist. This was not, he reminded himself, the way a Christian should be thinking. A devout Christian would consign them all to limbo, would deny there ever had been such as they. But this, he knew, was a viewpoint that he could not accept. He must still conceive of them as the ever-present enemy, and this was especially true in this place, the Desolated Land.

His fingers dropped to the purse suspended from his belt and beneath them he felt the crinkle of the pages that he carried. Here lay his faith, he thought, here, in this place where he sat, lay another faith. Perhaps a mistaken faith, perhaps a faith that should not be accepted, that instead should be opposed with every power at one's command, but a faith neverthe-less—a faith that man, in his ignorance, with no other faith, and yearning toward something that could intercede for him against the vastness of infinity and the cruelty of fate, had embraced despite all its cruelty and horror, thinking perhaps that any fate that was worth embracing must be horrible and cruel, for in those two qualities lay power, and power was something that man needed to protect himself against the outer world.

Here on this very ground, undoubtedly, had been performed certain hideous and repugnant rites that he had no knowledge of and was glad he had no knowl-edge of. Here humans may have died as sacrifices. Here blood had been spilled upon the ground, here obscene practices had been acted out, here monstrous ntities had trod with evil intent—and not only recently, but extending back into unguessed time, peraps into that time that anteceded mankind.

Daniel walked up close to where he was sitting, hrust down his head to nuzzle at his master. Duncan troked the big horse's head, and Daniel snorted oftly at him.

From the west a wolf howled, and it seemed that his time the howl was closer.

Conrad came striding up to stand near the horse nd man.

"We'll have to keep the fire burning high throughut the night," he said. "Wolves have a fear of fire."

"We have naught to fear of wolves," said Duncan. They are not driven by hunger. There is plenty for hem to pull down and eat out there in the woods."

"They are closing in," said Conrad. "I have been atching glimpses of their eyes."

"They are curious. That is all."

Conrad hunkered down beside Duncan. He pushed he head of his club back and forth upon the ground.

"What do we do tomorrow?"

"I suppose we go on hunting for Andrew's trail."

"And what if we don't find the trail?"

"We'll find it. There had to be a trail across these ills."

"What if enchantment closes the trail to us? Makes s not to see it."

"We escaped the enchantment, Conrad." Although, uncan reminded himself, he had entertained the ought, earlier in the day, that the enchantment might ill be with them.

"We are lost," said Conrad. "We don't know where e are. I don't think Andrew knows."

Out at the edge of the firelight circle two eyes leamed back at Duncan and then, almost instantly, ere gone.

"I saw one of your wolves just now," he said to onrad. "Or at least his eyes."

"Tiny has been watching," Conrad said. "Pacing ick and forth, He knows they are out there."

They were moving in closer now. The darkness a
the edge of the campfire circle was rimmed by shining
eyes.

Tiny went walking out toward them. Conrad called
him back. "Not yet, Tiny. Not quite yet."

Duncan rose to his feet.

"We're in for it," said Conrad quietly. "They ar
getting set to rush us."

Daniel switched around to face the gathering
wolves. He tossed his head, snorting in anger. Tiny
coming back, ranged himself by Conrad. His ruff wa
lifted and a growl gurgled in his throat.

One of the wolves paced forward. In the fireligh
his gray fur seemed almost white. He was large an
raw-boned, a death's head of a wolf. He seemed t
teeter forward, his great gaunt head thrust out, th
lips pulled back from the fangs, his eyes glittering i
the reflection of the flames.

Another wolf came up behind and to one side c
him, stopped with its head at the first wolf's shoulde.

Duncan drew his blade. The rasp of drawn met:
was harsh in the silence that had fallen on the clearin
The firelight glinted off the shining steel.

He said to the horse beside him, "Steady, Danie
steady, boy."

At a quick shuffle of feet behind him he risked
glance over his shoulder and saw that it was Andrev
He held the staff half lifted. The cowl had fallen t
his shoulders, and his graying hair was a halo in th
firelight.

From the darkness at the edge of the clearing
voice spoke, loud and clear, but using words tha
Duncan had never heard before—not English, neithe
Latin nor Greek, nor with the inflection of the Gaulis
tongue. Words that were harsh and guttural and with
snarl in them.

At the words the wolves came charging in: the bi
wolf that had first appeared paced by the second on
that had come up to stand with him, and others racin
out on each side, coming in half crouched, tensed t
leap, bursting from the dark at the signal or the con

122

mand of the one who had spoken from the darkness.

At Duncan's side, Daniel reared up, striking out with his front hoofs. Tiny was a streak of unleashed hatred lunging at the beasts. The big wolf rose, soaring effortlessly from the ground, his jaws aimed at Duncan's throat. The sword licked out and caught his outstretched neck, hurling him to one side with the impact of the thrust.

The second wolf, running beside him and leaping as he ran, crumpled under Conrad's club. Out in front of Conrad, Tiny seized a third by the throat and with a powerful toss of the head sent him spinning through the air.

Another wolf leaped at Duncan, fangs gleaming, mouth wide open for the strike. Even as Duncan lifted the blade, a spearlike stick came thrusting from one side and impaled the beast in its open mouth, ramming deep into its throat. The wolf folded in midair, but the impact of its leap carried it forward, taking the spear with it as it fell.

Duncan's foot caught on the falling stick and he was thrown to his knees. A wolf was rushing in at him and he jerked up the blade, but even as he did, Daniel reached out with a driving hoof, catching the animal behind its hunched shoulder blades. The wolf went down with a crunch of snapping bones.

Duncan surged to his feet, and as he did he saw Tiny on the ground, locked in battle with one of the beasts, and another charging in, with a raging Conrad standing close beside the dog, club lifted and ready for the charging wolf. And just beyond the embattled dog, Beauty was struggling frantically to tug free of one of the beasts that had caught her by a foreleg, with two other wolves rushing in upon her.

Duncan lunged to Beauty's aid, but he had taken no more than a step or two when a raging fury, brandishing two burning brands, streaked toward the burro's attackers. One of the brands went spinning through the air, turning end for end, and the two charging beasts sheered off.

"Meg!" Duncan shouted. "Meg, for the love of God,

watch out!" But she paid him no attention, running like the wind, her ancient body wobbling on her shaky legs that seemed to twinkle with her speed even as she wobbled. She lifted the one remaining brand and brought it down on the wolf that had Beauty by the leg. The wolf yelped and spun away, went whimpering out into the darkness.

From the darkness came again the loud, clear voice speaking in the unknown tongue, and as the words rang across the clearing, all the wolves turned about and ran.

Duncan came to a halt and turned slowly to his left. Daniel stood beside the fire, and a short distance from him Andrew had one foot on a dead wolf to hold it down while he tugged desperately to free the staff rammed deep into its throat.

Conrad and Meg were walking toward the fire, with Tiny trailing, while behind Tiny came the limping Beauty. Here and there lay the bodies of the wolves. One of them, possibly the one that Daniel had struck, was trying to pull itself along with frantically working forelegs, its hind quarters dragging.

As Duncan walked toward the fire, Andrew suddenly screamed, let go of the staff on which he had been tugging, and backed away from the dead wolf, his hands lifted to his face.

"No! No!" he screamed. "No, not that!"

Duncan ran toward him and then stopped short, staring at the dead wolf in shocked amazement and disbelief.

The body of the wolf was slowly changing and as he watched in horror, it became the body of a naked woman, with the hermit's staff still protruding from her mouth.

Beside Duncan, Meg chirped at him in a high and squeaky voice. "I could have told you, but I never had a chance. It happened all too fast."

Conrad stepped past Duncan, grasped the hermit's staff in one hamlike hand, and jerked it free.

The body of the wolf beyond the woman had turned into a man, and out beyond the two of them

124

the thing with the broken back that had been dragging itself away wailed suddenly in a human voice, a cry of pain and terror.

"I'll take care of him," said Conrad grimly.

"No," said Duncan. "For the moment, leave him be."

"Werewolves," spat Conrad. "They're only good for killing."

"There is something I have to find out," said Duncan. "There were a lot of them. Only a few of them attacked. The others hung back. If they had all come in . . ."

"Someone called them back," said Conrad.

"No, it wasn't that. Not that alone. There was something else."

"Here," said Conrad, holding out the staff to Andrew.

The hermit shrank away. "No, no," he wailed. "I do not want to touch it. I killed a woman with it."

"Not a woman. A werewolf. Here, take it. Hold fast to it. You'll never have another staff quite like it."

He thrust it out forcefully at Andrew and the hermit took it. He thumped it on the ground.

"I shall always remember," he pleaded.

"Good thing to remember," Conrad said. "A blow struck for our Lord."

Duncan walked out to the edge of the firelight, stood over the wailing man with the broken back, then slowly knelt beside him. The man was old. His arms and legs were thin as straws, his knees and elbows knobs. His ribs showed through his skin. His snow-white hair hung down to curl up at his neck and was plastered with sweat across his forehead. He looked at Duncan with fear and hatred in his shining eyes.

"Tell me," said Duncan, "who spoke out of the dark."

The man's lips pulled back to reveal his yellowed teeth. He snarled and spat.

Duncan reached out to grab him by the shoulder and he flinched away. He opened his mouth and

125

screamed, his head arched high, the cords in his neck standing out like ropes. White, foamy spittle gathered at the corners of his mouth and he screamed and moaned and clawed feebly at the ground to pull himself away. He writhed in agony.

A hand came down and grasped Duncan by the shoulder, hauled him to his feet.

"Here, let me," said Conrad.

His club came down and there was the sickening sound of a crunching skull. The man crumpled and lay still.

Duncan turned to Conrad angrily. "You shouldn't have done that. I told you not to."

"When you kill snakes," said Conrad, "you kill them. You do not coddle them."

"But there was a question."

"You asked the question and you got no answer."

"But he might have answered."

Conrad shook his head. "Not that one. He was too afraid of you."

And that was true, thought Duncan. The werewolf had been beside itself with fear. It had screamed and tried to claw itself away. It had writhed in agony.

Conrad touched him on the arm. "Let's go back to the fire. I have to see how Beauty is."

"She was limping. That was all. Meg saved her."

"Yes, I saw," said Conrad.

"How is Tiny?"

"A slit ear. A tooth mark here and there. He'll be all right. Just a little sore."

By the time they got back to the fire Andrew had piled on more wood, and the flames were leaping high. Andrew and Meg were standing side by side. Conrad went off to see about Beauty.

"That was a brave thing you did," Duncan told Meg. "Running out there to help Beauty."

"I had fire. Werewolves are afraid of fire."

She bridled at him. "I suppose you wonder why I helped. My being a witch and all. Well, I'll tell you. A little magic and some mild enchantments, those are all right with me. In my day I've done a lot of that. There

126

is nothing wrong with it. Many times it helps. But I told you I had no real evil and I meant that. Werewolves are evil and I cannot abide them. Mean, downright vicious evil. There's no call for anyone to be that evil."

"There was a pack of them," said Duncan. "A lot of them. I never knew that werewolves ran in packs, although perhaps they do. You were telling me about the camp followers who trailed in the wake of the Harriers. Could that be what accounted for so large a pack?"

"It must be that. They must have come swarming in from all over Britain."

"And you heard the voice?"

She put her arms around herself, hugging tight and shivering.

"You knew the words? You recognized the language?"

"Not the words," she said, "but the language, yes. A word here and there. It's a very ancient tongue."

"How ancient?".

"That I cannot tell you, sir. Not in years or centuries. It goes deep back. Spoken before any human spoke, perhaps before there were such things as humans."

"Primordial," he said. "The words of primordial evil."

"I do not know."

It was on the tip of his tongue to ask how she recognized the language, but he did not ask the question. There was no need to distress her further. She had been honest in her answers, he was sure, and that was good enough.

Conrad came back. "Beauty is all right," he said. "Her leg a little sore. We came out lucky."

The clearing was quiet. The humped bodies of the dead werewolves lay at the edge of the outer darkness.

"Perhaps," said Andrew, "we should bury them."

"You do not bury werewolves," Conrad said. "A stake through the heart, perhaps. Besides, we haven't any shovel."

127

"We'll do nothing," Duncan said. "We'll leave them where they are."

The chapel stood white in the flickering firelight. Duncan looked at the open door. The firelight did not reach deep enough into the interior to show the reversed crucifix and he was glad of that.

"I'll not sleep a wink this night," said Andrew.

"You had best," said Conrad roughly. "Come morning light, we have a long, hard day ahead. Do you think you can find that trail?"

Andrew shook his head in perplexity. "I am not sure. I seem all turned around. Nothing has looked right."

A wailing scream cut through the night, seeming to come from directly overhead, as if the screamer hung in the darkness over them.

"My God," yelped Andrew. "Not more. Not any more tonight."

The scream came again, a moan and whimper in it. It was the sort of sound that squeezed the heart and made the blood run cold.

A calm voice spoke to them from just inside the firelit zone.

"You have no reason to fear," it said. "That is only Nan, the banshee."

Duncan spun around to face the one who spoke. For a moment he did not recognize him. A little man with a cap that drooped, a pair of spindly legs, ears that were oversized.

"Snoopy," he said. "What are you doing here?"

"Hunting you," said Snoopy. "We've been hunting you for hours. Ever since Ghost told us he had lost track of you."

Ghost came fluttering down and beside him another figure, its darkness in contrast to the white of Ghost.

"It was pure happenstance," said Ghost, "that I ran into them."

"It was much more than happenstance," said Snoopy, "and you wouldn't understand. We have no time to explain."

Ghost floated lower until his white robe swept the

128

ground. Nan, the banshee, settled down, hunched herself along the ground toward the fire. She was repulsive. Her deep-set eyes glittered at them from beneath her shaggy brows. Thick black hair flowed down her back almost to her waist. Her face was thin and hard.

"Faith," she said, "and you were hidden well. It took us long to find you."

"Madam," said Duncan, "we were in no wise hiding. We simply reached here and camped the night."

"And a fine place you picked," said Snoopy, walking up to them. "You know you cannot stay here."

"We intend to," Conrad told him. "We fought off a pack of werewolves. We can handle whatever else comes."

"We have been looking for you, goblin," said Andrew. "Why were you not at the church, where you said you'd be?"

"I've been out spreading word that you'll need some help. And the way you've been fumbling around, you will need all the help that we can give."

"You found little help," Andrew said snappishly. "One beaten-up old banshee."

"I'll have you know, you twerp," said Nan, the banshee, "that I can give you ace and spades and beat you at hands-down."

"There'll be others later on," said Snoopy calmly. "They'll be there when you need them most. And you know you can't stay here. No matter what you say, in your ignorance and arrogance, we have to get you somewhere else."

"We know," said Duncan, "that this is a pagan shrine."

"More than that," Snoopy told him. "Much more than that. A place that was sacred to Evil before there were any pagans who might worship Evil. Here, in the days of the first beginning, gathered beings that would shrivel up your tiny souls were you to catch even the smallest glimpse of them. You desecrate the ground. You befoul the place. They will not suffer that you stay here. The werewolves were the first.

129

There will be others, not so easily beaten off as were-wolves."

"But there is the chapel . . ."

"They suffered the chapel to be built. They watched it being built by arrogant and misunderstanding men, by stupid churchmen who should have known far better. They lurked in the shades and watched it going up and they bided their time and when that time came . . ."

"You can't frighten us," said Conrad.

"Perhaps we should be frightened," said Duncan. "Perhaps if we had good sense we would be."

"That is right," said Meg. "You should be."

"But you came along with us. You did not protest when we . . ."

"Where else is an old and crippled witch to go?"

"You could have flown off on your broomstick," said Conrad.

"I never had a broomstick. Nor did any other witch. That is only one of the many stupid stories . . ."

"We can't move until we get some rest," said Duncan. "Conrad and I could go on, but the witch is feeble and Andrew has walked the livelong day. He is worn out."

"I had the strength to kill a werewolf," the hermit pointed out.

"You mean it, don't you?" Conrad said to Snoopy. "You're not just shoving us around."

"He means it," said Nan, the banshee.

"We could put Andrew up on Daniel," Conrad said. "Let Beauty carry Meg. She weighs no more than a feather. The packs we could carry. Beauty, even with a sore leg, could carry Meg."

"Then," said Snoopy, "let us be about it."

"I plead with you," said Ghost. "Please do. If you stay here you'll join me in death by morning. And you might not have the good fortune that I had to become a ghost."

13

After a time Duncan's eyes became acclimated to the darkness and he found that, after a fashion, he could see. That is, he could distinguish trees sufficiently not to run head-on into them. But there was no way to know the character of the ground underfoot. Time after time he tripped over a fallen branch or fell when he stepped into a hole. Rather than walking, it was like floundering. By keeping his eyes on Conrad's broad back and the whiteness of the pack that Conrad carried, he did not wander off. Had it not been for Conrad and the pack, he was sure he would have.

Snoopy led the way, with Ghost sailing along just above him, serving as a sort of beacon they could follow. Daniel followed Snoopy and Ghost, and Beauty trailed along behind her comrade, Daniel. Conrad and Duncan brought up the rear. Nan flew about somewhere above them, but she wasn't too much help. The rags she wore were either black or drab and could not be seen, and she had the disconcerting habit of letting loose upon occasion with dolorous wails.

Andrew had objected to riding Daniel, but when Conrad picked him up and heaved him into the saddle, he did not try to get off. He rode slumped over, his head nodding. Half the time, thought Duncan, the man's asleep. Meg lay lengthwise on the little burro, clinging like a leech, her arms around Beauty's neck. There was no saddle for Beauty, and her rotund little barrel of a body was not ridden easily.

Time stretched out. The moon slid slowly down the western sky. Occasionally night birds cried out, probably in answer to Nan's wailing. Duncan wished she would shut up, but there was, he knew, no way to make her do it, and besides, he didn't have the breath to shout at her. The walking was punishment. It was all up and down hills. Duncan had the impression that they were going in the same direction from which they had come, but he couldn't be sure about it. He was all mixed up. Thinking of it, it seemed to him that they had been mixed up for some time now.

If it had not been for the enchantment, they could have continued to the fen and down the strand. By this time, more than likely, they would be getting close to the fair and open land Snoopy had told them of, free at last of these tortured hills.

It was strange, he thought. The Harriers had made three attempts to stop them or turn them aside: the encounter in the garden near the church, the enchantment of the day before, the attack of the werewolves. But each attack had been feebler than he would have expected. The hairless ones had broken off the encounter in the garden without making too great an effort. The enchantment had failed—or maybe it had succeeded. Maybe all it had been intended to do was to get them off the trail they had been following. And back at the chapel, undoubtedly if all the werewolves had made a concerted attack, they could have wiped out the little band of humans. Before that could happen, however, they had turned tail and run, called off by the voice that cried out of the darkness.

There was something wrong, he told himself. None of it made sense. The Harriers had swept through this land, killing off the inhabitants, burning villages and farmsteads, making the area into a desolated land. Surely a band as small as theirs should not have been able to stand before them.

Except for the frog-mouth full of teeth that had stared out of the darkness at them, there had been no sign of the Harriers. He had no way of knowing, he admitted to himself, that frog-face had been a Harrier, although, since it resembled nothing else he had ever heard of, he supposed it was.

Did he and his band, he wondered, travel under some powerful protection? Perhaps the hand of God extended over them, although even as he thought it, he knew it to be a foolish thought. It was not often that God operated in such a manner.

It must be, he told himself, only half believing it, the amulet he had taken from Wulfert's tomb—a bauble, Conrad had called it. But it might be more than a bauble. It might be a powerful instrument of magic. Andrew had called it an infernal machine. Thinking of it as a machine, he had naturally thought that there must be some way to turn it on and make it operate. But it if were magic, as it might be, it would need no turning on. It would be operative whenever the occasion demanded that it should be. He had dropped it into the pouch in which he carried the manuscript and had scarcely thought of it since. But he could recognize the possibility that it was the magic that had protected them from the full wrath of the Harriers.

No Harriers, he had told himself. And yet, might not the hairless ones be Harriers, or at least one arm of the Harriers? Harold, the Reaver, had mentioned them as among those that had attacked the manor. It was entirely possible, Duncan told himself, that they were the fighting arm of the Harriers—the shock troops designed to protect the true Harriers while they gathered to participate in those mysterious rites of rejuvenation. If that, in fact, was what they were doing. He could not even be sure of that, he told himself. It was one of the theories that His Grace had mentioned.

Christ, he thought, if I could only know one thing for certain. If I could be sure of only one aspect of this tangled mess.

Wulfert—he was not even sure of him. Regarded by the village where he'd come to live as a holy man, not correcting the error that the villagers had fallen into. Not correcting it because it gave him safety. A wizard who was hiding out. Why should a wizard be hiding out? And, when one came to think of it, how about Diane? She had known that Wulfert was a wizard, had come seeking word of him. But when she gained the word, she had not followed up on it, but had gone flying off. Where was she now? If he could only talk to her, she might be able to explain some of what had been happening.

The moon by now was well down toward the western horizon, but there was still no hint of morning light. Were they ever going to stop? They'd been laboring through these hills for hours, and there was no indication that they were about to stop. How much distance did they need to put between themselves and the Chapel of the Jesus of the Hills to be safe from the jealous evil that protected it?

For some time now Nan had desisted from her wailing. They had emerged from the forest to come on one of the occasional clear spots they had found on the summit of some of the hills. The backbone of the hill reared up in a mass of rocky outcrops.

Looking up, Duncan saw Nan, a black bat of a woman, flying through the sky, outlined by the faintness of the moonlight.

What little wind there had been had died down, a signal of the coming dawn. A heavy silence reigned over everything. The only sound was the occasional ringing of Daniel's or Beauty's iron-shod hoofs as they came in contact with a stone.

Then, out of the moonlit sky, it came again, the sounds that Duncan had heard the night before: the sound of hoofbeats in the sky, the distant shouts of men, the distant baying of dogs.

Ahead of him, Conrad came to a halt and he saw that the others had come to a halt as well. Snoopy stood on a small rocky ridge ahead of them and was staring into the sky. Meg sat bolt upright on Beauty

134

and also stared skyward. Andrew remained slumped in the saddle, doubled over, fast asleep.

The shouting became louder, the baying swelled and deepened, and the hoofbeats were like faint thunder rolling down the heavens.

A shadowy tracery of something came over the treetops to the north, and as he watched, Duncan saw that there was only one horseman riding in the sky, standing straight in the saddle, brandishing a hunting horn and shouting to spur on the dogs that ran ahead of him—vicious, bounding hunting dogs that slavered on the trail of an unseen quarry. The great black horse galloped through the empty air with no ground beneath its pounding hoofs.

The horse and rider and the dogs swept toward the group standing on the hilltop and passed over them. There was no way to see the features of the man, the horse, or the dogs, for they all were black, like silhouetted shadows moving across the sky. The hoofbeats pounded so hard that they seemed to raise echoes among the hills, and the baying was a torrent of sound that engulfed them as they stood there. The rider raised the horn to his mouth and blew a single blast that seemed to fill the sky, and then the rider and his pack were gone. They disappeared over the southern tree line, and the sound gradually diminished with the distance until nothing could be heard, although it seemed to Duncan that he still heard the ringing of the hoofs long after the sound of them had gone.

Nan came tumbling out of the sky and landed beside Duncan. She skipped a step or two to gain her balance, stood in front of him, and craned her head upwards. She was jigging in excitement.

"Do you know who that was?" she asked.

"No I don't. Do you?"

"That was the Wild Huntsman," she screeched. "I saw him once, years ago. In Germany. That was when I was young and before I settled down. The Wild Huntsman and his hounds."

Meg had slipped off Beauty and was tottering toward them.

"He always was in Germany," she said. "He never was anywhere else. That proves what I've been telling you about all these things of evil gathering with the Harriers."

"Was he looking for us?" asked Conrad.

"I doubt it," said Meg. "He's not really hunting anyone or anything. He just rides the skies. He whoops and hollers and blows that horn of his and his dogs make such a racket they scare you half to death. But he doesn't mean anything by it. That's just the way he is."

"Who is he?" Duncan asked.

"No one knows," said Nan. "His name has been forgotten. He's been riding the skies so long there's no one who remembers."

Snoopy came scuttling down from the ridgetop.

"Let's get moving," he said. "It's just a little farther. We'll be there by first light."

"Where are you taking us?" asked Duncan. "We have a right to know."

"I'm taking you to where you should have been all the time. Back to the strand."

"But that, or just short of there, is where we ran into enchantment. They'll be waiting there for us."

"Not now," said Snoopy. "There's no one there right now. You'll be safe. They would not think that you would come back."

Ghost jiggled in the fading moonlight, just above their heads.

"That is right," he said. "All the blessed day not a sign of anyone at all. I'd say the way was clear."

"We'll have to rest," said Duncan, "before we try the strand. All of us are practically dead upon our feet from loss of sleep."

"Andrew's getting sleep," said Conrad.

"He's the only one of us," said Duncan. "He'll pay for it. When we get there he'll stand guard while the rest of us get some rest."

136

14

The slimy monster hurled itself out of the swamp, scaly, triangular, horned head, with fanged jaws and darting snakelike tongue, mounted on a barrel-sized snakelike body, towering above him, while he stood thigh-deep in water, the muck of the marsh sucking at his feet, anchoring him so he could not get away, but had to stand and face the monster. He bawled at the monster in anger and revulsion as it hung above him, hissing, dominating him, sure of him, taking its time, not in any hurry, hanging there like a stroke of certain doom while he waited with his toothpick of a sword— good steel, sharp and deadly and well fitted to his fist, but so small a weapon that it seemed unlikely it could inflict more than a scratch upon this scaly monstrosity that eventually would pick its time to strike.

The swamp was silent except for the hissing of the monster and the slow drip of water from its shining hide. It had a strange unearthliness, as if not entirely of the earth nor quite yet of some other place—a moment and a space poised on some freakish borderline between reality and unreality. Tendrils of trailing fog roiled above the black and stagnant water—black molasses water, too thick to be actual water, but a devilish brew that reeked and stank of foul decay. The

137

trees that grew out of the water were leprous, their gray and scaling trunks bearing the mark of an unknown and loathsome ailment with which the entire world on the other side of the borderline might be afflicted.

Then the head came crushing down with the body following, arcing and coiling and striking him as if some giant fist had descended on him, brushing aside his sword-arm, buckling his knees, throwing its smooth and muscular loops about his body, enfolding him in its strength, driving the breath out of his lungs, crushing his ribs, dislocating his shoulders, folding him in upon himself and a voice bawling, "Be careful of that dog. Tie him tight, but don't put a mark upon him. He's worth more than all of you together. If he be so much as bruised, I'll hang the man who does it by his thumbs."

There was sand in Duncan's mouth—sand, not water—and hands that held him, not the great snake body. He struggled, trying to lash out with arms and legs, but the hands held him so tightly that he could accomplish nothing. There was a knee thrust into the small of his back and another pressing on his shoulders. His face was pressed hard against the ground. His eyes came open and he saw a dead and fallen leaf, with an insect crawling slowly on it, fighting its way across its smooth and slippery surface.

"Tie that big one tight," said the bawling voice. And then, "That horse. Watch out. He'll kick the guts out of you."

Somewhere Tiny was growling fiercely, somewhere Daniel was fighting off, or trying to fight off, his captors. And from all around came thumping sounds and the grunts of struggling men.

Duncan felt heavy cords cutting harshly into his wrists, and then someone jerked him up and flipped him over. He lay on his back and stared up at the sky. At the periphery of his vision he saw the figures of uncouth men looming over him. From somewhere far off came an eerie keening.

He fought his body erect, pushing with hands lashed

behind his back to lever himself upright, till he was sitting flat upon his rump with his bound feet thrust out straight before him.

A few feet away lay Conrad, trussed up like a Christmas goose, but still struggling to break free.

"Once I get my hands on you," Conrad roared at the men who had just stepped away from him, "I'll rip your livers out."

"Friend Conrad," said one of the men, "I extremely doubt you shall have that chance."

There was something about the man that seemed familiar to Duncan, but his head was half turned away and he could not be sure. Then the man shifted slightly and he saw that it was Harold, the Reaver.

Duncan's mind struggled to grasp reality. But it was difficult to grasp reality, for the transition had been too swift. He had been dreaming—yes, that must be it, he had been dreaming—of confronting a snakelike monster that had lunged out of a swamp, the dream more than likely touched off by the similar monster he had seen emerging from the inky pool in the enchantment swamp. And then, suddenly, he had not been dreaming any longer, but was being caught and tied by this vicious, ragamuffin crew.

He glanced around him, trying to take in the situation at a glance. Andrew was tied to a small tree, his hands roped against the tree, other ropes about his middle. There was no sign of Meg, although she must be somewhere, and no sign of Daniel either, but the patient little Beauty stood hitched to another tree, a heavy rope looped, halterlike, about her head and neck. Out of the corner of his eye he could see Tiny, his four feet tied together, his jaws held shut by loops of cord pulled tightly about them. Tiny was struggling fiercely, throwing himself about, but there seemed little possibility the dog could fight his way to freedom. Conrad still lay a few feet away, looking more than ever like a Christmas goose ready for the oven.

They were at the edge of a small grove of trees at the beginning of the strand—the place where they had stopped in early morning light and flopped, without thought of breakfast or of fire, wanting only to catch a few hours of sleep while Andrew stood the guard.

Snoopy was nowhere in sight, nor was Nan, the banshee, nor was Ghost. Which, Duncan told himself, was no more than might have been expected. As soon as his charges were safely at the strand, Snoopy, perhaps accompanied by Nan, would have gone off to collect his band of Little People. Ghost more than likely was out on scout, alert to any danger. Ghost had said last night that he had seen no one during the entire day, that here they would be safe. And if that had been the case, Duncan wondered, where the hell had the Reaver and his men been hiding?

The Reaver was walking toward him, and he watched him as he came, puzzled at the emotions the man evoked in him—some fear, perhaps, certainly some hatred, but the fear and the hatred washed away by the utter contempt he felt for such a rogue. The Reaver was the scum of the earth, a vicious opportunist with no principles whatsoever: a nothing, less than nothing.

The Reaver stopped a few feet from him and stood, with his hands planted firmly on his hips, looking down at him.

"So, m'lord, how do you like it now?" he asked. "The tables now are turned. Perhaps you'd care to tell me what this is all about."

"I told you," said Duncan, "that night at the manor. We are bound for Oxenford."

"But you did not tell me why."

"I told you. We carry messages."

"And that is all?"

Duncan shrugged. "That is all," he said.

The Reaver stooped forward, placed one great hand on the pouch at Duncan's belt, with one wrench tore it free.

"Now we'll see," he said.

Taking his time, he carefully undid the buckles and opened the pouch. His hand dipped into it and brought out Wulfert's amulet. He dangled it on its chain, the

140

brilliant jewels set in it turned to fire in the fading sunlight.

"A pretty thing, forsooth," he said, "and perhaps valuable. Tell me what it is."

"A bauble only," Duncan said. "A piece crafted for its beauty."

And deep inside himself he prayed, *Not the manuscript! Please, not the manuscript!*

The Reaver dropped the amulet into his pocket, reached in the pouch again and brought out the manuscript.

"And this?"

"A few leaves of parchment," said Duncan, as smoothly as he could, "brought along for reading. A favorite of mine. I've had little time to read it."

"Bah!" said the Reaver in disgust. He crumpled the manuscript in his fist and tossed it to one side. The wind caught it and scudded it along the sand for a few feet. Then it caught on a small shrub and lodged there, the wind still tugging at it.

The Reaver's hand went in the pouch again, bringing out a rosary, the cross of ivory, the beads of amber. He examined his find carefully.

"Venerable?" he asked. "Perhaps sanctified by some holy man?"

"By His Grace, the archbishop of Standish Abbey," Duncan said. "Which makes it only moderately sanctified."

"Still a splendid piece of work," the Reaver said affably, dropping it into his pocket. "I might get a copper for it."

"It's worth much more than that," said Duncan. "You'd be a fool to sell it for a copper."

Next the Reaver came up with a clinking doeskin bag. "Now this," he said, a grin exposing his snaggle-teeth, "is more like it." He opened the bag and poured some of the coins into an open palm, poking at them with a finger of the hand that held the bag.

"A goodly sum," he said, "and welcome to a man in as straitened circumstances as I find myself to be."

141

He poured the coins back into the bag and dropped it, as well, into the pocket of his jacket.

Opening the pouch wide, he peered into it, reaching in a hand to explore the remaining items.

"Junk," he said contemptuously and tossed the pouch aside.

"And now the sword," he said. "A blade carried by a gentleman. Much better, I suppose, than the poor iron that we carry."

He stepped to one side and drew the blade from Duncan's scabbard. Squatting down in front of Duncan, he examined it with a practiced eye.

"Good steel," he said, "and serviceable. But where is the gold, where are the jewels? I would have expected a scion of the nobility to carry a better piece than this."

"Gold and jewels are for ceremony," Duncan told him. "This is a fighting weapon."

The Reaver nodded. "What you say is true. Sharp and with a needle point. Very good, indeed."

He flicked the sword point upward, thrust it forward an inch or two to prick against Duncan's throat.

"Let us now suppose," he said, "you tell me what is really going on. Where is the treasure that you seek? What kind of treasure is it?"

Duncan said nothing. He sat quietly—quietly while every instinct screamed for him to pull away. But if he flinched from the pointed steel, he told himself, there would be no purpose served. Flinch away and one flick of the Reaver's wrist would have the point against his throat again.

"I'll have your throat out," the Reaver threatened.

"If you do," said Duncan, "you'll foreclose ever finding out."

"How true," the Reaver said. "How very true, indeed. Perhaps skinning you alive would be a better way. Tell me, have you ever watched while a man was skinned alive?"

"No, I never have."

"It is not a pretty sight," the Reaver said. "It is done most slowly, a little at a time. There are various methods of procedure. Beginning at the toes or sometimes at the fingers. But that is tedious work for the skinner, who must be very careful since the technique is quite delicate. I think I might prefer, if I were the skinner, to begin at the belly or the crotch. Although quite complicated, I think I would prefer beginning at the crotch. That is a very tender region and it usually brings fast results. If we were to do it on you, where would you prefer we start? We'll accord you the courtesy of making your own choice."

Duncan said nothing. He could feel the sweat popping out along his forehead and he hoped it didn't show. For this, he sensed, was not idle talk. It was not meant to frighten him into talking. This butcher meant to do it.

The Reaver appeared to be in deep thought, mulling over the situation.

"Maybe it might be better," he said, "if we did it first on someone else and let you watch a while before we started in on you. Perhaps that great oaf over yonder. He'd be a good one to do it on. He has such a splendid hide. So much of it and in such good condition. Once a man had it off him, he could make a jacket of it. Or that piddling hermit, tied against the tree. He would scream louder than the oaf. He would squirm in agony. He would scream and ask for mercy. He would call most piteously on the Lord. He'd put on quite a show. Although I am undecided. The hermit's skin is so wrinkled that it would seem scarcely worth the effort."

Duncan still said nothing.

The Reaver made a deprecating gesture. "Oh, well," he said, "it's too late in the day to talk about it now. To do a first-rate skinning job good light is needed, and the sun's about to set. First thing in the morning, that is when we'll start. So we'll have the full day for it."

He lumbered to his feet, tucked Duncan's sword beneath his arm, patted his bulging jacket pocket, and made as if to turn away. Then he turned back and looked at Duncan, grinning at him.

"That'll give you the night to think it over," he said. "We can talk again, come morning."

He shouted to his men. "Einer and Robin," he bellowed, "you stand first watch over this precious haul of ours. Don't take your eyes off them. And I want no marks upon them. I want no injury to their hides. I want the pelts perfect when we strip them from them. And should you fail—should you let them, by some mischance, get away, or should you, in your fumbling way, abuse them in any way at all, I shall have your balls."

"Reaver," said Duncan, "you are misinformed. There is no treasure. Our journey is not a treasure quest."

"Ah, well," said the Reaver, "later we can judge as to that. Although I fear, if you finally should convince me that I am mistaken, it may be difficult to stick your hide back on you."

He walked a few steps out beyond the edge of the grove to reach the beginning of the strand and again raised his voice in a bellow.

"Cedric, for the love of Christ, why so far away? I said set up the camp nearby."

From a short distance away Old Cedric's piping voice answered him. "Here there was a small patch of grazing for the horses—we'll want to keep an eye on them—and a good supply of down wood ready for the fire."

The Reaver grumbled underneath his breath, then said, "Well, I guess it really makes no difference. These ones are securely bound. The Devil himself could not work them free. They'll be closely watched and we are just a step away."

Einer, the one who had been made to change his seat to make room for Duncan and Conrad that night at the manor house, said, "We could drag them into camp. It would be a pleasure."

The Reaver considered for a moment and then said, "No, I don't think so. There'll be two men at all times watching over them. Why should we waste our strength? Besides, here they'll have quiet to get their thoughts together and know their proper course, come morning."

144

As he went down the strand, others trailed after him. Einer and Robin, two lusty louts, stayed behind.

Einer said to Duncan, "You heard what he said. We want no shenanigans. I am under orders to make no marks on you, but at the least tomfoolery I'll feed you sand until you choke."

Conrad asked, "You all right, m'lord?"

"No talking," Robin, the guard, told them. "You are to keep your mouths shut."

"I'm all right," said Duncan. "So is Andrew. I don't see Meg."

"She's over toward the left, not far from Daniel. They have him tied up between two trees."

"I said no talking," Robin screamed, taking a quick step forward, brandishing a rusty claymore.

"Easy," Einer cautioned him. "The Reaver said no marks."

Robin pulled back, let the claymore fall to his side.

"M'lord," said Conrad, "it seems we face great peril."

"I am sure we do," said Duncan.

The manuscript was still where it had blown, tangled in the tiny shrub, held there by the pressure of the wind.

15

There was something stirring in the clump of willows at the outer edge of the grove. Duncan sat bolt upright, staring at the spot where he had seen the stirring, or thought that he had seen it. Watching intently, he could not be sure. A fox, he thought, although it seemed unlikely that a fox would creep in so close. Or perhaps some other animal, some small roamer of the night, out to find a meal.

The clump of tangled willows screened the Reaver's camp. Through the interlacing branches Duncan could see the flare of fire. Earlier the night had been loud with the shouting, the laughter and the singing of the men about the fire, but as the night wore on, the noise had quieted down.

The moon had risen earlier and now stood halfway up the eastern sky. The keening he had heard before still came intermittently and he now was certain that the sound came from somewhere in the fen.

His wrists were sore from straining against the ropes in the hope that he could loosen them, might even slip them off. But he no longer strained against them, for there was no give to them and he was convinced that there was no way of working free of them.

There had to be a way to escape, he told himself,

there simply had to be. For hours he had racked his brains to find the way. A sharp stone, perhaps, against which he could scrape his bonds, abrading them, finally cutting through them or damaging them so much they could then be broken. But there seemed to be no stones, only sand mixed with a little loam and clay. By intricate contortions he probably could slide his bound hands beneath his rump, double up his knees and thus be able to reverse the position of his hands, pulling them under and over his legs, getting them in front of him, where he could get at the rope that bound them with his teeth. But that, he knew, would be impossible with the two guards watching. As a matter of fact, he was not sure at all that it could be done. Or it was possible that if he could crawl to Conrad, either he could chew through Conrad's bonds or Conrad chew through his—more than likely Conrad chew through his, for Conrad had bigger teeth and a stronger jaw. But that, too, would be impossible with Einer and Robin watching.

He built up fantasies of rescue—of Snoopy coming back and being able to sneak up and cut the bonds of one of them, who could then engage the guards while Snoopy went on with the freeing of the others; of Ghost coming in and then streaking off for help, for any kind of help; of Diane plummeting down astride her griffin, armed with her battle axe; even of the Wild Huntsman and his pack of baying dogs, forsaking his eternal chase across the sky and rushing in to help. But none of this, he knew, was about to happen.

The chances were that there'd be no escape or rescue, and when morning came . . . But he refused to think of that, he shut his mind to it. It was the sort of prospect a man could not plan against. Thinking of it in those small chinks of time when he could not block his thinking of it, he admitted that it was unlikely he could stand up, in any decent sort of way, against the torture. And the worst of it, he thought, was that he had nothing he could tell the Reaver that would forestall the torture.

For there was no treasure, there had been no thought

of treasure. He wondered how the Reaver had picked up the idea they might be after treasure. Although, come to think of it, that would be almost automatic for a man of the Reaver's stripe. Ascribing his own motives and expectations to other men, it would not be unusual for the Reaver to sniff out the scent of treasure or the drive toward a treasure in anyone he met.

Tiny had quit his struggling some time before, although he had kept it up for a long while, and now lay quietly on his side. For a long time Conrad had not stirred; knowing Conrad, Duncan thought, he might have gone to sleep. Andrew hung against his tree, limp, the ropes supporting him. From the Reaver's camp came muted sounds of revelry, although more subdued than they had been in the evening.

The manuscript still was entangled in the low-growing shrub, the wind still fluttering the edges of its pages. Duncan ached to make some effort to conceal or hide it, but feared that any effort he might make to do so would call attention to it.

The guards had not been relieved and were getting restless. Quietly they had talked it over between themselves, wondering aloud if the Reaver might have forgotten to send out their replacements.

With some surprise, Duncan realized that he was hungry and thirsty. Thirst he could understand, but the hunger puzzled him. Surely a man in his position, facing what he faced, should not think of hunger.

How many days, he wondered, since he and Conrad had left Standish House? It seemed half of forever, but when he counted back it was only five or six, although he could not be sure. Somehow, when he thought of them, the days got tangled up. So little time, he thought, to get into so much trouble; so much time to have gone so short a distance on their journey.

Robin said to Einer, loudly enough for Duncan to catch the words, "They should have sent someone long ago to take our place. Probably, by this time, the lot of them are besotted on the wine that was given for all of us. And us not with a taste of it."

"I would not mind a cup of it," said Einer. "It is

seldom that we have wine. I had been looking forward to it. For months we have drunk nothing but ale until it lies sour upon the stomach."

"I have a mind," said Robin, "to go and get a gourd of it for us. In a moment I'd be back."

"The Reaver would take the ears off you if you left your post."

"The Reaver, whatever else you may say of him," protested Robin, "is a reasonable man and not one to exact undue suffering from his men. If I went and spoke to him of it, he might send out someone to take our place. He's simply forgotten how long he's had us out here."

"But the prisoners!"

"Not a one of them has stirred in the last hour. There's naught to fear from them."

"I still don't like the sound of it," said Einer.

"I'm going to get that wine," said Robin. "It's not fair to keep us out here while they lie guzzling. I'll be back in the shake of a wee lamb's tail. They all may be so sodden they'll take no notice of me."

"If there's any wine left."

"There should be. There were three casks of it."

"Well, if you're determined, then. But hurry. I still think it is a foolish thing to do."

"I'll be right back," said Robin.

He wheeled about and disappeared, moving hurriedly, blotted from Duncan's sight by the clump of willows.

Wine, thought Duncan. Who could they have encountered who would give them wine?

A faint rustling came from the willows. The fox, or whatever it might be, was still there, or had come back again.

Einer, who must have heard the rustling, started to turn, but the figure that rose out of the willows moved too fast for him. An arm went around his throat and metal flashed briefly before it disappeared with a thud, sinking into Einer's chest. The guard straightened momentarily, gurgling, then slumped and fell, to lie huddled on the sand. One foot jerked spasmodically, kicking at the earth.

The man who had risen from the willows ran toward Duncan and knelt beside him. In the light of the moon, Duncan caught a glimpse of his face.

"Cedric!" he whispered.

"As I told you once before," Cedric whispered back, "a small stroke here and there."

The knife in his hand sliced through the bonds that held Duncan's hands, then he turned to the feet and slashed the rope that held the ankles. He thrust the knife toward Duncan.

"Here," he said, "take this. You'll have need of it."

The old bee master rose and started for the willows.

"Wait, man!" whispered Duncan. "Stay and go with us. If the Reaver finds you out . . ."

"Nay. My bees. The bees still have need of me. They would be lost without me. And no one will notice. They all lie as if dead, badly in their cups."

Duncan surged to his feet. His legs seemed dead beneath him, numb from being bound so long. Old Cedric was already gone, vanishing in the willows.

Duncan ran to Conrad, pushed at him so he could reach his arms.

"What goes on, m'lord?"

"Quiet," Duncan whispered.

He cut the cords that bound Conrad's arms and handed him the knife.

"Free your legs," he said, "then cut loose the others. The second guard is coming back. I'll take care of him."

Conrad grabbed the knife. "Thank dear God," he said.

As he ran toward the willows, Duncan could hear the shuffling tread of Robin returning, floundering through the sand. Duncan stooped to scoop up the claymore that Einer had dropped. It was an awkward, heavy weapon that did not fit his fist. His numbed fingers had some difficulty grasping it, but finally he managed to get a good grip on it.

Robin began talking to Einer even before he rounded the willows.

"I took an unbroached cask of it," he crowed triumphantly. "No one noticed. Or I don't think they did. All of them are slobbered."

He grunted, shifting the cask from one shoulder to the other. "We have enough to last out the night," he said. "More than enough to last the night. There'll be some left over we can wash our feet in if we feel the urge."

He came around the corner of the clump of willows, and Duncan stepped swiftly forward. The stroke had no finesse, no fanciness, no swordsmanship. He simply crashed the edge of the claymore down on the top of Robin's head. The skull split with the sound of a ripe melon popping; the rusty iron stopped only when it reached the breast bone. The violence of the iron striking the heavy bone set up a vibration that made Duncan's forearm tingle. Robin made no sound. He fell like a tree before an axe. The cask hit the ground and bounced, rolling for a ways, its contents slopping in it.

Duncan bent over the body, reached for the hilt of Robin's blade and jerked it free. Then he ran for the manuscript, and with the two weapons tucked beneath his armpit, held by the pressure of his arm, he picked up the manuscript, folded it once, unneatly, and thrust it inside his shirt, where it lay against his skin.

Andrew was free, staggering about on unsteady legs, and so also was Meg. Conrad was bending over Tiny, carefully cutting the cords that held the big dog's jaws together. Duncan ran for Daniel, roped between two trees. As he approached, the horse shied away. Duncan spoke to him softly. "It's all right, Daniel. Take it easy, boy." He slashed at the ropes and as they came free, the horse lunged forward, then stood trembling. Beauty, already freed, trotted up, dragging the rope that had been her halter.

Conrad was moving toward Duncan, and Duncan held out one of the claymores toward him. Conrad raised his hand to show he had his club. "They left it lying there beside me." Duncan tossed one of the clay-mores to one side.

"What the hell's the matter with Andrew?" he asked. The hermit was stumbling about, looking at the ground.

Duncan hurried to him, grasped him by the arm. "Come on," he said. "We must get out of here."

"My staff," gasped Andrew. "I must find my staff."

He made a sudden lurch forward. "Ah, there it is," he said.

He grabbed it up and thumped it on the ground.

"Where to, m'lord?" asked Conrad.

"Back into the hills. We'll have a better chance there."

Conrad sprinted forward, snatched up Meg, threw her on Daniel's back. "Hang on tight," he said. "Stay low so a branch doesn't scrape you off. You'll have to cling with all your might, for you haven't got a saddle. I don't even know where the goddamn saddle is."

16

They halted in the clearing on the top of the rocky ridge where they had stopped the night before to watch the Wild Huntsman career across the sky. The moon was low in the west and a few birds were beginning to stir and twitter in the woods below them. Meg slid off Daniel, grateful for the halt, and Andrew sat down on a small boulder.

"They're all beat out, the both of them," Duncan told Conrad. "Maybe we should hole in here and wait to see what happens."

Conrad looked around. "Good place," he said. "We could get our backs against those rocks and hold them off, should they come upon us. Better than being caught out in the woods."

He held out his wrists for Duncan to see. They still carried ugly red welts from the bonds and the skin was abraded and bleeding. "I notice yours are the same," he said.

"They tied us tight," said Duncan. "If it hadn't been for Cedric . . ."

"He should have come along with us. If the Reaver finds him out . . ."

"Maybe he won't find him out. All of them were dead drunk. Someone had given them three casks of

153

wine. And of course, they'd have to try to drink it up. Who in the world would have given them wine?"

"Maybe they found it. In one of the burned homesteads."

"No. Einer, or was it Robin, said someone had given it to them."

"You asked Old Cedric to come along with us?"

"That's right. He said he couldn't. That his bees had need of him."

"Ghost didn't show up last night."

"Maybe he did and saw what had happened and went tearing off to try to locate Snoopy."

"Had he come down, he would have scared the Jesus out of those two guards. They'd have lit out."

Duncan shook his head. "What good would it have done? Even so, Ghost could have done nothing to cut us loose."

"Yes," said Conrad, "maybe that is it. Maybe he did show up and then left again. But what do we do now, m'lord?"

"We'll talk it over, think about it," Duncan said. "I don't know quite yet what we should do. Maybe find a place to hole up until the situation clears a bit."

"If it clears."

"We have to do something. We have no food, no blankets. Nothing. And the Reaver took the wizard's amulet."

"Small loss," said Conrad. "Just a pretty bauble."

"It may be more than that," said Duncan. "It may be a powerful talisman. It may have provided us protection. We were able to escape the enchantment, we defeated the hairless ones with ease, the werewolves turned tail and ran. It may have been the amulet that brought all these things about."

"It gave us no protection from the Reaver."

"That is right," said Duncan. "It did not help us against the Reaver. But I am sure it helped us with the others."

Andrew rose from his boulder and came over to where they were standing.

"I know," he said, "what you must think of me

154

There was no time for it to be done before, but now that we have a breathing space perhaps you may want to castigate me for the dereliction of my duty. I was the one who should have kept the watch. You left me on guard against any seeming danger. But I dozed. I caught a catnap, I am sure of that. That must have been the manner in which they came upon us, with me nodding while I should have been a-watch."

"So that is how it came about," rumbled Conrad. "I had wondered briefly on it, but had no time to think any further. So you were fast asleep. Why should you have needed sleep? You slept all the night before, slumped in Daniel's saddle."

"That is true, of course," said Andrew. "But it was not restful sleep. It was not the kind of sleep you judged it to be. Dozing was more like it. Not sound and solid sleep. Although I do not offer that as an extenuation of my failing. It all comes of a certain weakness in me, a weakness of the body. My mind may tell the body to perform, but the body fails. I am of not such stuff as martyrs may be made."

"And you also," said Conrad, "have a mouth that keeps running on."

"Think no further on it," Duncan said. "To each of us our weaknesses. In the end, it turned out all right."

"I shall endeavor," Andrew said, "to recompense for my failure in this instance. I shall try the harder to do my bounden duty as a soldier of the Lord. Henceforth, I swear to you, you may depend upon me in all surety."

"If it would make you feel any better," Conrad said, "I would be delighted to kick you in the rump. That might ease your conscience, which seems to be so sorely smarting."

"If you truly would, sir," said Andrew eagerly, "making certain that it is a lusty kick, with no power in it held back in consideration of me as a companion of the road."

He turned around and bent over, hiking up his robe to present his bare and scrawny bottom.

"Stop this buffoonery," snapped Duncan. "It is ill

behavior in a soldier of the Lord to present his bony
ass to his boon companions. Let down your robe and
straighten, like a man. Sir Hermit, henceforth I shall expect more propriety of you."

Andrew let down his robe and straightened up.

Conrad said to Duncan, "It might have been better,
m'lord, if you had allowed me. There must be something done to stiffen up his spine and make a better
soldier of him. And anyhow, a swift kick in the stern
never yet has failed to help a malefactor."

Duncan held up his hand for silence. "Listen," he
said. "Quiet, all of you, and listen."

Faintly, from far away, came the sound of shouting
and of screams. At times the sounds gained somewhat
in volume and at other times shrank to no more than a
whisper in the wind.

"From the strand," said Conrad. "It is from the direction of the strand."

They listened further. The distant and muffled yelling and screaming kept on. For a time it seemed to
stop and then it took up again and finally it did stop
and there was nothing to be heard.

"The Reaver's men," said Conrad. "They met up
with someone."

"Perhaps the hairless ones," said Andrew.

They stood for long moments listening, but nothing
further happened. The first light of the sun was flushing
the east and the birds were chirping in the woods below
them.

"We should know," said Conrad. "If the fight, if that
is what it was, has swept them from the strand, then
we could use it safely and make our way through these
cursed hills without all the labor that it would be to
climb them."

"Let me go," said Andrew. "I shall be very careful.
I shall not let them see me. Let me, please, to disclose
to you my newfound resolution to be a trustworthy
member of this company."

"No," said Duncan. "No, we stay here. We do not
move from here. We have no way of knowing what
might have happened. And should they come against

156

us, here at least we have a chance to make a stand against them."

Meg chirped at Duncan's elbow. "Then, dear sir, please let me be the one," she said. "Certainly, if they should come against us you could spare my feeble strength. But I can go and bring back to you a report of what happened with all the shouting and the yelling."

"You?" asked Conrad. "You can barely crawl about. All this time with us, you've ridden to preserve your little strength."

"I can manage it," protested Meg. "I can go through the underbrush like a scuttling spider. I can use what little magic I still may have left in me. I can get there and back, bringing word."

Conrad looked at Duncan questioningly.

"Maybe," said Duncan. "Maybe she could do it. Is it, Meg, something that you want to do?"

"Little enough I have done," said Meg. "So far I've been no more than a burden to you."

"We do need to know," said Duncan. "We could sit on this hilltop for days, not knowing. It is important that we know. But we can't split up our small force to send another one of us to scout the situation."

"If only Ghost were here," said Conrad.

"Ghost isn't here," said Duncan.

"Then I may go," said Meg.

Duncan nodded and she swiftly scuttled down the hill. For a time they stood and watched her as she darted through the trees, but finally she was lost from view.

Duncan walked back to a group of stone slabs that at one time had broken off and fallen from the rocky ridge. Choosing one of the slabs, he sat down upon it. Conrad seated himself on one side of him and Andrew on the other. Silently, the three of them sat in a row. Tiny came ambling around the mass of broken slabs and lay down ponderously in front of Conrad. Down the slope Daniel and Beauty cropped at a patch of scanty grass.

So here they were, thought Duncan, sitting side by

157

side on a slab of riven stone in a godforsaken wilderness, three adventurers and about as sorry a lot as ever could be found.

His belly ached with hunger, but he did not mention it to the others, for without a doubt, they were hungry, too, and there was no sense talking of it. Before the day was over, certainly by tomorrow, they would have to find some food. Tiny might be able to pull down a deer if one was to be found, but thinking back on it, Duncan remembered that they had seen no deer nor any other game except occasional rabbits. Tiny could catch rabbits and did, for his own eating, but probably would not be able to catch enough of them to provide food for everyone. Probably there were roots and berries and other provender in the woods that could ease their hunger, but he would not know where to look or what to choose, and he doubted that any of the others did. Perhaps Meg could be of help. As a witch, she might have knowledge of the food provided by the woods, for she would have been concerned with finding certain materials that went into her potions.

He thought of what they'd do next and of the way ahead, and found that he was shuddering away from it. They had made little progress so far, and in making the little that they had, they had run into a lot of trouble. Now they would be traveling without Wulfert's amulet and without it, the trouble might get worse. The amulet, he was convinced, had helped them with the hairless ones, the enchantment and the werewolves, and yet, come to think of it, he knew that he was wrong. The amulet could not have been of help with the hairless ones, for it was not until after their encounter with them that he had acquired it. Although that, he thought, might have been simply happenstance. Certainly the amulet must have been some protection against the enchantment and the werewolves. Perhaps the victory over the hairless ones could be explained by something else—perhaps by Diane and her griffin. The hairless ones, until the last moment, probably had not expected to face Diane and the griffin along with the rest of them. Yes, he said to himself, thinking foggily, that must be the explanation.

And yet, with the amulet or without it, he knew he would go on, by whatever means, under no matter what kind of circumstances. He had no choice; he had fought out the issue that night when he'd lain in the hermit's cave. The long history of his heritage made no other decision possible. And when he went on, the others would go with him—Conrad, because the two of them were close to being brothers, Andrew because of the mad obsession with being a soldier of the Lord. And Meg? There was no reason for Meg to continue with them, no advantage for her to gain, but he was sure she would.

The sun had climbed far up the sky and there was a drowsiness in the air—a soft, warm drowsiness. Duncan found himself nodding, half asleep. He pulled himself erect, drew in great breaths of air to force himself back to wakefulness, and in a few minutes' time was nodding once again. His body ached and his wrists were sore from the chafing of the bonds. His gut was an empty howl of hunger. He craved sleep. If he could only go to sleep, he thought, maybe when he woke the soreness and the ache, perhaps even the sharpness of the hunger, would be gone. But he could not go to sleep, he must not sleep. Not now. Not yet. Later there would come a time for sleep.

Beside him Conrad came to his feet, staring down the slope. He took a half-step forward, as if unsure of himself, then he said, "There she is."

Duncan forced himself upright and stared down the slope with Conrad. Andrew did not stir. He was doubled over, hands grasping his staff, his head almost to his knees, fast asleep.

At the edge of the forest below them, Duncan saw faint movement. Then, as he watched, he saw that it was Meg. She was toiling up the hill, bent over, almost crawling. She fell and struggled to her feet and came on again, moving slowly and tortuously.

Conrad was running down the hill. When he reached her he lifted her, cradling her in his arms, leaping up the hill with her. Carefully he laid her down in front of Duncan. When she struggled to sit erect, he helped her, lifting her into a sitting position.

She looked up at them with beady eyes. Her jaw worked and a harsh sound came out of them.

"Dead," she said.

"Dead?" asked Duncan. "The Reaver's men?"

"All of them," she whispered in harsh tones. "Laid out on the strand."

"All of them?"

"All of them. Dead and bloody."

17

The wind off the fen fluttered the rags that clothed some of the humped figures lying on the sand—not all of them, for it was apparent that some of the dead were hairless ones, and they had no rags to flutter. Huge black birds perched upon the corpses or hopped angrily about among them; and there were other birds as well, although they were not noticeable at first, little birds of the forest and the strand that hopped or ran about, pecking with their vicious little beaks at morsels scattered on the ground or at the pools of black, coagulated blood that lay puddled on the sand. The bodies lay within a small area, as if the Reaver's band had come together to present a solid front to the massed attack, which must have come on them from three sides, giving them no way to escape except into the fen, which would have been death itself. Luggage and saddlebags, pots and pans, blankets, pieces of clothing, drinking mugs, and weapons lay scattered all about. The campfire still smoldered feebly, sending up thin threads of tenuous, finespun smoke. Far up the strand a half dozen horses stood with shot hips and hanging heads. There was no sign of the rest of the horses; by now they could be widely scattered. Against a tumbled pile of firewood lay carelessly stacked saddles, saddle blankets and other harnesses.

Duncan stopped when he came around the clump of willows, and the others stopped with him, staring at the scene of carnage. Looking at the grotesque scattering of bodies, Duncan felt the bitter taste of bile rising in his throat and hoped he would not vomit, for that would be a disgraceful thing to do. Although he had read in the history scrolls at Standish House the lurid, spine-chilling accounts of battles and the somber, black descriptions of their aftermath, this was the first time he had seen at firsthand the butchery of combat.

It was strange, he thought, that it should affect him so. He had felt nothing like this in the garden skirmish with the hairless ones or in beating off the werewolves. Only a few hours ago he had cleaved the skull of the unsuspecting Robin, and it had been no more than a detail, a necessary job that must be done in the struggle for survival. But this was different. There was nothing personal about this. He was not involved. This was death on a fairly massive scale, the evidence of death and the violence that had brought it on this short stretch of ground between the flatness of the fen and the sharply rising ground.

Here lay the men, he told himself, who had threatened violence and torture to himself and the others with him, and, staring at the small patch of crumpled bodies, he tried to tell himself that he was glad this had happened to them, that it freed him of his fear, that it might even be, in some way, a product of his hatred of them, but he found, surprisingly, that he could not hate the dead.

It was not that he had never known human death before. He had first met it when he was ten or so, when Old Wells had come to his chamber, where he was hiding, and taken him to that great room where his grandfather lay dying. The rest of the family had been there, but he had seen no face clearly except for the hawklike face of the old man who lay upon the bed. Thick, tall lighted tapers stood at the four corners of the bed, as if the old man who lay there might have already died, the flickering light of the tapers doing little to beat back the gloom of death. His Grace had stood beside the bed, draped in his brilliant yet somber robes of office, muttering Latin prayers for the solace and the benediction of the dying man. But it had been his grandfather he had watched, the only one he had really seen, a frail old body surmounted by the fierceness of the hawklike face. And yet despite the desperate fierceness of the face, a shell-like man, a man made out of wax, a waxen replica of a man already gone.

Conrad touched his arm. "M'lord," he said.

"Yes," said Duncan. "I am sorry. I was thinking."

They walked forward slowly, tramping ponderously, and at their approach the large black scavengers, squawking in outrage at this disturbance of their feast, spread their ragged wings and pumped them mightily to lift their heavy bodies. The smaller birds waited for a time in an attempt to brazen out the intrusion, and then they, too, flew away in a blizzard of whirring wings.

White and empty faces, some of them with the eyes already plucked out of them by the ravenous birds, stared uncomprehendingly at them here and there from the heap of tangled bodies.

"The thing that we now must do," said Conrad, "is find what they have taken from us—your sword, the amulet on which you place so much trust, Daniel's saddles, our blankets, some food for us to eat. And then we can leave this place behind us, thankful that it all is done."

Duncan stopped and Conrad went ambling on, circumnavigating the area of the dead. Meg scuttled about, humped over, resembling in certain ways the scavengers that had flown away, snatching up items that she found lying on the ground. Andrew stood a little way in the rear, leaning pensively on his staff, his peaked face peering out from beneath the cowl. Tiny trotted at Conrad's heels, snarling softly at the tangled dead.

"M'lord," said Conrad. "Please come, m'lord."

Duncan hastened around the heap of dead to reach Conrad's side. He looked down at the body indicated

163

by Conrad's pointing finger. The eyes in the body's head came open and looked up at him.

"The Reaver," said Conrad. "The son-of-a-bitch still lives. Shall I finish him?"

"There's no need to finish him," said Duncan. "He's not leaving here. His last hour is upon him."

The Reaver's mouth worked and words came dribbling out.

"Standish," he said. "So we meet again."

"Under somewhat different circumstances than the last time. You were about to skin me."

"They betrayed me, Standish." The words ran out and the Reaver closed his eyes. Then the words took up again, but the eyes stayed closed. "They said for me to kill you, but I did not kill you."

"And I'm to feel great charity because of that?"

"They used me, Standish. They used me to kill you. They had no stomach for the job themselves."

"Who are the 'they' that you talk about?"

The eyes came open again, staring up at Duncan. "You'll tell me something true?" the Reaver asked. "You'll swear it on the Cross?"

"For a dead man, yes. I'll swear it on the Cross."

"Is there any treasure? Was there ever any treasure?"

"There is no treasure," Duncan said. "There never was a treasure."

The Reaver closed his eyes again. "That's all I needed. I simply had to know. Now you can let that great lout who stands beside you . . ."

Conrad lifted up his club.

Duncan shook his head at him.

"There's no need," he said. "There is nothing to be gained."

"Except the satisfaction."

"There'd be," said Duncan, "no satisfaction in it."

Andrew had moved up to stand beside them. "Some last words should be said," he told Duncan softly. "Last rites for the dying. I am not equipped nor empowered to do it. But surely some small words . . ."

The Reaver opened his eyes again, but they did not

164

stay open. The lids simply fluttered, then went shut again.

"Get that sanctimonious bastard out of here," he muttered, his words so low they could scarcely be heard.

"You're not welcome," Conrad said to Andrew.

"One last mercy," whispered the Reaver.

"Yes, what is it, Reaver?"

"Bash in my goddamn head."

"I would not think of doing it," said Conrad.

"I lie among my dead. Help me die."

"You'll die soon enough," Conrad told him.

Andrew dropped his staff, snatched at the club in Conrad's hand, wrested it from him. The club went up, came down.

Conrad stared in astonishment at his empty hand.

"A final word?" asked Duncan. "This is your last rite?"

"I gave him mercy," Andrew said, handing back the club.

18

They camped some distance up the strand, out of sight of the huddled dead. Night had closed down and from across the fen came the far-off keening. The wind-blown firelight flickered, reaching to the upsurge of the soaring cliffs, to the rim of the far, flat fen.

The fen was a fearsome place, Duncan told himself, sitting by the fire, fearsome in its far-reaching flatness, in its empty loneliness, a stretch of watery wilderness that reached as far as one could see—not a lake, nor yet a marsh, but a place of many little ponds and sluggish streams, separated with rank-growing marsh grasses and sedges, flecked here and there by small groves of willows and other water-loving shrubs and trees. Dropped in the middle of it, a man would be hard put to find his way safely out.

Conrad, sitting across the fire from Duncan, said, "We came out of it well, m'lord. We not only saved our necks, but got back all of our belongings—your sword, the amulet—plus some other welcome plunder."

"I'm sorry about Old Cedric," Duncan said.

"We should have stayed to bury him," said Andrew. "If not the others, at least Cedric. He deserved that much from us."

166

"We would have done him no great favor," Conrad told the hermit. "No matter how deep we might have dug his grave, the wolves would have him out of it in a day or two."

"It was getting late," said Duncan. "We had only a couple of hours till dark. I wanted to be well up the strand before the sun had set."

Ghost came floating in. He hovered between them and the fen.

"Well, finally," said Andrew, considerably disgusted. "Where have you been all this time? We have been in trouble . . ."

"In trouble I knew you were," said Ghost. "I came back last night and glimpsed the trouble you were in. I did not show myself, for immaterial as I am, I knew that I, all by myself, could be of no help at all. So immediately I went off in search of Snoopy or perhaps of others of his kind, hoping to summon them to provide what aid they could. But I could not find them . . ."

"That Snoopy!" Andrew said. "He is as worthless and as irresponsible as you are, yourself. I tell you, he is not one to trust. No good will ever come of him."

"He helped us the other night," said Duncan. "At the Jesus of the Hills. He warned us to get out of there. He showed us the way."

"Well, every now and then," conceded the hermit, "he may be of some small help. When the notion strikes him. But he's no one to depend on. You'll break your neck if you depend on him. There's a deep sense of mischief in him."

"I am happy to report," said Ghost, "that there is no present danger. Whatever hairless ones there may be still about are well beyond the hills, on the other side of them."

"The hairless ones were here this morning," Conrad said. "They did in the Reaver."

"That I know," said Ghost. "But they did not linger. They now are far away."

"The Reaver and his men may have been hiding in the rift," said Duncan. "That may be why no one

167

saw them. You are sure the hairless ones are not hiding in the rift?"

"Sure I am," said Ghost. "I just came from there. The selfsame thought had occurred to me. I am straight from there. I traveled its entire length." He shuddered. "A terrifying place," he said.

"Beyond it," said Duncan, "there should be a castle. That is what Snoopy said."

"What once had been a castle. A ruin now, no more. The stones have fallen in. It's no better than a mound. Trees grow out of it and mosses cover it."

Meg, crouched in a place of her own beside the fire, away from the rest of them, was muttering to herself. She had picked up some pebbles and seemed to be playing some sort of game with them.

"You are casting runes," said Andrew, distaste in his voice. "What do they tell you? What do you see for us?"

"Trouble," said the witch. "New trouble. Great trouble."

Duncan said, "We've had our trouble, old grandmother. We have had our share of it."

"No one has his share of it," said Meg. "It's not equally divided. Some know nothing but travail and trouble, others none at all."

"Can you tell us what shape it may take?" asked Conrad. "So we can be ready when it strikes."

"The runes do not tell me that much. Only that trouble lies on the road ahead."

"A fake you are," said Andrew. "It all is fakery. Those are not runes you have. They are no more than pebbles. Runes are stones that have certain magic marks upon them."

"That's unkind of you to say," Duncan told the hermit. "We must think the woman knows her art."

"Well spoke," said Meg, "and I thank you, sire. One who knows the art can pick up any stone and it will serve the purpose. The secret lies not in the stone at all, but in the knowledge of the thrower."

"One thing you may tell me," Duncan said. "I think

that you might know. What is this keening we hear from off the fen? It has the sound of sorrow in it."

"It is sorrow," said Meg. "It is sorrow for the world. For all life upon this Earth. For men and everything that now exists or that existed before there were any men."

"You speak sacrilege," said Andrew. "I've heard this somewhere before, not too long ago, and then I did not speak of it. But now I speak of it. The Book tells us there was no life before men, that all life was created on the selfsame day. In Genesis, it is written . . ."

Duncan interrupted him. "Softly, my friend," he said. "There are some great doctors, students of the rocks, who think otherwise. They have found imprints on the stones . . ."

"Also I have heard of that," said Andrew wrathfully. "I place no credence in it. It all is sophistry."

"Each man to his own belief," said Duncan. "We will not argue it." He said to Meg, "Sorrow, you say. From whom or whence comes this sorrow?"

"I do not know," said Meg. "That is hidden from me. What I do know is that in many places in the world there come these sounds of sorrow. Desolate places, lonely and forsaken places. A wailing for the world."

Duncan sat and listened to the wailing for the world. It seemed to come from some distant place, not necessarily from the fen, although it came across the fen—perhaps, he thought, from some secret place where the miseries and the disappointments of the world came to a common focus. A wailing for all the events that could have been, but did not come to be, for the crusade that never got off to a decent start, leaving Jerusalem still in the hands of infidels; for the Iberian ships that never clove the ocean waves to those ports and the unknown lands that still were waiting for them; for the Europe that still lay stagnant, plowing its worn-out soils with the plows that had been used for centuries, with the peasantry, for the most part, still huddling in dark and noisome hovels; with pools of paganism still remaining, some of them

169

almost within the shadow of the magnificence of churches that had been reared up, with Christian sweat and prayer, to proclaim the glory of the Lord.

An evil force, His Grace had said, that battened and fattened on mankind's misery, that moved upon strategic crisis points to guarantee continuation of the misery. That Evil in the past had struck in many places, at strategic points, and now it had struck in Britain. What factors were there that might make Britain a strategic place to strike? Britain, through all history, had been a place of quiet, a backwater of the world, where there might be local squabbling and some small clash of arms, but an area that had never loomed large in the consideration of the world.

"Fair sir," said Ghost, moving over to him, "I believe I have not done too badly. I have been faithful in my scouting. I have ever told you truth."

"You have been loyal," said Duncan, "although I do not understand your loyalty. There is no reason in the world you should be loyal to me."

"You told me once, however, that you would not invite me to go along with you, although you said you saw no way that you could stop me going. It was not a remark, I know, that was meant to be unkind, but ever since it has rankled in my breast."

"And what do you think that I should say?" asked Duncan. "That given another chance, I would have invited you? I don't know if I can say that, although I can say something else. I am glad you chose to come along."

"You truly mean that, sir?"

"I most sincerely mean it, Ghost."

"Then," said Ghost, "I shall continue with a lighter heart. When would you estimate, sir, we will arrive in Oxenford? I am very anxious to hunt out a reverend doctor there and discuss my case with him."

"At the rate that we've been going, we may never get there."

"You cannot mean that, sir."

"No, I suppose I don't. Someday we will be in Oxenford."

170

But even as he said it he wondered if they would. They had covered, so far, not too many miles, and if they took too much longer, Bishop Wise might well be dead before the manuscript could be placed into his hands. And should the good bishop not be there, their journey would have been a foolish errand at the best.

It would help, he thought, if they could only know the location of the Horde of Harriers. They must be somewhere in northern Britain, perhaps in congregation for that strange procedure that would bring about their rejuvenation. It certainly must now be time, he thought, for the procedure to begin, for surely they had carved out to its fullest extent that area of desolation designed to protect them from any interference. It might be, he thought, that the Harriers had thrown roadblocks in his path for the simple reason that he was inadvertently heading straight for their congregation, thereby posing that possibility of interference they must guard against. If it could only be known where they were, he and his band could swing wide around them, and the Harriers then might let them be.

He thought back once again along the trail that they had traveled, hoping by doing this to pick up some clue that would be useful in planning their further progress. But in thinking back along their trail, he thought again of Diane and her griffin. And try as hard as he might to see her simply as an incident of their travel, his mind hung back and clung to the memory of her. He tried to rebuild her in his mind, to re-create the memory that he held of her, but he found that he was unable to accomplish this. All that remained was the memory of the axe that she had carried and the griffin she had ridden. What color was her hair? He was astonished to find that he did not know. What color were her eyes? Again he could not say. And the shape of her face, he found, now had quite escaped him. Thinking back, he realized that he had thought of her, had even watched for her, every day since they first had met—which had been just a few days earlier, but which seemed, for some reason, to be much longer ago than it was in actuality.

Why, he wondered, was he so obsessed with her—not knowing in his own mind that he was obsessed with her, but still thinking of her, in idle moments, each day since he had seen her.

"M'lord," said Conrad, "a fog is beginning to roll in. We must keep sharp watch tonight."

What Conrad said was true. In the last few minutes, a fog had risen from the fen high into the air and now was creeping in toward them. From the fen still came, somewhat muffled by the rising, thickening fog, the keening sound—the wailing for the world.

19

They reached the end of the strand when the sun was well down the western sky, and entered the rift. It was a narrow cleft between two towering walls of rock, as if sometime in the far past a giant, wielding a heavy sword, had cleft the mountain in a single stroke. Blowing sand from the strand had drifted for a short distance into the rift, lying in ripples and low dunes, pocked by the tracks of men and horses, probably made by the Reaver's band. But within a few rods the sand ended and the bottom of the rift was a solid rock. For a short stretch it would be as level as a floor, then would be rough and broken for a time, often almost blocked by slabs of stone that in the past peeled off the rocky walls and tumbled down into the bottom of the cleft. There was no vegetation—no blade of grass, no small shrubs or trees rooted desperately to the walls of solid rock. A steady, relentless wind funneled through the rift, moving from the fen. High in the chasm, the rushing winds howled and wailed, at times shrinking to a whisper, at others rising to a shrill and doleful lamentation.

They took up automatically the order of march they had used since starting from the village—Tiny leading, but staying much closer than he had in open country, with Conrad following, behind Conrad, Beauty and the hermit, going in single file now, for often there was not room for them to walk side by side. Behind the two of them came Duncan, with Daniel close upon his heels, Meg huddled on the horse's back, clutching the saddle to guard against a misstep that might be brought upon Daniel by the uneven footing.

The rift lay in deep twilight. Only for a few moments during the day, when the sun was directly overhead, did any sunlight ever reach the floor. The upper portions of the eastern wall were lighted by the sun, but as the day went on, the shadow crept higher up the wall, with the slice of sunlight growing less and less and the shadow deepening in the lower reaches of the rift.

Duncan had the feeling that they were walking in the bottom of a well, isolated from the world outside, cut off from all that might be happening there—cut off, perhaps, but not protected, for the place, he knew, could be a trap.

They had routinely taken up their accustomed order of march, and while that might have been all right in more open country, Duncan realized that it was wrong here. With room to maneuver, Daniel, bringing up the rear, could swing about to face any danger that might come up behind him. Here he had little room to maneuver; there were places on the trail where he would have been unable to turn around. Duncan squeezed himself against the right hand wall of rock and when Daniel, seeing him stop, also stopped, his master urged him ahead. "It's all right, boy," he told the horse. "I want to take up the rear." If danger presented itself at the head of the march, he told himself, Tiny and Conrad could hold it off until he could manage to join them.

Stepping carefully, almost daintily, Daniel walked past him, his hairy body pressing Duncan hard against the rock wall. Duncan said to Meg, "Keep close watch ahead. If anything appears to be happening up there, let me know at once."

Overhead the wind moaned and screamed. Except for that, however, the only sounds were the ring of Daniel's iron-shod hoofs against the rock, the pitter-patter clacking of Beauty's little hoofs as she hurried along.

Plodding along behind Daniel, Duncan put his hand down to the belt pouch, which he had retrieved and resewn onto his belt, felt beneath his fingers the yielding crackle of the manuscript. Shifting his hand down, he encountered the small bulk of Wulfert's amulet, recovered from the Reaver's pocket. At the feel of it he felt reassured. Something had operated to bring them safely through all the dangers they had faced, and he felt certain that it could not have been happenstance alone. Could it have been the amulet? Might it not, through the years that it had lain in Wulfert's tomb, have reinforced its magic, as a good brandy might acquire better flavor and bouquet from aging? But magic or not, he told himself, potent or weak, he felt the better for having it again.

Time went on and the shadow crept slowly up the left wall of the rock. There was no sign that the rift was coming to an end; no daylight loomed ahead. They perforce were going at a slow rate, but by this time they should be nearing the end. What was it Snoopy had said, only five miles or so? Although, as Andrew insisted, one probably could not place much reliance upon anything that the goblin said. If the goblin were anywhere close to right, even at their slow rate they should have covered the distance by this time. For a moment Duncan entertained the fantasy that the rift would never end; that there was a magic laid upon it that would keep it going on forever; that they would never reach the end of it.

For considerable time it had seemed to him that the sounds made by the wind in the upper part of the chasm had been changing, becoming no longer merely the sound of wind, but the sound of voices, as if a congress of damned souls might be screeching and shrieking, yelling back and forth in unintelligible words.

A lull came in the wind and the sound ceased and for a long moment all was deathly quiet. To Duncan it seemed that the silence was more terrifying than the howling and the shrieking. The hoofbeats of Daniel and Beauty rang out sharp and clear, like the beating of a drum by which they marched to an unknown, but a certain doom.

Again the wind took up and the voices came once more, if they were voices and not his imagination. And now above the shrieks of fear and the screams of agony one voice boomed out, drowning all the others. The voice kept saying, "Holy! Holy! Holy!" the one word repeated over and over again, each repetition of it embodying an ecstatic and terrifying fervor. At times it seemed to Duncan that the one word was quite clear, and at other times he could not be entirely certain of it, although a moment later he would be convinced that he had heard the word correctly. But whether clear or uncertain, it carried in it that unsettling, almost embarrassing fervor of euphoric rapture—the kind of rapture to which a condemned soul might give expression should it suddenly and unexpectedly be raised from the torture of Purgatory to the very gates of Heaven.

Duncan put his hands to his ears to shut out the sound of that joyous paean, and when he took them away a few moments later, Conrad was shouting up ahead.

"Light!" he was yelling. "I can see light. We are coming to the end."

Staring fixedly ahead, Duncan could see no light, although that was not greatly to be wondered at, for here the trail was exceptionally narrow and Daniel's big body filled the most of it, blocking his view. But in a short while he could distinguish a faint glimmer that made the walls of stone a little brighter. The ecstatic voice still was shouting "Holy! Holy! Holy!" but as the light grew stronger, the sound lost its strength and some of its ecstasy and finally faded out entirely. The shrieking of the wind came to be no more than a mumble and the damned souls grew silent and ahead he could see a glimpse of the green and pleasant land that Snoopy had told them of.

It was, in all truth, a green and pleasant land, a wide sweep of valley backdropped by the hills through which they had come. Before them lay the ruins of the castle against which they had been warned by the goblin.

The castle was little more than the mound that Ghost had described. Two crumbling turrets still stood guard at each end of it, but between the turrets, the stone lay heaped in an untidy pile, the rough edges of the fallen stones rounded and modified by weather. But the thing that caught Duncan's attention was the well-spaced standing stones, no longer upright, but canting at various angles. At one time, it was apparent, the entire castle had been surrounded and fenced in by a circle of massive stones of the kind that one might see, or so it was said, at Stonehenge and on a smaller scale in many other places. But this circle was larger than the one at Stonehenge, if traveler's tales could be credited, perhaps a great deal larger, for this castle circle once had enclosed many acres. In an earlier day, Duncan thought, it must have been an impressive sight, but now, like the castle, it was considerably dismantled. The lintel stones, with the slow canting of the uprights, had fallen from their places and lay half buried on the surface, or, not falling entirely free, still lay with one end propped against a standing stone.

The sun was no more than a few minutes above the western horizon, and shadows were lengthening and growing deeper in the valley. Just beyond the castle ran a quiet river, unhurried in its flow, with small flocks of ducks flying above it, and others floating on its surface. Behind him Duncan could hear the subdued mumble of the wind blowing through the rift.

He walked forward to join Conrad. Tiny had trotted on ahead, quartering the slope of hillside below them, nosing out the land.

"I would say we should go down to the river and

camp the night," said Duncan. "Get an early start, come morning."

Conrad nodded his agreement. "It will be good," he said, "to have some open land. Now we can make better time."

"We need to," Duncan said. "We have wasted a lot of time."

"If we could have caught some of the Reaver's horses."

"We tried," said Duncan. "They were having none of us."

"We still can make good time," said Conrad. "We have good legs."

"The hermit will hold us up."

"We could put him up with Meg on Daniel. That horse could carry both of them and never notice."

"We'll see about it," said Duncan. "The hermit would raise hell. He wants to be the same as you and I."

"I'll grant him that," said Conrad, "if he'd just keep up with us."

They started down the slope, the others trailing along behind them. They had reached the bottom of the slope and started out across the valley when Meg let out a shriek.

They whirled about.

Filing out of the timbered hill to the east of the rift came a long rank of hairless ones, and behind them loomed a bank of fog, or what appeared to be fog, disturbed and agitated, as if some sort of commotion were taking place inside of it. Tendrils of it spurted out in front of the rolling bank so that the slouching hairless ones seemed to be wading knee-deep through a patch of ground mist. In the broken rifts of the swirling fog could be caught occasional glimpses of obscene monstrosities—an impression of teeth, of horns, of beaks, of glittering eyes.

Conrad sucked in his breath. "Magic," he said.

The rest of the band was piling down the hill. They reached Duncan and Conrad and swung into line to face the oncoming hairless ones, who were backed by the roiling cloud of smoky fog.

"We make our stand here?" Conrad asked.

"We might as well," said Duncan. "There's no place to retreat. If we ran, they'd pull us down."

"The ruins of the castle," suggested Conrad. "We could place the mound at our back. Here they'll sweep around our flanks. They'll be down on us like wolves."

"There isn't time to reach the castle," Duncan said. "Besides, Snoopy warned us of the castle."

Daniel was at his right hand, Andrew at his left, Beauty and Meg next, with Conrad and Tiny anchoring the left.

"Meg, what are you doing here?" demanded Duncan. "Get out of here. Run for your life."

She cackled at him. "I can bite and scratch," she squealed. "I can kick. I can summon up some magic."

"A pox on your magic," Andrew told her. "Those coming at us are the ones with magic."

The hairless ones came slowly down the hill with their lumbering gait, the clubs in their hamlike fists held ready. Behind them rolled the cloud of fog that now seemed shot through with lightning bolts, flaring as it seethed. Within it loomed horrific shapes, revealed momentarily by the lightning flares, then shut from sight by the roiling of the fog.

The last rays of the sun still touched the top of the hills to the north, but in the valley, shadows were beginning to creep across the land.

Duncan held his sword at ready and was pleased to find that there was no fear in him. It was useless, he told himself, to attempt to make a stand before such a force. The hairless ones would strike them and for a moment there would be a flurry of fighting, then the hairless ones and the monstrosities coming on behind them would roll over their thin line and that would be the end of it. But what was a man to do? Run, to be hunted down and dragged down, like a fleeing animal? Collapse upon his knees and plead for mercy when he knew there would be no mercy? Simply stand and take death as it came? No, by God, he told himself, he'd fight and when it was all over, once it all was known, there'd be no shame at Standish House.

For a moment he remembered, as clearly as if he stood before him, that old man at Standish House, with his plumb-line upright body, his rugged face with the short clipped mustache, his gray hair and the clear, honest grayness of his eyes. The kind of a man, Duncan knew, that a son could never shame.

He raised his sword as the foremost hairless one came toward him. Another step, he told himself. The hairless one took the other step, his club raised and already beginning to come down. Duncan chopped with his blade. He felt, rather than saw, the striking into flesh. Then the hairless one was falling and another took his place. The sword slashed out again, missed the stroke that he had intended, deflected by the club, but took off the club arm just above the elbow. Beside him Daniel was screaming in battle rage, as only a fighting horse could scream, standing on his hind legs, striking out with his forelegs, crushing skulls, bowling over the hairless ones as they leaped at him. To Duncan's left Andrew was tugging to free his staff from the belly of one of the attackers. Another hairless one aimed a club at him as he was tugging at the staff, but before the club could strike Duncan brought his sword down, slicing open the throat of the thing that held the club.

Duncan lost track of time. There was no past, no future, simply a bloodstained, straining present in which he thrust and struck, as if somewhere back there someone was lining up the hairless ones for him to strike at, as if it were some sort of silly game, replacing the one that went down with another that came charging in upon him to supply him with another target for his swordsmanship. It seemed to him incredible that he could keep on, but he did keep on.

Quite suddenly there was in front of him not a hairless one, but a spitting, vicious fury that was all claws and fangs, black as the deepest pit of night, oozing loathsomeness, and in a flare of blinding hatred, a hatred he had not felt against the hairless ones, he brought down the blade upon it, hewing it in half.

Something struck him from one side and he lost his balance, going over. As he scrambled to his feet, he saw what had struck him. A raging griffin, poised with beating wings over the swirling cloud of fog, which was still streaked by lightning flashes, was reaching down with grasping claws and stabbing beak, slashing, clawing, stabbing, rending the things that hid inside the cloud. Leaning from the griffin's back, a woman clad in a leather jacket, the red-gold glory of her hair streaming in the battle wind, wielded a shining battle axe that was smeared with the red of blood and black ichor such as had spouted from the body of the spitting fury Duncan had killed.

As Duncan surged to his feet he heard the thunder of hoofs coming from above him, as if they were riding down the sky, the sudden blaring of a hunting horn, and the deep bay of hunting dogs.

He took a step forward and stumbled again, coming down with one knee across the fallen body of the hermit. Ahead of him a hairless one was shambling forward, rocking on his bowed legs, heading for Tiny, who was systematically tearing apart a horror that squealed and shrieked. Duncan lunged to his feet, surged toward the hairless one. The point of his blade took it in the throat, and the club, coming down, thudded into the ground, falling short of Tiny.

Then the thunder of the hoofs and the deep hoarse baying of the hunting dogs seemed to fill the valley, and down out of the sky they came—black silhouettes of horse and rider and hunting dogs—fog-draped shadows that still had some substantiality, and a howling wind came with them that almost blew Duncan from his feet.

The Wild Huntsman and his pack swooped down to tear through the roiling bank of fog that concealed the hideous shapes with the obscene teeth and beaks and talons, emerged again, climbing in the sky, then wheeled to return.

Atop the griffin, her high-lifted battle axe dripping

blood and ichor, Diane shouted at Duncan. "The castle! Run for your life. Run to the castle!"

Duncan turned to pick up Andrew, but the hermit was getting to his feet, using his staff to pull himself erect. One side of his face was raw, the blood dripping from his wispy beard onto his tattered robe.

"To the castle," Duncan shouted at him. "Run. As fast as you can go."

Diane still was shouting, "Everyone to the castle. It's your only chance."

Duncan reached for Daniel, grabbed him by the mane.

"Daniel, come," he shouted.

There were no longer any of the hairless ones charging in upon them. The fog bank lay in tatters, the lightning flashes gone, and a mass of dark shapes were hopping and running, crawling and wriggling up the hillside.

Duncan spun around to look for Conrad and saw him limping toward the ruined castle, one hand gripping the collar of a raging Tiny, dragging the dog along. Meg and Beauty were running a footrace for the castle, Meg hobbling and wobbling in a frantic effort to keep pace with the little burro. Andrew stumped along behind them, angrily striking at the ground with his staff.

"Come, Daniel," Duncan said and set off at a swinging pace, the big horse following.

Looking over his shoulder, Duncan saw the Huntsman and his pack in a sharp climb up the sky. He heard a swirl of leathery wings and saw Diane and the griffin also heading for the castle.

The canted standing stones were just ahead of him and as he ran toward them, he wondered what kind of safety might be offered by the castle. If the Evil forces and the remaining hairless ones attacked again, and probably they would as soon as they had reassembled, he and his band would have to fight again. They would be fighting, this time, with the castle mound to protect their backs, but even so, how long could they hope to stand against such a force? It was sheer good luck they had made the stand they had. Had it not been for the intervention of Diane and the Huntsman, they now would all be dead. And the Wild Huntsman, he wondered. Why had this wild rider of the skies taken a hand in it? What interest could have brought him to it?

He looked quickly behind him and saw the irregular lumps of the dead hairless ones lying in a ragged row. The hairless ones and the other things as well—the spitting fury that he had sliced in two, the squawling thing that Tiny had torn apart, and perhaps there were others of them, too.

He passed between two of the standing stones, Daniel pacing at his side, and as he stepped between them, the grass beneath his feet turned from unkempt meadow grass to a well-kept, pampered velvet lawn.

Startled, he looked up and gasped at what he saw. The castle mound was gone. In its place stood a splendid castle, a building out of fairyland, brand new and shining, stone steps leading up to a great front entrance that was agleam with candlelight and with lights showing as well in some of the many windows.

The griffin stood humped upon the lawn in front of him and Diane, in her leather breeches and her leather jacket, her hair a golden glory in the fading light from out the west, still carrying the gory battle axe, was walking across the lawn toward him.

She stopped a few feet from him and made a little curtsy.

"Welcome," she said, "to the Castle of the Wizards."

All the rest of them were there, standing on the sweep of immaculate lawn, their heads tilted up to stare at the castle, all of them, more than likely, as puzzled as he was.

He still was carrying the naked sword in his fist, and he lifted it, unthinking, to place it in the scabbard, but Diane made a motion to stop him.

"Not," she said, "until you wipe it clean. Here." One hand went to her throat and pulled free the white stock that she wore.

"Use this," she said, holding it out to him.

"But I would not want to . . . "

"Go ahead," she said. "I have plenty of others. This is an old one, anyhow."

"I could manage with some grass."

She shook her head and he took from her the length of fabric. It was fine of weave and silky to the touch.

"With your permission, ma'am," he said.

Carefully he wiped and polished the blade until there was not a fleck upon it.

"Give the rag to me," she said. Hesitantly, he handed the stained piece of cloth to her and she, in turn, used it to clean the battle axe.

"It was good sport," she said. "Good hunting."

He shrugged in bewilderment. "Yes, it turned out that way. We were in a bad way for a time, until you and the Huntsman showed up. Tell me, what has the Huntsman to do with all of this? For that matter, what have you? And this castle . . . "

"I've told you," she said. "This is the Castle of the Wizards. Once you pass the magic circle you stand on enchanted ground."

Conrad came limping up, followed by Tiny.

"What happened to you?" asked Duncan.

Conrad swung slowly around to show the bloody gash that ran from thigh to knee. "Something raked me. I think that thing, whatever it was, that Tiny tore apart. But you are all right, m'lord."

"Knocked down by a griffin's wing, that's all."

He put his hand up to his forehead and it came away sticky with clotting blood.

"I'm sorry about that," said Diane. "At times Hubert tends to get a little awkward. But it's really not his fault. He is so old, you know." She said to Conrad, "You better had come in. That gash . . . "

"It will heal," said Conrad. "I have taken worse."

"There could be poison in it. There are unguents that will take care of that. I'm well schooled in salves and potions."

"My thanks," said Conrad, trying to be courtly, but not quite making it.

184

Glancing back at the circle of standing stones, Duncan saw that now they were all in place and correctly seated. Now there was no cant to them. Lying squarely on top of them, in their proper places, were the lintel stones. All the stones, the lintels and the standing ones, were new and white, shining faintly in the fading light, as if they had been carved only yesterday.

"I don't understand," he said to Diane. "The stones all standing, the castle new and shining, this lawn, the stone benches on the lawn, the shrubs and trees, the little pools, the paths, all so neatly landscaped."

"It is an enchanted place," she said. "A special place. Outside the magic circle it all seems a ruin, as it rightly should be, for it was raised many centuries ago. But once inside the circle it is as it always has been since the day it was created. Here time and the ravages of time are held at bay. At one time many powerful wizards lived here and they possessed great secrets. They could hold the world and time at arm's length. They could . . . "

"At one time, you said. And now?"

"Now one wizard still lives here. He is the last of them."

He started to ask another question, but clamped shut his mouth before the words came out.

She laughed a merry laugh at him. "You were about to ask about myself."

"I have no right, milady."

"I don't mind telling you. I have wizard blood."

"You a wizard?"

She shook her head. "No. I have tried to be. I wanted to be. I have found I'm not. Wulfert. You remember that I asked of Wulfert."

"Yes, I do remember."

She said, "Wulfert was my great-grandfather. But we stand here talking when we should be going in. Your big comrade needs something on that wound. And there may be other injuries. You have a scratch upon your head. All of you, I suppose, are half starved."

Conrad brightened visibly. "I could do with food,"

185

he said. "And a little drink should you have it. Fighting's thirsty work."

"You must excuse him," Duncan said. "He has no shame at all."

"We have no staff," said Diane. "Not a single servant. There was a day when the castle did have servants everywhere, when there were people here who might have need of servants. But now there really is little need of them and it is hard to find the kind of faithful servitors that one would want. There is not a great deal to do. The preparation of food, the making of beds, such small chores as that. The enchantment takes care of all the rest."

"In a rough fashion, milady," said Conrad, "m'lord and I can cook, and I suppose old Meg as well. The hermit I don't know about. At best he is a simple soul."

"Well, get along," said Diane. "The larder is well stocked. It always is well stocked. We'll not go hungry."

With Duncan on one side of her, Conrad on the other, she led the way toward the long flight of broad, wide steps that went up to the castle's entrance. Meg fell in behind them.

"We'll find meat for the dog," said Diane. "The lawn will provide good pasturage for the horse and burro."

"We thank you, milady," Duncan said. "Your hospitality is above and beyond all courtesy. What you did in helping us today . . . "

"The help was mutual," she said. "You did as much for us as I and Hubert did for you. You lured the Evil out and struck a mighty blow against them. You made them smart. Cuthbert will be pleased. It is something he would have done himself had he not been so old and feeble and so very much alone. You see, I am the only one he has. All his old comrades are gone."

"Cuthbert?"

"He is the wizard that I spoke of. The last of a mighty band of wizards. But now all the rest are gone

186

and he had lost much of his former power because of the loss of his companions, although he would deny that should it be mentioned. I am very careful not to mention it."

"You say he is old and sick. I did not know . . ."

"Wizards are not supernatural beings," said Diane. "Certainly you know that. They are merely men of great knowledge in certain arcane subjects and therefore able to accomplish many wondrous things, but they are not immune to the common ills and woes of mankind. I had meant to come back to the church and village where we first met, but when I returned I found Cuthbert very ill and have remained here since, nursing him."

"And how is he now?"

"Much better, thank you. It's his own fault, perhaps. When I leave he forgets to eat. He gets so busy that he forgets to eat. Old as he is, he needs proper nourishment."

They came to the foot of the long stairs and began to climb them. Halfway up, Duncan looked back and saw that outside the circle of standing stones stood a heavy growth of trees.

"Those trees were not there before," he said.

"What trees?" Diane asked.

"The trees outside the circle."

"You don't understand," she said. "From this place you see everything the way it was when the castle was created. At the time it came into being this land was wilderness, with only a few wild tribes or occasional hunters following the few paths that ran across it."

They continued their climb and finally came to the great entrance, which led into a large room, a sort of reception hall, thought Duncan. The floor was of well-fitted, colorful flagstone, and from it ran up several other short stone staircases leading to other parts of the castle. Candelabra set in the walls flared with thick waxen candles, lending a soft light to the hall.

In the center of the hall stood a six-foot column of stone, three feet through, and at the sight of what crouched atop it, Duncan and all the others stopped short in their tracks.

"Come on," said Diane impatiently. "It is only Scratch. There is no need to fear him. I assure you he's quite tame and harmless."

Slowly they went forward, the creature on top of the column watching them intently. The creature spoke to them. "Only Scratch, she says, and she speaks right, as she always does, for she is a very truthful and even a kindly person. You see before you, either for your pity or your contempt, a demon straight from the pits of Hell."

"He always dramatizes," said Diane. "He stops all who visit to tell his story to them. There's no one now, of course, who can judge how true it is, but he has much to tell. Give him the opportunity and he'll talk an arm off you."

"But what is he?" asked Duncan.

"He is what he told you, a demon out of Hell. He has served as doorkeeper here for almost as long as the castle has existed."

"That is what they designate me," said Scratch, "but I keep no door. I am chained here to this column as a subject for ridicule by humans, who more often than not make great sport of me. Rather, it seems to me, I should be an object of deep pity, the most unfortunate of creatures, a runaway from my place of origin, but not a true resident of this palace of opulence and glory. Gaze upon me, please, and see if I tell you wrong. See my crumpled horn, observe the hump upon my back, the clubfoot that I carry, my crippled hands, clenched and held as in a vise by arthritis, the result of the foul and damp and chilly climate of this most barbarous of countries."

"Scratch, shut up," Diane said sharply.

"And please," said Scratch, "look upon my tail which, along with his horns, is the pride of any demon. Look upon it and tell me if it seems a thing of pride. Broken in three places and never set properly, although the setting of it would have been as child's play for any competent chirurgeon."

"Scratch," said Diane, "I command you to be silent. Stop this endless chatter. Our guests have no interest in you."

All that Scratch had said of himself, Duncan saw, was true. The last third of his tail took the form of an amazing zigzag, as if it had been broken and no attempt made to reset the bones, or if an attempt had been made, it had been very badly done. His left foot was clubbed, at least three times as large as it should have been, and with a misshapen hoof enclosing the malformation. Above the clubfoot a long chain was riveted, hanging in a loop to the floor, the other end of it set into a heavy metal staple sunk into the stone. An unsightly hump rode his shoulder blades, forcing the upper half of his body into an awkward forward thrust. The left horn atop his head was perfectly formed, short, but stout, the other horn distorted and grown to greater size, ridged with ugly wrinkles like the markings on a clam shell, and bent close against his forehead. His outthrust hands were twisted and bent, the fingers convulsively half closed.

Conrad moved closer to the column, reached up to touch one of the crippled hands. "You poor son-of-a-bitch," said Conrad.

Diane spoke coldly. "Let us proceed. He is no one to waste your pity on."

20

First Diane administered to the wounds, smearing
salve on Conrad's gash, swabbing off Andrew's
abraded face and rubbing soothing unguent on it,
cleaning out the small cut on Duncan's head. Meg,
who had come through without a scratch upon her,
sat in a chair too high for her, with her feet dangling
off the floor, cackling as she recalled her part in the
battle.

"Faith," she said, "the old girl knew what she was
about. I got well down to the ground, well out of all
harm's way. I killed no single one of them, for I had
not the strength to do it, but I discommoded them. I
found a stout branch that had fallen from a thorn tree
and from where I crouched upon the ground, I
cracked them in the shins. They did not know what
hit them, and I whacked with all the strength I had in
my scrawny arm. But I made them hop and flinch,
and as they hopped and flinched, m'lord smote them
with his blade or the hermit speared them with his
staff."

"Always in the gut," said Andrew proudly. "The
gut is a soft place and easily penetrated with a determined blow."

"I don't know how you managed it," said Diane. "I got there as quickly as I could, but . . . "

"Our arms were strong," said Conrad sanctimoniously, "because our cause was just."

The doctoring over, they explored the larder and found a haunch of beef, well roasted, a large loaf of wheaten bread, a wheel of cheese, a platter of fried fowl left over from the day before, a small pigeon pie, a keg half full of pickled herring, and a basket of juicy pears.

"Cuthbert, when he does not forget to eat," said Diane, "is a trencherman of note. He likes good food and, too often, far too much of it. He is no stranger to the gout."

Now they sat around the table in the kitchen, where Diane had done her doctoring, the medications pushed to one end of the table, the food set on the other.

"I must beg your pardon," Diane said, "for serving you in such a lowly place, but the dining room is far too splendid. It makes me a bit self-conscious. It is too splendid a room for my taste and, I would suppose, for yours as well. Also, once the meal is done, there is much china and silver to be washed and dried and put away again. It is too much work."

"Cuthbert?" asked Duncan. "You have spoken of him often. When will we be able to talk with him? Or will we?"

"Most certainly," said Diane, "but not tonight. There was a time when he would sit up half the night, working at his desk, but of late years he has taken to going to his bed at the coming of first dusk. The man is old and needs his rest. And now suppose you tell me all that's happened since the day I first met you in the orchard. There have been rumors, of course, of the things that you have done, but you know how rumors are. Not to be relied upon."

"Nothing great," said Duncan. "We have, it seems, stumbled from one disaster to another, but each time have managed to escape by the skin of our teeth."

They told her, chiming in on the story by turns,

while she sat listening intently, her head bent forward, the flare of the candles making another flame of her shining hair. One thing Duncan did not tell her, and the others did not think to, or noticing that he had omitted it, made no mention of it—and that was about the finding of the amulet in Wulfert's tomb.

Watching her as she listened, Duncan debated whether he should go back along the story's trail and tell her of the amulet, but in the end he refrained from doing so. Certainly, he knew, it was a thing that would greatly interest her, and perhaps she had a right to know—most surely had the right to know if Wulfert truly had been kin of hers, as she had said.

Finally, when the story was all done, she asked of Wulfert. "You remember that I was seeking him," she said, "or rather, some word of him, for he must have long since been dead. You, Sir Hermit, before we were interrupted by the hairless ones, seemed to indicate that you knew of him. For some reason you did not explain, you appeared to be greatly distressed."

Andrew lifted his head, looking across the table at the sternness of Duncan's face.

"Only, milady," he said smoothly, "that I had heard of him, knew that he was buried in the village cemetery. My distress was that the village had regarded him as a saintly man. It was a shock to learn that he had been, instead, a wizard."

"You were outraged to learn that he was a wizard and no holy man?"

"Milady," said Andrew, "I and the people of my village were only simple folk. Perhaps even ignorant folk. We did not know of wizards. We had thought . . . "

"I can guess what you had thought," said Diane. "And it seems that I remember you saying that he was placed in a tomb, that the village built a tomb for him because he was thought a saintly man."

"That is right," said Andrew, "but an oak fell and shattered it. In some great storm, perhaps."

"There is a story, perhaps no more than a legend,

192

that he carried with him a piece of wondrous magic. Had you ever heard of that?"

"No ma'am, I don't recall I ever had."

"I imagine not," said Diane. "He would have kept it secret. I suppose it now is lost. Oh, the pity of it!"

"Why the pity, ma'am?" asked Conrad.

"The legend says that it was designed as a weird against the Horde of Evil, known in these parts as the Harriers."

"And," said Duncan, "you hoped to recover it."

"Yes," she said, "that had been my hope. There now is need of it."

Duncan felt the others looking at him.

"Even had you found it," he said, "it might be of little value. One would have to know how to put it to most effective use."

"No, I think not. I think the mere possession of it would be quite sufficient. The magic rests in the talisman itself, not in the user of it."

"Perhaps you should search the tomb," said Conrad, skating on thin ice.

"Perhaps," said Diane. "I had thought of that. I had meant to go back again. But after the incident in the garden plot with the hairless ones, I had the frantic feeling that Cuthbert needed me, so I flew directly here. I found that he did indeed have need of me. I have nursed him ever since."

She made a motion with her hands. "Although I doubt the searching of the tomb would be of any use. Even had the talisman been buried with him, which it might not have been, when the oak fell upon the tomb its contents would have been revealed to anyone who might want to investigate. Certainly there would have been in the village those with a ghoulish twist of mind. Undoubtedly, had it been there, it would have been filched long since."

"What you say may well be true," said Andrew, "but of this talisman you speak of I have never heard."

"A tomb robber," said Diane, "would not reveal himself."

"I suppose not," Andrew said.

No one was watching him any more, Duncan saw. The deed had been done. Rightly or wrongly, the lie had been told. To the man, they had backed him in his secrecy. Of them all, only Meg had said nothing and she, he knew, would not go against the rest of them. His fingers itched to go to the pouch at his side, touch the slight bulge of the amulet to assure himself that it still was there. But he fought successfully against doing it.

Tiny, who had gulped down a generous helping from the roast, earlier had been lying, asleep or half-asleep, in one corner of the kitchen, but now, Duncan noted, he was gone. More than likely he had gone out exploring. The castle had a lot of nooks and crannies that he could snoop in.

"There is one thing that intrigues me," Duncan said to Diane. "I asked you earlier, but you had no chance to answer. It concerns the Huntsman. Why should he get himself involved?"

"He hates the Evil," Diane told him. "As do many of the others of us. The Little Folk—you'll find few of them who have any liking for the Evil. Basically they themselves are not evil; only different. There are certain naturally evil beings, of course, like the were-wolves, the ghouls, the vampires, and others who would willingly align themselves with the Harriers, holding them in high regard and believing that they may be one with them. But the Little Folk are decent people and so is the Huntsman."

"I have wondered," Duncan said, "if he could have been watching us all the time. We saw him a few nights ago and I am certain, at an earlier time, I heard him in the sky."

"He could have been."

"But why should he bother with us?"

"He is a free spirit, the Huntsman. I know very little about him, although I met him briefly a few years ago. He originated, I believe, in the Germanies, but I can't be sure of that. Maybe sometime in the past he may have witnessed some of the ravages

194

brought about by the Harriers and has been watching them ever since."

"A crusader for the right?"

"No, I'd scarcely call him that."

"In any case," said Andrew, "we are appreciative of the part he played today."

"This Evil," said Duncan. "I wonder what it really is."

"Cuthbert, if you asked, probably could tell you much better than I can," said Diane.

"Our archbishop at the abbey back home suggested that the creatures may feed on the misery of the world and that they will go to any lengths to keep that misery going."

"I have heard that," Diane said, "but Cuthbert is an expert on the Evil. He has spent long years in the study of it. He has at hand much documentation bearing on it. He's the one to ask about it."

"Would he be willing to discuss it with us? Many experts grow somewhat jealous of the body of knowledge they have acquired."

"Yes, I think he will."

A burst of savage barking came from far away. Conrad leaped to his feet. "That's Tiny," he said. "I'll take care of him. There are times when he hasn't got good sense."

Turning, he ran out the door and the others pelted after him. "Sic 'em, boy!" yelled Meg.

"No, not that," snapped Conrad. "Don't encourage him."

They ran down a hall and across the magnificent dining hall, coming out on the circular corridor that fronted on the huge reception hall.

There they sighted Tiny. He was in front of the demon's column, his rear thrust high into the air, his front feet thrust out on the floor, his muzzle resting on them. His tail was waving frantically in good fun, and every now and then he lifted his head from his paws to unloose a half-playful, half-savage barking at the crouching Scratch.

Conrad went clattering down the staircase to the

hall. "Tiny, cut it out," he yelled. "Tiny, you damn fool. Leave Old Scratch alone."

The demon sang out at him in protest. "Not Old Scratch. That is another demon entirely. That is the full-fledged Devil. To call me Scratch was a play on words. The ones who finally trapped and caught me would guffaw and roll upon the floor in laughter when they called me Scratch. For reasons that I do not entirely understand, it was a great joke to them. But they called me Young Scratch, to distinguish me, you understand, from the other one. But finally it became simply Scratch and that I have been ever since. Which is not an appellation that I enjoy overmuch, but since I have been stuck with it all these years I must live by it."

Conrad strode across the floor to Tiny, grabbed him by the collar and hauled him to his feet. "Shame on you," he said. "Here he is, chained to this stone, while you are running free. You should be ashamed."

Tiny fawned on Conrad, but he did not look ashamed.

Duncan, coming up behind Conrad, said to Scratch, "You seem to be all right. Did he try to harm you?"

"Not in the least," said the demon. "He was only engaged in some doggish fun. I did not mind at all. He had no intent to hurt me, nor, I believe, to even frighten me. In his doggish mind, he only played a game with me."

"That's generous of you," said Duncan.

"Why, thank you, sir. It is very decent of you to say so."

"And by the way," asked Duncan, "is it true, as you said, that you are a demon from the very pits of Hell? And if that is so, how come you here?"

"That is a long story and a sad one," said Scratch. "Someday, when you have the time, I will relate to you the whole of it. I was an apprentice demon, you must understand, assigned to the antechambers of the Infernal Regions to learn my vocations. But, I fear, I did very badly at it. So to speak, I was all thumbs. I never did get anything quite right. I suppose I never really got into the spirit of the job. I was always in the doghouse. Constantly I was reprimanded for my lack of honest zeal."

"Maybe you were not cut out to be a demon." '

"That may well be. But being a demon, I had little choice. There were few other occupations that were open to me. I would have you believe that at all times I did my valiant best."

"So what happened?"

"Why, I ran away. I couldn't take it any longer. One day I just cut out. And do you know, sir, and this was the unkindest cut of all—I don't believe they made any great effort to run me down and haul me back."

"Except for the chain, you have good treatment here?"

"Except for the chain, I would say so. I know that I am somewhat better treated here than a human would be treated should he find himself in Hell."

21

Cuthbert lay propped up in bed by two pillows placed atop one another against the headboard. He wore a nightcap of startling red and a nightgown with ruffles at the throat and wrists. He was a sunken man. His eyes were sunken deep beneath white, bushy eyebrows, the cap coming down so far upon his forehead that it seemed to rest upon the eyebrows. His face was sunken so that his cheekbones could be seen, the skin drawn tightly over them, his nose stabbing out like a beak, the mouth a furrow between the stabbing nose and outjutting chin. His chest was sunken, his shoulders rising above it in their bony knobbiness. Beneath the coverlet his stomach was so flat and sunken that the pelvic bones stood out, making twin humps beneath the bedclothes.

He cackled at Duncan, then spoke in a raspy voice, "So. Diane tells me you smote them hip and thigh. That's the way to do it. That's the one language that they understand."

"My band and I," said Duncan. "I did not do it all alone."

"You'll see the others of them later," Diane told the wizard. "They are a motley group."

198

She said to Duncan, "You do not mind if I call them a motley group?"

"I suppose you could call them that," said Duncan, not too well pleased.

"You told me of them," Cuthbert said to Diane. "A dog and horse and also a little burro. I'll want to see them, too."

"The dog, perhaps," said Diane. "Certainly not the horse."

"I want to see the entire tribe of them," insisted Cuthbert. "I want to gaze upon this little band that smote them hip and thigh. By gad, it does me good to know there are such still in the land. Not running squealing from them, but standing up to them."

"The horse and burro would have trouble getting here," protested Diane. "All those stairs."

"Then I'll go and see them."

"You know, sire, you must not exert yourself."

He grumbled at her with mumbling words. He said to Duncan, "This is what happens when a man grows old. You can't exert yourself. You can't walk to the water closet. You must squat upon a pot to pee. You must move slowly and you must remain in bed. You must eat soft foods because your gut will not handle honest meat. You must be sparing with the wine. You must do not a single thing that you may enjoy, but many that you don't."

"In a short while," said Duncan, "it would be my hope and prayer that you'll again be doing all the things you most enjoy. But you must take what care you can . . ."

"You're in league with her," Cuthbert accused him. "Everyone is in league with her. She can twist a strong man about her little finger. Look at her, the hussy, all that golden hair and the way she bats her eyes."

"You know, sire," said Diane sharply, "that I never bat my eyes. And if your behavior does not improve considerably I shall cook you up a mess of greens and feed them to you for supper. And see you eat them, too."

"You see," Cuthbert said to Duncan. "A man hasn't

got a chance. Especially should he grow old. Take care you do not advance beyond the age of thirty. And now suppose you tell me about your little band and this great battle."

"We would not have survived the battle," Duncan said, "had it not been for Diane and her griffin and the Wild Huntsman . . . "

"Ah, the Huntsman—a stout fellow, that one. I well remember the time . . . " He speared Duncan with a sharp glance. "Don't tell me you're the Huntsman. A close relative, perhaps, but surely not the Huntsman. You can't fool me with your tales. I know the Huntsman. You can't palm yourself off . . . "

"Sire," said Diane, "I told you of this gentleman. He's not the Huntsman nor did he claim to be. You're imagining again. Duncan Standish is the scion of a great house in the north."

"Yes, yes," said Cuthbert, "now I do recall. The Standish, you say. The Standish, yes, I have heard of them. If you are of that house, what are you doing here? Why did you not tarry in the safety of the north, behind the castle walls?"

"I go with messages to Oxenford," said Duncan.

"Oxenford? Oxenford. Yes, I know of Oxenford. A great company of distinguished scholars. I have friends in Oxenford."

He let his head drop back on the pillow and closed his eyes. Duncan looked questioningly at Diane and she signaled patience.

After a time the wizard stirred on the pillows, opened his eyes and hauled himself into a more upright position. He looked at Duncan.

"You're still here," he said. "I thought you might have left. You sat throughout my nap. You must excuse me, sir. Unaccountably, at times, I fall into these little naps."

"You feel better now, sire?"

"Yes, much better now. Diane told me you had a question for me."

"It's about the Horde of Evil. My archbishop told me . . . "

200

"And what archbishop might that be?"

"His Grace of Standish Abbey."

"A fuddy-duddy," said the wizard. "A blathering fuddy-duddy. Do you not agree?"

"At times I have thought him so."

"And what does he say of the Horde of Evil?"

"Very little, sire. He knows not what it is. He believes it feeds on human misery and that the devastations, which come at regular intervals, may be periods when it rejuvenates itself."

"You would have me tell you what the Evil is?"

"If you know, sire."

"Of course I know. What do you think I and my band of now-dead brethren have been doing all these years? The answer, of course, is that we have been performing many tasks and digging deep for truth. In the course of our work we have not ignored the Evil. What would you know of it?"

"What it is, sire. Where it came from. Where did it start?"

"It came here from the stars," the wizard said. "This we do know. Why it came we are not certain. It may have been driven from the stars by a stronger force against which it could not stand. Or it may have run so rampant in its rapacity among the stars that there was nothing left for it to feed upon and so, rather than face starvation, it sought out another world and by pure chance, or perhaps not so much by chance, came upon this poor world of ours, where it found the teeming life that could provide the misery that it needed to feed upon and grow. Apparently it has done well here. With the weight of this world's misery it has increased in strength and numbers with the passing of each century. If something is not done soon it will swallow all the life of Earth and then, perhaps, be forced to go again among the stars to seek another world.

"It came here an untold time ago. Of the years that it's been here, we have no measure. When man arose, with his greater capacity for misery—a greater capacity than our friends, the beasts, although they, too, can suffer misery—it began to reap a richer harvest and in consequence has waxed the fatter, and now there seems but little prospect that it can be stopped or stood against. That is why I treasure so greatly the stand you made against it, the evidence that there are men who still will stand fast against it, with no fear in their hearts."

"But you are wrong," said Duncan. "I did have fear."

"And yet you stood."

"Sire, there was nothing else to do. We had no place to run."

"You're a truthful man," the wizard said. "It takes a truthful man, and a courageous one, to confess the fear within him. But, then, you are a puissant warrior."

"That I'm not," said Duncan. "Trained in arms, of course, but until this journey I had never drawn a blade in anger. Rather, I am a farmer. I'm much more interested in growing better beef and mutton, raising better crops . . . "

"It is well," said Cuthbert. "Britain, and the world, has need of farmers such as you. More need, perhaps, than for those who can wield a mighty blade. And yet, also, you are proficient with the blade."

He said to Diane, "Greens, you say. I will not eat your greens. Greens and pottage and sometimes gruel, that is all you ever feed me." He said to Duncan, "How can you expect a man to keep up his strength with such hog slop as that?"

Duncan said, "It may be that your stomach . . . "

"What does a minx like her know of a grown man's stomach? Meat, that's what I need. Good red meat, not done to a crisp, but pink throughout and with blood upon the trencher."

"I fed you meat," Diane reminded him, "and you threw it up."

"Badly cooked," he said. "Very badly cooked. Give me a properly cooked haunch of beef or a saddle of mutton and . . . "

His mind seemed to jump. He said to Duncan, "You asked me another question. What was it, now?"

"I had another question. Several other questions. But I had not asked them yet. My archbishop . . ."

"So, we're back to that old woman of a churchman once again."

"He said that the devastations the Evil causes may be for the purpose of rejuvenation, setting up an area where there will be no interference in their rejuvenation procedure. That there they grow in strength, and perhaps in numbers, so they'll be ready for more centuries of their evil-doing."

"I've heard the theory," said the wizard, "and in certain instances there may be some truth in it, although it seems more likely that the devastations serve another purpose, probably designed to block developments that might, in the long run, improve the lot of mankind.

"In this instance, in this present devastation, I am certain that the devastation is not for rejuvenation if, in fact, it ever is. This time the Evil is running very scared. It is frightened of something that will happen. It is gathering its forces to prevent the happening. And yet, for some reason, the Evil appears very much confused, uncertain of itself, as if some unforeseen event had come about that makes all its planning go for naught.

"I was pleased, to tell you the truth, when the devastation started in this area, for now, I told myself, it would be easier to study it at firsthand rather than from old records and the observations of others, who may not have been as accurate in what they had written down as might be desirable. Here was the chance of a lifetime for such a one as I, but I was hampered greatly by the lack of trusty associates. I told myself, however, that I could do the work alone, for I had many years of experience in such a labor. So I worked on it . . . "

"You worked too hard," said Diane. "That's what's the matter with you now."

The wizard's mind jumped. "We were talking about the Huntsman," he said. "Do you know he once spent a week with us? There were several of us then and

203

sometimes we'd have guests of a slow weekend. But the Huntsman was no invited guest. He dropped in. He came riding in one evening on his horse and with all those dogs of his. They landed in the big dining room you saw, where we were just finishing a well-cooked meal. The dogs jumped up on the sideboard and made off with a platter of partridge, a ham, and a venison pot roast, and fought one another up and down the hall for each one's fair share of it, while those of us at table sat petrified with the gaucherie of it. The Huntsman, meantime, hoisted a small keg of beer to drink directly from the bung-hole, pouring it directly down his throat and I swear you could hear the glugging of it when it hit his stomach. Although after that first onslaught it all got straightened out and we had a jolly week of it, with those dogs eating us out of house and home and the Huntsman drinking us out of house and home. But we didn't mind too much, for the Huntsman told us tales that thereafter, for a full year's time, we recited to one another, savoring them again."

"You must have had good times in those days," said Duncan, saying the first thing that came to mind.

"Oh, we did," the wizard said. "You must ask me about that night when a band of drunken rogues brought the demon to us. Having tired of him themselves, and looking to get rid of him, they thought it a splendid joke to bring him as a gift to us. By the way, you have met the demon, have you not?"

"Yes, I have," said Duncan.

"As demons go," the wizard said, "he is not a bad sort. He claims he has not a single vicious bone in his body and while I'd not go so far as that . . . "

"Sire," said Diane, in a gentle voice, "you were talking about the Horde of Evil."

Cuthbert seemed somewhat surprised.

"Were we?" he asked. "Is that what we were talking of?"

"I believe it was," said Duncan.

"As I was saying," said the wizard. "Or was I saying it? I just cannot remember. But, anyhow, I think it likely that most people have no real idea of how a congress of wizards live. I would imagine they might equate a wizard's castle with a monastery where the little monks wind their silent ways through mazes of doctrinal theology, clutching their ragged little souls close within their breasts, scarcely daring to breathe for fear they will draw into their lungs a whiff of heresy. Or they might think of a castle such as this as a place of hidden trapdoors, with sinister figures, black draped and cowled, hiding around corners or ambushed behind the window drapes, with sinister winds whistling down the corridors and hideous odors billowing from thaumaturgic laboratories. It is, of course, nothing like unto either one of these. While this place now is quiet from lack of occupants, there was a day when it was a gleesome place, jocular and laughter loving. For we made a jovial group when we put our work aside. We worked hard, it is true, for the tasks we set ourselves were not easy ones, but we also knew how to spend merry hours together. Lying here, I can call the roll of those old companions. There were Caewlin and Arthur, Aethelbehrt and Raedwald. Eadwine and Wulfert—and I can think of them all most kindly, but for Wulfert I feel remorseful pangs, for while what we did was necessary, it still was a hard and sad action to be taken. We turned him out the gate . . . "

"Sire," said Diane, "you have forgotten that Wulfert was kin of mine."

"Yes, yes," said Cuthbert. "I forget again and my tongue runs on. It seems to me that lately I do much forgetting." He made a thumb at Diane and said to Duncan, "That is quite correct. Wizard blood runs in her veins, or perhaps you already know. Mayhaps she had told you."

"Yes, she had," said Duncan.

The wizard lay quietly on the pillows and it seemed the talk had ended, but again he stirred and spoke.

"Yes, Wulfert," he said. "He was like unto a brother to me. But when the decision came to be made, I sided with the others."

205

He fell into a silence and then again he spoke. "Arrogance," he said. "Yes, it was his arrogance. He set himself against the rest of us. He set his knowledge and his skills against our skills and knowledge. We told him that he wasted time, that there was no power in his talisman, and yet, setting at naught our opinions and our friendships, he insisted that it had great power. He said it was our jealousy that spoke. We tried to reason with him. We talked to him like brothers who held great love of him. But he'd not listen to us, stubbornly he stood against us all. Granted that this talisman of his was a thing of beauty, in more ways than one, since he was a magnificent craftsman, a skilled worker in the arcane, but it takes more than beauty . . ."

"You are sure of that?" asked Diane.

"My dear, I am sure of it. A petty power, perhaps. He claimed that this silly talisman of his could be used to go against the Horde of Evil and that was pure insanity. A mere petty power, is all. Certainly nothing that could be used against the Evil."

"How is it," Diane asked, "that you never spoke to me of this before? You knew I was seeking word of him, that I hoped to find the talisman."

"Why should I cause you pain?" the wizard asked. "I would not have said it now, but in my silliness and weakness, it slipped out of me. I would not willingly have spoken, for I knew how loyal you were to him. Or to his memory. For I suppose he now is dead. I think you told me that."

"Yes, for a century or more. I found where he was buried. In the village just beyond the hills. The last years of his life he posed as a saintly man. The village would have run him out if they'd known he was a wizard."

The old man's eyes were misted. A tear went running down one wasted cheek.

He waved a hand at them. "Leave me now," he said. "Go. Leave me with my grief."

22

He had a problem, Duncan told himself, and the fact he had a problem worried him a lot. He should not have this kind of problem—it was not in his nature to follow a course that would result in such a problem. All his life he had been frank and forthright, saying exactly what he thought, holding back no truth, telling no lies. And this was worse than a simple lie; this was dishonesty.

The amulet—perhaps the talisman, for that was how Cuthbert had described it—did not belong to him. It belonged to Diane, and every fiber in him cried out for him to hand it back to her. It had been constructed by her great-grandfather and should be passed on to her. And yet he had said nothing about having it, had set the course for the rest of his band to say nothing of it, either.

Cuthbert had said it had no power, that its fabrication had been a failure. And yet Wulfert, Diane's great-grandfather, had been willing to accept banishment from the congress of wizards rather than admit that it had no power.

It was because of the nagging feeling, almost a conviction, that it did have a very potent power, he knew, that he had acted as he had. For if the talisman had

207

any kind of power at all, could afford its bearer even the slightest protection, then, he told himself, he had a greater need of it than had anyone. Not he, of course, but the manuscript—for that was the crux of it, the manuscript. He must get it to Oxenford and there was nothing that he could ignore, nothing at all, that would help him get it there.

It was not for himself alone that he, who had never been dishonest, now was dealing in dishonesty. In the library back at Standish House His Grace had said that in the manuscript lay mankind's greatest hope—perhaps the one last hope remaining. If that were true, and Duncan had no doubt it was, then dishonesty was a trivial price to pay to get the writings of that unknown follower of Jesus into the hands of Bishop Wise.

And yet Duncan did not like it. He felt, somehow, unclean. Unworthy and unclean, fouled with deceit and shiftiness, skulduggery and trickery.

What was right? As he thought of it, the line between right and wrong became blurred and smeared, and it never had been that way before with him. He had always known, instinctively, without being told, what was right and what was wrong. There had been no blurring, there had been no smear. But his prior decisions in this regard, he realized, had always dealt with simple considerations in which there had been no complicating factor. But here there was a complicating factor that, in no way, he could quite fit into place.

He sat on the bottom step of the great stone stairway that led up to the castle's entrance. In front of him swept the verdant greenness that ran from where he sat to the edge of the sweeping circle of standing stones ringing in the castle's park. Through the park ran curving paths and walkways paved with bricks. Spotted about the smoothness of the lawn were stone benches, pools, and spouting fountains, rose-covered bowers, flowering gardens, and clumps of shrubs and trees set tastefully in the great green expanse of grass.

It was a beautiful place, he thought—not a place of natural beauty, but a place of artificial beauty, made so, not perhaps by man, as would be the case in other castle parks and gardens, but by the wizardry of a congress of men skilled in bringing about events that stood beyond the natural.

There was in it a peace and restfulness that he would not have thought possible in the domain of wizardry. And yet, he told himself, it would have been wrong for him to think so, for wizards were not necessarily evil men, although there had been some, if history told true, who had turned to evil. The temptation to evil, he realized, would always have been present among men who held such large-scale powers as they, but that did not mean evil was inherent in them; perhaps only a small fraction of them had ever turned to evil. Their powers were great because of the knowledge that they held and this might be, he told himself, why wizards were in such bad repute. The general populace, the great mass of common men, viewed all great power and all extensive knowledge with suspicion; they viewed with suspicion anything they could not understand, and the knowledge held by wizards was unimaginably beyond the understanding of the rest of mankind.

Down near the standing stones, Conrad and Tiny were playing. Conrad was throwing a stick for Tiny, and Tiny, beside himself with joy, for there were not often times when he could play, went racing after the stick when Conrad threw it, bringing it back in his mouth, gamboling and frisking in an ecstasy of fun that somehow did not fit in with the disposition of a war dog. To one side stood Daniel and Beauty, watching the play. Daniel, it seemed to Duncan, was looking on disdainfully, as if he recognized that such behavior was beneath Tiny's dignity. Beauty, however, did not seem to mind. At times she cropped a mouthful of grass, but for the most part watched with uncommon interest. Probably, Duncan thought, if Conrad were to throw a stick for her, she would run and fetch it, too.

A short distance from Daniel and Beauty, Hubert, Diane's griffin, was lying on the lawn, the eagle head held high, the long whip of a tail curled halfway around his body as a cat would curl its tail when lying down, the jutting, rounded lion hips tawny against the greenness of the grass.

Behind him, Duncan heard a faint sound and turned his head. Diane was coming down the steps, but a different Diane. She was clothed in a filmy, clinging gown that reached from neck to toes, belted at the waist. Leaf green it was, the pale yellow-green of the first spring leaves of the willow tree. Her flame-colored hair almost shouted against the pale softness of the fabric.

Duncan came swiftly to his feet. "Milady," he said, "you are beautiful. Beautiful and charming."

She laughed lightly at him. "I thank you, sir. Who, I ask you, could be beautiful in buckskins?"

"Even then," he said, "you had a charm about you. But this—I cannot tell you."

"It's not often," she said, "that I can dress like this, or have occasion to. But with a house of guests, what other could I do?"

She sat down upon a step and he sat beside her.

"I was watching Conrad and Tiny at their play," he said.

"They are a pair," she said. "You have known them long?"

"Conrad and I since we were boys," he told her. "We were inseparable. And Tiny since he was a pup."

"Meg is in the kitchen," she said, "cooking up a mess of sauerkraut and pig knuckles. She says it has been years since she has had her fill of such a dish. I wonder, do you like it?"

"Exceedingly," said Duncan. "And what of the hermit? I've not seen him all the day."

"He's wandering," said Diane. "All about the grounds. He stands, leaning on his staff, staring off at nothing. Your hermit is a troubled man."

"A befuddled man," said Duncan. "Unsure of himself. Torn by many questions. He cannot quite determine the condition of his soul. He tried for long, by various means, to be a holy man, and now he has be-

210

come a soldier of the Lord and it's a profession he's uneasy at."

"Poor man," she said. "He has within himself so much good and no way to express it. And Cuthbert? How did you like Cuthbert?"

"Impressive," Duncan said. "Although, at times, difficult to understand. Difficult to follow."

"He's senile," said Diane.

Duncan shot a quick astonished glance at her. "You are sure of that?" he asked.

"Well, aren't you?" she asked, in turn. "A brilliant mind, sharp and clever, but now dulled by time and sickness. He cannot follow up his thoughts. At times he's irrational. I watch him closely, lest he hurt himself."

"He did seem to have some trouble."

"The last of a long line," she said, "that persisted over hundreds of years. Now all are gone except for Cuthbert. They tried to keep the congress going, bringing in young apprentices, but it never worked. There are few outstanding wizards any more. It takes a special kind of man to be a wizard. A capacity to absorb vast amounts of arcane knowledge and to work with it. Perhaps something more than that. An instinct for wizardry, perhaps. A distinctive turn of mind. There may be few people in the world today who have that turn of mind."

"How about yourself?"

She shook her head. "Women seldom can accomplish wizardry. That turn of mind, perhaps. Not the kind of mind that a woman has. It may have to be a man's mind. The mind of the male animal may be shaped and pointed in a slightly different direction than a woman's mind. I tried, of course, and they let me try, for while they were forced to banish Wulfert, they held a high respect for him, even in his banishment. He was the most accomplished wizard of them all. And while I could grasp some of the concepts, could perform certain little magics, put together some of the more simple of the manipulations, I was not cut out for wizardry. They did not tell me this. In time to come they would have had to tell me, but I did not force them to. I realized it myself, that I could never be anything other than a poor apprentice wizard. And there's no room in the world for inefficient apprentices."

"But you are a resident of the wizards' castle."

"A courtesy," she said. "A sincere and heartfelt courtesy. Because I have Wulfert's blood in me. When my parents died of a plague that swept the countryside, Cuthbert left the castle for the first time in his life, for the only time, for he has not left it since, and claimed me as a descendant of his great, good friend who by that time, I now know, had long since been dead. The last of the wizards raised me here and because I loved them I tried to learn their skills, but couldn't. All this I tell you about Cuthbert coming to get me, I've been told, for I was then too young to remember it. Not only did they raise me here and care for me, but they gave me as well old Hubert, who was Wulfert's griffin, left behind when my great-grandfather had to leave this place, for he could not take a griffin with him."

"The day will come when Cuthbert will die," said Duncan gently. "What about you then? Will you continue to stay on?"

"I don't know," she said. "I have seldom thought upon it. I have tried to keep from thinking on it. With Cuthbert gone, it would be lonely here. I don't know what I'd do. There'd be no place in the outside world for me. I am not used to it, would not know what to do, have had no chance to know what one should do. And I could not for long keep hidden that I had wizard blood in me. The outside world, I am afraid, would not take kindly to me if that were known."

"The world can be cruel," said Duncan. "I wish I could tell you that it isn't, but it is."

She leaned toward him, kissed him swiftly on the cheek. "The world can be kind," she said. "You have been kind to me. You have talked of my problem with a very gentle kindness."

"I thank you, milady," said Duncan gravely. "I

thank you for your words. And for the kiss. It was a lovely kiss."

"You make fun of me," she said.

"Not at all, Diane. It is true gratitude, the more grateful because I have done nothing to deserve it."

"Cuthbert," she said, changing the subject abruptly, "has expressed a desire to see you."

"It must be soon," said Duncan. "We tarry here too long. We must be on our way."

She protested, somewhat flustered. "Why so soon? You should take several days to rest. All of you need rest. You've had no easy time."

"We've been held up," said Duncan, "by many misadventures. By this time we should have been in Oxenford."

"Oxenford can wait," she argued.

"I'm sorry, milady, but I don't believe it can."

She rose swiftly to her feet. "I must be going in to see how Cuthbert is. I cannot leave him long."

"I'll go with you," he said. "You said he wanted to see me."

"Not now," she told him. "I'll call you when he is ready for you."

As Duncan crossed the reception hall, Scratch, the demon, perched upon his pedestal, called out to him.

"Are you in a hurry, sire?" he asked. "Would you, perhaps, have a little time to spare? If so, it would be merciful of you to halt a while and chat. Despite all this magnificence of stone and fancy scrollwork, despite the elevated and exalted throne they have provided for me, there are times when the hours hang heavy on my hands."

Duncan altered his course and walked toward Scratch's column. "I have not a thing to do," he said. "Mistress Diane is gone to see how the wizard fares and my companions apparently have pursuits of their own. I would treasure a little time with you."

"Now, that is fine," the demon said. "Two men with the selfsame thought, a way in which to pleasantly while away some time. But there's no need for you to stand there, getting a crick in your neck from staring up at me. If you'd only help me down, we could sit on that stone bench a step or two away. My chain is long enough for me to reach it handily and with some to spare."

Duncan moved closer to the column and reached up

his hands. The demon leaned forward and Duncan grasped him about the waist and helped him down.

"Except for this clubfoot of mine, which additionally is weighted down by the chain, I could get down quite easily myself," said Scratch. "In fact, I often do, but not in a manner that you could call easily." He held out his arthritis-crippled hands. "And these don't help, either."

They walked to the bench and sat down, side by side. Scratch lifted his clubhoof and crossed his knees. He jiggled the hoof up and down and the chain clanked.

"I was explaining to you the other day," he said, "that my name is Scratch—formerly Young Scratch, now simply Scratch, but never Old Scratch, for that is the vulgar designation of His Nibs, who runs the Infernal Operation. Since the name has been given me, I suppose I must abide by it, but I have never liked it. It is the kind of name one might give a dog. Why, even milady's griffin is given the honest name of Hubert, which is a far better name than Scratch. Through the years I have squatted on my column and have thought, among many other things, of a name that I'd enjoy bearing. A more suitable name, with more dignity and a more euphonious sound. I have paraded hundreds of names through my mind, taking my time, for I have all the time there is, weighing each name as I think of it, twisting and turning it in my mind, so I can get a critical look at it from every angle, rolling it around in my mouth to get the sound and feel of it. And after all these years and all the examination, I think I have finally found a name that would fit me well and that I'd be proud to have. I'll wager you cannot guess what that name might be."

"I have no faintest idea," said Duncan. "How could I have?"

"It is Walter," said Scratch triumphantly. "It is a splendid name. Do you not think it is? It has a full round sound to it. It is a name that is complete of itself and not a bobtailed name. Although I am aware it could be shortened to Walt. If I had such a name I

215

should frown upon its shortening. It is not a fancy name. It has no flair to it. It is a solid name, an honest name, fashioned to fit a solid and an honest man."

"So that is how you spend your time," said Duncan. "Thinking up a new name for yourself. I suppose it is as good a device as any to make the time go by."

"It is only one of many things I do," said Scratch. "I do a lot of imagining. I imagine how it might have been for me had events gone differently. If I had worked out as an apprentice demon, if I could have cut the mustard, by now I would be a senior demon or, just possibly, a junior devil. I would be much larger than I am now, although maybe there would not have been that much change in size. I am a runt, you know; I have always been a runt. It may be that therein lies my trouble. Perhaps a runt is foreordained to failure, perhaps a runt never can make good. But even when I know this, I still can keep on imagining. I can envision myself as a senior demon or a junior devil, with a big paunch of a belly and hair upon my chest and a very dirty laugh. That's one thing I never was able to achieve, that very nasty laugh that can chill a human's blood and shrivel up his soul."

"You seem to me," said Duncan, "to be quite philosophical about your plight. You have not grown bitter. Many lesser ones would have grown bitter. And you do not whine for pity."

"What would be accomplished," asked Scratch, "should I rant or rave or whine? No one would love me more; in fact, they'd love me less. No one loves a bellyacher. Although I do not know why I talk of love, for there's no one who loves me. Who could love a demon? There are those who may feel some small pity of me, but pity is not love. What they mostly do is laugh at me—at my twisted tail, at my clubhoof, at my crumpled horn. And laughter, my lord, is very hard to take. If they'd only shrink from me in horror, or even in disgust, I'd be better satisfied. I could live with that."

"I have not laughed at you," said Duncan, "nor

have I felt overwhelming pity for you. But I'll not claim I love you."

"That is not expected," said Scratch. "I would have some suspicion of a human who professed love for me. I then would look for motive."

"And well you might," said Duncan, "but since I have proclaimed no love of you and thus have not attempted to put you in my debt, could I ask an honest question?"

"I would be pleased to have you."

"Then what can you tell me about the Horde of Evil? I would imagine that in this castle, from wizard talk, you may have heard some mention of it."

"That I have. What is it you would know? Although it occurs to me you may know something of it personally. I have been informed that you and your band stood them off not too long ago."

"Only a small party of them, mostly the hairless ones, although there were others. I don't know how many of them or how many kinds."

"The hairless ones," said Scratch, "if I correctly catch the meaning of your term, are the slogging infantry, the guards, the skirmishers who do the initial dirty work. In a certain sense they are not true evil beings, not really of the Horde. All they have is bone and muscle. They have little magic in them, perhaps none at all."

"And the rest of them? I talked with one who'd seen these others. Or told me that he had. He talked of imps and demons and I doubt that he is right. He was only using names he knew, generic names for evil. In our encounter outside the wall, I killed one of these others and Tiny killed another and they were not imps or demons. I know not what they were."

"You're quite right," said Scratch. "They are neither imps nor demons. Imps and demons are of this world and these other ones are not. You know, of course, that the Horde came from the stars."

"So I've been told," said Duncan.

"They are the spawn of other places, other worlds, which I suspect are not like our world. So it only stands to reason that the Evil they spawned is unlike the evil of the Earth. They come in inconceivable shapes and forms. The very alienness of them is sufficient to clot one's lifeblood. Their habits and their motives and their modes of operation, I presume, as well, would not conform to the habits, the motives and the operations of an evil thing of Earth. In going up against them you are encountering a sort of creature you can never have imagined, perhaps could not possibly imagine."

"Someone told me," Duncan said, "that they are no horde at all; they really are a swarm. What could be meant by that?"

"I do not really know," said Scratch. "I have, you must understand, no real knowledge of them. It's only what I've heard."

"I realize that. But about a swarm. Prior to being told that they were more like a swarm than horde, I had talked with a venerable bee master and he talked of swarming bees. In this wise, could there be some connection?"

"There is one thing," said Scratch, "although it was a short conversation only that I chanced to overhear. It might, just possibly, bear on this swarming matter."

"Please go on," said Duncan. "Tell me what it was."

"At those times," said Scratch, "when the Horde is in the process of devastating an area, in the way it has devastated northern Britain, the members of the Horde at times are prone to come together, to form a sort of living mass. Perhaps like unto a swarm of bees. The ones who talked of this, having heard of it from a few widely separated and isolated observations, were very puzzled by the reported action. At other times, it appears, the individual members of the Horde, when there is no devastation going on, seem to work alone or in small parties, only a few of them together. But when they are about a devastation, they do collect, or so observers say, into a massive swarm . . ."

"Now, wait a minute," Duncan said. "I think there might be a clue to that. A learned man told me, not long ago, that they devastated an area to make them-

218

selves secure so they can engage in a rejuvenation process, a retreat of sorts, he said, as fathers of the church sometimes hold retreats. Do you suppose . . . "

"You know," said Scratch excitedly, "you may have something there. I have never heard of their rejuvenation rites. But that could well be it. A coming together of the entire community of Evil, a close coming together, a personal contact, one to one, and from that contact they might gain an unknown strength, a renewing of themselves. What do you think? It sounds reasonable to me."

"That had been my thought. I'm glad you share it with me."

"That might explain the swarming."

"I think it could. Although there are so many factors, so many things of which we have no understanding and perhaps never will."

"That is true," said Scratch, "but it's a good hypothesis. One that could be worked on. You talked with Cuthbert. What had he to say of it?"

"We did not talk about the swarming. At the time I did not know of it and if he did, he did not mention it. I brought up the rejuvenation theory, but he seemed to think little of it. He said the Horde was frightened of something, probably was getting together to move against it, but for some reason had become confused. Tell me something, Scratch. If you were forced to take sides in this matter, if there were no way in which you could avoid taking sides, which side would you choose?"

The demon jiggled his hoof up and down and the chain clanked. "This may sound strange to you," he said, "but if forced to take a stand I'd stand in with you humans. My heritage may be evil, but it's a human evil, or at least an earthly evil. I could not stomach associating with an alien evil. I'd not know them and they'd not know me and I'd be uncomfortable with them. Evil may be evil, but there are various kinds of it and they can't always come together."

Steps sounded on the stairs coming down from the balcony into the reception hall, and Duncan looked

219

around. Still dressed in her green gown, Diane seemed to be floating down the stairs. Only the tapping of her sandals betrayed her walking.

Duncan got off the bench and Scratch also clambered off to stand stiffly beside him.

"Scratch," asked Diane, "what are you doing off your pillar?"

"Milady," Duncan told her, "I asked him to come down and sit with me. It was more comfortable for me. That way I did not need to stand, craning up my head to look at him."

"Has he been pestering you?"

"Not at all," said Duncan. "We've had a pleasant talk."

"I suppose," said Scratch, "I'd best get up again."

"Wait a second," Duncan said, "and I'll lend you a hand."

He reached down and hoisted the demon so he could catch hold with his crippled hands and scramble back atop the pillar.

"It was good talking with you," Duncan said. "Thanks for giving me your time."

"That is gracious of you, my lord. We will talk again?"

"Most assuredly," said Duncan.

The demon squatted atop the pillar and Duncan turned back to Diane. She was standing in the entrance waiting for him.

"I had thought," she said, "we might take a turn around the grounds. I'd like to show them to you."

"I'd be delighted," said Duncan. "It is kind of you."

He offered her his arm and they went down the stairs together.

"How is Cuthbert feeling?" Duncan asked.

She shook her head. "Not as well as yesterday. I am worried for him. He seems so irrational. He's asleep now. I waited to come down until he was asleep."

"Could my visit with him . . . "

"Not at all," she said. "His ailment grows upon him. It progresses day by day. Occasionally he has a good day, but not too often now. Apparently he has not been himself since I left to go in search of Wulfert. I suppose I should not have left him, but he said he'd be all right, that he could get along without me."

"You have great love of him?"

"You must remember, he has been a father to me. Since the time I was a babe. The two of us are family."

They reached the bottom of the stairs and now turned to the left to follow a path that led to the back of the castle park. The lawn ran down to just short of the river, fenced in by the ring of standing stones.

"You think, undoubtedly," she said, "that I am harsh with Scratch."

"It seems to me you might have been, a little. Certainly he has a right to come down off his pillar and sit upon a bench."

"But he pesters everyone," she said. "It is seldom now that we have visitors, but in the olden days there were many who came to the castle, and he always pestered them, wanting to pass the time of day with them, hanging onto them as long as possible to engage them in his silly jabber. Cuthbert felt, and I think the others did as well, that he was an embarrassment."

"I can see how that might be," said Duncan, "but he really is all right. I'm not an authority on demons, naturally, so I can't . . ."

"Duncan."

"Yes?"

"Let's stop all this foolish chatter. There's something that I have to tell you, and if I don't tell it to you now, I'll never have the strength to."

She had halted at the bending of the path, opposite a large clump of birch and pine. He swung about to confront her and saw that her face was drawn and white.

"There can't anything be that bad," he said, startled by the look of her.

"Yes, there can be," she told him tightly. "You remember just an hour or so ago you said that you

221

must be leaving soon, and I said there was no hurry, that you should stay a while and rest."

"Yes, I remember that."

"I should have told you then. But I couldn't tell you. I simply couldn't say the words. I had to leave to try to find the courage."

He started to speak, but she held up a hand to stop him.

"I can't wait," she said. "There can be no further talk. I must tell you now. Duncan, it is this: you can't leave. You can never leave this castle."

He stood stupid in the path, the words not sinking in, refusing to sink in.

"But that can't be," he said. "I don't . . ."

"I can't say it any plainer. There's no way for you to leave. No one can help you leave. It's a part of the enchantment. There's no way to break it . . ."

"But you were just telling me you had visitors. And you, yourself . . ."

"It takes magic," she told him. "Your personal magic, not someone else's magic. It takes an arcane knowledge that one holds oneself. The visitors have had that kind of knowledge, that kind of magic. Because of that, they could go where no others could. I have some of that knowledge myself, also a special dispensation . . ."

"You mean because none of us has that knowledge . . ."

She nodded, tears in her eyes.

"And you can't help us? The wizard can't help us?"

"No one can help. The ability must be yours."

Suddenly anger flared within him, blinding him.

"Goddamn it, then," he yelled, "why did you tell us to run for the castle? You knew what would happen. You knew we would be trapped. You knew . . ."

He stopped in mid-sentence, for he doubted she was hearing him. She was weeping openly, head bowed, arms hanging at her side. Just standing there, all alone, and weeping.

She raised a tearstained face to look at him, cringing away from him.

222

"You would have been killed," she said. "We broke the Harrier line, but they'd have been back again. It was only a momentary battle lull. They'd have returned and hunted you down, like wild animals."

She reached out for him. "You understand?" she cried. "Please do understand!"

She took a step toward him and he put his arms around her, drawing her close against him, holding her tightly. She bowed her head against him, weeping convulsively, her body shaking with the sobs.

Her muffled voice said, "I lay awake last night, thinking of it. Wondering how I could have done it, how I'd ever tell you. I thought perhaps I could ask Cuthbert to tell you. But that wouldn't have been right. I was the one who did it, I should be the one to tell you. And now I have—and now I have . . . "

24

They sat in silence for a time after Duncan had
finished telling them—not so much a shocked silence
as a benumbed silence.

Meg was the first to speak, attempting to cast a
cheerful light on it. "Well, I don't know," she said,
"It's not too bad. There are a lot worse places for an
old bag such as Meg to live out her final days."

They disregarded her.

Finally Conrad stirred and said, "You say one has
to have some knowledge of the arcane arts. What are
the chances that we could acquire that knowledge?"

"I'd say not too good," said Duncan. "I suspect it
would have to be a detailed and specific knowledge,
perhaps well backgrounded by even other knowledge.
Not all of us could learn these arts, perhaps not any
of us. And who is there to teach us? Cuthbert is old
and dying. Diane's knowledge is too small. I gather
that it is not the knowledge that she has, but a special
dispensation, that enables her to come and go."

"I suppose that's right," said Conrad, "and, any
how, it would take too long a time. We haven't got
that kind of time."

"No, we haven't," said Duncan. "Two dying men—
a dying man here and another one at Oxenford."

"And what about Tiny? What about Daniel and Beauty? They could not be taught the arts. Even could we go we couldn't leave them behind. They're a part of us."

"Probably we could take them with us," Duncan said. "I don't know. There is Diane's griffin; he can come and go. Certainly he does not know the arts."

"Even if there is none to teach us," Andrew said, "there are books. I found the library this morning. A huge room and tons of writing."

"It would take too long," objected Duncan. "We'd have to sift through heaps of scrolls and might not recognize what we sought even should we find it. And there's no one to guide us in our studies. There'd also be the problem of language. Many of the books, I suspect, may be written in ancient tongues that now are little known."

"For myself," said Andrew, "for me, personally, this turn of events is no great tragedy. Quite willingly, if there were no other considerations, I could settle down here, for it is a pleasant place and I could carry on my profession here as well as elsewhere. But for the two of you I know it is a matter of great importance to get to Oxenford."

Conrad pounded the ground with his club. "We have to get to Oxenford. There has to be a way. I, for one, will not give up and say there is no way."

"Nor will I," said Duncan.

"I had a premonition of this," Andrew told them. "Or if not of this, of something very wrong. When I saw the birds and the butterfly . . ."

"What the hell," asked Duncan, "have birds and butterflies got to do with it?"

"In the woods," said Andrew. "In the forest just beyond the standing stones. The birds sit frozen in the branches, not moving, as if they might be dead, but they have a live look to them. And there was a butterfly, a little yellow butterfly sitting on a milkweed pod. Not stirring, not moving. You know the way a butterfly will sit, slowly moving its wings up and down, not very much, but some motion to them. This one did

225

not move at all. I watched for a long time and it did not move. I think I saw, although I could not be sure, a thin film of dust upon it. As if it had been there a long time and dust had collected on it. I think the woods are part of the enchantment, too, that time has stopped there except for the people—and Hubert. Everything else is exactly the same as it was on the day this castle was created by enchantment."

"The stoppage of time," said Duncan. "Yes, that could be it. The castle is brand new, so are the standing stones. The chisel marks still fresh upon them, as if they had been carved only yesterday."

"But outside," said Conrad, "in that world we left to walk into this world, the castle lies in ruins, the stones have tumbled down. Tell me, m'lord, what do you think is going on?"

"It's an enchantment," said Meg. "A very potent one."

"We've beaten enchantments before," said Conrad. "We beat the enchantment that came upon us as we approached the strand."

"That was but a feeble spell," said Meg, "designed only to confuse us, to get us off the track. Not a well-constructed spell, not carefully crafted as this one surely is."

Duncan knew that what she said was true. Despite all their whistling past the graveyard, despite all of Conrad's bravado, the firm confidence they showed for one another's benefit, this was an enchantment they were not about to break.

They sat crouched in a row on the bottom step of the stairway that came down from the entrance. Before them ran the measured velvet of the lawn. Daniel and Beauty were at the foot of the park, near the standing stones, filling their bellies with succulent grass. Hubert, the griffin, still lay where he had been earlier in the day. Grown stiff with age, he did not move around too much.

"Where's Tiny?" Duncan asked.

"The last I saw of him," said Conrad, "he was digging out a mouse. He's around somewhere."

So here they were, Duncan told himself, caught in as pretty a mousetrap as anyone could want. This way not only would the manuscript never get to Oxenford, but it would be lost to mankind as well. All that would remain would be the two copies made at the abbey's scriptorium.

His father, at Standish House, and His Grace, at the abbey, would wait for word of him and Conrad, and there would be no word; there never would be word. They would have gone into the Desolated Land and that would be the last of them. Although perhaps, just perhaps, there might be a way for word to be gotten out. Diane could get out, could go out and return. At least, should she be willing, she could carry word to Standish House, perhaps carry the manuscript as well. There still might be time for someone else to get to Oxenford with it. Not through the Desolated Land, for that route had proved too dangerous; the chances of traversing it were slight. Despite the swarming pirates, it might be carried by ship. There still might be enough time left to pull together a fleet of fighting ships, manned by men-at-arms, to get through the pirate packs.

"M'lord," said Conrad.

"Yes, what is it?"

"A delicate matter."

"There are no delicate matters between you and me. Speak up. Tell me what you were about to."

"The Horde," said Conrad, "does not want us to get to Oxenford—well, maybe not actually to Oxenford, maybe they just don't want us to get anywhere. They've tried to block us at every turn. And now perhaps we're blocked for good. They'll have no more trouble from us."

"That's true. But what's your point?"

"The Lady Diane."

"What about the Lady Diane?"

"Could she be in league with them? Is this but a clever trick?"

Duncan flushed in anger, opened his mouth to speak and then held back the words.

Andrew hurriedly said, "I think not. To me it is inconceivable. Twice she aided us in battle. She would not have done this had she been in league with them."

"I think you probably are right," said Conrad. "It's only that we must consider every angle."

In the silence that followed, Duncan's mind went back again to his half-formed plan to get the manuscript to Oxenford by some other route. It wouldn't work, he knew. Diane, without question, could carry it to Standish House, could acquaint his father with what had happened to him and Conrad, but it seemed hardly likely that the manuscript could be carried to Oxenford by sea. His father and the archbishop had given that possibility full consideration and apparently had decided that it would be impossible. It might be that his father would decide to attempt it by land once again, sending out a small army of men-at-arms, but that sort of venture, it seemed to Duncan, would have little chance of success. The Reaver's band of thirty men or more had been easily wiped out. That his own small group had gotten as far as it had, he was convinced, was due only to the protection afforded by the talisman.

Or, wait a moment, he told himself. If Diane could take the manuscript to Standish House, she could take it just as easily to Oxenford. At Oxenford she could deliver it by hand to Bishop Wise and wait to bring back the word.

But, thinking this, he knew that none of it was possible, knew that he had been doing no more than conjuring up fantasies in a desperate effort to find some solution to his problem.

He could not hand over the manuscript to Diane—nor, perhaps, to any other. He could not give it to someone he could not trust and in this place, other than Conrad, whom could he trust? Diane had lured him and his party into this circle of enchantment. And now she said that she was sorry, had even wept in saying she was sorry. But expressions of sorrow come easily, he told himself, and tears just as easily.

And that was not all. The manuscript had been

given into his keeping and it must stay that way. He was the one who had sole responsibility for it; it was a sacred trust he could share with no one else. In his mad groping for some way out of his predicament, he had forgotten, for the moment, the holy vow he implicitly had taken when His Grace had handed him the parchment.

"Another thing," said Conrad. "Could the demon help us? He might have a trick or two up his sleeve. If we appealed to him, if we were able to offer him the payment of setting him free, if we could . . ."

"With a demon I'll not deal," snapped Andrew. "He is a filthy beast."

"To me," said Duncan, "he seems a decent chap."

"You cannot trust him," Andrew said. "He would play you false."

"You said we could not trust Snoopy either," Conrad reminded him. "Yet if we'd paid attention to Snoopy, we'd not be where we are now. He warned us against the castle. He told us not to go near it."

"Have it your own way," whined Andrew, "but leave me out of it. I'll have no traffic with a demon out of Hell."

"He might have a way to help us."

"If he did, there'd be a price attached. Mark my word, there'd be a price to pay."

"I'd be prepared to pay the price," said Conrad.

"Not the kind he'd ask," said Andrew.

It was no good, Duncan told himself. Scratch, decent chap though he might be—something of which they could not be certain—would not be able to help them. Nor could anyone. Diane, if she had been able, would have opened a path for them. And if she were unable, so would be all the others of them. An enchantment of this sort, he told himself, if it were to have any value, would have to be foolproof and tamperproof.

Despite all his daydreaming, all his wishful thinking, the matter now was closed, the venture cancelled out. They could not leave the castle, the manuscript would not get to Oxenford, the one last hope of mankind, as His Grace had termed it, now had flickered out.

He rose heavily to his feet and started up the stairway.

"Where are you going, m'lord?" Conrad asked.

Duncan didn't answer him, for there was no answer. He had no idea where he might be going or what might be his purpose. He had no thought at all. It was as if his mind had been wiped clean of every thought he had. The only thing he knew was that somehow he must get away, although he did not know from what. And even as he thought this, he knew that he would be unable to get away from anything.

He kept on plodding up the stairs.

He had almost reached the entrance when he heard the scream—a ululating wail laden with an unsupportable terror, the kind of half screech, half howl a condemned soul might utter, interspersed with squeals of stricken horror. The sound nailed him to the spot, petrified and stupefied, terror-stricken by the horror of it.

The screaming was coming from somewhere inside the castle, and the first thought he had was of Diane. But it was not Diane, he realized; the sound was too full-throated, too deep to be made by a woman. Cuthbert, he told himself—it had to be the wizard.

With a superhuman effort he broke the chain of terror that held him in place, forced his legs to move, and went leaping up the stairs. As he burst through the entrance into the hall, he saw that it was Cuthbert. The old man was running along the balcony above the hall. He wore the long white nightgown with ruffles at the throat and wrists, the flaming red nightcap askew upon his head. His hands were lifted high, as if raised in horror, and his face was so twisted it seemed scarcely human. From his foam-flecked, frothing lips issued a stream of screams and squeals, and then, in mid-scream, he went over the balustrade that closed in the balcony and spun in the air, cartwheeling through the emptiness, his scream becoming one loud, persistent screech that did not end until he

230

hit the floor. Then the scream cut off and he lay, a huddled, crumpled figure all in white except for the red nightcap.

Duncan rushed forward, and out of the corner of his eye he caught sight of Diane, still clad in her filmy gown of green, running down one of the staircases from the balcony.

He reached Cuthbert and went to his knees beside him, reaching out his hands to lift the body, but stopping when he saw the rivulet of blood that came from beneath the shattered head to run along the polished flagstones. Then, more slowly, he reached out again and turned the body, saw what had happened to the head and face and then let it roll back again to its original position.

Diane was racing toward him and, getting to his feet, he leaped to intercept her. He caught her in his arms and held her while she beat at him with her fists.

"Don't look," he told her sharply. "You don't want to look."

"But Cuthbert . . . "

"He is dead," said Duncan.

Above him he heard a creaking, and looking up, he saw that a part of the balcony balustrade was swaying. Even as he watched it came crashing down. Shards of shattered stone skittered across the floor, and from somewhere within the castle's bowels came a groaning sound. Then one of the pillars that stood along the wall of the reception hall tieing the hall and balcony together slowly, gracefully peeled itself off the wall and toppled, not with a rush, but settling slowly, describing a polished arc, as if it were tired and lying down to rest. It struck the floor with violence despite its graceful fall and came apart, the broken debris flying out to roll across the flagstones.

"Let's get out of here," yelled Conrad. "The whole damn place is beginning to fall down."

From deep within the castle came the moaning of strained and shifting masonry, the moans punctuated by unseen crashes. Out of the walls of the hall blocks of stone were coming loose and moving, the entire wall writhing as the blocks continued their shifting.

"M'lord!" yelled Conrad. "M'lord, get a move on, for the love of God!"

Duncan moved as if in a dream, heading for the entrance, dragging Diane with him. Behind him came thunderous crashes as the castle continued to collapse. Meg was scuttling out the entrance, followed closely by Andrew. Conrad was hurrying toward Duncan, intent on grasping him and propelling him to safety.

A bawling voice rang through the hall.

"Help me!" the voice bawled. "Do not leave me here."

Duncan, still with a grip upon Diane, swung around to see where the voice came from.

Scratch, the demon, had jumped down off his pedestal and was on the floor, his back toward them, his hands upon the chain, leaning backward, heels dug in, tugging futilely at the chain in an effort to free it from the stone.

Duncan gave Diane a shove toward the entrance. "Run!" he shouted. "Don't look back, just run."

He leaped for the demon and the chain, but Conrad got there first. He shoved the demon to one side, wrapped the chain around his fists, and reared back on his heels, throwing the weight of his massive body against the staple fastened in the pillar. The links of the chain hummed and whined with the strain he put upon them, but the staple held.

Duncan, moving in behind Conrad, also grasped the chain. "Now," he said. The two of them threw their weight against the staple but it did not stir.

"No way," gasped Conrad. "We can't pull it out."

"Hang on. Keep it taut," said Duncan. He stepped around Conrad to position himself between Conrad and the staple. He drew his sword and lifted it high above his head, then struck at the chain with all his strength. Sparks flew as the blade's edge struck the iron, but the sword skidded along the length of chain and the links held. Duncan struck again and again sparks flew, but the chain still stayed intact.

One wall of the reception hall was down and stones were falling from the ceiling, bouncing on the flagstones. Stone dust floated in the air, and the floor was covered with tiny bits of fragmented masonry. Any minute now, Duncan knew, the entire structure would collapse upon them.

"Let the damn chain be," wailed the demon. "Cut off my hoof to free me from the chain."

Conrad grunted at Duncan. "He's right," he said. "That's the only way. Cut off his goddamn foot."

Duncan spun around, ducked behind Conrad.

"Fall down," he yelled at Scratch. "Hold up the foot so I can make a cut at it."

Scratch sprawled full length on the floor and held up the clubhoof. Duncan raised his blade for the stroke. Someone joggled him. He saw that it was Andrew.

"Get out of the way," Duncan shouted at him. "Give me room."

But Andrew did not move. His staff was poised above his head and he brought it down in a vicious sweep. It struck the outstretched chain and at the blow the chain shattered into bits, tiny shards of metal spewing out along the floor.

Still holding the staff in his right hand, Andrew reached down with his left, grabbing the demon by the arm, and headed for the entrance, dragging the freed Scratch along behind him.

"Run for it!" yelled Conrad, and Duncan ran, with Conrad close behind him. Ahead of them Andrew loped along with surprising speed, still hauling along an outraged demon, who screamed to be let loose, that he could make it by himself. As they burst out the entrance and started down the stairway, the reception hall caved in upon itself with a thunderous roar. Small fragments of broken stone went whizzing past them, and a cloud of dust belched out of the entrance.

By this time Andrew had let go of Scratch, and the demon, despite his clubfoot, was scrambling frantically down the stairs. On the lawn at the foot of the stairs, Meg was kneeling with her arms locked around

Diane's knees to keep her from struggling free. Behind Duncan and Conrad the castle continued crashing in upon itself. The central tower had already fallen and the walls were buckling.

Reaching the foot of the stairs, Duncan ran to reach Diane. He grasped her arm.

"You can't go back in," he said.

"Cuthbert," she said. "Cuthbert."

"She tried to break away and go back," said Meg. "I had to hold her. I had to seize violently upon her. She almost got away."

"It's all right now," said Duncan. "All of us are out."

He grasped Diane by both shoulders, shook her.

"It's all over now," he told her. "We can't help him. We never could have helped him. He died when he hit the floor."

Daniel and Beauty were at the foot of the park, standing beside one another, staring up toward them, watching the crumbling of the castle. Tiny was loping up the park toward them, his ears laid back, his tail standing out behind him. Hubert, the griffin, did not seem to be about.

Scratch hobbled over to confront Andrew. He stood before him, his head tilted up to look at him.

"I thank you, reverend father," he said, "for freeing me. That is a truly miraculous staff you have."

Andrew made a choking sound, as if he had swallowed something that tasted very bad. His face twisted in disgust and he had the look of a man who, any minute now, might fall down dead.

"It was not death I feared," said Scratch. "I doubt I would have died. It was something worse than death. Death is something that holds no fear for me, for I doubt I'll ever die. In a truly horrible way, I suppose I am immortal. But if the castle had crashed down upon me, I'd have been imprisoned there until the very stones should rot away with time and . . . "

Andrew made a croaking sound and swung his arm, as if to banish the demon forever from his sight.

"Leave me alone," he moaned. "Begone, foul demon, from me. I want no sight of you again."

"You do not even want my thanks?"

"Least of all I want your thanks. I want nothing of you. Forgetfulness is all I ask from you."

"But Andrew," said Conrad, walking up to him, "all this poor creature tries to do is express his gratitude. It is not mete you take such an attitude toward him. Demon he may be, but surely you must agree it is to his credit to feel gratitude. And he says right—you have a miracle of a staff. Why had you not told us before it held such puissant power?"

"Begone!" howled Andrew. "All of you begone. I want not to have you gaze upon me. I do not wish you to be the witnesses to my shame."

He turned about and started walking down the park. Conrad made as if to follow him, but Duncan signed him to desist.

"But there's something wrong with him," protested Conrad.

"In time he'll let us know," said Duncan. "Now all he wishes is to be left alone. Give the man some time."

Diane pulled herself away from Duncan and looked at him with level eyes.

"I'm all right now," she said. "It now is at an end. I know what happened. With the death of the final wizard, the enchantment now is ending."

The sun had been shining brightly, only halfway down the western sky, but now it seemed to be getting dark and the sun was gone.

The crashes from the castle were fewer, and in the deepening dark it no longer was a castle, but a heap of rubble, with only two towers still standing. A faint haze of white stone dust still could be seen hanging over the shattered masonry.

Conrad plucked at Duncan's sleeve. "Look, the standing stones," he said. Duncan looked toward the foot of the park and saw that the standing stones were no longer standing as they had been. Many of them were canted at an angle and the lintels had fallen off them.

He turned back to stare at the castle and in the moonlight (the moonlight!) he saw it as a mound—saw it as he first had seen it when they'd come out of the chasm with the windy voice in the upper reaches of its walls chanting, "Holy! Holy! Holy!"

"So it ends," said Diane, her voice small and soft. "The last wizard is dead and the enchantment gone. The castle a mound, as it has been for centuries."

"There are fires," said Conrad, and, indeed, there were, many little campfires gleaming in the dark on the hillside between the mounded castle and the hills.

"The Horde?" the demon asked. "Waiting there for us?"

"I think it unlikely," said Duncan. "The Horde would have no need of fires."

"More than likely," Conrad said, "it is Snoopy and his gang."

Duncan said to Scratch, "There's no need for you to stay. We placed no price upon the freeing of you. We have no claim upon you. If there's somewhere you want to go . . ."

"You mean you do not want me?"

"It's not that," said Duncan. "Should you want to stay with us, you're welcome."

"I thought, perhaps, the hermit. He is not happy with me. Although I cannot understand . . ."

"He's only dramatizing," said Conrad. "Showing off a little. He'll get over it."

"I have nowhere else to go," said Scratch. "I have no other friends. I can, mayhaps, be of some small service to you. I can fetch and carry."

"Stay, then," said Duncan. "Our company becomes more diverse as we proceed upon the journey. We can make room for a demon."

The ground beneath his feet, Duncan realized, no longer had the even smoothness of a lawn. It was rough and humpy, covered by wild grasses and low-growing ground cover that rasped, as he moved, against his boots. Somewhere, off in the distance, an

236

owl was hooting, and in the hills above the castle mound a wolf howled mournfully.

The moonlight was bright, the moon a night or two from fullness, and to the south he caught a glimpse of the river, shining like a mirror.

Saved again, he thought, jerked out of the jaws of disaster by the most unlikely of events, the castle's enchantment broken by the death of the last of those who had held it together. Cuthbert had committed suicide, whether intentionally or in a fit of insanity, there was no way of knowing. But it had been suicide. He had hurled himself from the balcony to the floor below.

Diane moved close to him and he put an arm about her, held her tightly. She leaned her head upon his shoulder.

"I am sorry," he said. "Sorry that it happened this way."

"I should have known," she said. "I should have realized that one day Cuthbert would be gone and the castle gone with him. I guess I did know, way back in my mind, but I didn't allow myself to even think of it."

He stood, holding her closely, trying to give her the little comfort that he could, looking out beyond the canted standing stones to the fires that blazed along the slope.

"There must be a lot of them out there," he said. "Snoopy told us he'd collect an army."

"Duncan," asked Diane, "have you seen Hubert anywhere?"

"No, I haven't. He must be around. He was out there just a while ago with Daniel and Beauty."

She shook her head against his shoulder. "I don't think so. I think I've lost him, too. He was one with the castle. He'd been here so long."

"As soon as it is light," said Duncan, "we'll look for him. He may wander in before the night is over."

"There's someone coming," Conrad said.

"I don't see anyone."

"Just the other side of the standing stones. Snoopy, more than likely. I think we should go out to meet

237

them. They won't want to pass beyond the stones. They know something's happened, but they can't know quite what."

"There's no danger now," said Diane.

"They'd not know that," Conrad said.

Conrad started down the slope and the rest of them followed. They passed between the standing stones and now it could be seen that a band of half a dozen little figures stood there waiting for them.

One of them stepped forward, and Snoopy's voice spoke to them in a scolding tone. "I warned you," he said. "Why can't you pay attention? I warned you to shun the castle mound."

25

Snoopy knelt on the ground beside the fire and swept an area clear of litter with his hand.

"Watch closely," he said. "I'll draw a map to show you the situation."

Duncan, standing to one side, bent over to stare at the smooth place on the ground, remembering how the goblin had drawn a map for them that first day they'd met in the chapel of the church.

Snoopy picked up a stick, stabbed a hole into the ground. "We are here," he said. He drew a ragged line along the map's northern edge. "There are the hills," he said. To the south he drew a snaky line. "That's the river." To the west he made a sweeping line, running south, then turning west and looping to the north.

"The fen," said Conrad.

Snoopy bobbed his head. "The fen."

He ran the stick along the line that represented the hills, curved it east, made a tight loop, and continued south of the snaky line that was the river.

"The Horde," he said, "is stretched out along that line. They have us hedged in north and east and south. Mostly hairless ones, with some of the other Horde members mixed in. They have us backed against the fen."

"Any chance of breaking through?" asked Conrad.

Snoopy shrugged. "We haven't tried. Anytime we want to, we can. We can filter out, a few here, a few there. They won't even try to stop us. We're not the ones they want. It is you they want. They lost you here; they know you couldn't have gotten out of this pocket. Perhaps they think you may be hiding in the mound. If that's the case, they tell themselves, the time will come when you must move out. They know you'll have to surface sometime and then they'll have you. And you can't filter out as we can."

"You mean," said Duncan, "that they've just been sitting there and you've been just sitting here?"

"Not entirely," said Snoopy. "Not us just sitting here, I mean. We've got dozens of magics set out for them, foolish little traps that will not really hold them, but that can hamper and confuse them, slow up any progress they might make. Some of the traps are mean as sin. They know they're there and don't want to tangle with them until they have to. If they start to move anywhere along their line, we'll know."

"You're sticking out your necks for us," said Duncan. "We had not intended that you should. Help us, of course. We were glad of the help you gave us. But we never expected this."

"As I told you," Snoopy said, "we can back off anytime we want to. There's no overwhelming danger for us. You're the ones who are in danger."

"How many of your people do you have here?"

"A few hundred. Maybe a thousand."

"I wouldn't have dreamed you could get together that many. You told us the Little Folk have small love of humans."

"I also told you, if you recall, that we have less love of the Horde. Once the word got started that here was a small band of humans marching into the face of the Horde, the news ran on all sides like wildfire. Day after day our people came flocking in, singly and in little bands. I will not try to deceive you. My people will not fight to the death for you. Actually they have

240

but little stomach for fighting. They've never been a warrior people. But they'll do what they can."

"For which," said Duncan, "they have our gratitude."

"If you'd only pay attention to what we tell you," said Snoopy, testily, "you would be better off. I told you, specifically, to stay away from the castle mound. Don't go near it, I told you. From what you've told me, it was only by incredible human luck that you won free of it." He shook his head. "I do not understand this human capacity for luck. Our people never have that kind of luck."

"We had but little choice," Conrad pointed out. "If we'd not sought refuge in the castle, we'd have been massacred."

"If you could have gotten across the river . . . "

"There was no possibility of that," said Duncan. "The Horde contingent would have run us down. They were re-forming even as we ran."

"From what we found on the field of battle," Snoopy said, "you wreaked a deal of damage on them."

"Only for a time," said Conrad. "We could not have held. Even as it stood, Diane and the Huntsman saved us. The unexpected violence of their attack . . . "

Snoopy nodded his head emphatically. "Yes, I know. I know."

"This time," Duncan promised, "we'll pay a closer attention to you. We'll follow your counsel. What do you suggest?"

The goblin rocked back and sat upon his heels. "Not a thing," he said. "I have no suggestions."

"You mean nothing at all? No plan at all?"

"I've thought it over well," said Snoopy. "So have the rest of us. We held a council on it. We spoke for long, we thought extremely hard. We have nothing to offer. We fear your goose is cooked."

Duncan turned his head to look at Conrad.

"We'll find a way, m'lord," said Conrad.

"Yes, of course," said Duncan, wondering as he said

241

it if this might be some ghastly joke the Little Folk
were playing on them. A joke or just the brutal truth?

"In the meantime," said Snoopy, "we'll do what we
can for you. We've already found a blanket for the
Lady Diane to shield her from the cold, for that flimsy
gown she wore was no protection whatsoever. Without the blanket she would have frozen before the
night was over."

Duncan straightened up from the position he had
assumed to study Snoopy's map. The fire was burning
high. Daniel and Beauty were standing companionably
together, heads hanging, across the fire from him.
Tiny lay curled up, half asleep, not far from Conrad.
Around the fire sat and crouched a number of the
Little People—goblins, gnomes, elves, sprites and pix-
ies—but the only one he recognized was Nan, the
banshee. She sat huddled close to the fire, her wings
wrapped neatly about her. Her eyes, so black they
seemed to be polished gems shining in the firelight,
peered out from beneath a shock of disordered, coal-
black hair.

He tried to read the faces, but could not make them
out. If there was friendliness, he failed to see it. Nor
did he see hatred. They simply sat there, staring, waiting. More than likely watching, he told himself, to
see what the humans were about to do.

"These lines that hem us in," Conrad said to
Snoopy. "Surely they cannot be made up of the entire
Horde."

"No," said Snoopy. "The main Horde is across the
fen, west of the fen, moving northward up its shore."

"Closing us in from the west."

"Perhaps not. Ghost has been keeping watch of
them."

"Ghost has been working with you? Where is he
now?"

Snoopy waved a hand. "Out there somewhere,
watching. He and Nan have been our eyes. They've
kept us well informed. I had hoped that there might be
other banshees. They would have been useful. But

Nan is the only one who came. You can't count on them. They're an ugly lot."

"You said that the main Horde may not be blocking us on the west. How is that?"

"Ghost thinks that tomorrow or the next day they'll move farther north, leaving the west bank, directly across from us, free. But why are you so interested? You could not hope to cross the fen. No one in his right mind would try to cross the fen. It is mud and swamp and water and shifting sands. There are places where there is no bottom to it, and you can't know, until you come upon them, where those pits may be. One spot may be solid footing, but the next one is muck that seizes you and holds you. Once he sets foot into the fen, one has no chance of coming out alive."

"We'll see," said Conrad. "If that's the only hope, we'll try it."

"If Hubert is still around," said Duncan, "Diane could go out on patrol with Ghost and Nan. That would give us one more set of eyes."

"Hubert?"

"Diane's griffin. He was not around after the castle fell."

"We'll look for him tomorrow," Snoopy said.

"I'm afraid," said Diane, "that he'll not be found."

"Nevertheless, we'll look," Snoopy promised. "We'll try to make up as well for all you lost."

"We lost everything," said Conrad. "Blankets, cooking utensils, food."

"It will be no problem," said the goblin. "Some of our people right now are working on a set of buckskins for milady. The gown she wears is useless for this sort of life."

"It's kind of you," said Diane. "One thing else I beg of you. A weapon."

"A weapon?"

"I lost my battle axe."

"I don't know about a battle axe," said Snoopy. "But perhaps something else—a blade, perhaps."

"A sword?"

243

"Yes, a sword. I think I know of one I can lay my hands upon."

"It would be gracious of you."

Snoopy grumbled. "I don't know what's the use of all of this. You're caught within a trap. To my way of thinking, there is no way to get out of it. When the Horde decides to move in, they'll squeeze you like a bunch of grapes."

Duncan looked around the campfire circle. All the Little People crouched there were bobbing their heads in agreement with Snoopy.

"I never saw such a bunch of quitters in all my life," said Conrad scornfully. "Hell, you're ready to give up without even trying. Why don't you all take off? We'll get along without you."

He turned and walked out into the darkness.

"You must excuse my friend," Duncan told those huddled at the fire. "He is not one to accept defeat with any grace."

Just beyond the fire a figure moved furtively out of the trees, stood there for a moment, then scuttled back again. Duncan hurried in his direction and stopped at the edge of the grove from which the figure had emerged.

He called softly. "Andrew, where are you? What is wrong with you?"

"What do you want with me?" asked Andrew in a pettish voice.

"I want to talk with you. You've been acting like a spoiled child. We have to get to the bottom of it."

Duncan walked a few steps into the grove. Andrew moved out from behind a tree. Duncan came up to him, stood facing him.

"Out with it," he said. "What is chewing on you?"

"You know what's chewing on me."

"Yes, I think I may. Let us talk about it."

The firelight did not reach the spot where they stood, and all that Duncan could see of the hermit was the white blob of his face, but in the faintness of the light he could read no expression.

"You remember that night we talked in my cell,"

said Andrew. "I told you how I had tried hard to be a hermit. About how I tried to read the early fathers of the Church. About how for hours on end I sat staring at a candle flame, and how none of it seemed to be of any use at all. I think I told you I was a failure as a hermit, that my early hope to be at least a slightly holy man had come to nothing. I probably told you that I was poor timber for a hermit, that I was not cut out to be a holy man. I am sure I told you all of this and perhaps a great deal more. For I was sore of heart and had been for some time. It is no easy matter for a man to spend the greater part of his life at his profession and in the end to know that he has failed, that all his time and effort have gone for naught, that all his hopes and dreams have vanished with the wind."

"Yes, I remember some of it," said Duncan. "I think, in telling it now, you have embellished it a bit. I think that having felt yourself a failure as a hermit, you then jumped at the slightest chance to become a soldier of the Lord. And if that is what you really are, although I'm not too sure of the proper definition, you have done rather well at it. You have no occasion to be out here now sulking in the brambles."

"But you do not understand."

"Please enlighten me," said Duncan drily.

"Don't you see that all the staring at the candles paid off in the end? The candle business, and perhaps some of the other things I did. Perhaps the fact that I willingly took the road as a soldier of the Lord. I'm not sure that I am a holy man—I would not be so brash as to claim I am. It might be sacrilegeous to even hint I am. But I do have powers I did not have before, powers that I had no suspicion that I had. My staff . . ."

"So that is it," said Duncan. "Your staff broke the demon's chain. Broke it after a full blow of my sword did nothing but strike a shower of sparks from it."

"You know, if you'll but admit it," Andrew said, "that the staff itself could not have fazed the chain. You know that the answer must be either that the staff itself suddenly has acquired a magic, or that the man who wielded it . . . "

"Yes, I do agree," said Duncan. "You must have certain holy powers for the staff to accomplish what it did. But, for God's sake, man, you should be glad you have."

"But don't you see?" wailed Andrew. "Don't you truly see my predicament?"

"I'm afraid this entire thing escapes me."

"The first manifestation of my power resulted in the freeing of a demon. Can't you understand how that tears me up inside? That I, a holy man, if a holy man I am, should use this power, for the first time, mind you, to free a mortal enemy of Holy Mother Church?"

"I don't know about that," said Duncan. "Scratch does not appear to be a bad sort. A demon, sure, but a most unsuccessful demon, unable to perform even the simple tasks of an apprentice imp. Because of that he ran away from Hell. And to demonstrate how little he was missed, what a poor stick of a demon he had turned out to be, the Devil and his minions did not turn a hand to haul him back to his tasks in Hell."

"You have tried to put a good face on it, my lord," said Andrew, "and I thank you for your consideration. You're an uncommon kindly man. But the fact remains that a black mark has been inscribed against me."

"There are no black marks," said Duncan with some irritation. "This is about as silly an idea as I have ever heard. There's no one sitting somewhere, inscribing black marks against you or anyone else."

"Upon my soul," said Andrew, "there is such a mark. No one else may know, but I know. There is no way for me to wipe it out. There is no eraser that will obliterate it. I'll carry it to my death and, mayhaps, beyond my death."

"Tell me one thing," said Duncan. "It has puzzled me. Why, seeing that the sword had failed, did you wield the staff? Did you have some sort of premonition, some sort of inner light . . . "

"No, I did not," said Andrew. "I was carried away,

is all. Somehow or other, I don't know why, I wanted to get into the act. You and Conrad were doing what you could and I felt, I suppose, although at the time I was not aware of it, that I should do what I could."

"You mean that when you dealt such a mighty blow with that staff of yours that you were trying to help the demon?"

"I don't know," said Andrew. "I never thought of it in that way. But I suppose I was trying to help him. And, realizing that, my soul is wrung the harder. Why should I try to help a demon? Why should I lift a finger for him?"

Duncan put out a hand and grasped the hermit's scrawny shoulder, squeezed it hard. "You are a good man, Andrew. Better than you know."

"How is that?" asked Andrew. "How does helping a demon make me a good man? I would have thought it made me worse. That's the entire trouble. I gave aid to a minion out of Hell, with the reek of sulphur still upon him."

"One," said Duncan, "that had forsaken Hell. That turned his back upon it, renouncing it. Perhaps for the wrong reasons, but still renouncing it. Even as you and I renounce it. He is on our side. Don't you understand that? He stands now with us. One with the mark of evil still upon him, but now he stands with us."

"I don't know," said Andrew doubtfully. "I'd have to think on that. I'd have to work it out."

"Come back to the fire with me," said Duncan. "Sit by the fire and be comfortable while you work at it. Get some warmth into those shivering bones of yours, some food into your belly."

"Come to think of it," said Andrew, "I am hungry. Meg was cooking up a mess of sauerkraut and pig's knuckles. I could taste them, just thinking of them. It has been years since I have eaten kraut and knuckles."

"The Little Folk can't offer you kraut and knuckles, but there is a venison stew that is monstrous good. There's enough of it left, I'm sure, to more than fill your gut."

247

"If you think it would be all right," said Andrew. "If they'd make room for me."

"They'll welcome you," Duncan assured him. "They've been asking after you." Which was not exactly true, but it was a small untruth and it could do no harm. "So come along." Duncan put an arm around the hermit's shoulder and together they walked back to the fire.

"I'm not yet clear in mind," warned Andrew, stubborn to the last. "There is much to puzzle out."

"Take your time," said Duncan. "You'll get it straightened out. You'll have the time to mull it over."

Duncan escorted him across the cleared area around the fire at which he'd talked with Snoopy. Diane and Nan were sitting together and he took him over to them.

"Here's a hungry man," he said to Nan. "Could there still remain a bowl of stew?"

"More than a bowl," said the banshee. "More than even he can eat, hungry as he looks." She said to Andrew, "Sit down close to the blaze. I will get it for you."

"Thank you, ma'am," said Andrew.

Duncan swung about and looked for Conrad, but was unable to locate him. Nor could he find Snoopy among the scattered Little People.

The moon had moved well up in the sky. It must be almost midnight, Duncan told himself. Within a short time all of them should be settling down to get some sleep, for they'd need to be up by dawn. What they'd do he had no idea, but as quickly as possible they had to have a course of action planned. Conrad, he thought, might have turned up some new piece of information, and it was important that he see him soon.

It was just possible that Conrad had wandered over to another fire. Purposefully he set out for the nearest one. He had gone only a couple of hundred feet or so when someone hissed at him from the darkness of a clump of bushes. Swiftly he swung around, his hand going to the sword hilt.

"Who's there?" he challenged. "Show yourself."

248

A deeper shadow detached itself from the bushes. Moonlight shimmered on the crumpled horn.

"Scratch, what are you doing here?" Duncan asked.

"Waiting for you," the demon said. "I have a thing to tell you. Quietly. Not too loud. Squat down so we can talk."

Duncan squatted to face the dumpy little figure. The demon leaned forward painfully, head thrust forward by the hump upon his back.

"I have been listening," he said. "You are in trouble."

"It's nothing new," Duncan told him. "We always are in trouble."

"But this time facing powerful forces on all sides of you."

"That is true."

"No way to escape?"

"So the Little People tell us. We do not take their word entirely."

"There is a way across the fen," said Scratch.

What was going on? What was Scratch attempting to do here? Shut up in the castle for centuries, how would he know about the fen?

"You do not believe me," said the demon.

"It's hard to. How could you know?"

"I told you once that someday I would tell you of my adventures. We never got around to it."

"You did tell me that. I'd be delighted to hear the tale you have to tell. But not now. I'm looking for Conrad."

"Not all of it now," said Scratch. "Just a part of it. You must know that once I fled from Hell the word got around in human circles there was a demon loose —a fugitive demon from whom the protection of Old Scratch had been withdrawn, fair game for anyone who could lay hands upon him. I was hunted mercilessly.

"That's how I came to know about the fen. At this very place, the south end of the fen, I hid for several years; until I felt that I was safe, that everyone had forgotten me, that the trail had grown cold and the

249

hunt been given up. So I came out of the fen and, wouldn't you know it, almost immediately was gobbled up."

"But the fen is death," said Duncan. "Or so we have been told."

"If one knows the way . . . "

"And you know the way?"

"A water sprite showed me. A grumpy little sprite, but he took pity on me. One must be careful, but it can be done. There are certain landmarks . . . "

"It's been a long time since you've been in the fen. Landmarks can change."

"Not these. There are certain islands."

"Islands change. They can shift or sink."

"The hills come down to the fen and stop. But a part of them, very ancient parts of them, still remain, much worn down and lower than the hills. These are the islands that I speak of. They stand solid through the ages. All rock, they cannot sink. Rock ledges run underwater between them, connecting them. The ledges are what you follow to get across the fen. They are covered by water and just by looking, you cannot see them. One must know."

"Deep water?"

"Up to my neck in places. No deeper."

"All the way across? To the western shore?"

"That is right, my lord. A hidden ridge of rock, a part of the ancient hills, but there are tricky places."

"You'd recognize the tricky places?"

"I am sure I can. I have a good memory."

"You would lead us, show us the way?"

"Honored sir," said Scratch, "I owe you a debt I had never hoped I could repay. Showing you across the fen would be only partial payment. But if you would accept . . . "

"We do accept," said Duncan. "If events so order themselves . . . "

"Events?"

"It may be the main Horde of Harriers will block our way. They are moving up the west bank of the fen. If they should continue moving north, as they were when last seen, then, with your help, we can cross the fen and be clear of them."

"There is one thing else."

"Yes?"

"At the western edge of the fen stands a massive island, much larger than the others. It is guarded by dragons."

"Why dragons?"

"The island," said Scratch, "is a wailing place. The Place of Wailing for the World."

26

Diane, Meg, and Nan were sitting together by the fire, a little apart from the others, when Duncan returned, trailed by the limping, lurching Scratch. A short distance off, Andrew was stretched out on the ground, covered by a sheepskin, fast asleep and snoring. A long, slender fold of black velvet lay on Diane's lap.

Meg cackled at Duncan. "You should see what Diane has. You should see what Snoopy gave her."

She gestured at the fold of velvet.

Duncan turned to look at Diane. Her eyes were sparkling in the firelight and she smiled at him. Carefully she unfolded the velvet to reveal what lay within it.

The naked blade shone with a hundred fiery highlights and a nest of inset jewels glinted in the hilt.

"I told him," she said, "that it was too magnificent for me, but he insisted that I take it."

"It is splendid," Duncan said.

"The goblins have guarded it for years," said Nan, "as a sacred treasure. Never, in their wildest dreams, did they ever think they'd find a human they would want to give it to." She shrugged. "Of course it is far too massive for a goblin or any other of our kind to ever think of wielding."

252

Duncan went down on his knees in front of Diane, reached out to touch the blade.

"May I?" he asked.

She nodded at him.

The steel beneath his fingers was cold and smooth. He ran his fingers along its length in something that was close to a caress.

"Duncan," Diane said in a hushed voice, "Duncan, I'm afraid."

"Afraid?"

"Afraid I know what it is. Snoopy didn't tell me."

"Then," said Duncan, "I don't think you should ask."

He picked up one end of the velvet and folded it back to cover the sword.

"Cover it," he said. "It is a precious thing. It should not be exposed to the damp night air. Snug it safe and tight."

He said to Meg, "There is something I should ask you. Some days ago you told us about the wailing for the world. You told us very little. Can you tell us more of it?"

"No more than I told you then, my lord. We spoke of it when we heard the keening from the fen."

"You said there were several such wailing places, probably widely separated. You seemed to think one of the wailing places was located in the fen."

"So it has been told."

"Who is it that does the wailing?"

"Women, my lord. Who else would wail in this world of ours? It is the women who have cause for wailing."

"Do you have a name for these wailing women?"

Meg wrinkled up her face, trying to remember. "I believe there is a name for them, my lord, but I don't think I've ever heard it."

"And you," Duncan said to Nan. "You banshees are wailers."

"Wailers, yes," said Nan, "but not for the entire world. We have trouble enough to wail for those who need it most."

253

"Perhaps the entire world stands in need of wailing, of a crying out against its misery."

"You may be right," the banshee told him, "but we wail at home, on the land we know, for the widow left alone, for the hungry children, for the needy old, for those bereft by death. There is so much to wail over that we can take care of only those we know. We crouch outside the lonely cottage that is overrun by grief and need and we cry out against those who have occasioned the grief and need and we . . ."

"Yes, I understand," said Duncan. "You know nothing of the wailing for the world?"

"Only what the witch has told you."

A soft step sounded behind Duncan, someone moving lightly.

"What is this about the wailing?" Snoopy asked.

Duncan swiveled around to face the approaching goblin. "The demon says there is a wailing in the fen."

"The demon's right," the goblin said. "I have heard it often. But what has that to do with us?"

"Scratch tells me the fen can be crossed. He claims he knows the way."

Snoopy puckered up his face. "I doubt that," he said. "It has always been told the fen is impassable."

"But you do not know for sure?"

"I do not know for sure. No one has ever been fool enough to try. No one ever puts a boat upon its waters, for there are lurking dangers there that rise up to seize one."

"Then," said Duncan, "look upon a fool. I am about to try."

"You'll be swallowed up," said Snoopy.

"We'll be swallowed up in any case. You say the Horde pens us in. That leaves the fen the only way to go."

"With the main body of the Horde on the western shore?"

"You told me Ghost had reported they were moving north. If they continue to move north, if they move far enough to the north, the way will be clear."

254

"The ones surrounding us are beginning to move in," said Snoopy. "A closing of the net. There is some movement from the east. They've tripped some of our magic traps."

"Then all the more reason," said Duncan, "for trying the fen. And as quickly as we can."

"If the forces surrounding us know that you are here, and most certainly they must for otherwise there would be no movement, then surely the main body on the fen's western bank also must know."

"But the Horde on the western bank can have no idea we will try to cross the fen."

Snoopy threw up his hands in disgust. "Go on," he growled. "Do what you wish. You will in any case. You do not listen to me. You have never listened to me."

"I'm sorry," Duncan said. "You offer no alternatives. The fen does offer an alternative. I have decided I will go. The demon will go with me to point the way. Conrad, I am sure, will come along."

"And so will I," Diane said softly. She said to Snoopy, "You spoke of buckskins for me. When will they be ready? I can not essay the fen in such dress as this."

"By first morning light," said Snoopy. "Our people have been working all the night."

"We can't leave by morning light," said Duncan, "although I would like to. Before we leave a search for the griffin must be made."

"There has been searching in the night," said Snoopy. "He has not been found. At the first hint of dawn the area will be swept again. We have slight hope of finding him. He was tied too closely for too long to the wizards and the castle. He was old and worn out with long service and may not have wished to survive the castle. It is unlikely he would have survived with the final wizard gone. Milady, I think, shares our beliefs."

"Yes, I do," said Diane. "But without Hubert I still will go."

"You could ride Daniel," Duncan said.

"No. Daniel is your horse. He's too accomplished a war-horse to be hindered by a rider save that he and the rider fight as one. In all the encounters on this journey you have never ridden him. The two of you have fought side by side. That is as it should be."

"I will go with you," said Nan. "The fen holds no terrors for me, since I can fly above it, although haltingly and with no grace at all, flapping like a crow. Perhaps I can be of some help in spying out the land."

"And since I started this adventure with you," Snoopy said, "you cannot leave me out."

"There is no need," said Duncan. "You have little faith in what is proposed and certainly you should stay here to direct your people."

"There is no need of my direction," Snoopy told him. "In truth, I never have directed them. I simply sent out a call for their gathering. And they came, as if to a picnic, for the adventure they might find. But they are not ones who will face up to great danger. Rather, being wise people, all of them, they run from danger. To tell you the honest truth, they're beginning to scatter now. By the time you are gone, they will be as well."

"Then, in good common sense, why don't you scatter with them? We thank you for the thought of going with us, but it is beyond . . . "

Snoopy broke in with a fine display of rage. "You would deprive me of a feat of which I can talk for years, with all the others of them sitting about to listen intent on every word as it drops from off my lips? The life of the Little Folk, as you are wont to call us in your patronizing manner, is a boring life. We have but few occasions to perform feats of derring-do. Few of us ever have the chance of becoming even minor heroes. It was different in those days before you humans came and pushed us off our land. The land was then our own and we played out upon it our little dramas and our silly comedies, but now we can do none of this for we have not the room, and halfway through are certain to run into some stupid, loutish human who

256

reminds us of our present poor estate and thereby robs us of what little fun we're having."

"Well, all right, then," said Duncan, "if that's the way it is. We'll value your company. Although I must warn you that somewhere along the way we may meet with dragons."

"I give that for dragons," said Snoopy, snapping his fingers.

Twigs snapped in the darkness and Conrad came blundering into the firelit circle. He made a thumb, pointing into the air above him.

"See who I've found," he said.

They all looked up and saw that it was Ghost, who floated down to mingle with them.

"I had given you up, my lord," he said to Duncan. "I searched and searched for you, but there wasn't any trace. But even as I searched I held true to the task I had been assigned. I watched the Horde, in its many various parts, and lacking anyone to whom I could report, since you were gone, I passed my knowledge on to Snoopy. He was as puzzled as I was as to what could have happened to you, but he had suspicions that your disappearance had something to do with the castle mound and this has now been confirmed by Conrad, whom I was delighted to stumble on just a while ago and . . ."

"Hold up," said Duncan, "hold up. There's word I want from you."

"And I, my lord, have word to give you. But first I must ask, for mine own peace of mind, if you still intend, despite the many interruptions, to continue on to Oxenford. I still retain the hope of getting there for, as you know, I have many troublesome questions to ask the wise ones there. Troublesome questions for me, perhaps, but I hope not for them. It is my most earnest dream they can give me answers that will set me more at ease."

"Yes," said Duncan, "we do intend to continue on to Oxenford. But now my question. What about that part of the Horde traveling up the west bank of the fen?"

"They continue north," said Ghost. "They've picked up speed. They are traveling faster now."

"And show no sign of stopping?"

"There is no sign of their slackening their pace. They continue lunging onward."

"That settles it," said Duncan, with some satisfaction. "We start tomorrow, as soon as we are able."

27

At the first paling of the eastern sky, they searched for Hubert. They swept the grounds surrounding the castle mound and the stretch of river meadows below and to every side the castle without finding a trace of the griffin. There were, now, fewer of the Little People than there had been the night before, but those who were left aided in the search with a will. Once the search was done, they disappeared, drifting off with no one able to mark their going. All that remained to show they had ever been there were a dozen smoldering, dying campfires spread out on the slope above the castle mound.

Duncan and Conrad pulled their small force together and started out, heading for the fen. To the north loomed the great mass of the hill through which Duncan and his band had passed, its western end cut off sharply where it met the fen. To the south the river wound lazily through the marshy meadows.

The band traveled spread out now rather than in a column, through open land broken here and there by small groves of trees and sparse woodland, the space between covered by low ground cover and patches of hazel. The morning, which had dawned clear and bright, became dismal as heavy clouds moved in from

259

the west, not covering the sun, but dimming it so that it became little more than a pale circle of light.

Less than an hour after starting, they heard the first faint sound of wailing. Subdued by distance, it still was clear, a far lament of loneliness with an overtone of hopelessness, as if the cause of wailing would never go away, but would endure forever.

Walking beside Duncan, Diane shivered at the sound of it.

"It goes through one," she said. "It cuts me like a knife."

"You've never heard it before?" he asked.

"Yes, of course, at times. But from far off and I paid no attention to it. There are always funny noises coming off the fen. I had no idea what it was and . . ."

"But the wizards would have known."

"Knowing, they might not have told me. Except when I went to search for Wulfert, I seldom left the castle. In many ways, although I was not aware of it, I lived a protected life."

"Protected? You, a warrior maid . . . "

"Don't mistake me," she said. "I am no forlorn waif, no damsel in distress. I rode on certain forays and I learned the art of arms. And that reminds me, there's something I must thank you for. You believed with me in the blade."

She carried it naked in her hand, for there was no scabbard for it. She cut a small figure with it and it flashed even in the faint sunlight.

"It is a good piece of steel," he said.

"And that is all?"

"Snoopy told you nothing. You should ask no further."

"But there was a sword lost long ago and . . . "

"There have been many swords and many of them lost."

"All right," she said. "That's the way we leave it?"

"I think it's for the best," said Duncan.

They had been breasting the uplift of a long and gentle swale and now they came to the top of it, all of them bunched together and staring toward the west,

260

where they could see the thin faint blueness of the fen. At the bottom of the uplift lay a long thin strip of forest lying between them and the fen, running from the cut-off mass of the northern range of hills as far south as they could see.

Scratch edged up to Duncan, tugging at his jacket for attention.

"Scratch, what do you want?" asked Duncan.

"The woods."

"What about the woods?"

"It wasn't there before. I remember from the time that I was here. There wasn't any woods. The land ran smooth down to the fen."

"But that was long ago," said Conrad. "A long, long time ago."

"Several centuries," said Diane. "He's been chained in the castle for that long."

"In several centuries," said Duncan, "a woods could have grown up."

"Or he remembers incorrectly," said Conrad.

Andrew growled at them, thumping his staff on the ground. "Pay no attention," he said, "to that imp of Satan. He is a troublemaker."

"Meg," asked Duncan, "do you know about this woods?"

"How could I?" asked the witch. "I've not been here before."

"It looks all right to me," said Conrad, "and I always am the first to sniff out trouble. Just an ordinary woods."

"I can detect nothing wrong with it," said Snoopy.

"I tell you," shrilled Scratch, "it was not there before."

"We'll proceed cautiously," said Conrad. "We'll keep on the watch. To get to the fen, it is quite clear that we must make our way through the woods."

Duncan looked down at Scratch, who still was standing close beside him, still with a hand upon the jacket as if he meant to tug it once again. In the other hand he held a long-handled trident, its three tines barbed and sharp.

"Where did you get that?" asked Duncan.

"I gave it to him," said Snoopy. "It belonged to a goblin that I know, but it is too heavy and awkward for such as we to wield."

"Giving it to me," said Scratch, "he remarked that it was appropriate to me."

"Appropriate?"

"Why, certainly," said Snoopy. "You are not up, my lord, on your theology."

"What has all of this got to do with my theology?" asked Duncan.

"I may be wrong," Snoopy told him, "but I thought it was an old tradition. I happened, not too long ago, upon a scroll that I supposed, from what I saw of it, must have recorded Bible stories. I did not take the time to puzzle out any of the barbarity of your written language, but I did look at the pictures. Among them I found a drawing, rather crudely done, showing demons, such as this friend of ours, pitchforking a number of disconsolate humans into the flames of Hell. The instruments the demons used to do the forking very much resembled this trident that our present demon holds. That is all I meant when I suggested that such a weapon might be appropriate to him."

Duncan grunted. "Let's be on our way," he said.

A faint path, seemingly one that was not often traveled, angled down the gentle slope toward the woods. From a short distance off the edge of the woods seemed quite ordinary. It seemed in no way different from any other patch of woodland. The trees were ancient, with a hoary look about them, thick through at the butt, quickly branching to form a heavy tangle of interlocking branches. The faint pathway they had been following continued on into the thickness of the woods, providing enough clearance through the tangle for a man to follow it with ease.

"You're quite certain," Duncan asked Scratch, "that this woods was not here when you last saw this place? Can you be absolutely sure this is the place you saw?"

Scratch lifted his clubfoot and scratched the other leg with the misshapen hoof.

"I am fairly certain sure," he said. "I doubt I could be mistaken."

"In any case," Conrad pointed out, "we shall have to cross it if we are to reach the fen."

"That is true," said Duncan. "Conrad, I think you and Tiny should take the point, as you always do. The narrowness of the path means that we must go in single file. Diane and I will guard the rear. Don't let Tiny get too far ahead of you."

Meg, who had been riding Daniel, slipped off his back.

"You'd better get back on," said Conrad. "We'll be moving out."

"All the more reason why I should not be in the way of a fighting horse," said Meg. "I can hobble by myself through this small patch of woods."

"I'll walk beside her," said Andrew, "to help her on her way."

"Why, thank you, kind sir," said Meg. "It is not often that an old bag such as I has offer of an escort."

"Meg," asked Duncan, "is there something wrong? You would not encumber Daniel, you tell us. Is it that . . ."

The witch shook her head. "Nothing wrong at all, my lord. But these woods are close quarters."

Duncan made a sign to Conrad, who moved out, walking down the path, with Tiny stalking close ahead of him. The others fell into line. Diane and Duncan brought up the rear, with the crippled demon limping painfully ahead of them, using the reversed trident as a staff to help himself along.

The woods held a somber sense, such as one would expect of a woods in autumn, the sense of the dying, drifting leaf, of the frost-shriveling of the little plants that grew on the forest floor. But otherwise there seemed to be nothing and that, thought Duncan, in itself was not wrong, for that was the way that it should be. Most of the trees were oaks, although there were other scattered kinds. The path, he told himself, was the sort of trail that deer, over the years, might beat out for themselves, going in single file, stepping in one another's tracks. A hush hung over everything. Not even a leaf was rustling and that, Duncan thought, was strange, for there seldom was a time when leaves did not do some rustling. Even on the calmest day, with no wind at all, in an utter quietness, somewhere in a woods a leaf would rustle for no apparent reason. Fallen leaves, lying on the path, muffled their footfalls and no one spoke a word. The hush of the woods had imposed a hush on the people who entered it.

As is the case with most woodland trails, the path was a crooked one. It dodged between trees, it wound around a fallen, moldering forest giant, it avoided lichen-covered boulders, it clung to the slightly higher ground, skirting the small wet areas that lay on the forest floor—and in doing all of this it wound a twisted way.

Duncan, bringing up the rear, with Diane just ahead of him and ahead of her the limping, lurching demon, stopped and turned halfway around to view the path behind him. For, unaccountably, he felt an itching between his shoulder blades, the sort of feeling a receptive man might have from something watching him. But there was nothing. The path, the little that he could see of it, was empty, and there was no sign that any other might be near.

The feeling, he told himself, came about from the almost certain knowledge that in a very little time the entire area held by the Little Folk would be swarming with the hairless ones and other members of the Horde, closing in to make their kill. The Little Folk, more than likely, by now had cleared the area. They had started sifting out before the night was over and by the time he and his band had left, there had been none about—none but Snoopy, who now was marching up there in front with Conrad, and Nan, who presumably was flying about to spy out whatever might be happening. The magic traps the Little Folk had set out might impede the Horde for a time, but perhaps for only a few hours at the best. The traps, wicked and mean as some of them might be, could not stand for long against the more powerful and subtle magic of the

Horde. In the final reckoning, all the traps would be little more than minor nuisances.

He put his hand to his belt pouch, felt the small, round hardness of Wulfert's talisman, the yielding softness of the manuscript, listening to its crackling rustle as he pressed his fingers to it.

If only Scratch should be right, he told himself—if they could cross the fen, if the main body of the Horde kept moving northward up the west margin of the fen —then they still would have a chance. With the south open for the run to Oxenford, there still would be a chance to carry out the mission. It was the only chance they had, he reminded himself. There were no alternatives. There were no choices, no decisions to be made.

With one last look down the empty path behind him, he turned about and hurried to catch up with Diane. As he hurried along the path, he caught the first faint sound of wailing he had heard since they'd entered the woods. It seemed farther off than ever, a mere whisper of a sound, muted and broken up by the denseness of the trees.

Suddenly, ahead of him, the heavy growth lessened, and he stepped out into a small clearing, an almost circular clearing, as if in some time long past a woodsman had chopped down the trees and hauled off the logs to make a cleared circle in the forest.

The rest of the band had stopped and were clustered in the center of the clearing. As Duncan stepped smartly forward to join them, he glanced around and it seemed that the circle was hemmed in by larger and thicker trees than they had passed through heretofore. The trunks of the trees were huge and they grew almost cheek by jowl; their massive interlocking branches, springing from the trunks only a few feet above the ground, formed an impenetrable hedge that held them locked inside the circle.

He hurried up to Conrad. "What are we stopping for?" he asked. "Why don't you continue on? We have to reach the fen."

"There is no path," said Conrad. "A path comes into the clearing, but there is none leading out."

"And now," said Andrew, thumping his staff upon the ground with an exasperation summoned up to mask his fear, "there's none coming in, as well."

Duncan spun around and looked back the way he'd come and saw that Andrew was right. The trees, somehow, had moved in and closed together to block out the path they had been following.

"With a great deal of work," said Conrad, "we could wriggle our way through. But it would be difficult for Daniel. He can't get down on his hands and knees and crawl as can the rest of us. We'll have to do some chopping to make a way for him. Even without the work of chopping, progress will be slow."

Meg came hobbling up. "It's witchery," she said, "and a most convincing witchery. Had it been otherwise than cunning, I would have smelled it out."

Snoopy jumped up and down in rage, flapping his arms. "It's them double-dipped-in-damnation gnomes," he howled. "I told them and told them no traps need be laid against the fen, for none of the Horde was there. Concentrate, I told them, on that stretch of ground north of the river meadow. But they did not listen. Gnomes are arrogant and they never listen. They laid this intricate trap to snare the Horde and now we're caught instead. Now the gnomes are gone, scattered like all the rest of them, and they cannot be gotten to spring and free the trap."

"You are sure of that?" asked Duncan.

"Sure of it I am."

"How can you be so sure?"

"Because I know the gnomes. Cross-grained folk they are. And skilled in very complex magic. No other of our people could do the kind of work required to lay out a belt of forest and to . . . "

The sound of flapping wings cut him short and everyone looked up to see what was going on. It was Nan, coming down in an awkward plunge, wings windmilling desperately to check her speed and to maintain her balance. She landed sprawling, falling forward on her face. Once on her feet, she lurched forward to meet them.

"The Horde is coming in!" she shrilled. "The Horde is on the way! They're pouring down the hill, moving toward the woods."

"Now what do we do?" yapped Andrew. "What do we do now?"

"We quit our blubbering," said Conrad gruffly, "and remember we are soldiers of the Lord."

"I'm no soldier of the Lord," yelled Scratch, "but if it comes to fighting, I'll fight by the side of those who are. Given the necessity, I can be a very dirty fighter."

"I just bet you can," said Meg.

"Let us hope," said Duncan, "that the magic of the gnomes can work as effectively against the Horde as it seems to work with us and . . . "

He stopped in mid-sentence, staring at the trees.

"My God," he whispered, "will you look at that!"

There had been, he remembered, many years ago, a roving artist who had stopped at Standish House for a bite of food and a night of shelter and wound up staying on for months, finally ending up at the abbey, where he undoubtedly still was, working at the scriptorium, drawing sketches and doing miniature paintings and other nonsensical conceits with which the monks fancied up their manuscripts and scrolls. As a boy, Duncan recalled, he had spent much time with the artist, whose name he had forgotten after all these years, hanging over the little desk on which he worked, watching in fascination the magic lines of his pencil sketching scenes and people unlike anyplace or anyone he had ever seen before. The sketch that had intrigued him the most, which the artist had given him, had depicted a group of trees that had somehow turned into rather frightening people—trees with faces that had only a rough, but frightening, equivalence to the faces of people, their limbs becoming arms, their branches many-fingered grasping hands. Trees turned into monsters.

And now here, in this magic forest of the gnomes, the trees were assuming the guise of monsters just as those trees the artist sketched had. The trunks bore flabby faces: loose-lipped, ravening mouths, most of them toothless, although a few of them had fangs; bulbous, obscene noses sprawling over half the face; ghoulish, spiteful eyes. Now there was a rustling of leaves as the limbs and branches of the trees became the arms and hands of monsters, some with fingers, some with claws, some with tentacles, and all of them waving in a frenzy of sudden energy, reaching out to grasp one, to claw one to his death.

They were hemmed in by monsters that were trees, or trees that were trying to be monsters.

"Them stinking gnomes," raged Snoopy, "they have no decency at all. This magic of theirs cannot distinguish between friend and foe."

From far away, apparently from the edge of the woods, back toward the slope they had descended, came muffled screaming.

"That's the hairless ones," said Conrad. "They have reached the woods and met the trees."

"Or the trees," said Andrew. "The hairless ones did not strike me as ones who would do much screaming."

"Meg, can you do anything?" Duncan shouted at the witch. "Do you have the spells to overcome this magic?"

Andrew strode forward toward the trees opposite their entry point into the circle, brandishing his staff at them and intoning Latin phrases, the most atrocious Latin, Duncan told himself, that he had ever heard.

"Shut up!" Duncan yelled at him, and to Meg, he said, "Is there any way that you can help?"

"I can but try," Meg told him. "As I've explained before, my powers are very feeble. My witchery trappings all were taken from me."

"Yes, I know," said Duncan. "You have told us that. All the bat's blood, all the polecat dung, all the rest of it. But there must lie within you a power that does not need these trappings."

He yelled at Andrew, "Desist from that silly blather. This is not a place where churchly mouthings will do us any good."

268

Meg said in a small voice, "Perhaps the two of us together?"

A faint tendril of fog came drifting through the trees at that point where they had entered the clearing.

Conrad came up to stand beside Duncan and Diane. "That fog," he said, "is the fog of the Horde. You remember, when we fought before the castle mound. It has the same smell as it had then. They came at us in a rolling bank of fog and . . . "

"I don't remember any smell," said Duncan.

"Well, I do," said Conrad. "I have a sharper nose than you have."

"The Horde is trying to get through the woods," said Diane. "They may be held up for a while, but perhaps not for long. Snoopy told us none of the magic traps could really stop the Horde."

Snoopy said, "This one will hold a little longer than the others. Those crazy gnomes really put their heart into this one. All their efforts put the one place it wasn't needed. If it hadn't been for them, we would have reached the fen by now."

"Maybe Meg can witch a path for us," said Conrad.

"Not with Andrew bellowing out that obnoxious Latin," said Duncan. "We'll have to shut him up."

Something very violent was taking place within that section of the woods through which they'd come. The trees were shaking furiously, their branches whipping all about. The mouths in the trunks of the trees were opened wide as if to scream, but no sound came out, although there were other sounds—the crunch and swish of lashing branches, sudden screams and grunts.

"It's the hairless ones," said Conrad. "They are breaking through."

He shifted the club in his hand and took a quick step forward.

Over the top of the trees came a torn black rug, flapping furiously, plopping down toward them. Twin heads reached out for them, needle teeth rimming the open mouth, wings with hooked claws slashing at the air.

"Look out!" howled Conrad.

269

Diane stepped swiftly to one side as the ragged rug hovered just above her. Her sword flashed high and came down like a blade of light. It struck the flapping wing and sheared it off. The creature went lopsided, skidding through the air. Duncan's sword swung up to meet it. One of the heads came off and the remainder of the already shorn wing. The creature flopped to the ground. Conrad brought his club down on the remaining head and the thing skittered about the clearing, twisting and turning, hopping in the air and somersaulting like a chicken with its head lopped off.

Duncan saw that his blade was smeared with the sticky black ichor he had seen when he'd killed the squalling, flapping thing in the fight at the castle mound.

He threw a quick glance skyward and saw that another of the flying rugs had cleared the trees and hung above the clearing, but even as he saw it the rug veered off, heading back across the trees.

Meg and Andrew, he saw, were standing side by side, facing the opposite side of the clearing, Andrew furiously shaking his staff and bawling out his Latin, while Meg waved her arms in cabalistic gestures and cried out a high sing-song of words so twisted and kinky that they seemed to Duncan, listening to them, to be beyond the range of human tongue.

More fog was rolling into the clearing. Between the trees, low down against the ground, came a pointed head with a cruel beak, sinuous, like a snake, scuttling forward on little lizard's feet. The head reared up, surging from side to side, as if seeking, rearing itself to strike. Diane leaped forward and the glistening blade came down in a long, smooth swing. The beaked head popped into the air, fell to the ground and bounced, a flood of thick, blackish ichor pouring in a flood from the severed neck. But the long, twisting, snakelike body, propelled by its many little feet, kept on coming out. As its forepart fell to the ground, the rest of it, emerging from the trees, piled upon itself.

The trees were whipping violently, as if beaten by a vicious wind, the mouths still open and working in their silent screaming, the branches swaying furiously, the hands making grasping motions. At times screams, often cut off abruptly, sounded from the depths of the woods. One giant branch, with a dozen hands attached, heaved into the air. Grasped by the hands was the twisting, broken body of a hairless one. Another hairless one staggered through the trees, going to its knees, then rising swiftly, shuffling toward them, a club gripped in its hand.

Duncan sprang forward to meet it, but Conrad was there before him. Before the hairless one could lift its club, Conrad aimed a blow at it. The sound of a crunching skull sounded distinctly and the hairless one staggered forward, falling, but behind it was another one and another and another. The hairless ones had broken through the woods and were coming with a rush.

Duncan saw a lifted arm, with a club poised in its fist, and swung his blade in instinctive defense. The arm came off and the falling club struck his left shoulder a glancing blow. Out of the corner of his eye he saw Diane to one side and slightly behind him, her sword flashing as it struck. A hairless one came at him and he skipped aside to dodge the swinging club, caught the charging enemy in the throat with his sword point. But there was still another one behind the one that he had stabbed, and this time, he knew, the club would find its mark before he could lift his blade. And even as he thought this, two plunging, striking hoofs came across his shoulder, one of them striking the hairless one squarely in the face. Daniel's body crashed into Duncan and he went down on hands and knees, with the great horse's body looming over him, snorting with rage, striking with his hooves and teeth.

Conrad, he saw, also was on the ground, crawling, with his right arm dangling limply. Standing on spraddled legs above him was a hairless one, with the club already lifted and starting to come down. Duncan lunged upright, hurling himself forward, but he knew he'd be too late. Before he could intervene, the lifted

271

club would come thudding down on Conrad's head. Out of nowhere, a dark, stout body was suddenly between Conrad and the hairless one, the trident thrusting upward, propelled by both hands and with all the power in Scratch's muscular body. The tines caught the hairless one squarely in the throat, just below the chin, driving deep, the full length of the tines.

A bellow rang out—Andrew's voice—"A path! We have got a path!"

Duncan now was on his feet, his attention divided between Andrew's sudden bellow and the harpooned hairless one, which slowly tipped backward, its club fallen from its hand, as Scratch still clutched the trident's shaft, tugging furiously to disengage the tines. Just beyond Conrad, Tiny leaped from the body of a hairless one that he had downed, crouching for a new attack.

For the moment, it seemed, there was nothing to attack. There were no more hairless ones. Rolling fog still poured from out the forest and the trees still were thrashing furiously, but the small band of hairless ones who had broken through now were lying on the ground, either dead or dying.

Andrew still continued shouting, "We have a path! We have a path!"

"Head for that path," yelled Duncan. "All of you. Get out of here."

He took a quick stride to one side, grasped Conrad around his massive body and heaved him to his feet. Even as Duncan lifted him, the big man still was scrambling wildly to retrieve his fallen club. He grasped it in his left hand and staggered forward, his right arm still dangling at his side. By main strength, Duncan awkwardly got him turned around.

"Andrew has a path," he told him. "Get out there and follow it."

Tiny came up, his face wrinkled in doggish worry. He pushed himself close against the tottering Conrad, trying to support him.

Scratch was there, too, dragging the trident with one hand, wedging himself between Tiny and Conrad.

"Here," he said to Conrad, "lean upon my shoulder."

Duncan reached out and took the club from Conrad's hand.

"I'll carry this," he said. "Lean on the demon. He is stout and strong. He can give you help."

"I need no help," growled Conrad.

"The hell you don't," said Duncan.

Conrad put his left hand on Scratch's shoulder, started hobbling away.

Duncan swung around. Diane, he saw, had hold of Daniel's forelock, was leading the big horse across the clearing, toward Andrew's path. Off to one side, Snoopy was racing toward the path, driving Beauty before him.

For one last look, Duncan swung around. The wood still was in violent commotion and the fog still was seeping out of it. But coming out of it were no more hairless ones, no more snaky creatures with cruel beaks.

They had to get out of there fast, he knew. The magic built into the forest by the gnomes might not hold much longer, and once it failed the way would be open for the Horde to come down upon them.

Give us time, he prayed. Time to get through the woods and to reach the fen.

For once they reached the fen, they probably would be safe. Even if the hairless ones or others of the Horde tried to follow them across the water, defense against them would be relatively simple.

He felt a hand upon his arm.

"Come on, Duncan," said Diane. "The others all are on the path."

Wordlessly he turned and followed her.

The path was narrow, with only scant room for one person to push his way through. Daniel, Duncan thought, might have some trouble.

Ahead of him he heard the others making their way down the path. Snoopy had said, in his anger, he remembered, that the stupid gnomes had built a trap that could not distinguish between friend and foe—

273

and in this Snoopy had been wrong. It had not yielded to the magic of the Horde, but had paid attention to Meg's witchery and Andrew's howled-out Latin.

Slowly he backed down the path, watching behind him. And as he backed the path closed in behind him. Trees materialized or shifted to block the way and heavy growth closed in.

He turned and said to Diane, "Let us run for it."

Ahead of them he saw open sky, and a moment later they burst from the woods. The others were ahead of them, running down the slope, Conrad loping in the rear, using his left hand to cradle the useless right arm.

Scratch ran ahead of all of them, racing for the fen. At its edge, he halted for a moment and looked about, as if searching for a landmark. Then he ran along its shore for a little way and plunged into the water, the others following.

When they reached the shore, Diane and Duncan walked out into the water, which came barely to their ankles. As they went farther, in places it became deeper, but never more than knee-deep. Ahead of them lay a small rocky island, and when the others reached it they clambered over it and disappeared. A few minutes later Diane and Duncan reached the island, climbing over the piled-up rocks. On the other side they found the rest of them, huddled out of sight —Daniel standing in the water just beyond the island, effectively hidden by the tumbled rocks.

Scratch reached up and pulled them down. "We'll hide here," he said. "If the Horde doesn't see us, they probably will not try to venture out. They'll have no idea the fen can be crossed."

They lay behind the rocks and watched. The woods still existed, although from their distance, there was no sign of the commotion within it, except for tiny puffs of fog still issuing from it.

Again they could hear the wailing. At times it was fairly clear and loud, at other times faded.

Snoopy came crawling up the rocks to stretch himself beside Duncan.

"Those crazy gnomes," he said, "built better than they knew. Even the witch could not detect the magic of the woods. And they still are standing up."

Even as he spoke, the woods vanished, disappearing in their entirety. The slope on which they had stood lay quite bare except for a scattered band of hairless ones, and behind them other creatures half obscured by fog.

The hairless ones moved down the slope, shambling along. At the edge of the fen they stopped, staring across the water, then began running up and down the shore, like quartering dogs seeking out a scent. After a time they went back up the slope, walking through the fog bank, which moved to follow them. In a little time they and the fog bank disappeared over the crest of the slope and did not reappear.

"We'll wait here until evening falls," said Scratch. "It won't be long. The sun is not far from down. Then we'll move out. It never gets quite dark out here. There is always some reflection from the water."

Conrad was sitting on a rock near the edge of the island, hunched over, hugging his injured arm close against his body. Duncan made his way down to him.

"Let me see that arm," he said.

"The damn thing hurts," said Conrad, "but I don't think it's broken. I can move it if I have to, but it hurts when I do. A club caught me, on the fleshy part of the arm, just below the shoulder."

The upper arm was so swollen that the skin was shiny. An angry red welt, beginning to change to purple, covered the area from the shoulder to the elbow. Duncan squeezed the arm gently and Conrad flinched.

"Easy there," he said.

Duncan took the elbow in his palm, worked it slowly up and down.

"It's not broken," he said. "You're a lucky man."

"He should have it in a sling," said Diane. "It's easier that way."

She reached into the pocket of her new buckskin

275

jacket, brought out the filmy green gown she'd worn.

"We can use this," she said.

Conrad looked at it. "I couldn't," he moaned. "If back home, the word got out . . . "

"That's nonsense," she said. "Of course you can."

Duncan laid the club beside Conrad. "Here's your club," he said.

"Thanks," said Conrad. "I would have hated to lose it. The best of wood, well seasoned. I spent hours shaping it."

Working swiftly, Diane fashioned a sling from the gown, eased it around the arm, tied it at the shoulder.

She laughed gaily. "A bit too much material," she said. "It'll hang on you like a cape. But you'll have to put up with that. I will not tear it up. There may be a time I'll need it."

Conrad grinned at her.

"Everyone must be hungry," he said. "Beauty's down there with Daniel. Someone should take off her packs. We have some food in there."

"No cooking, though," said Duncan. "We can't show any smoke."

Conrad grunted. "No wood to burn, anyhow. The packs must have something we can choke down without cooking."

As evening came down Duncan and Diane sat together on a boulder at the water's edge. They had been silent for a time. Finally Diane said, "Duncan, about that sword. The one that Snoopy gave me."

"Yes. What's wrong with it?"

"Nothing. Absolutely nothing. But it's strange."

"It's unfamiliar to you."

"It's not that. It's—how do I say this? It's as if someone's helping me. As if another arm than mine is wielding it. As if someone steps inside me and helps me handle it. Not that I haven't control of it, for I have. But as if someone's helping."

"That's your imagination."

She shook her head. "I don't think so. There was a sword that was thrown into a lake . . . "

"That's enough," said Duncan sternly. "No more fantasy. No more."

"But Duncan, I'm afraid."

He put an arm around her, held her close against him. "It's all right," he said. "Everything's all right."

28

I t was, Duncan told himself, like walking through a painting, one of the blue pastel landscapes with an overtone of faery that hung in one of the sitting rooms at Standish House, precious little canvases that had been painted so long ago and hid away so long that no one now could remember who the artist might have been. Not much contrast in color, all executed in various hues of blue, with the only other color a pale moon of rather sickly yellow glinting through the blue of clouds and sky. No contrasts, nothing but subtle gradations of color, so that viewed from a distance the canvas seemed to be little more than a smudge of blue. Closer up one could make out the details and only then could there be some appreciation of what the painter might have had in mind. There had been one of them, he remembered, very much like this, a flat watery landscape showing little but the expanse of water, with deeper tones that hinted at a distant shoreline, and in the sky, as here, the sickly yellow moon.

They had been making their way through the water for hours, keeping very much in line, following close upon one another's heels, each turning as the one ahead of him turned in order to stay on the narrow underwater ledge of rock along which Scratch was feeling his way at the head of the column.

Besides the moon, there were a few stars in the sky, although at times the drifting, filmy clouds blotted out the most of them. But the flat, smooth surface of the fen, acting like a mirror, picked up and reflected every splinter of light that fell upon it. With eyes now well adjusted to the dark, it did not seem that they were moving through night at all, but through twilight, through that time of day, that particular moment, when the last deepening of twilight gives way to final night.

Diane was at the head of the column, close behind Scratch, while Duncan was last in line, with Andrew just ahead of him. The hermit, it seemed to Duncan, was becoming tired. He stumbled every now and then and was doing a lot more splashing with his staff than seemed necessary. Before too long, Duncan knew, they would have to stop to rest. He hoped that soon they would reach another of the little rocky islands. Since they had left the first island, they had come to and passed over two others. He had no idea if there were more ahead. He hoped there were, for Andrew certainly had need of rest, and perhaps some of the others as well. Conrad, despite his rugged strength, must be experiencing heavy going with his injured arm.

The water was not deep, seldom more than above his knees, but the going was slow and laborious, for with each step it was necessary to reach out and feel for solid footing before putting down one's weight.

There had been no interruptions. Twice great bodies had hurled themselves out of the fen, but had been prevented from reaching those upon the ledge of rock by the shallowness of the water. One of them Duncan had not seen, since it had hurled itself at the head of the column. He had only heard the furious splashing as the creature fought to drive itself across the ledge. The other he had seen only momentarily and in the poor light had been unable to gain more than a fleeting impression of it. The body had been huge and

279

thick, the head vaguely toadlike. His strongest impression had been of the single, fist-sized eye that for a moment had been caught in the moonlight, blazing red like an angry jewel.

All the night they had heard the far-off wailing for the world, and now it seemed to Duncan that they must be getting closer to it. It was louder and did not fade in and out as it had before. Now it kept on and on, the wailing varying in pitch but never going away. If one concentrated on it, Duncan told himself, it could be not only an annoying, but an unnerving sound. In the last hour or so it had seemed to him that he was, in a degree, becoming accustomed to it. One can get used to almost anything, he thought. Or maybe he only hoped so.

Ahead of him Andrew stumbled and went to his knees. Moving quickly, Duncan seized him and pulled him to his feet.

"You're getting tired," he said.

"I am tired," whined the hermit. "Tired in body and in soul."

"I can understand about the body," Duncan said. "What's this business of the soul?"

"The good Lord," said Andrew, "has been pleased to show me that through all my years of unremitting and conscientious labor I have acquired some small measure of a certain holiness. And how have I used it? How have I put to use this feeble power of mine? I'll tell you how. By freeing a demon from his chains. By overcoming, or helping to overcome, a vicious and a devious heathen magic, but only with the aid of one sunk deep in witchery. It is an evil thing to collaborate with a witch or any other force or practitioner of evil, my lord. It is worse to take some credit to myself for something that well might have been done by witchery alone, for I have no way of knowing to what degree, if any at all, I was responsible for the opening of the path that freed us from the forest."

"One of these days," said Duncan harshly, "this overwhelming self-pity that you feel will be the death and the damnation of you. Remember, man, that you are a soldier of the Lord—self-proclaimed, perhaps, but still, in your mind, a soldier of the Lord."

"Yes," said Andrew, "a soldier of the Lord, but a poor one. A little fumbling, inept soldier who quakes inside himself with fear, who finds no joy in it, who drives himself to be what he may not be."

"You'll feel better," said Duncan, "once you've had a chance to rest. It has been a bitter day for us and you no longer young. You've shown the true spirit of a soldier in bearing up so well."

"It might have been better," said Andrew, "if I'd remained in my simple cell and not gone adventuring. This journey has revealed to me more of my true self than is comfortable to know. I have accomplished nothing and . . . "

"Now, hold up," Duncan told him. "It would appear to me that you have accomplished quite a lot. If you had not freed the demon he would not have been able to guide us across the fen."

Andrew brightened up. "I had not thought of that," he said, "although to accomplish that I gave aid and comfort to an imp of Satan."

"He doesn't belong to Satan any longer. Remember that. He ran away from Hell."

"But still he is a thing of wickedness. He has no grace within him and no possibility . . ."

"If by that you mean he is not a convert to Christianity, it is true he's not. But in view of what he has done for us, we must count him as a friend and ally."

"My lord, at times it seems to me that you have strange values."

"Each of us," said Duncan, "must decide upon our own values. Take it easy now. If you should stumble once again, I'll be here to fish you out."

Following the still tottery, fumbling hermit, Duncan gazed out across the fen. It was a place of flatness, a great expanse of limpid water stretching out on every side, broken here and there by darker splotches that probably were beds of reeds growing in a patch of shallow water or small islands of willows rooted in a mud flat.

The wailing continued, rising, falling, a lonely sound that could twist the heart of one who allowed himself to listen to it and to nothing else. After a time, even listening to it peripherally, the sound seemed to acquire a weight, as if it were a physical substance that bore down upon one. Duncan found himself wondering if it might be the weight of the wailing, pressing on the fen, that made it so flat and featureless. Nothing, he told himself, not even a watery wilderness such as this, could stand unaffected beneath the weight of the wailing for the world.

Ahead of him loomed a pile of rocks, another island, with those ahead of him clambering over it. He increased his stride, caught Andrew's arm, assisting him over the great slabs of riven stone. He found a flat slab that made a good seat and swung Andrew around and sat him down upon it.

"You stay here and rest," he told him. "Don't move until I come to get you. You're all tuckered out."

Andrew did not answer. He hunched up his knees, put his arms down on them and bent his head to rest it upon the folded arms.

Duncan clambered up the rocks and found the rest of the company on the other side, settling down to rest. He said to Snoopy, "I think we should hold up for a while. Everyone must be tired. Andrew is about played out."

"So are the others," Snoopy said. "Big and tough as he may be, Conrad has almost had it. That arm is hurting him a lot. You'll have to talk with Scratch. Reason with him a little. He's hell-bent for going on. That demon is all whang-leather. He doesn't know what tired is. He could keep on forever. He'll want to go on after we rest only for a short while."

"What's his hurry?"

"I don't know. We must be better than halfway across by now. It is hard to judge. Everything looks the same here. There aren't any landmarks."

"I'll talk with him. He may have a reason. Have you seen anything of Nan?"

Snoopy made a face. "I think she's gone."

282

"You mean she left us?"

"I can't be sure, but I think maybe. She's not a good flyer. You know that. A flitterer rather than a flyer."

"Yes, I know."

"Over land, where she can come down anywhere or anytime she wishes, she wouldn't mind. But here, if she had to come down, there is nothing solid to set down on, only water. Banshees hate the water. Besides, there's danger here."

"You mean the things that rushed us."

"Well, yes, those. We're fairly safe from them so long as we are on the ledge. Here they can't get at us. The water is too shallow and they're too big. Otherwise, we'd have been gobbled up."

"There are other dangers?"

Snoopy twitched his shoulder. "I don't know. Stories. There are all sorts of stories about the fen. No one knows about it and that's how the stories start. No one ventures into it."

"And you think Nan is gone?"

"I think so. I don't know. She didn't tell me one way or the other."

"Maybe she figured she had done enough for us."

"That could be true," said Snoopy.

Duncan worked his way down the island to the water's edge. There he found Scratch perched on a boulder. He hunkered down beside him.

"The folks are fairly well beat out," he said. "Is there any reason we can't stay here until daylight, get some rest?"

"We should get across as fast as we can," said Scratch. "Look ahead there." He pointed and Duncan peered in the direction he was pointing. "See those peaks over there? Three peaks. They are hard to make out."

Duncan shook his head. "I'm not sure I can. One minute I think I see something and the next I don't."

"The peaks are the Island of the Wailing for the World."

"The place where the dragons are."

"That's exactly it," said Scratch. "They may not see us in the dark. Dragons maybe can see in the dark. I'm not sure. But if so, not very well. If we could reach the island before dawn we might not have too bad a time with them. But if they spot us open in the water and we still have a long way to go they'll peck us to death; they'll get us one by one."

"We'd have a better chance if we were on the island that they guard?"

"Yes, a better chance. They couldn't fly at us. They've got a big wingspread and they can't get in close to the island's rocky crags. They'll come at us, of course, on the ground, but they'll be easier to handle there. Kill a couple of them and the others may sheer off. Basically dragons are a cowardly lot."

"Then you think we should push ahead?"

"What's to hold us up?"

"Andrew is on his last legs. Conrad is hurting a lot and is getting shaky."

"Put one of them on the horse."

"Meg already is riding Daniel. She doesn't weigh much more than a feather, of course, but I'd hate to put more weight on him. I'd hate to tire him out. He's the best fighter that we have. When it comes time to face the dragons, I want him there and able to fight the best he can."

"My lord," said Scratch, "I think it is important that we make a try to reach that island not later than dawn."

"Once we get to the wailing island, how much farther across the fen?"

"A short distance. A mile or so. It's hard by the western shore."

"From the island we could make a run for the shore despite the dragons?"

"If they saw us leaving the island they might not be after us so hard. Their job is to guard the island. Leaving it, we'd no longer be a threat. I think it might work out that way. I'm just guessing."

From overhead came a soft rustling. Duncan looked up and saw Ghost floating in.

"I bring sad tidings," said Ghost. "The unexpected has come about." He paused dramatically.

"All right," said Duncan. "Quit your silly posing, catch your breath, and dump all the misery on us."

"My breath I do not need to catch," said Ghost. "As you well know, I have no breath to catch. And I have no intent to dump misery on anyone at all. I only tell you truth."

"Then out with it," said Duncan impatiently. "Tell us this great truth."

"The Horde has ceased its northward progress and has turned back," said Ghost. "It is encamped on the western shore opposite the wailing island and its components are beginning to form into a massive sphere."

"My God," said Duncan, "a swarm. They are starting to form a swarm."

"A swarm?" asked Ghost.

"Yes, a swarm." Duncan turned to Scratch. "You told me about their swarming habits."

"I told you what I'd heard," said Scratch.

"A defensive swarming, you said. Gaining strength by personal, almost one-to-one contact of all the members of the Horde. A pulling together. A gathering to face danger."

"That," said Scratch, "was the interpretation I had heard put upon it."

"Against us, for the love of God," said Duncan.

"If any of this that I earlier told you is true," said the demon, "I would assume the defense would have to be against us. We're the only possible danger around."

"Cuthbert told me the Horde was running scared," said Duncan. "He had no idea of what it might be scared. But why should they be scared of us? They have faced us and beaten us. We have fled repeatedly from them. What danger do we pose?"

"There is ample evidence of their fear of you," said Ghost. "They have never really come against you, not the members of the Horde. Only a few of them, a half-dozen at the most. They have sent the hairless ones against you and the hairless ones may not even

285

be members of the Horde. They may be no more than beings created by their magic—foot soldiers, the carriers-out of orders who may not have the sense to know of fear."

"What the ghost says is true," the demon said. "If the Horde had no fear of you, you'd have been dead days ago."

"What do you do now?" asked Ghost. "They lie in wait for you."

"We can't retreat," said Duncan. "We've come too far to think of turning back. The quicker we get across the fen, the quicker we'll confront them. We may be able to slip past them. I don't know. The one thing we can't do is give them time. It may take them a while to complete the swarming."

"When you face them, what will you do?" asked Ghost. "My shrunken soul, if I still have any soul at all, shrinks even further at the thought of it."

"We'll do what we can," said Duncan. "Maybe when we face them we'll know what we should do."

He leaped to his feet.

"Be ready to show us the way," he said to Scratch. "We are going on, right now."

29

The wailing had become louder and heavier— heavier in the sense that it seemed to press down harder on the earth and water and all those things that lived or traveled on the land and water, as if a great invisible hand, with its palm spread wide, was pushing down, squeezing all that lay beneath it.

Conrad stumbled and pitched forward, his hand slipping from Duncan's shoulder, which it had been gripping for support. Duncan thrust himself forward and sidewise in an attempt to block Conrad's fall and got one arm around him, but it slipped away, and the impact of the big man's fall shoved them both into the water.

It was the third time Conrad had fallen since they had started the grueling drive to reach the wailing island before dawn set in. On several other occasions Duncan had been able to catch him soon enough to prevent a fall.

Now Duncan struggled up out of the water and by hauling and shoving got Conrad on his knees. The big man snorted and coughed, spitting out the water he had swallowed.

"M'lord," he wheezed, "why not go on without me?"

"Because we started this together," said Duncan, "and we are, by God, finishing it together."

Conrad struggled up, stood swaying on his feet.

"It's the arm," he said. "The pain of it has drained my strength. I am shaken by a fever. Go ahead. I can follow after. On hands and knees, if need be, but I'll follow after."

"I'll carry you if I have to."

"M'lord, you can't carry me. It would be like carrying a horse."

"Or drag you by the heels," said Duncan.

"Where's my club?" asked Conrad.

"Snoopy's carrying it."

"It's too heavy for Snoopy. He might drop it and it could float away from him."

"Look," said Duncan. "There's the wailing island, dead ahead of us. A half a mile away. That's as far as we have to go. And we'll get there in time. There's no sign of dawn as yet."

"Where are the dragons?" Conrad asked. "There should be dragons. Scratch said so. I heard him say it."

"Come on," commanded Duncan. "Get your legs moving. Get going. Grit your teeth and move. Lean on me."

"It's not right I should lean on you, m'lord."

"Goddamn it, lean on me," yelled Duncan.

Conrad lurched forward, leaning heavily on Duncan, breathing hard, shivering and shaky. Step by step they inched themselves along.

They had fallen a little behind the others, but not by much. The line of march was moving slowly. Everyone was worn down by this terrible trek across the fen, Duncan told himself. Somewhere near the head of the line, Diane was shepherding Andrew along, keeping him awake, keeping him from falling, keeping him going.

So far there had been no sign of dragons. Maybe, Duncan told himself, there would not be any dragons. Although that, he knew, was more than one could hope for.

If only the wailing would stop, he thought, stop at least for a minute to give one a slight breathing space. The wailing and the pressure, the sense of the weight of wailing bearing down upon one, the pressure that held the fen tideless and motionless, flat and calm, a great palm pressed against the water.

Then, for some reason that he didn't know, in an intuition that came to him as unquestioned truth, an intelligence that suddenly blossomed in his brain, he knew that it was not the wailing alone that was pressing down upon him, but the misery of the world—all the misery and hate, all the terror, all the pain and guilt—somehow collected, drawn from all the peoples of the world and concentrated here, funneling down upon this island just ahead, to present itself, to make the force of itself known. As if, he thought, here all the people of the world were coming to confessional, seeking the solace and the comfort that might be gained from such a rite, and, perhaps, getting it, in at least some degree, from the wailing that came off the island. Were the misery and guilt, the pain and terror, he wondered, here converted into wailing and given to the winds to be swept away?

It was a stunning knowledge and he fought against it, for it was horrible, it was unreasonable and not possible, it was unseemly that such a thing could be—shameless, an obscenity, a barbarity. It was a wonder, he thought, that the island did not writhe in throes of agony, that the fen did not steam and boil under the impact of this stream of misery.

And yet, struggle as he might against this unbidden knowledge, he knew it to be true, and knowing this, the pressure seemed greater and more oppressive, more unrelenting than it had been before.

A short distance ahead a small island loomed, no more than a tiny clump of rocks jutting out of the water only a hundred yards or so from the wailing island. Looking up, Duncan looked again at the three sharp peaks of the bigger island, outlined as deep blue spires against the paler blue of sky. The moon was almost down; it swam just a hand's breadth above the darkness of the western horizon. Looking toward the east it seemed to him that just possibly dawn might be breaking soon. He could not be certain, but it ap-

peared that the eastern sky was lightening, the first
faint hint of a rising sun.

The stubby dark form of the demon climbed the
little rocky islet just ahead and disappeared down its
far side. Behind him came Daniel, with Meg clinging
like a bug upon his back. Behind Daniel was Beauty,
mincing daintily along, choosing her footsteps precisely and with grace. The whiteness of the pack
strapped to her back glimmered in the dark. Then
Diane, supporting the stumbling Andrew, who still
carried his staff, clutching it in a death grip despite
his feebleness. And behind these two came the spidery
figure of Snoopy, skittering busily from rock to rock,
with Conrad's club carried precariously upon a shoulder, the club threatening every now and then to over-
balance him.

Tiny came splashing back through the water to see
how Duncan and Conrad were making out, his forehead all wrinkled up with worry. He nuzzled gently at
Conrad.

"It's all right," said Conrad, speaking to him with
teeth clenched against the pain. "Go ahead now.
Catch up with the others."

Satisfied, Tiny turned and trotted through the water.

They came up to the small clump of rocks. "Take
it easy," Duncan said to Conrad. "Grab tight hold of
me. I can take your weight."

"Yes, m'lord," said Conrad.

"Be sure of your footing before you move," said
Duncan. "You can't fall down and hurt that arm
again."

They worked their way slowly and carefully up the
rocks, went cautiously down the other side, were in
the water once again. Those ahead of them were more
than halfway to the wailing island.

There had been no dragons. Thank God, said Duncan to himself, there have been no dragons.

"Just a little ways farther," he said to Conrad.
"Then we can rest. Get some sleep."

He had not thought, he remembered, that it would

be this way. Two days, he had figured, when they had started out, for them to cross the fen. But instead they had crossed it, or almost crossed it, in a single night.

He had been watching his feet, he realized, as if watching them might tell him how best to place them. Now, looking up, he saw that those ahead of him had stopped, all of them with their heads bent back, staring up into the sky. Diane had let loose her hold on Andrew, who had fallen and was floundering in the water. Daniel was rearing on his hind legs and Meg was sliding, as if in slow motion, off his back, to sprawl into the waters of the fen. Directly above Daniel was a black shape against the sky, a batlike shape with wings far stretched out, curved tail lashing behind it, vicious head thrust out.

"Stay here!" Duncan yelled at Conrad. "A dragon! Stay here."

He wrenched himself free of Conrad's clutching hand, leaped forward, sword rasping from its sheath. Beneath him one foot skidded on the slippery underwater rock and as he tried to right himself, the other foot also slipped and he went down upon his back, the water closing over him.

He tried to rise, feeling a sense of blind panic washing over him, and slipped again. A shrill scream split the silence and he saw that the dragon, gripping Beauty with its two taloned feet, was beating its wings frantically to lift itself. Daniel, rearing high, had seized the dragon's neck with his teeth and was hanging on. As Duncan watched, the struggling dragon lifted Daniel off his feet and then sank down again. To one side Duncan saw the flash of Diane's sword. As she swung, a second dragon, seeking to avoid the blow, slithered sideways, almost crashing into the water. The sweep of one of its wings knocked Diane off her feet.

Conrad was running toward Daniel and as Duncan watched, he launched himself into the air, his one good arm reaching out. The arm encircled the dragon's neck and the dragon sprawled in the water, unable to beat its way to safety with Conrad's added weight.

Beauty had ceased her screaming. Her limp body, released by the dragon, bobbed in the water, which was being thrashed into foam by the dragon's struggles to escape. Tiny leaped at the dragon's throat, his head making a slashing motion. The dragon stiffened, tried frantically to hump itself out of the water, and then collapsed and lay still. The dragon that had attacked Diane was beating its way upward. Diane had regained her feet.

There was a sound of wings above him, and looking up, Duncan saw that the air seemed full of dragons circling swiftly in upon them, heading for the kill. And this, he knew, was the end of it; this was where the journey ended. His company, beaten down by the long night of travel, caught in the open no more than a hundred feet from the safety of the wailing island, could not stand against such an attack. Bitterness flared so deeply within him that he tasted gall inside his mouth. Roaring out a challenge that had no words, a berserker roar of hate, he lifted his sword arm high, running forward to take his stand with the others of the band.

From overhead, above the circling dragons, somewhere in the deep blueness of the sky, came the sudden clatter of driving hoofs, a wild bugling and the baying of a hundred hunting hounds.

The dragons broke their circling, milling wildly as they sought to get away, and down through them, scattering them, came the Wild Huntsman on his neighing charger whose pounding hoofs struck sparks in the air. The horse and huntsman swooped so low that for a moment Duncan caught sight of his face, eyes glowing wildly under bushy brows, beard blowing back across his shoulder in the wind of his own charge. Then the horse, with frenzied hoofs, was climbing into the blue again, the Huntsman flourishing his horn in hand. The dragons were fleeing wildly from the hunting dogs that bayed them down the sky.

The rest of his band, Duncan saw, was lunging

through the water toward the safety of the island, Diane dragging a limp and struggling Andrew, Conrad plunging steadily ahead on his own.

Duncan waded out and seized Beauty. When he touched her he knew that she was dead. Her body floated and he towed her to shore. There he sat down and laid her head across his lap. He put down a hesitant hand and stroked her, pulled gently at her long and silky ears. No more, he thought, the little mincing feet, dancing along the trail ahead of him. The least and the humblest of them all and now it had come to this.

A soft nose nuzzled his shoulder and he turned his head. Daniel snorted softly at him. He reached up a hand to stroke the horse. "We've lost her, boy," he said. "We have lost our Beauty."

30

Duncan was walking down a woodland path when he met the giant. It was early spring and all the trees had the soft, green-yellow, lacy look they have when the leaves first start unfurling from the buds, and there were many flowers—the floor of the woods carpeted with flowers of every hue—little flowers that nodded at Duncan as he went past, as if they had seen him and wanted to say hello. The woods were a friendly place, fairly open, with a lot of space for light and air, not one of your thick, somber, even threatening woods that all the time is closing in as if they meant to trap the traveler.

Duncan didn't know where the woods were, he didn't know where he had started from nor where he might be going; it was enough that he was there. He walked in the present moment only and that, he thought, was good. He had no past to be remorseful over, he had no future he must fear.

And then the giant came into sight and each of them walked forward until they confronted one another. The path was narrow and there was not room for the both of them. To pass by one another the both of them, or at least one of them, must step aside. But neither of them did. They stopped, facing one another,

294

Duncan glaring up at the giant, the giant glaring down at him.

Then the giant reached down with an enormous hand, lifted him, and shook him. He shook him lustily. Duncan's head snapped back and forth and his legs were jerking every which way. His arms did not move because the giant's great fist was holding them tightly in its grasp.

And the giant was saying, "Wake up, my lord. Wake up. There is someone here to see you."

Duncan tried to crawl back into the dream again. "Leave me be," he mumbled. But the giant said, "Wake up. Wake up. Wake up." And the funny thing about it was that it was not the giant's voice that was speaking, but another grating voice that he thought he recognized. It seemed to him it must be Scratch's voice. The shaking kept right on, someone shaking his shoulder rather violently.

He opened one eye and saw Scratch bending over him. He opened the other eye and saw that he was lying flat upon his back, with a projection of rock hanging over him.

"You're awake now," said Scratch. "Stay awake. Don't fall back to sleep."

The demon squatted back upon his heels, but he did not make a move to leave. Scratch stayed there, watching him.

Duncan pulled himself to a sitting position, lifted a fist to rub his eyes. He was on a small bench of stone with another outcropping of stone extending over him. Beyond the outcrop the sun was shining brightly and almost at his feet he saw the water of the fen. A little distance off Conrad lay huddled on one side, with a sleeping Tiny squeezed very close against him. Andrew was on his back, with his mouth wide open, snoring.

Duncan started to get up and then sat back, faint with the panic that had flooded over him. He had gone to sleep, he realized, perhaps all of them had fallen into exhausted sleep, with no proper precautions taken. No guard had been set, no one had spied out the land. They must have simply fallen down and slept. And that, he knew, was inexcusable of him, a failure as a leader.

He asked in a weak voice, "Is everything all right?"

"Everything's all right," said Scratch. "I stood the watch while my companions slept."

"But you were tired as well."

Scratch shook his head. "Not tired. A demon does not know fatigue. But there are people waiting, sire. Otherwise I'd not have wakened you."

"Who's waiting?"

"Some old women. Rather nice old women."

Duncan groaned and rose to his feet.

"Thank you, Scratch," he said.

Where the slab on which he had been lying ended, a path began, and he stepped out onto it. As soon as he left the protection of the overhanging ledge of stone the pressure and the weight of the wailing struck him, although there was no wailing now. And if there were no wailing, he asked himself rather numbly, how could there be weight and pressure? Almost instantly he had the answer—not the pressure of the wailing, but the pressure and the weight of the world's misery flowing in upon this place, flowing in to be exorcised, to be canceled by the wailing. The pressure seemed so great that momentarily he staggered under it and became, as well, aware of the sadness of it, an all-encompassing sadness that damped every other feeling, that set the joy of life at naught, that made one numb with the enormity of the hate and terror in the world.

The women that Scratch had mentioned were standing, the three of them, just up the path that led from the fen's edge into the island's height. They were dressed in flowing gowns that came down to their ankles, very simple gowns, with no frills or ruffles on them, that once had been white but now were rather grimy.

They carried baskets on their arms, standing there together, awaiting him. He squared his shoulders against the pressure of the misery and marched up the path to face them.

When they were face-to-face they stood silent for a moment, he and the three of them, looking one another over.

They were no longer young, he saw; it had been a long time since they had been young, if ever. They had the look of women who never had been young. Yet they were not hags, despite the wrinkles on their faces. The wrinkles, rather, gave them dignity, and there was about them a calmness that was at odds with the concentrated misery pouring in upon this place.

Then one of them spoke, the one who stood slightly in the forefront of the three.

"Young man," she asked, "can you be the one who did violence on our dragons?"

The question was so unexpected and the implication so incongruous that Duncan laughed involuntarily. The laugh was short and harsh, little better than a bark.

"You should not have," the woman said. "You have badly frightened them. They have not as yet returned and we are very worried of them. I believe you killed one of them, as well."

"Not until it had done its best to kill us," said Duncan sharply. "Not until it had killed little Beauty."

"Beauty?" asked the woman.

"A burro, ma'am."

"Only a burro?"

"One of my company," said Duncan. "There is a horse and dog as well, and they also are of our company. Not pets, not animals, but truly part of us."

"Also a demon," said the woman, "an ugly club-footed demon that challenged us and threatened us with his weapon when we came down the path."

"The demon also," said Duncan. "He, likewise, is one of us. And, if you will, with us also is a witch, a goblin and a hermit who thinks he is a soldier of the Lord."

The woman shook her head. "I have never heard the like," she said. "And who, may I ask, are you?"

"Ma'am, I am Duncan of the House of Standish."

"Of Standish House? Then why are you not at

Standish House rather than out here in the fen harassing inoffensive dragons?"

"Madam," he said evenly, "I can't imagine how you fail to know, but since you don't, I'll tell you. Your inoffensive dragons are the most bloodthirsty raveners I have ever happened on. Further I will tell you that while we had the right good will to harass them handsomely, it was not we who really did the job. We were too worn out from the crossing of the fen to do it creditably. It was the Wild Huntsman who put the run on them."

They looked at one another, questions in their faces.

"I told you," said one of the others who stood behind the one who had been speaking. "I told you I heard the Huntsman and the baying of his hounds. But you said that I was wrong. You said the Huntsman had not the hardihood to approach this island, to interfere with us and the work that we are doing."

"Your work," said Duncan, "is something in which I have some interest. You are the wailers for the world?"

"Young Standish," said the spokeswoman, "this is something with which you should not concern yourself. The mysteries in which we are engaged is not a subject to be pondered by mortals. It is bad enough that your earthly feet have violated the sacred soil on which you stand."

"And yet," said one of the others, "we are able to forgive you your sacrilege. We extend, symbolically, our hospitality. We have brought you food."

She stepped forward and placed the basket that she carried on the path. The other two set their baskets down beside it.

"You can eat it with no fear," said the one who had first set down the basket. "There is no poison in it. It is wholesome, solid food. There is enough natural misery in this world. We do not need, of ourselves, to compound it further."

"You should be the ones who know," said Duncan, not realizing until he'd said it how ungracious it must sound.

298

They did not answer him and seemed about to go, but he made a motion asking them to stay.

"One thing," he said. "Have you by any chance, seen from your vantage point upon the island, any evidence of the Horde of Harriers?"

They stared at him in wonder, then one of them said, "This is silly, sisters. Certainly he must know about the Horde. This deep in the Desolated Land, he must be well aware of them. So why don't we answer him?"

"It can do no harm," said the spokeswoman. "There is nothing he, nor anyone, can do. The Horde, Sir Duncan, lies just across the fen, on the western shore, a short distance from this place. They must know that you are coming, for they've formed into a swarm, although why they should swarm for the likes of you is more than I can understand."

"A defensive swarm?" asked Duncan.

The spokeswoman asked sharply, "How do you know about defensive swarms?"

Duncan laughed at her.

"Save your laughter, young man," she told him. "If you cross that stretch of water to face them your laughter will be out of the other corner of your mouth."

"And if we go back," said Duncan, "your precious dragons will be the death of us."

"You're obnoxious and ill-mannered," said one of the three, "to speak thus of friends of ours."

"Friends of yours?"

"Why, most certainly," said one of them. "The dragons are our puppydogs, and without the Horde, through all the centuries, there'd be less misery in the world."

"Less misery . . . " And then he understood. Not a confessional to ease the pain and supply the comfort, not an exorcism of fear and terror, but a reveling in the misery of the world, rolling happily in the distress and sadness as a dog would roll in carrion.

"Vultures," he said. "She-vultures." And was sick of heart.

Christ, was there anything that was decent left?

Nan, the banshee, keened for the widow in her humble cottage, for the mother who had lost her child, for the old and weary, for the sick, for the abandoned of the world, and whether the keening was of help or not, it was meant to help. Nan and her sister banshees were the mourners for those who had no others who would mourn for them.

But these—the wailers for the world, who wailed either by themselves or by a more extensive sisterhood or by means of some infernal machine that made modulated wailing sounds—he caught the vision of some great complicated piece of machinery with someone turning a long and heavy crank to produce the wailing —these used the misery of the world; they sucked it in and funneled it to this place where they wanted it to be, and there they luxuriated in it, there they rolled in it and smeared themselves with it, as a hog would bury itself in repulsive filth.

The three had turned about and were going up the path, and he waved an angry arm at them.

"Filthy bitches," he said, but he said it underneath his breath, for it would do no good to yell at them— no harm, perhaps, but no good, either—and they were not the ones he should be concerned about. They were filth that one passed by, filth that one stepped around and tried not to notice. His concern lay beyond this island.

He stepped forward swiftly and, lifting the baskets one by one, hurled them out into the waters of the fen.

"We gag upon your hospitality," he told, between clenched teeth, the women walking up the path. "We need no crusts of bread you toss to us. We damn you all to Hell."

Then he turned about and went down the path. Scratch and Conrad were sitting side by side upon the ledge on which they'd slept.

"Where are the others?" he asked.

"The hermit and the witch have gone to bring in Beauty's pack," said Scratch. "They spotted it. It had been floating in the water and came to shore just down

300

the beach. There may be something in it still fit to eat."

"How are you feeling?" Duncan asked Conrad.

The big man grinned at him. "The fever's gone. The arm feels better. Some of the swelling's down and the pain is not as bad."

"Milady," said Scratch, "went off in that direction." He made a thumb to show the way she'd gone. "She said something about spying out the land. Before I woke you up. She has been gone for quite some time."

Duncan looked at the sky. The sun was halfway down from noon. They had slept a good part of the daylight hours away.

"You stay here," he said. "When the others come in keep them here as well. I'll go and find Diane. That way, you said."

The demon nodded, grinning.

"If there's anything to eat," said Duncan, "eat it. We must be on our way. We have no time to lose."

"M'lord," said Conrad, "you plan to beard the Horde?"

"There's nothing else to do," said Duncan. "We have no other choice. We can't go back and we can't stay here. This island is an abomination."

Conrad grinned wolfishly. "I shall be close beside you when we go in," he said. "I need but one arm to swing a club."

"And I as well," said Scratch. "Snoopy was right in what he said in giving me the pitchfork. Appropriate, he said. And it is that. It fits my hands as if it had been made for me."

"I'll see you soon," said Duncan.

He found Diane on a small headland that overlooked the fen, back the way they'd come. She was sitting on a small rocky upthrust and turned her head when she heard his step behind her.

"Is it time to go?" she asked.

"Almost," he said. "In just a little while."

"I don't know," she said. "This facing of the Horde . . ."

"There's something I must tell you," he said. "Something I must show you. I should have long ago."

301

He put his hand into the pouch at his belt, took out the talisman and held it out to her.

She drew her breath in sharply, put out a hand toward it and then drew back the hand.

"Wulfert's?" she asked.

He nodded.

"How did you get it? Why didn't you tell me?"

"Because I was afraid," said Duncan. "Afraid that you might claim it. I had need of it, you see."

"Need of it?"

"Against the Horde," he said. "That was the purpose for which Wulfert made it."

"But Cuthbert said . . ."

"Cuthbert was wrong. It has protected us against the Horde from the day I found it. They have sent their minions against us, but with a few exceptions, no members of the Horde have come against us. They have kept well away from us."

She put out both her hands and took it from him, turning it slowly, the embedded jewels blazing as the sunlight caught them.

"So beautiful," she said. "Where did you find it?"

"In Wulfert's tomb," he told her. "Conrad hid me in the tomb after I was knocked out in the garden fight. Where we first met, remember?"

"What a strange thing to do," she said. "To hide you in a tomb."

"Conrad sometimes does strange things. They usually are effective."

"And you found it there by accident?"

"When I came to I was lying on it and it was uncomfortable. I thought it was a rock someone had chucked into the tomb. At first I had meant to give it to you, if we found you again. But, then, when it became apparent . . ."

"I understand," she said. "And now you think you can use it against the Horde. Perhaps destroy them?"

"I'm gambling on it," Duncan said. "I think so. It is apparent something has been protecting us. It must be the talisman. I think we have a weapon feared by the Horde. Why else would they swarm against us?"

"So Wulfert was right all along," she said. "The others all were wrong. They threw him out when he was right."

"Even wizards can be wrong," he said.

"One thing," she said. "Tell me why you're here. What brought you here? What is going on? Why is it so important that you get to Oxenford? You never told me that. Or Cuthbert. Cuthbert would have been interested. He had many friends in Oxenford. He wrote to them and they wrote to him. Over the years he had corresponded with them."

"Well," he said, "there is this manuscript. The story is a long one, but I'll try to tell it quickly."

He told her quickly, condensing it, using as few words as he could.

"This doctor in Oxenford," she said. "The one man in all the world who can authenticate the manuscript. Have you got his name?"

"His name is Wise. Bishop Wise. An old man and not too well. That's why we are in such a hurry. He is old and ill; he may not have too long. His Grace said his sands were running out."

"Duncan," she said in a small voice. "Duncan . . ."

"Yes? You know the name?"

She nodded. "He was Cuthbert's old friend, his good friend."

"Why, that is fine," he said.

"No, Duncan, it is not. Bishop Wise is dead."

"Dead!"

"Some weeeks ago Cuthbert got the word," she told him. "Word his old friend had died. More than likely before you set out from Standish House."

"Oh, my God!" he said, going down on his knees beside her.

A pointless trip, he thought. All of this for nothing. The man who could have authenticated the manuscript dead before they even had set out. Now the manuscript would not be authenticated. Not now. Perhaps never. A hundred years from now there might be another man, or there might never be another man such as Bishop Wise. His Grace would have to wait, Holy

Church would have to wait, the Christian world would have to wait for that other man, if there should ever be one.

"Diane," he said, choking. "Diane!"

She reached out and pulled his head into her lap, held him there, as a mother might a child.

"Go ahead and weep," she said. "I'm the only one to see. Tears will do you good."

He did not weep. He could not weep. Rather, bitterness swept in and gripped him, twisting him, rankling his soul. Until now, until this very moment, he realized, he had not known or had not let himself know how much the manuscript had meant to him—not as an abstract thing holding potential good for all the world, but to him personally. To him, Duncan Standish, as a Christian soul, as one who believed, however marginally, that a man named Jesus once had walked the Earth, had said the words He was reported to have said, had performed His miracles, had laughed at wedding feasts, had drunk wine with His brothers, and finally had died upon a Roman cross.

"Duncan," Diane said softly. "Duncan, I mourn as well as you."

He lifted his head and looked at her.

"The talisman," he said.

"We will use the talisman as Wulfert meant it should be used."

"It's all that's left," he said. "At least some good may come out of this journey."

"You have no doubts of the talisman?"

"Yes, there may be doubts. But what more is there to do?"

"Nothing more," she said.

"We may die," he said. "The talisman may not be enough."

"I'll be there," she said. "I'll be there beside you."

"To die with me?"

"If that is how it happens. I don't think it will. Wulfert . . . "

"You have faith in him?"

"As much faith as you have in your manuscript."

"And after it is over?"

"What do you mean? Once it is over?"

"I'll go back to Standish House. And you?"

"I'll find a place. There are other wizard castles. I'll be welcome."

"Come home with me."

"As your ward? As your mistress?"

"As my wife."

"Duncan, dearest, I have wizard blood."

"And in my veins runs the blood of unscrupulous adventurers, martial monsters, reavers, pirates, the ravishers of cities. Go far enough back and God knows what you'd find."

"But your father. Your father is a lord."

For a moment Duncan envisioned his father, standing tall-tree straight, whiffling out his mustache, his eyes gray as granite and yet with a warmth within them.

"A lord," he said, "and yet a gentleman. He'll love you as a daughter. He never had a daughter. He has no one but me. My mother died years ago. Standish House has waited long for a woman's hand."

"I'll need to think," she said. "One thing I can tell you. I love you very much."

31

The swarm rested on top of a small ridge, back from the edge of the fen. It was a terrifying sight—black and yet not entirely black, for through it ran strange flickerings, like the distant flaring of heat lightning such as one would see far off, coloring the horizon, on a summer night. At times the swarm seemed to be substantial, a solid ball of black; at other times it appeared curiously flimsy, like a loose ball of yarn, like a soap bubble very close to bursting. It seemed, even when it appeared to be most solid, to be in continual motion, as if the creatures or the things or whatever it might be that made it up, were continually striving to place themselves in more advantageous positions, rearranging themselves, shuffling about to attain a more ideal configuration. Watching it, one at times could see, or imagine he saw, a shape, an individual member of the swarm, although never for long enough to be entirely sure what it might be. And that, thought Duncan, was perhaps as well, for the glimpses that he got were of shapes and structures so horrifying, so far beyond anyone's most outrageous imaginings, that they made the blood run cold.

He spoke to those who clustered about him. "All of you know what we are to do," he said. "I will carry the talisman, holding it high, presenting it. I will walk in front, going slowly. Thus," he said, holding it high so that all could see. In the last rays of the setting sun, the jewels in the talisman caught fire, blazing like a mystic flame with all the colors of a rainbow, but brighter, far brighter than a rainbow.

"And if it doesn't work?" growled Conrad.

"It *must* work," Diane told him coldly.

"It must work," Duncan agreed calmly. "But, on the off-chance that it doesn't, everyone run like hell. Back into the fen, back toward the island."

"If we can run," said Conrad. "I won't run. The hell with running . . . "

A hand reached up and snatched the talisman out of Duncan's grip.

"Andrew!" Duncan roared, but the hermit was rushing forward, running toward the swarm, the blazing talisman held high in one hand, his staff flailing in the other, his mouth open and screaming words that were not words at all.

Conrad was raging. "The stupid, show-off son-of-a-bitch!" he howled.

Duncan leaped forward, racing to catch Andrew.

Ahead of him a lightning stroke flared. In its afterglow Duncan saw Andrew stand for a moment, burning in bright flames. Then, as the flames snuffed out, the hermit was a smoking torch of man, a torch a vagrant gust of wind had blown out, with tendrils of greasy smoke streaming from his upraised arms. The talisman was gone and Andrew slowly crumpled, fell in upon himself into a mound of charred and smoking flesh.

Duncan threw himself flat on the ground and the wild, terrible thought ran through him: It had not been Wulfert's talisman, it had not been the talisman that the Horde had feared; it had not been the talisman that had protected them in their long journeying through the Desolated Land. He should have known, he told himself. On the strand the Horde—it must have been the Horde—had used Harold the Reaver to obtain the thing they feared, the one thing they had not dared to try to seize themselves. And they had gotten the talisman, but had left it there upon the strand, as a thing of little value.

The one thing they had not gotten was the manuscript!

The *manuscript,* he thought. The manuscript, for the love of God! It had been the manuscript that the Horde had attempted to destroy, to negate, to obliterate. That had been the purpose of this latest desolation—desolate the northern part of Britain and then, having isolated it, move on Standish Abbey, where the manuscript was housed. But by the time they were ready to move on Standish Abbey, the manuscript, the original manuscript written by the little furtive figure who had scurried about to watch and listen, was no longer there. The Horde seemed much confused, Cuthbert had said, uncertain of itself. And that was it, of course. The manuscript, they had learned or somehow sensed, was no longer where it had been, but was being carried through the very desolation the Horde had brought about.

Little furtive man, little skulking, skittering man—Duncan said to that one who so long ago had lurked, jackallike, about the company of Jesus, who had never been one of that company nor had tried to be one of them, who had only watched and listened and then had sat huddled, in some hidden corner, to write what he had seen and heard—you did better than you knew. Writing down the words of Jesus exactly as He spoke them, with no variation whatsoever, with no paraphrasing, reporting every gesture, every movement, even the expression on His face. For that, Duncan realized, was the way it had to be. It had to be the truth, it had to be a report of events exactly as they were if it were still, centuries later, to retain the magic, recapture the glory and the power, present the full force of the Man who had spoken.

Why, he asked that little skulking man, why did you never let me see your face? Why did you keep turning from me, why did you keep your face in shadow so that I could not know you? And that, he thought, that

308

was a part of it as well, that was the way it had to be. For this little furtive man sought no glory for himself; all would have been for naught if he had sought the glory. He must remain, forever, the truly faceless man.

Duncan thrust his hand into the pouch, his fingers closing on the manuscript, bringing it out, the crinkling, crackling mass of it. Rising to his feet, he held it high above his head and with a bellow of triumph, charged the looming swarm.

Ahead of him the great, dark, shifting ball of the swarm flared with its many lightning strokes and with each stride he took, the flares grew ever brighter, but staying within the swarm itself, never reaching out. The same flaring strokes that had run the length of the rolling fog on the slope above the castle mound, flares such as the one that had reached out to turn Andrew into a smoking torch, but now they did not reach out.

Suddenly the flaring all came together and when that happened the swarm was turned into a ball of exploding fire. It burst apart and there were many smoldering fragments flying in the air, falling all about him, smoking and shriveling as they struck the ground, to lie there for a moment, writhing as if in agony, then going quiet and dead.

The Horde was gone and in the twilight that came creeping in with the going of the sun there came a putrid stench that rolled like a fog over everything.

Duncan let his arm fall to his side, still clutching the wrinkled manuscript, wrinkled from being clutched too tightly.

A wailing scream rose in the twilight, not the wailing for the world, but another wailing, a wailing very close.

Duncan turned and saw Meg crouched above the stinking mound that had been Andrew and knew that the wailing came from her.

"But why?" asked Diane, coming up beside him. "A hermit and a witch?"

"He gave her a bite of cheese that first day we

found her," Duncan said. "He offered her his arm to help her along the forest trail. He stood side by side with her to witch a path out of the forest clearing. Is that not enough?"

32

S o the manuscript would not now be authenticated. With Bishop Wise dead in Oxenford, there was no one now to put the stamp of truth upon it. It would be returned to Standish Abbey and for years it would lie there, perhaps housed in an ornate coffer, unannounced to the world and unknown because there'd be no one who could say it was true or false, an actual document or a pious fraud.

And yet, Duncan told himself, so far as he was concerned it had been authenticated. For it had been the truth of it, the authenticity of it, the proven words and acts of Jesus, that had brought about the Horde's destruction. Anything less than that, he told himself, would have made no mark upon the Horde.

He touched his fingers to the pouch at his side and beneath the pressure heard the reassuring rustle of it. So many times, he thought, he had done this very thing and listened to the crackle of the parchment, but never with the thankfulness and the surety that he felt now.

Diane stirred at his side, and when he put an arm around her she came close to him.

The fire blazed high, and off to one side Scratch had raked off a bed of coals and was engaged, with

311

Conrad's help, in frying fish that he and Conrad had caught out of a little stream after begging the loan of Duncan's shirt to improvise a net.

"Where is Ghost?" asked Duncan. "He was around for a while, but now he's disappeared."

"You won't see him," said Diane. "He's off to haunt a castle."

"A castle. Where did he find a castle?"

"The castle mound," said Diane. "He came to me to ask for my permission."

"And you gave it to him?"

"I told him it was not mine to give, but to go ahead. I told him that I couldn't see any way to stop him."

"I told him that very thing," said Duncan, "when he wanted to go to Oxenford with us. I'm surprised he would settle for a castle. He wanted to go to Oxenford so badly."

"He said that he wanted a home. He wanted a place to haunt. Said he had been hanged to a small-sized tree and you couldn't haunt a tree, especially a little bitty one."

"It seems to me I've heard that plaint before. What would Cuthbert think of it?"

"I think that Cuthbert, if he knew, might be rather pleased. But Ghost, poor thing, he wanted it so badly. He said he had no home . . . "

"If you listen to him," Duncan said, "he will wring your heart. I'm glad to be shut of him. He was nothing but a pest."

"How about Scratch?" Diane asked. "What will happen to him?"

"He is coming along with us. Conrad invited him."

"I'm glad of that," said Diane. "He and Conrad have gotten to be pals. And that is good. Scratch, despite being a demon, is not too bad a being."

"He saved Conrad's life back there in the clearing," Duncan said. "Conrad is not about to forget such an act as that."

"And Conrad was nice to him back there at the castle," said Diane. "So were you. Everyone else, up to that time, had treated him absolutely rotten."

Meg brought them fish on birch bark platters and squatted down in front of them.

"Don't eat too soon," she warned them. "Let it cool a bit."

"And you?" asked Diane. "What are you going to do now that the adventure's over? Scratch is coming with us."

"Standish House," said Duncan, "could use a resident witch. We've not had one for years."

Meg shook her head. "I've been thinking. I've wanted to talk with you about it. I have no hut, you see; no place at all to live. I have not a thing at all. But Andrew had a cell. Do you suppose he'd mind? I think I know where it is. If not, Snoopy said he'd show me."

"If that is what you want," said Duncan, "I think Andrew might be happy to know that you were there."

"I think," said Meg, "that he might have liked me just a little bit. Back, that first time we met, he took this piece of cheese out of his pocket. It had lint upon it from the pocket and there were teeth-marks on it, for he'd been nibbling on it and he gave it to me and he . . . "

Her voice broke and she could speak no more. She put her hands to her eyes and, swiftly rising, hobbled off into the darkness.

"She was in love with Andrew," Diane said. "Strange, that a witch and hermit . . . "

"We all were in love with him," said Duncan, "cross-grained as he might have been."

Cross-grained and a soldier of the Lord. A soldier of the Lord to the very last, insisting that he was a soldier of the Lord when he still was a hermit. Rushing to his death as a soldier of the Lord. Andrew and Beauty, Duncan thought—a soldier of the Lord and a little patient burro.

I'll miss them both, he thought.

From far off, faint in a vagrant wind, came the keening of the wailing for the world. Now, Duncan told himself, as the years went on, there'd be less wailing for the world. Still some misery in the world, but

313

with the Horde no longer on the Earth, less and less of it. Less for the she-vultures on the island to wallow in, less for them to smear upon themselves.

Diane set the plate of fish down upon the ground, plucked at Duncan's sleeve.

"Come with me," she said. "I can't do this all alone. I must have you standing by."

He followed her around the fire to where Snoopy sat eating fish. Diane walked to a place in front of him. She held out the naked sword, cradled in her hands.

"This is too precious a blade," she said, "to belong to any human. Would you take it back into the custody of the Little People? Keeping it until there's need of it again."

Snoopy carefully wiped his hands, held them out to take the sword. Tears stood in his eyes.

"You know, then, milady, who it once belonged to?"

She nodded, not trusting herself to speak.

"Willingly, then," said Snoopy, "we will take it back. We will guard it well and reverence it. Someday it may be there'll be another hand that is worthy to hold it. But no one ever more than yours, milady."

"You will tell the Little People," said Diane, "how much they honored me."

"It was because we trusted you," said Snoopy. "You were not unknown to us. You'll be found at Standish House?"

"Yes," said Diane. "We're leaving in the morning."

"Someday we'll come and visit you," said Snoopy.

"We'll be waiting for you," said Diane. "There'll be cakes and ale. There'll be dancing on the green."

She turned away and went back to Duncan. She took him by the arm. "And now," she said, "I'm ready for tomorrow."

About the Author

Clifford D. Simak is a newspaperman, only recently retired. Over the years he has written more than 25 books and has some 200 short stories to his credit. In 1977 he received the Nebula Grand Master award of the Science Fiction Writers of America and has won several other awards for his writing.

He was born and raised in southwestern Wisconsin, a land of wooded hills and deep ravines, and often uses this locale for his stories. A number of critics have cited him as the pastoralist of science fiction.

Perhaps the best known of his work is *City*, which has become a science-fiction classic.

He and his wife Kay have been happily married for almost 50 years. They have two children—a daughter, Shelley Ellen, a magazine editor, and Richard Scott, a chemical engineer.